Publisher's Note

Ancient Chinese classic poems are exquisite works of art. As far as 2,000 years ago, Chinese poets composed the beautiful work *Book of Poetry* and *Elegies of the South*. Later, they created more splendid Tang poetry and Song lyrics. Such classic works as *Thus Spoke the Master* and *Laws Divine and Human* were extremely significant in building and shaping the culture of the Chinese nation. These works are both a cultural bond linking the thoughts and affections of Chinese people and an important bridge for Chinese culture and the world.

Mr. Xu Yuanchong has been engaged in translation for 70 years. He won the Lifetime Achievement Award in Translation conferred by the Translators Association of China (TAC) in 2010, and won the "Aurora Borealis" Prize for Outstanding Translation of Fiction Literature, conferred by the Federation of International Translators (FIT) in 2014. He is honored as the only expert who translates Chinese poems into both English and French. After his excellent interpretation, many Chinese classic poems have been further refined into perfect English and French rhymes. This collection of Classical Chinese Poetry and Prose gathers his most representative English translations. It includes the classic works *Thus Spoke the Master, Laws Divine and Human* and dramas such as *Romance of the Western Bower, Dream in Peony Pavilion, Love in Long-life Hall* and *Peach Blooms Painted with Blood*. The largest part of the collection includes the translation of selected poems from different dynasties. The selection includes various types of poetry. The selected works start from the pre-Qin era to the Qing Dynasty, covering almost the entire history of classic poems in China. Reading these works is like tasting "living water from the source" of Chinese culture.

We hope this collection will help English readers "understand, enjoy and delight in" Chinese classic poems, share the intelligence of Confucius and Lao Tzu (the Older Master), share the gracefulness of Tang poems, Song lyrics and classic operas and songs and promote exchanges between Eastern and Western culture. We also sincerely invite precious suggestions from our readers.

出版前言

中国古代经典诗文是中国传统文化的奇葩。早在两千多年以前，中国诗人就写出了美丽的《诗经》和《楚辞》；以后，他们又创造了更加灿烂的唐诗和宋词。《论语》《老子》这样的经典著作，则在塑造、构成中华民族文化精神方面具有极其重要的意义。这些作品既是联接所有中国人思想、情感的文化纽带，也是中国文化走向世界的重要桥梁。

许渊冲先生从事翻译工作70年，2010年荣获"中国翻译文化终身成就奖"，2014年荣获国际译联颁发的"北极光"杰出文学翻译奖。他被称为将中国诗词译成英法韵文的唯一专家，经他的妙手，许多中国经典诗文被译成出色的英文和法文韵语。这套"许译中国经典诗文集"荟萃许先生最具代表性的英文译作，既包括《论语》《老子》这样的经典著作，又包括《西厢记》《牡丹亭》《长生殿》《桃花扇》等戏曲剧本，数量最多的则是历代诗歌选集。这些诗歌选集包括诗、词、散曲等多种体裁，所选作品上起先秦，下至清代，几乎涵盖了中国古典诗歌的整个历史。阅读和了解这些作品，即可尽览中国文化的"源头活水"。

我们希望这套许氏译本能使英语读者对中国经典诗文也"知之，好之，乐之"，能够分享孔子、老子的智慧，分享唐诗、宋词、中国古典戏曲的优美，并以此促进东西文化的交流。也敬请读者朋友提出宝贵意见。

PROJECT FOR TRANSLATION AND PUBLICATION
OF CHINESE CULTURAL WORKS
中国文化著作翻译出版工程项目

CLASSICAL CHINESE POETRY AND PROSE

BOOK OF POETRY

TRANSLATED BY XU YUANCHONG

许译中国经典诗文集

诗经 ｜ 许渊冲 译

五洲传播出版社
China Intercontinental Press

中华书局
Zhonghua Book Company

Contents
目　　录

Preface 1
Book of Songs
Songs Collected South of the Capital,
Modern Shaanxi and Henan 15
    Cooing and Wooing 15
    Home-going of the Bride 16
    Mutual Longing 17
    Married Happiness 18
    Blessed with Children 18
    The Newly-wed 19
    The Rabbit Catcher 20
    Plantain Gathering 20
    A Woodcutter's Love 21
    A Wife Waiting 22
    The Good Unicorn 23

卷一

序　393
国　风

周　南 403
    关　雎 403
    葛　覃 404
    卷　耳 405
    樛　木 406
    螽　斯 407
    桃　夭 408
    兔　罝 409
    芣　苢 409
    汉　广 410
    汝　坟 411
    麟之趾 412

BOOK OF POETRY

Songs Collected South of Shao, Modern Henan 24
    The Magpie's Nest 24
    The Sacrifice 24
    The Grasshoppers 25
    Sacrifice before Wedding ... 26
    The Duke of Shao 27
    I Accuse 27
    Officials in Lamb Furs 28
    Why Not Return? 29
    An Old Maid 30
    The Starlets 30
    A Merchant's Wife 31
    A Deer Killer and a Jadelike Maiden 32
    The Princess' wedding 32
    A Hunter 33

Book of Songs
    Songs Collected in Bei, Modern Hebei 34
        Depression 34

召南 413
    鹊巢 413
    采蘩 414
    草虫 414
    采蘋 415
    甘棠 416
    行露 417
    羔羊 417
    殷其雷 418
    摽有梅 419
    小星 420
    江有汜 420
    野有死麕 421
    何彼襛矣 422
    驺虞 423

卷二

国风
    邶风 424
        柏舟 424

My Green Robe 35		绿 衣 425	
A Farewell Song................36		燕 燕 426	
Sun and Moon 37		日 月 427	
The Violent Wind 38		终 风 428	
Complaint of a Soldier 39		击 鼓 429	
Our Mother 40		凯 风 430	
My Man in Service............41		雄 雉 431	
Waiting for Her Fiance......42		匏有苦叶 432	
A Rejected Wife 43		谷 风 433	
Toilers 45		式 微 435	
Refugees 45		旄 丘 435	
A Dancer............................46		简 兮 436	
Fair Spring........................47		泉 水 437	
A Petty Official..................48		北 门 438	
The Hard Pressed 49		北 风 439	
A Shepherdess 50		静 女 440	
The New Tower 51		新 台 441	
Two Sons in a Boat............52		二子乘舟 441	

Songs Collected in Yong, Modern Shandong................53

　　A Cypress Boat 53

　　Scandals 53

　　Duchess Xuan Jiang of Wei......54

鄘 风 443

　　柏 舟 443

　　墙有茨 444

　　君子偕老 444

9

BOOK OF POETRY

Trysts 56

Misfortune 57

Duke Wen of Wei...............57

Elopement.........................58

The Rat 59

Betrothal Gifts...................60

Patriotic Baroness Mu of Xu...61

Songs Collected in Wei, Modern Henan 63

Duke Wu of Wei 63

A Happy Hermit 64

The Duke's Bride 65

A Faithless Man 66

A Lovesick Fisherman.........69

A Widow in Love 70

The River Wide 70

My Lord 71

A Lonely Husband 72

Gifts 72

Songs Collected around the Capital, Modern Henan 74

The Ruined Capital 74

My Man Is Away 75

What Joy 76

桑　中 445

鹑之奔奔 446

定之方中 447

蝃　蝀 448

相　鼠 449

干　旄 449

载　驰 450

卫　风 452

淇　奥 452

考　槃 453

硕　人 454

氓 455

竹　竿 457

芄　兰 458

河　广 459

伯　兮 459

有　狐 460

木　瓜 461

王　风 463

黍　离 463

君子于役 464

君子阳阳 465

In Garrison 77

Grief of a Deserted Wife 78

Past and Present 79

A Refugee 80

One Day When I See Her Not 81

To Her Captive Lord 81

To Her Lover 82

Book of Songs
Songs Collected in Zheng, Modern Henan 83

A Good Wife 83

Cadet My Dear 83

The Young Cadet 84

Hunting 85

Qing Warriors 87

Officer in Lamb's Fur 87

Leave Me Not 88

A Hunter's Domestic Life 88

Lady Jiang 89

A Joke 90

Sing Together 90

扬之水 465

中谷有蓷 466

兔 爰 467

葛 藟 468

采 葛 469

大 车 469

丘中有麻 470

卷 三
国 风

郑 风 472

缁 衣 472

将仲子 473

叔于田 474

大叔于田 474

清 人 475

羔 裘 476

遵大路 477

女曰鸡鸣 477

有女同车 478

山有扶苏 479

萚 兮 480

BOOK OF POETRY

A Handsome Guy 91

Lift up Your Robe.............91

Lost Opportunity..............92

A Lover's Monologue..........93

Wind and Rain.................93

To a Scholar 94

Believe Me..........................94

My Lover in White............95

The Creeping Grass 96

Riverside Rendezvous........96

Songs Collected in Qi, Modern Shandong.................98

   A Courtier and His Wife 98

   Two Hunters 98

   The Bridegroom 99

   Nocturnal Tryst 100

   A Tryst before Dawn 100

   Incest 101

   Missing Her Son 102

   Hunter and Hounds........103

   Duchess Wen Jiang of Qi ... 104

   Duke of Qi and Duchess of Lu 104

狡 童................480

褰 裳................481

丰................481

东门之墠................482

风 雨................483

子 衿................483

扬之水................484

出其东门................485

野有蔓草................485

溱 洧................486

齐 风........................ 488

鸡 鸣................488

还................489

著................489

东方之日................490

东方未明................491

南 山................491

甫 田................492

卢 令................493

敝 笱................494

载 驱................495

The Archer Duke............105

Songs Collected in Wei, Modern Shanxi..................107
　A Well-drest Lady and Her Maid.........107
　A Scholar Unknown........107
　A Scholar Misunderstood...108
　A Homesick Soldier.........109
　Gathering Mulberry........110
　The Woodcutter's Song....111
　Large Rat........................112

Songs Collected in Tang, Modern Shanxi....................114
　The Cricket.....................114
　Why Not Enjoy?.............115
　Our Prince......................116
　The Pepper Plant.............117
　A Wedding Song.............117
　A Wanderer....................118
　An Unkind Lord in Lamb's Fur......................119
　The Peasants' Complaint....120
　To His Deceased Wife.....121
　The Russet Pear Tree........121

猗 嗟......................496

魏 风................497
葛 屦
..........................497
汾沮洳....................498
园有桃....................499
陟 岵......................499
十亩之间................500
伐 檀......................501
硕 鼠......................502

唐 风................504
蟋 蟀......................504
山有枢....................505
扬之水....................506
椒 聊......................507
绸 缪......................507
杕 杜......................508
羔 裘
..........................509
鸨 羽......................510
无 衣......................511
有杕之杜................511

13

An Elegy..........122

Rumor..........123

Songs Collected in Qin, Modern Shaanxi 125

Lord Zhong of Qin 125

Winter Hunting 126

A Lord on Expedition 126

Where Is She? 128

Duke Xiang of Qin 129

Burial of Three Worthies ..130

The Forgotten 131

Comradeship 132

Farewell to Duke Wen of Jin ..133

Not As Before 134

Songs Collected in Chen, Modern Henan 135

A Religious Dancer 135

Secular Dancers 135

Contentment 136

To a Weaving Maiden 137

A Date 137

The Evil-doing Usurper 138

Riverside Magpies 139

The Moon 139

葛 生..........512

采 苓..........513

秦 风..........514

车 邻..........514

驷 驖..........515

小 戎..........515

蒹 葭..........517

终 南..........518

黄 鸟..........519

晨 风..........520

无 衣..........521

渭 阳..........522

权 舆..........522

陈 风..........524

宛 丘..........524

东门之枌..........525

衡 门..........525

东门之池..........526

东门之杨..........527

墓 门..........527

防有鹊巢..........528

月 出..........528

The Duke's Mistress.........140

A Bewitching Lady..........141

Songs Collected in Kuai, Modern Henan...................142

The Last Lord of Kuai......142

The Mourning Wife 142

The Unconscious Tree......143

Nostalgia 144

Songs Collected in Cao, Modern Shandong............................145

The Ephemera 145

Poor Attendants 145

An Ideal Ruler 146

The Capital 147

Songs Collected in Bin, Modern Shaanxi 149

Life of Peasants................149

A Mother Bird.................152

Coming Back from the Eastern Hills 153

With Broken Axe 155

An Axe-handle.................156

The Duke's Return 157

Like an Old Wolf 158

株林...............529

泽陂...............530

桧风 531

羔裘...............531

素冠...............531

隰有苌楚...............532

匪风...............533

曹风 534

蜉蝣...............534

候人...............535

鸤鸠...............536

下泉...............537

豳风 538

七月...............538

鸱鸮...............541

东山

...............542

破斧...............544

伐柯...............545

九罭...............545

狼跋...............546

Book of Odes
First Decade of Odes
To Guests 160

Loyalty and Filial Piety 161

The Envoy 162

Brotherhood 163

Friendship and Kinship ... 165

The Royalty 166

A Homesick Warrior 168

General Nan Zhong and His Wife 170

A Soldier's Wife 172

Fish and Wine 174

Second Decade of Odes 175
Southern Fish Fine 175

Longevity 175

卷 四

小 雅
鹿鸣之什 548

鹿 鸣 548

四 牡 549

皇皇者华 550

常 棣 551

伐 木 553

天 保 554

采 薇 556

出 车 557

杕 杜 559

南 陔(佚) 560

白华之什 561

白 华(佚) 561

华 黍(佚) 561

鱼 丽 561

由 庚(佚) 562

南有嘉鱼 562

崇 丘(佚) 563

南山有台 563

由 仪(佚) 564

Southernwood 177

The Heavy Dew 178

The Red Bow 179

Our Lord Visiting the School 180

General Ji Fu 181

General Fang 183

Great Hunting 185

Royal Hunting 187

Third Decade of Odes 189

The Toilers 189

Early Audience 190

Water Flows 190

The Crane Cries 192

To the Minister of War 193

The White Pony 193

Yellow Birds 194

A Rejected Husband 195

Installation 196

蓼 萧 564

湛 露 565

彤弓之什 567

彤 弓 567

菁菁者莪 568

六 月 569

采 芑 570

车 攻 572

吉 日 574

鸿 雁 575

庭 燎 576

沔 水 577

鹤 鸣 578

卷 五

小 雅

祈父之什 579

祈 父 579

白 驹 580

黄 鸟 581

我行其野 581

斯 干 582

The Herdsmen's Song 199

Fourth Decade of Odes 201
To Grand Master Yin 201
Lamentation 204
President Huang Fu 208
Untimely Rain 210

Counselors 213
Reflections 215
The Banished Prince 217
Disorder and Slander 220
Friend or Foe? 222
A Eunuch's Complaint 224

Fifth Decade of Odes 226
Weal and Woe 226
The Parents' Death 227
East and West 228
Banishment to the South ...231

Injustice 232
Don't Trouble 234
A Nostalgic Official 234
Bells and Drums 236
Winter Sacrifice 237

无 羊 585
节南山 586
正 月 588
十月之交 592
雨无正 594

小旻之什 597
小 旻 597
小 宛 599
小 弁 600
巧 言 602
何人斯 604
巷 伯 606

谷 风 607
蓼 莪 608
大 东 610
四 月 612

北山之什 614
北 山 614
无将大车 615
小 明 616
鼓 钟 617
楚 茨 619

Spring sacrifice at the Foot of the Southern Mountain...240

Sixth Decade of Odes............243
    Harvest...........................243
    Farm Work....................244
    Grand Review 246
    A Noble Lord 247

    The Royal Toast 248
    The Love-birds 249
    The Royal Banquet 250
    On the Way to the Bride's House
   251
    Blue Flies........................253
    Revelry 253

Seventh Decade of Odes.......257
    The Fish among the Weed....257
    Royal Favours 257
    Admonition.....................259
    The Unjust Lord..............261

信南山
...................................621

甫　田.............................622
大　田.............................624
瞻彼洛矣..........................625
裳裳者华..........................626

卷　六

小　雅
桑扈之什 628
    桑扈..................................628
    鸳鸯..................................629
    頍弁..................................630
    车辖
   631
    青蝇..................................632
    宾之初筵..........................633

    鱼藻..................................635
    采菽..................................636
    角弓..................................637
    菀柳..................................639

都人士之什 641

Men of the Old Capital ...262

My Lord Not Back 263

On Homeward Way after Construction 264

The Mulberry Tree...........265

The Degraded Queen 266

Hard Journey 268

Frugal Hospitality 269

Eastern Expedition 270

Famine 271

Nowhere but Yellow Grass....271

Book of Epics

First Decade of Epics............274

 Heaven's Decree 274

 Three Kings of Zhou 276

 The Migration in 1325 B.C. 279

 King Wen and Talents 281

 Sacrifice and Blessing.......282

 King Wen's Reign 284

 The Rise of Zhou.............285

都人士.....................641

采 绿.......................642

黍 苗 643

隰 桑.......................644

白 华.......................645

绵 蛮.......................646

瓠 叶.......................647

渐渐之石..................648

苕之华.....................648

何草不黄..................649

卷七

大 雅

文王之什........................652

 文 王.......................652

 大 明.......................654

 绵.............................656

 棫 朴.......................659

 旱 麓.......................660

 思 齐.......................661

 皇 矣.......................663

The Wondrous Park.........289
  King Wu 290
  Kings Wen and Wu 291
Second Decade of Epics.........294
  Hou Ji, the Lord of Corn ...294
  Banquet............................297
  Sacrificial Ode 298
  The Ancestor's Spirit 300
  King Cheng......................301
  Duke Liu 302
  Take Water from Far Away...305
  King Cheng's Progress 306
  The People Are Hard Pressed
 308
  Censure............................310
Third Decade of Epics..........314
  Warnings..........................314
  Admonition by Duke Wu of Wei
 317
  Misery and Disorder........322
  Great Drought.................326
  Count of Shen 330
  Premier Shan Fu 333

  灵　台......................666
  下　武......................667
  文王有声..................668
生民之什 670
  生　民......................670
  行　苇......................673
  既　醉......................674
  凫　鹥......................675
  假　乐......................677
  公　刘......................678
  泂　酌......................680
  卷　阿......................681
  民　劳
 683
  板..............................685
荡之什 688
  荡..............................688
  抑
 690
  桑　柔......................693
  云　汉......................697
  崧　高......................700
  烝　民......................702

21

BOOK OF POETRY

The Marquis of Han 336
Duke Mu of Shao 339
Expedition against Xu 341
Complaint against King You
.... 343
King You's Times 346

Book of Hymns

Hymns of Zhou 349
First Decade of Hymns of Zhou
.... 349
  King Wen's Temple 349
  King Wen Deified 349
  King Wen's Statutes 350
  King Cheng's Inaugural Address
.... 350
  Mount Qi 351
  King Cheng's Hymn 351
  King Wu's Sacrificial Hymn
.... 352
  King Wu's Progress 352
  Kings Cheng and Kang ... 353

韩奕 705
江汉 707
常武 709
瞻卬
.... 711
召旻 713

卷八

颂
周颂 715
清庙之什
.... 715
  清庙 715
  维天之命 716
  维清 716
  烈文
.... 717
  天作 718
  昊天有成命 718
  我将
.... 719
  时迈 719
  执竞 720

Hymn to the Lord of Corn 354

Second Decade of Hymns of Zhou 355

Husbandry 355

King Kang's Prayer 355

The Guest Assisting at Sacrifice 356

Thanksgiving...................356

Temple Music..................357

Sacrifice of Fish 358

King Wu's Prayer to King Wen 358

King Cheng's Sacrifice to King Wu 359

Guests at the Sacrifice......360

Hymn to King Wu Great and Bright..............................360

Third Decade of Hymns of Zhou 362

Elegy on King Wu 362

King Cheng's Ascension to the Throne 362

思 文 721

臣工之什 722

臣 工................................722

噫 嘻...............................723

振 鹭 723

丰 年...............................724

有 瞽...............................724

潜 725

雍 726

载 见 727

有 客...............................727

武 728

闵予小子之什 729

闵予小子............................729

访 落 729

King Cheng's Consultation 363
King Cheng's Self-criticism 364
Cultivation of the Ground ...364
Hymn of Thanksgiving....366
Supplementary Sacrifice ..367
The Martial King.............367
Hymn to King Wu 368
King Wu's Hymn to King Wen 368
The King's Progress..........369

Hymns of Lu........................370
　Horses.......................370
　The Ducal Feast...............371
　The Poolside Hall 373
　Hymn to Marquis of Lu ...376

Hymns of Shang 381
　Hymn to King Tang 381
　Hymn to Ancestor...........382
　The Swallow 383
　The Rise of Shang............384
　Hymn to King Wu Ding ...387

敬 之 730
小 毖 731
载 芟 732
良 耜 733
丝 衣 734
酌 735
桓 735
赉 736
般 736

鲁 颂 738
　駉.................738
　有 驳 740
　泮 水 741
　閟 宫 743

商 颂 748
　那.................748
　烈 祖 749
　玄 鸟 751
　长 发 752
　殷 武 754

CLASSICAL CHINESE POETRY AND PROSE

BOOK
OF POETRY

TRANSLATED BY XU YUANCHONG

China Intercontinental Press   Zhonghua Book Company

Preface

Few people in Europe and America know that the earliest anthology of verse in the world is the *Book of Poetry* compiled in China 2500 years ago. This book consists of 305 poems dating from 1713 B.C. ("The Rise of Shang") to 505 B.C. ("Comradeship"). It is divided according to the type of music into four main sections: 160 *Songs* sung by the people in 15 city states and collected by royal musicians; 74 *Odes* and 31 *Epics* sung by the nobles at court or at banquets, and 40 *Hymns* used during sacrifice to the gods and ancestors. The section of *Hymns* is subdivided into "Hymns of Zhou," "Hymns of Lu" and "Hymns of Shang," the last of which is said to be the oldest, dating from between the 17th and the 12th century B.C.

Songs of the early Western Zhou Dynasty composed from the 11th to the 9th century B.C. include all the "Hymns of Zhou", a small part of the *Epics* and a few lyrical *Songs*. The majority of these songs are narrative or historical poems, the most outstanding being "Hou Ji, the Lord of Corn," "Duke Liu," "The Migration in 1325 B.C.," "the Rise of Zhou" and "Three Kings of Zhou" in the *Epic*, all of which describe the founding of the Zhou House. Songs of the later Western Zhou period during the 9th and 8th centuries B.C. include most of the *Epics* and practically all the *Odes* as well as a few folk *Songs*. Some *Epics* and *Odes* extol the military prowess of King Xuan who reigned at the end of the 9th and the beginning of the 8th century and led expeditions against the frontier tribes. "Expedition against Xu" describes his attack on the Xu tribes in the east, in which we find the embryo of Sun Wu's military strategy; "General Ji Fu" narrates King Xuan's northern expedition against the Huns and "General Fang" his southern campaign against the Chu tribes. These spirited, vigorous yet dignified *Odes* were composed by officials or historians, for example, "General Ji Fu" by Zhang Zhong, "Count of Shen" and "Premier Shan Fu" by General Ji Fu. Although competent enough, they cannot compare with soldiers' song like "A Homesick Warrior,"of which the last stanza was considered as the most beautiful verse in the *Book of Poetry*.

The best verse comes from the *Book of Songs* collected in the Eastern Zhou Dynasty from the 8th to the 6th century B.C. Most of the folk songs, written in a simple and natural style, reflect the life and struggle, labor and love, joys and sorrows of the people in ancient times. For instance, "Life of Peasants" gives a fairly comprehensive picture of the work of the peasants; "The Woodcutter's Song" satirizes against those idle and greedy lords, "Plantain Gathering" sings of the labor of women who gathered plantain seed; "A Deer Killer and a Jadelike Maiden" describes a hunter's love, "Cooing and Wooing" narrates the life and love of a young man and a fair maiden from spring to winter and their joy at wedding; "The Peasants' Complaint" expresses the sorrows of peasants, "Complaint of a Soldier" that of a homesick soldier, "A Farewell Song" and "My Green Robe" describe grief at parting and over death.

As Confucius said, "Poetry may serve to inspire, to reflect, to communicate and to admonish," we may say that the *Book of Songs* serves chiefly to reflect the life of the labouring people, to inspire them to do good and to admonish the rulers against doing wrong. For instance, the first and second sections reflect the domestic life of the ancient Chinese people, the third to fifth sections serve to admonish the lords of their faults, the seventh and twelfth sections are mostly love songs, the thirteenth and fourteenth sections reflect the general decay of the State and the last section inspires the people to admire their Duke.

The *Book of Odes* serves chiefly to communicate, to admonish and to reflect the life of the nobles. For instance, the first decade contains six Odes used at the royal banquet, the second decade includes two Odes used in district entertainment and two describing the royal hunting, the third decade contains an official's complaint against the disorder of the time ("The Toilers") and a soldier's against the minister of war ("To the Minister of War"), the fourth decade is composed of complaints against King You and his favorite Lady Shi of Bao (from "To Grand Master Yin" to "A Eunuch's Song"), the fifth decade consists of Odes of the oppressed nobles and "Revelry" is a very good picture of the dissipation of the time, the sixth decade is remarkable for "Harvest" and "Farm Work," and the last decade is chiefly censure on King Li's misgovernment, "A Homesick Warrior," "A Soldier's Wife," etc. might be classified as *Epics* for they describe the life of soldiers and generals.

The *Book of Epics* records historic deeds and reflects the life of the rulers. For instance, in the first decade there are six epic odes about King Wen, two about King Wu and two about their ancestors King Tai and King Ji ("The Migration in 1325 B.C.", "The Rise of Zhou"). In the second decade "Hou Ji, the Lord of Corn" tells us the story of Hou Ji, Lord of Grain or Corn, founder of the Zhou House, there are three epic odes about King Cheng, and another three are censures on King Li. The first three epic odes in the third decade are admonitions against King Ping, King Li and King Xuan respectively, the next three epic odes record the deeds of "Count of Shen," "Premier Shan Fu" and "The Marquis of Han" and the last two are censures on King You.

The *Book of Hymns* serves chiefly to glorify the ancestors of the rulers and inspire their descendents to worship them as gods. The book is subdivided into three sections: "Hymns of Zhou," "Hymns of Lu" and "Hymns of Shang." In the first decade of the "Hymns of Zhou" there are three odes singing the praises of King Wen, three of King Wu, four of King Cheng and one of Hou Ji, Lord of Grain or Corn. The second decade begins with an ode on husbandry and ends with a hymn to King Wu sung to the music regulating the dance in the temple. Other *Hymns* are sacrificial odes. The third decade is said to be composed by the Duke of Zhou himself as regent. The first seven Hymns are all concerned with King Cheng, his ascension, his consultation with his ministers, his self-criticism, his cultivation of the ground and his thanks-giving sacrifice. The last four are said to belong to the same series as "Hymn to King Wu Great and Bright, "sung to accompany the dance in honor of King Wu.

The "Hymns of Lu" contains only four odes celebrating Duke Xi of Lu, who was in fact a mediocre ruler, but as the descendent of the Duke of Zhou, he wes privileged to employ royal ceremonies and sacrifices, which was condemned by Confucius.

The "Hymns of Shang" contains five oldest *Hymns* in the Book. Some critics said the "Hymns of Shang" were written in the eighth century B.C. by Shang descendents in the State of Song, but there is no authentic proof for it.

Two devices are commonly employed in the *Book of Poetry*, the frequent use of simile and metaphor, and the practice of "evocation" or "association," that is, starting a song by evoking images quite apart from the central subject. "Large Rat" is a good example of a song in which an animal is compared to certain type of man. Sometimes the images first mentioned are related to the general theme like this, but again there may be no close connection between them, for instance, the grasshopper in "The Rat" is not closely related to the wife's longing for her husband. Certain images have emotional associations, others are chosen solely for the sake of rhyme.

Another striking feature of the Songs is the repetition of whole phrases and stanzas, done perhaps simply for effect. Occasionally a few words of the first stanza are altered to show the development of some action, or to introduce a new rhyme or produce a more melodious effect. The form of repetition varies: sometimes certain stanzas are repeated, sometimes a few lines only, sometimes whole lines and phrases as in "Plantain Gathering" and "An Old Maid."

The metres of traditional Chinese poetry may be roughly divided into tetrasyllabic, pentasyllabic and heptasyllabic lines as well as lines of irregular length. The tetrasyllabic lines were the earliest and most songs in the *Book of Poetry* are in this form, which had already reached maturity. Those four-character lines have only two feet each; hence the rhythm is brisk compared with the five-and seven-character lines which won popularity later. The great majority of the songs in this book are rhymed, but the rhyme schemes show a rich variety. Rhymes may be at the end of every line or every other line, certain stanzas retain the same rhyme throughout, elsewhere rhymes come in the middle of a line, and sometimes they are reinforced by alliterations.

The vocabulary of the *Book of Poetry* is a rich one; so notably is the use of epithets, double-adjectives, rhyming words and alliterations, which are employed in a variety of ways to heighten the descriptive effect or musical quality of the songs. In addition there are choruses and refrains too, another characteristic feature of folk-poetry.

This anthology was highly appraised by later generations and came to exercise a great influence on Chinese poets through the ages. For instance, we may compare the follow verse from (A) the *Book of Poetry* with (B) later poems.

1. A. How mighty did King Wu appear
     With his warriors and cavaliers
     Guarding his four frontiers! —"Hymn to King Wu"
   B. Where are my warriors brave to guard my four frontiers!
     —"Song of the Big Wind" by Liu Bang (256–195 B.C.), the
     first emperor of Han Dynasty

2. A. The present not enjoyed at all,
     We'll miss the passing days. —"The Cricket"
   B. Enjoy the present time with laughter!
     Why worry about the hereafter? —*19 Old Poems*

3. A. You go home with a sigh…
     When your car disappears,
     I stand there long in tears. —"A Farewell Song"
   B. Holding your band I sigh again;
     Letting it go, my teardrops rain. —"Su Wu to His Wife"

4. A. Three years I was his wife
     And led a toilsome life.
     Each day I early rose
     And late I sought repose. —"A Faithless Man"

B. At daybreak, I begin to weave;
   At night the loom I dare not leave.
   I've finished five rolls in three days,
   Yet I am blamed for my delays. —"Peacocks Southeast Fly"

5. A. Beneath my door of single beam
   I can sit and rest at my leisure;
   Beside the gently flowing stream
   I drink to stay hunger with pleasure. —"Contentment"

B. Into my courtyard no one should intrude,
   Nor rob my private rooms of peace and leisure.
   After long years of abject servitude,
   Again in nature I find homely pleasure.
   — "Return to Nature" by Tao Qian (365–427)

6. A. The bright moon gleams;
   My dear love beams.
   Her face so fair,
   Can I not care? —"The Moon"

B. The waves of Mirror Lake look like moonbeams;
   The maiden's dress like snow on waterside.
   The rippling dress vies with the rippling stream,
   We know not which by which is beautified.
   —"Song of the Southern Lass" by Li Bai (701–762)

7. A. Lofty is Mountain Tai
   Looked up to from Lu State.
   Mounts Gui and Meng stand nigh
   And eastward undulate. —"Hymn to Marquis of Lu"

B. O Peak of Peaks, how high it stands!
   One boundless green overspreads two states.

A marvel done by Nature's hands,

Over light and shade it dominates.

—"Gazing at Mount Tai" by Du Fu (712–770)

8. A. The eastern sun is red;

The maiden like a bloom

Follows me to my room.

The maiden in my room

Follows me to the bed. —"Nocturnal Tryst"

B. When doors were locked and incense burned, I came at night;

I went at dawn when windlass pulled up water cool.

—"Poem to one unnamed" by Li Shangyin (812–858)

9. A. Large rat, large rat,

Eat no more millet we grow!

Three years you have grown fat.

No care for us you show. —"Large Rat"

B. The rats in the public granary so fatted grow,

When they see man came in, they do not run away.

The soldiers not provided, the people hungry go.

Who allow them to eat so much from day to day?

—"The Rats in Public Granary" by Cao Ye (816–875)

10. A. On poplars by east gate

The leaves are rustling light.

At dusk we have a date;

The evening star shines bright. —"A Date"

B. Last festival of Vernal Moon,

The blooming lanterns bright as noon,

The moon above a willow tree

Shone on my lover close to me.

—"Mountain Hawthorn" by Ouyang Xiu (1007–1072)

PREFACE

From the examples cited above, we can see what great influence the *Book of Poetry* has exercised on Chinese poets through the ages. Influential as it was, it was not translated into English until the 18th century by Sir William Jones (1746–1794) who rendered a fragment of the book into two versions, one verbal and the other metrical. In the 1860s James Legge (1814–1897) had his verbal version of *The Shi King or the Book of Ancient Poetry* published in Hong Kong, and his metrical version published in London in 1871 and reprinted in New York in 1967. His is a scholarly rendition which reads unlike the simple and plain original. In 1891 appeared *The Shih Ching or Classic of Poetry* translated by C.F.R. Allen, and *The Shi King, the Old "Poetry Classic" of the Chinese* translated by William Jennings, both published in London. Allen assumes the liberty to vary from the words and sense of the original, and his metrical version is more like adaptation than translation.

When the 20th century opened, in 1906 appeared in London the *Book of Odes, Shih-king* translated by L.Cranmer-Byng, whose metrical version is not so free in sense nor so regular in form as Allen's. In 1913 appeared at Boston *Lyrics from the Chinese* translated by Helen Waddell, who omits a great deal in her version though she adds little or nothing, and who makes an organization of her own. Her book found a large sale and reached its sixth printing in 1934. On the other hand, Louis S. Hammond pushed the close translation to the extreme. She tried to use one syllable in English to represent one word in Chinese and at the same time preserve the original rhyme scheme in her translation. For example, the first stanza of her version of "Toilers" reads as follows:

Oh woe! Oh woe!

> Why not go?
> Because of you
> We are drenched with dew.

Almost all the earlier translators tried to render the *Book of Poetry* into English thyme. Ezra Pound (1885–1972) was the first after Legge to render Chinese poetry into free verse in *The Classic Anthology as Defined by Confucius* published in 1915 at Cambridge and reprinted in 1954 by Harvard University Press. In spite of its extravagant errors, his book possessed abundant color, freshness and poignancy, but it is rather his recreation than his translation. Another remarkable free verse translator was Arthur Waley (1889–1966), whose version of *The Book of Songs* was published in London in 1937. In his book he said, "the essentials of English poetry are rhyme, stress and alliteration, whereas those of Chinese poetry are rhyme, length of line and tone." But he did not use rhyme in his translation, for "if one uses rhyme, it is impossible not to sacrifice sense to sound." As to stress, he made one stressed syllable represent one word in Chinese. But neither Pound nor Waley knew that beauty in sense could not be preserved at sacrifice in sound. The *Book of Poetry*, as a whole, was written in rhyme, so no English version could reproduce an effect similar to the original if no rhyme were used. On the contrary, rhymes or beauty in sound would help to bring out the beauty in sense. For instance, we may read Waley's version of "Cooing and Wooing":

> "Fair, fair," cry the ospreys
> On the island in the river.
> Lovely is this noble lady,
> Fit bride for our lord.

> In patches grows the water mallow;
> To left and right one must seek it.
> Shy was this noble lady;
> Day and night he sought her.
>
> Sought her and could not get her;
> Day and night he grieved.
> Long thoughts, oh, long unhappy thoughts,
> Now on his back, now tossing on to his side.
>
> In patches grows the water mallow;
> To left and right one must gather it.
> Shy is this noble lady;
> With great zithern and little we hearten her.
>
> In patches grows the water mallow;
> To left and right one must choose it.
> Shy is this noble lady;
> With gongs and drums we will gladden her.

If you compare Waley's version with mine in this book, you will find that Waley has sacrificed both sense and sound for "fair, fair" is neither faithful to the original in sense nor so beautiful in sound as "cooing" which rhymes with "wooing." In other words, by using rhymes both the beauty in sense and that in sound are preserved. This is an example to show that beauty in sound may help to bring out beauty in sense. Waley did not know that a water bird would cry and a turtledove would coo in spring to find a mate and the water plant would emerge on water in summer, so he said in line 6 "one must seek it," which is not related neither to the hero nor to the heroine of this song. According to my interpretation, "seek" should be read "flow" and its subject should be "water" instead of "one," so the first two lines of the first two stanzas show the time of wooing. In the last two stanzas the water plant was gathered in autumn and the lute and zither were played on the occasion of the engagement and bells would ring and drums would beat on the occasion of the wedding in winter. But we can find no trace of engagement and wedding in Waley's version, so we may say that he has not preserved the beauty of the original, neither in sense nor in sound. What is true of Waley's version is equally true of other free verse translations. Therefore, we may come to the conclusion that without a deep understanding of Chinese culture, no translator would be competent to translate the *Book of Poetry*.

The poetry in the Book is susceptible of various interpretations, so a poem may have different English versions, and that is the reason why this anthology is different from my previous edition entitled *The First Branch Blooming on Earth*.

The *Book of Poetry* formed an important part of the education of Chinese intellectuals for thousands of years and became one of the classical canons of Confucianism. In this book the ancients learned the way how to regulate a family and how to govern a state, which may be summed up in two words: "rite" and "music." "Rite" imitates the order of the universe; "music" imitates the harmony of nature. All things burst forth in spring, grow in summer, mature in autumn and rest in winter, so man should woo in spring, love in summer, be engaged in autumn and wedded in winter in accordance with rite and with the accompaniment of music as shown in *Song* 1. Thus we see rite is instituted to secure the mean. in man's desires and music to secure the mean in man's sentiments. Music is benevolence and rite is justice externalized. If a state is governed with rite and music, the people will be just and benevolent and the world will be peaceful and happy. Rite and music are the essence of Confucianism or traditional Chinese culture. In comparison with them, government and law are but secondary. The main function of government and law is but to provide the conditions that make rite and music possible. Educated in Confucianism, China has been standing among the great powers for thousands of years, outshining Egypt and India, Greece and Rome which have only a glorious past, and America and England, France, Germany and Russia which have only a glorious present. From this we can see what an important role the *Book of Poetry*, gem of Chinese culture, will play if translated into an English version as beautiful as the original in sense, in sound and in form.

Xu Yuanchong
Peking University
April 18, 1993

BOOK OF SONGS

Songs Collected South of the Capital, Modern Shaanxi and Henan

Cooing and Wooing*

By riverside a pair
Of turtledoves are cooing;
There is a maiden fair
Whom a young man is wooing.

Water flows left and right
Of cresses here and there;
The youth yearns day and night
For the maiden so fair.

His yearning grows so strong,
He cannot fall asleep,
But tosses all night long,
So deep in love, so deep!

Now gather left and right
Cress long or short and tender!
O lute, play music light

---

* The young man made acquaintance with the maiden in spring when turtledoves were cooing (Stanza 1), wooed her in summer when cress floated on water (Stanza 2) and yearned for her until they were engaged in autumn when cress was gathered (Stanza 4) and married in winter when cresses were cooked (Stanza 5).

For the fiancée so slender!

Feast friends at left and right
On cresses cooked tender!
O bells and drums, delight
The bride so sweet and slender!

Home-going of the Bride*

The vines outspread and trail
In the midst of the vale.
Their leaves grow lush and sprout;
Yellow birds fly about
And perch on leafy trees.
O how their twitters please!

The vines outspread and trail
In the midst of the vale.
Their leaves grow lush on soil,
So good to cut and boil
And make cloth coarse or fine.
Who wears it likes the vine.

I tell Mother-in-law
Soon I will homeward go.
I'll wash my undershirt

---

* Going back to her parents' home was an important event for a bride after her wedding.

And rinse my outerskirt.
My dress cleaned, I'll appear
Before my parents dear.

Mutual Longing*

Wife: "I gather the mouse-ear
With a basket to fill.
I miss my husband dear
And leave it empty still."

Man: "The hill I'm climbing up
Has tried and tired my horse.
I'll drink my golden cup
So as to gather force."

"The height I'm climbing up
Has dizzied my horse in strife.
I drink my rhino cup
Lest I'd think of my wife."
"I climb the rocky hill;
My wornout horse won't go.
My servant's very ill.
O how great is my woe!"

---

* A wife was longing for the return of her husband while he was longing for her on his homeward way.

Married Happiness*

Up crooked Southern trees
Are climbing creepers' vines;
On lords whom their wives please,
Quiet happiness shines.

The crooked Southern trees
Are covered by grapevines;
On lords whom their wives please,
Greater happiness shines.

Round crooked Southern trees
Are twining creepers' vines;
On lords whom their wives please,
Perfect happiness shines.

Blessed with Children**

Insects in flight,
Well you appear.
It is all right
To teem with children dear.

Insects in flight,
How sound your wings!

---

* A wife was to her lord as the vine was to the tree.
** The poet wished the family to be blessed with as many children as a swarm of insects.

It is all right
To have children in strings.

Insects in flight,
You feel so warm.
It is all right
To have children in swarm.

The Newly-wed*

The peach tree beams so red,
How brilliant are its flowers!
The maiden's getting wed,
Good for the nuptial bowers.

The peach tree beams so red;
How plentiful its fruit!
The maiden's getting wed;
She's the family's root.

The peach tree beams so red;
Its leaves are lush and green.
The maiden's getting wed;
On household she'll be keen.

---

* Under the Zhou Dynasty (1121–255 B.C.) young people were married in spring when the peach tree was in flower. This was the first nuptial song in Chinese history, in which the beauty of the bride was compared to that of peach blossoms.

The Rabbit Catcher*

Well set are rabbit nets;
On the pegs go the blows.
The warrior our lord gets
Protects him from the foes.

Well set are rabbit nets,
Placed where crossroads appear.
The warrior our lord gets
Will be his good compeer.

Well set are rabbit nets,
Amid the forest spread,
The warrior our lord gets
Serves him with heart and head.

Plantain Gathering**

We gather plantain seed.
Let's gather it with speed!
We gather plantain ears.
Let's gather them with cheers!

---

* This was a song in praise of a rabbit catcher, fit to be a warrior and compeer of the lord. It set forth the influence of the lord as so powerful and beneficial that individuals of the lowest rank might be made fit to occupy the highest positions.

** This song was sung by women while gathering plantain seed which was thought to be favorable to child-bearing and difficult labors.

We gather plantain seed.
Let's rub it out with speed!
We gather plantain ears.
Pull by handfuls with cheers!

We gather plantain seed.
Let's fill our skirts with speed!
We gather plantain ears.
Belt up full skirts with cheers!

A Woodcutter's Love*

The tallest Southern tree
Affords no shade for me.
The maiden on the stream
Can but be found in dream.
For me the stream's too wide
To reach the other side
As River Han's too long
To cross its current strong.

Of the trees in the wood
I'll only cut the good.
If she should marry me,

---

* The legend said that there was a Goddess on the River Han. Here the woodcutter compared the maiden he loved to the inaccessible Goddess.

Her stable-man I'd be.
For me the stream's too wide
To reach the other side
As River Han's too long
To cross its current strong.

Of the trees here and there
I'll only cut the fair.
If she should marry me,
Her stable-boy I'd be.
For me the stream's too wide
To reach the other side
As River Han's too long
To cross its current strong.

A Wife Waiting*

Along the raised bank green
I cut down twigs and wait.
My lord cannot be seen;
I feel a hunger great.

Along the raised bank green
I cut fresh sprigs and spray.
My lord can now be seen,

---

* A wife tried to dissuade her lord from leaving her again by cooking for him a red-tailed fish to show the unfed flame of her heart.

But soon he'll go away.

"I'll leave your red-tailed fish:
The kingdom is on fire."
"If you leave as you wish,
Who'll take care of your sire?"

The Good Unicorn*

The unicorn will use its hoofs to tread on none
Just like our Prince's noble son.
Ah! they are one.

The unicorn will knock its head against none
Just like our Prince's grandson.
Ah! they are one.

The unicorn will fight with its corn against none
Just like our Prince's great-grand-son.
Ah! they are one.

---

* The unicorn was a fabulous animal, the symbol of all goodness and benevolence, having the body of a deer, the tail of an ox, the hoofs of a horse, one horn in the middle of the forehead. Its hoofs were mentioned because it did not tread on any living thing, not even on live grass; its head because it did not butt with it; and its horn because the end of it was covered with flesh, to show that the creature, while able for war, would have peace. This song celebrated the goodness of the offspring of King Wen (1184–1134 B.C.), founder of the Zhou Dynasty.

Songs Collected South of Shao, Modern Henan

The Magpie's Nest*

The magpie builds a nest,
Where comes the dove in spring.
The bride comes fully-drest,
Welcomed by cabs in string.

The magpie builds a nest,
Where dwells the dove in spring.
The bride comes fully-drest,
Escort'd by cabs in string.

The magpie builds a nest,
Where lives the dove in spring.
The bride comes fully-drest,
Celebrated by cabs in string.

The Sacrifice**

Gather southernwood white
By the pools here and there.
Employ it in the rite
In our prince's affair.

---

* The newly-wed were compared to magpie and dove or myna. The bride came escorted and welcomed by cabs and the wedding was celebrated by cabs.
** This song narrates the industry of the chambermaids assisting the prince in sacrificing.

Gather southernwood white
In the vale by the stream.
Employ it in the rite
Under the temple's beam.

Wearing black, glossy hair,
We're busy all the day.
With disheveled hair
At dusk we go away.

The Grasshoppers*

Hear grassland insects sing
And see grasshoppers spring!
When my lord is not seen,
I feel a sorrow keen.
When I see him downhill
And meet him by the rill,
My heart would then be still.

I go up southern hill,
Of ferns I get my fill.
When my lord is not seen,
I feel a grief more keen.
When I see him downhill

---

* A wife was longing for her lord from autumn when grasshoppers sang, to spring when fern was gathered, and to summer when herb was gathered.

And meet him by the rill,
My heart with joy would thrill.

I go up southern hill;
Of herbs I get my fill.
When my lord is not seen,
I feel a grief most keen.
When I see him downhill
And meet him by the rill,
My heart would be serene.

Sacrifice before Wedding*

Where to gather duckweed?
In the brook by south hill.
Where to gather pondweed?
Between the brook and rill.

Where to put what we've found?
In baskets square or round.
Where to boil what we can?
In the tripod or pan.
Where to put offerings?
In the temple's both wings.
Who offers sacrifice?
The bride-to-be so nice.

---

* According to ancient custom, the bride-to-be should gather duckweed and offer it as sacrifice in the temple three months before her wedding.

The Duke of Shao*

O leafy tree of pear!
Don't clip or make it bare,
For once our Duke lodged there.

O leafy tree of pear!
Don't break its branches bare,
For once our Duke rested there.

O leafy tree of pear!
Don't bend its branches bare,
For once our Duke halted there.

I Accuse**

The path with dew is wet;
Before dawn off I set;
I fear nor dew nor threat.
Who says in sparrow's head
No beak can pierce the roof?
Who says the man's not wed?

---

* The Duke of Shao was a principal adherent of King Wen. The love of the people for the memory of the Duke of Shao made them love the tree beneath which he had rested.

** A young woman resisted an attempt to force her to marry a married man and she argued her cause though put in jail and brought to the judge's hall.

He jails me without proof.
He can't wed me in jail;
I'm jailed to no avail.

Who says in the rat's head
No teeth can pierce the wall?
Who says the man's not wed?
He brings me to judge's hall.
Though brought to judge's hall.
I will not yield at all.

Officials in Lamb Furs*

In lamb and sheep skins drest,
With their five braidings white,
They come from court to rest
And swagger with delight.

In sheep and lamb skins drest,
With five seams of silk white,
They swagger, come to rest
And take meals with delight.

In lamb and sheep furs drest,
With their five joinings white,

---

* It was said that this song was a satire on those officials who did nothing but swagger, take meals and rest without delight.

They take their meals and rest
And swagger with delight.

Why Not Return?*

The thunder rolls away
O'er southern mountain's crest.
Why far from home do you stay,
Not daring take a rest?
Brave lord for whom I yearn,
Return, return!

The thunder rolls away
By southern mountain's side.
Why far from home do you stay,
Not daring take a ride?
Brave lord for whom I yearn,
Return, return!

The thunder rolls away
At southern mountain's foot,
Why far from home do you stay
As if you'd taken root?
Brave lord for whom I yearn,
Return, return!

---

* A young wife was longing for the return of her husband absent on pubic service.

An Old Maid*

The fruits from mume-tree fall,
One-third of them away.
If you love me at all,
Woo me a lucky day!

The fruits from mume-tree fall,
Two-thirds of them away.
If you love me at all,
Woo me this very day!

The fruits from mume-tree fall,
Now all of them away.
If you love me at all,
You need not woo but say.

The Starlets**

Three or five stars shine bright
Over the eastern gate.
We make haste day and night,
Busy early and late.
Different is our fate.

---

* According to ancient custom, young people should be married in spring. When mume fruit fell, it was summer and maidens over twenty might get married without courtship.
** This was a complaint of petty officials who should get up by starlight and go to bed by starlight.

The starlets shed weak light
With the Pleiades o'erhead.
We make haste day and night,
Carrying sheets of bed:
No other way instead.

A Merchant's Wife*

Upstream go you
To wed the new
And leave the old,
You leave the old:
Regret foretold.

Downstream go you
To wed the new
And forsake me.
You forsake me;
Rueful you'll be.

By-stream go you
To wed the new
And desert me.
You desert me.
Woeful you'll be.

---

* This was the complaint of a woman deserted by her husband who went upstream and downstream for commerce.

A Deer Killer and a Jadelike Maiden*

An antelope is killed
And wrapped in white afield.
A maid for love does long,
Tempted by a hunter strong.

He cuts down trees amain
And kills a deer again.
He sees the white-drest maid
As beautiful as jade.

"O soft and slow, sweetheart,
Don't tear my sash apart!"
The jadelike maid says, "Hark!
Do not let the dog bark!"

The Princess' wedding**

Luxuriant in spring
As plum flowers o'er water,
How we revere the string

---

* A hunter killed a deer, wrapped it in white rushes and offered it as present to a beautiful maiden. The last stanza described their lovemaking implicitly.

** This song described the marriage in 683 B.C. of the granddaughter of King Ping (769–719 B.C.) and the son of the Marquise of Qi. The silken thread forming a fishing line might allude to the newly-wed forming a happy family.

Of cabs for the king's daughter!

Luxuriant in spring
As the peach flowers red,
The daughter of the king
To a marquis' son is wed.

We use the silken thread
To form a fishing line.
The son of marquis is wed
To the princess divine.

A Hunter*

Abundant rushes grow along;
One arrow hits one boar among.
Ah! what a hunter strong!

Abundant reeds along the shores!
One arrow scares five boars.
Ah! what a hunter one adores!

---

* This was a song sung during the hunting season in spring.

Songs Collected in Bei, Modern Hebei

Depression*

Like cypress boat
Mid-stream afloat,
I cannot sleep
In sorrow deep.
I won't drink wine,
Nor roam nor pine.

Unlike the brass
Where images pass,
On brothers I
Cannot rely.
When I complain,
I meet disdain.

Have I not grown
Firm as a stone?
Am I as flat
As level mat?
My mind is strong:
I've done no wrong.

I'm full of spleen,

---

* This song may be interpreted either as complaint of a man or of a woman. Some say it was the forerunner of *Departure in Sorrow* by Qu Yuan (340–278B.C.).

Hated by the mean;
I'm in distress,
Insulted no less;
Thinking at rest,
I beat my breast.

The sun and moon
Turn dim so soon,
I'm in distress
Like dirty dress.
Silent think I:
Why can't I fly?

My Green Robe*

My upper robe is green;
Yellow my lower dress
My sorrow is so keen;
When will end my distress?

My upper robe is green;
Yellow my dress with dots.
My sorrow is so keen;
How can it be forgot?

The silk is green that you,

---

* This was the first elegy in which a widower missed his deceased wife who had made the green robe and yellow dress for him.

Old mate, dyed all night long;
I miss you, old mate, who
Kept me from doing wrong.

The linen coarse or fine
Is cold when blows the breeze.
I miss old mate of mine,
Who put my mind at ease.

A Farewell Song*

A pair of swallows fly
With their wings low and high.
You go home in your car;
I see you off afar.
When your car disappears,
Like rain fall down my tears.

A pair of swallows fly;
You go home with a sigh.

---

* This was the first farewell song in Chinese history, written by Duchess Zhuang Jiang whose beauty was described in Poem "The Duke's Bride" and who bore no children but brought up the son of Duchess Dai Wei, who became Duke Huan of Wei and was murdered by his half brother on the 16th day of the 3rd moon in 719 B.C. In this farewell song the duchess related her grief at the departure of Duchess Dai Wei, obliged to return to her native State of Chen after her son's death. The "late lord" here refers to their husband.

When they fly up and down,
I see you leave the town.
When your car disappears,
I stand there long in tears.

A pair of swallows fly,
Their songs heard far and nigh.
You go to your home state;
I see you leave south gate.
When your car disappears.
Deeply grieved, I shed tears.

My faithful sister dear
With feeling e'er sincere,
So gentle and so sweet,
So prudent and discreet!
The thought of our late lord
Strikes our sensitive chord.

Sun and Moon*

Sun and moon bright,
Shed light on earth!
This man in sight
Without true worth
Has set his mind

---

* This song was the complaint of a wife abandoned by her husband.

To be unkind.

Sun and moon bright,
Cast shade with glee!
This man in sight
Would frown at me.
He's set his mind
To leave me behind.

Sun and moon bright
Rise from the east.
This man in sight
Is worse than beast.
His mind is set
All to forget.

Sun and moon bright
From east appear.
Can I requite
My parents dear?
My mind not set,
Can I forget?

The Violent Wind*

The wind blows violently;

---

* This is the description of a feminine mind after a man's flirtation with her.

He looks and smiles at me.
With me he seems to flirt;
My heart feels deeply hurt.

The wind blows dustily;
He's kind to come to me.
Should he nor come nor go.
How would my yearning grow!

The wind blows all the day;
The clouds won't fly away.
Awake, I'm ill at ease.
Would he miss me and sneeze!

In gloomy cloudy sky
The thunder rumbles high.
I cannot sleep again.
O would he know my pain!

Complaint of a Soldier*

The drums are booming out;
We leap and bound about.
We build walls high and low,
But I should southward go.

We follow Sun Zizhong

---

* A soldier of the State of Wei repined over his separation form his family after the war made on the State of Chen in 718 B.C.

To fight with Chen and Song.
I cannot homeward go;
My heart is full of woe.

Where stop and stay our forces
When we have lost our horses?
Where can we find them, please?
Buried among the trees.

Meet or part, live or die;
We made oath, you and I.
Give me your hand I'll hold
And live with me till old.

Alas! so long we've parted,
Can I live broken-hearted?
Alas! the oath we swore
Can be fulfilled no more.

Our Mother*

From the south blows the breeze
Amid the jujube trees.
The trees grow on the soil;
We live on mother's toil.

From the south blows the breeze

---

* Seven sons blamed themselves for the unhappiness of their mother in her state of widowhood.

On branches of the trees.
Our mother's good to sons;
We are not worthy ones.

The fountain's water runs
To feed the stream and soil.
Our mother's seven sons
Are fed by her hard toil.

The yellow birds can sing
To comfort us with art.
We seven sons can't bring
Comfort to mother's heart.

My Man in Service*

The male pheasant in flight
Wings its way left and right.
O dear one of my heart!
We are so far apart.

See the male pheasant fly;
Hear his song low and high.
My man is so sincere.
Can I not miss him so dear?

Gazing at moon or sun,

---

* A wife deplored the absence of her husband in service and celebrated his virtue.

I think of my dear one.
The way's a thousand li.
How can he come to me?

If he is really good,
He will do what he should.
For nothing would he long.
Will he do anything wrong?

Waiting for Her Fiance*

The gourd has leaves which fade;
The stream's too deep to wade.
If shallow leap
And strip if deep!

See the stream's water rise;
Hear female pheasant's cries.
The stream wets not the axle straight;
The pheasant's calling for her mate.

Hear the song of wild geese;
See the sun rise in glee.
Come before the streams freeze
If you will marry me.

I see the boatman row

---

* A maiden was waiting at the ferry for her fiance to come across the stream.

Across but I will wait;
With others I won't go:
I will wait for my mate.

A Rejected Wife*

Gently blows eastern breeze
With rain 'neath cloudy skies.
Let's set our mind to please
And let no anger rise!
Who gathers plants to eat
Should keep the root in view.
Do not forget what's meet
And me who'd die with you!

Slowly I go my way;
My heart feels sad and cold.
You go as far to say
Goodbye as the threshold.
Is lettuce bitter? Nay,
To me it seems e'en sweet.
Feasting on wedding day,
You two looks as brothers meet.

The by-stream is not clear,
Still we can see its bed.

---

* This was the plaint of a wife rejected and supplanted by another whom she addressed in lines 5–6 of the 3rd stanza.

Feasting your new wife dear,
You treat the old as dead.
Do not approach my dam,
Nor move my net away!
Rejected as I am,
What more have I to say?

When the river was deep,
I crossed by raft or boat;
When't was shallow, I'd keep
Myself aswim or afloat.
I would have spared no breath
To get what we did need;
Wherever I saw death,
I would help with all speed.

You loved me not as mate;
Instead you gave me hell.
My virtue caused you hate
As wares which did not sell.
In days of poverty
Together we shared woe
Now in prosperity
I seem your poison slow.

I've vegetables dried
Against the winter cold.
Feast them with your new bride,

Not your former wife old.
You beat and scolded me
And gave me only pain.
The past is gone, I see,
And no love will remain.

Toilers*

It's near dusk, lo!
Why not home go?
It is for you
We're wet with dew.

It's near dusk, lo!
Why not home go?
For you, O sire,
We toil in mire.

Refugees**

The high mound's vines appear
So long and wide.
O uncles dear,
Why not come to our side?

Why dwell you thereamong

---

* This was a plaint of toilers in the service of the marquis of Wei.
** It was said that this was a complaint of the refugees in the State of Wei.

For other friends you make?
Why stay so long?
For who else' sake?

Furs in a mess appear;
Eastward goes not your cart.
O uncles dear,
Don't you feel sad at heart?

So poor and base appear
We refugees.
O uncles dear,
Why don't you listen, please?

A Dancer*

With main and might
Dances the ace.
Sun at its height,
He holds his place.

He dances long
With might and main.
Like tiger strong
He holds the rein.

---

* It was said that this was a censure against the State of Wei for not giving offices equal to their merit to its men of worth but employing them as dancers.

A flute in his left hand,
In his right a plume fine,
Red-faced, he holds command,
Given a cup of wine.

Hazel above,
Sweet grass below.
Who is not sick for love
Of the dancing Beau?
Who is not sick for love
Of the Western Beau?

Fair Spring*

The bubbling water flows
From the spring to the stream.
My heart to homeland goes;
Day and night I seek to dream.
I'll ask my cousins dear
How I may start from here.

I will lodge in one place,
Take my meal in another,
And try to find the trace
How I parted from mother.

---

* A daughter of the House of Wei, married in another state, expressed her longing to revisit Wei.

I'll ask about aunts dear
On my way far from here.

I'll lodge in a third place
And dine in a fourth one.
I'll set my cab apace;
With axles greased 'twill run.
I'll hasten to go home.
Why should I not have come?

When I think of Fair Spring,
How can I not heave sighs!
Thoughts of my homeland bring
Copious tears to my eyes.
I drive to find relief
And drown my homesick grief.

A Petty Official*

Out of north gate
Sadly I go.
I'm poor by fate.
Who knows my woe?
Let it be so!
Heaven wills this way.

---

* An officer of Wei set forth his hard lot and his silence under it in submission to Heaven.

What can I say?

I am busy about
Affairs of royalty.
When I come from without,
I'm blamed by family.
So let it be!
Heaven wills this way.
What can I say?

I am busier about
Public affairs, but oh!
When I come from without,
I'm given blow on blow.
Let it be so!
Heaven wills this way.
What can I say?

The Hard Pressed*

The cold north wind does blow
And thick does fall the snow.
To all my friends I say:
"Hand in hand let us go!

---

* The hard-pressed people left the State of Wei in consequence of the prevailing oppression and misery. The first two lines in all the stanzas are a metaphorical description of the miserable condition of the State. Foxes and crows were both creatures of evil omen.

There's no time for delay;
We must hasten our way."

The sharp north wind does blow
And heavy falls the snow.
To all my friends I say
"Hand in hand let's all go!
There's no time for delay;
We must hasten our way,"

Red-handed foxes glow;
Their hearts are black as crow.
To all my friends I say
"In my cart let us go!
There's no time for delay;
We must hasten our way."

A Shepherdess*

A maiden mute and tall
Trysts me at corner wall.
I can find her nowhere;
Perplexed, I scratch my hair.

The maiden fair and mute
Gives me a grass-made lute.

---

* This was the first in Chinese song which the poet showed his participation in the feeling of things.

Playing a rosy air,
I'm happier than e'er.

Coming back from the mead.
She gives me a rare reed,
Lovely not for it's rare:
It's given by the fair.

The New Tower*

How bright is the new tower
On brimming river deep!
Of youth she seeks the flower,
Not loathsome toad to keep.

How high is the new tower
On tearful river deep!
Of youth she seeks the flower,
No stinking toad to keep.

A net for fish is set;
A toad is caught instead.
The flower of youth she'll get,
Not a hunchback to wed.

---

* This was a satire against Duke Xuan of Wei who took his eldest son's bride as his own and built a new tower by the Yellow River to welcome her in 699 B.C. Here the toad and the hunchback refer to the duke and the flower of youth to his eldest son.

Two Sons in a Boat*

My two sons take a boat;
Downstream their shadows float.
I miss them when they're out;
My heart is tossed about.

My two sons take a boat;
Far, far away they float.
I think of them so long.
Would no one do them wrong!

---

* Duke Xuan of Wei who had taken his eldest son's bride as his own plotted to get rid of this son by sinking his boat, but his younger brother, aware of this design, insisted on going in the same boat with him, and their mother, worried, wrote this song.

Songs Collected in Yong, Modern Shandong

A Cypress Boat*

A cypress boat
Midstream afloat.
Two tufts of hair o'er his forehead,
He is my mate to whom I'll wed.
I swear I won't change my mind till I'm dead.
Heaven and mother,
Why don't you understand another?

A cypress boat
By riverside afloat.
Two tufts of hair o'er his forehead,
He is my only mate to whom I'll wed.
I swear I won't change my mind though dead.
Heaven and mother,
Why don't you understand another?

Scandals**

The creepers on the wall

---

* This song of a determined woman was mistaken for that of a chaste widow.
** After the death of Duke Xuan of Wei, the beautiful duchess had illicit connections with his son and gave birth to three sons and two daughters, the youngest daughter being Baroness Mu of Xu who wrote the Poem "Patriotic Baroness Mu of Xu". These connections raised scandals in the inner hall of the ducal palace.

Cannot be swept away.
Stories of inner hall
Should not be told by day.
What would have to be told
Is scandals manifold.

The creepers on the wall
Cannot be rooted out.
Scandals of inner hall
Should not be talked about.
If they are talked of long,
They'll be an endless song.

The creepers on the wall
Cannot be together bound.
Scandals of inner hall
Should not be spread around.
If spread from place to place,
They are shame and disgrace.

Duchess Xuan Jiang of Wei*

She'd live with her lord till old,
Adorned with gems and gold.
Stately and full of grace,

---

* This was a portrait of the beautiful Duchess Xuan of Wei. The first stanza described her arrival at the new tower (see Poem "The New Tower").

Stream-like, she went her pace.
As a mountain she'd dwell;
Her robe became her well.
Raped by the father of her lord,
O how could she not have been bored!

She is so bright and fair
In pheasant-figured gown.
Like cloud is her black hair,
No false locks but her own.
Her earrings are of jade,
Her pin ivory-made.
Her forehead's white and high,
Like goddess from the sky.

She is so fair and bright
In rich attire snow-white.
O'er her fine undershirt
She wears close-fitting skirt.
Her eyes are bright and clear;
Her face will fascinate.
Alas! fair as she might appear,
She's a raped beauty of the state.

Trysts*

"Where gather golden thread?"
"In the fields over there."
"Of whom do you think ahead?"
"Jiang's eldest daughter fair.
She did wait for me 'neath mulberry,
In upper bower tryst with me
And see me off on River Qi."

"Where gather golden wheat?"
"In northern fields o'er there,"
"Whom do you long to meet?"
"Yi's eldest daughter fair.
She did wait for me 'neath mulberry,
In upper bower tryst with me
And see me off on River Qi."

"Where gather mustard plant?"
"In eastern fields o'er there."
"Who does your heart enchant?"
"Yong's eldest daughter fair.
She did wait for me 'neath mulberry,
In upper bower tryst with me
And see me off on River Qi."

---

* It was possible that this song was constructed to deride the licentiousness that prevailed in the State of Wei.

Misfortune*

The quails together fly;
The magpies sort in pairs.
She takes an unkind guy
For brother unawares.

The magpies sort in pairs;
The quails together fly.
For master unawares
She takes an unkind guy.

Duke Wen of Wei**

At dusk the four stars form a square;
It's time to build a palace new.
The sun and shade determine where
To build the Palace at Chu,
To plant hazel and chestnut trees,
Fir, yew, plane, cypress. When cut down,

---

* The beautiful Duchess Xuan Jiang of Wei (see Poems "The New Tower", "Two Sons in a Boat", "Scandals", "Duchess Xuan Jiang of Wei") was first raped by Duke Xuan of Wei (master) and then by his son(brother). She was not so fortunate as quails and magpies which have a faithful mate.

** After the defeat and death of Duke Yi of Wei in 659 B.C., Duke Wen succeeded him, moved the capital to Cao and built a new palace in Chu. As he was diligent and sympathetic with the people, the State of Wei became prosperous under his reign.

They may be used to make lutes to please
The ducal crown.

The duke ascends the ruined wall
To view the site of capital
And where to build his palace hall.
He then surveys the mountain's height
And comes down to see mulberries.
The fortune-teller says it's right
And the duke is pleased with all these.

After the fall of vernal rain
The duke orders his groom to drive
His horse and cab with might and main.
At mulberry fields they arrive;
To farmers he is good indeed
He wishes husbandry to thrive
And three thousand horses to breed.

Elopement*

A rainbow rose high in the east;

---

* This was said to be a protest of Duchess Xuan Jiang against Duke Xuan of Wei who raped her (see Poem "The New Tower"). A rainbow was regarded by ancient people as an emblem of improper connections between man and woman, and it was held un-lucky to point to a rainbow in the east. The clouds bringing fresh showers to thirsting flowers were compared to love-making.

None dared to point to it at least.
I went to wed like others
And left my parents and my brothers.
The morning clouds rose in the west;
The day with rain would then be blest.
I went to wed another
When I left my father and mother.

Did I know I'd be raped by such a man
Who would do whatever he can!
He is a faithless mate.
Is it my fault or fate?

The Rat*

The rat has skin, you see?
Man must have decency.
If he lacks decency,
Worse than death it would be.

The rat has teeth, you see?
Man must have dignity.
If he lacks dignity,
For what but death waits he?

The rat has limbs, you see?

---

* This was a satire against the ruling class of the State of Wei who, without propriety, was not equal to a rat.

Man must have propriety.
Without propriety,
It's better dead to be.

Betrothal Gifts*

The flags with ox-tail tied
Flutter in countryside.
Adorned with silk bands white,
Four steeds trot left and right.
What won't I give and share
With such a maiden faire?

The falcon-banners fly
In the outskirts nearby.
Adorned with ribbons white,
Five steeds trot left and right,
What won't I give and send
To such a good fair friend?

The feathered streamers go down
All the way to the town.
Bearing rolls of silk white,
Six steeds trot left and right.
What and how should I say
To her as fair as May?

---

* This song described how a young lord sent betrothal gifts to his fiancee.

Patriotic Baroness Mu of Xu*

I gallop while I go
To share my brother's woe.
I ride down a long road
To my brother's abode.
The deputies will thwart
My plan and fret my heart.

"Although you say me nay,
I won't go back the other way.
Conservative are you
While farsight'd is my view?"

"Although you say me nay,
I won't stop on my way.
Conservative are you,
I can't accept your view."

I climb the sloping mound
To pick toad-lilies round.

---

* Baroness Mu of Xu, daughter of Duchess Xuan Jiang (see Poem "Scandals") of Wei, complained that the deputies of Xu did not allow her to go back to Wei to condole with her brother Duke Wen on the desolation of his State after the death of Duke Dai in 659 B.C., and to appeal to a mighty State on its behalf. It was contrary, however, to the rules of propriety for a lady in her position to return to her native State, so she picked toad lilies which might, it was said, assuage her sorrow.

Book of Poetry

Of woman don't make light!
My heart knows what is right.
My countrymen put blame
On me and feel no shame.

I go across the plains;
Thick and green grow the grains.
I'll plead to mighty land,
Who'd hold out helping hand.
"Deputies, don't you see
The fault lies not with me?
Whatever may think you,
It's not so good as my view."

Songs Collected in Wei, Modern Henan

Duke Wu of Wei*

Behold by riverside

Green bamboos in high glee.

Our duke is dignified

Like polished ivory

And stone or jade refined.

With solemn gravity

And elevated mind,

The duke we love a lot

Should never be forgot.

Behold by riverside

Bamboos with soft green shade.

Our duke is dignified

When crowned with strings of jade

As bright as stars we find.

With solemn gravity

And elevated mind,

---

* This song was written in praise of Duke Wu who ruled the State of Wei in 811–751 B.C.. The duke cultivated the principles of government. The people increased in number, and others flocked to the State. In 770 B.C. when King You of Zhou was killed by a barbarian tribe, the duke led his army to the rescue of Zhou and rendered such great service against the enemy that King Ping appointed him a minister of the royal court.

The duke we love a lot
Should never be forgot.

Behold by riverside
Bamboos so lush and green.
Our duke is dignified
With gold- or tin-like sheen.
With his sceptre in hand,
He is in gentle mood;
By his chariot he'd stand;
At jesting he is good,
But he is never rude.

A Happy Hermit*

By riverside unknown
A hermit builds his cot.
He sleeps, wakes, speaks alone;
Such joy won't be forgot.
By mountainside unknown
A hermit will not fret.
He sleeps, wakes, sings alone:
A joy never to forget.

---

* It was said that this song was directed against Duke Zhuang of Wei, who did not walk in the footsteps of his father Duke Wu, and by his neglect of his duties led men of worth to withdraw from public lire into retirement.

On wooded land unknown
A hermit lives, behold!
He sleeps, wakes, dwells alone
A joy ne'er to be told.

The Duke's Bride*

The buxom lady's big and tall,
A cape o'er her robe of brocade.
Her father, brothers, husband all
Are dukes or marquis of high grade.

Like lard congealed her skin is tender,
Her fingers like soft blades of reed;
Like larva white her neck is slender,
Her teeth like rows of melon-seed,
Her forehead like a dragonfly's,
Her arched brows curved like a bow.
Ah! dark on white her speaking eyes,
Her cheeks with smiles and dimples glow,

The buxom lady goes along;
She passes outskirts to be wed.

---

* This was the first description of a beautiful lady in Chinese poetry. The beautiful lady was married to Duke Zhuang of Wei who reigned in 757–735 B.C. but she bore no children and brought up Duke Huan who was murdered by his half-brother in 718 B.C. (see Poem "A Farewell Song")

Four steeds run vigorous and strong,
Their bits adorned with trappings red.
Her cab with pheasant-feathered screen
Proceeds to the court in array.
Retire, officials, from the scene!
Leave duke and her without delay!

The Yellow River wide and deep
Rolls northward its jubilant way.
When nets are played out, fishes leap
And splash and throw on reeds much spray.
Richly-dressed maids and warriors keep
Attendance on her bridal day.

A Faithless Man*

A man seemed free from guile;
In trade he wore a smile.
He'd barter cloth for thread;
No, to me he'd be wed.
I saw him cross the ford,
But gave him not my word.
I said by hillside green:
"You have no go-between.

---

* A woman who had been seduced into an improper connection, now cast off, related and bemoaned her sad case.

Try to find one, I pray.
In autumn be the day."

I climbed the wall to wait
To see him pass the gate.
I did not see him pass;
My tears streamed down, alas!
When I saw him pass by,
I'd laugh with joy and cry.
Both reed and tortoise shell
Foretold all would be well.
"Come with your cart," I said,
"To you I will be wed."

How fresh were mulberries
With their fruit on the trees!
Beware, O turtledove,
Eat not the fruit of love!
It will intoxicate.
Do not repent too late!
Man may do what he will;
He can atone it still.
No one will e'er condone
The wrong a woman's done.

The mulberries appear
With yellow leaves and sear.
E'er since he married me,

I've shared his poverty.
Deserted, from him I part;
The flood has wet my cart.
I have done nothing wrong;
He changes all along.
He's fickle to excess,
Capricious, pitiless.

Three years I was his wife
And led a toilsome life.
Each day I early rose
And late I sought repose.
But he found fault with me
And treated me cruelly.
My brothers who didn't know
Let their jeers at me go.
Mutely I ruminate
And I deplore my fate.

I'd live with him till old;
My grief was not foretold.
The endless stream has shores;
My endless grief e'er pours.
When we were girl and boy,
We'd talk and laugh with joy.
He pledged to me his troth,
Could he forget his oath?

He's forgot what he swore.
Should I say any more?

A Lovesick Fisherman*

With long rod of bamboo
I fish in River Qi.
Home, how I long for you,
Far-off a thousand li!

At left the Spring flows on;
At right the River clear.
To wed they saw me gone,
Leaving my parents dear.

The River clear at right,
At left the Spring flows on.
O my smiles beaming bright
And ringing gems are gone!

The long, long River flows
With boats of pine home-bound.
My boat along it goes.
O let my grief be drowned!

---

* A daughter of the House of Wei, married in another state, expressed her longing to revisit the scenes of her youth, where she had rambled in elegant dress between River Qi and the Spring. It was said that the daughter was Baroness Mu of Xu (see Poem "Patriotic Baroness Mu of Xu").

A Widow in Love*

The creeper's pods hang like
The young man's girdle spike.
An adult's spike he wears;
For us he no longer cares.
He puts on airs and swings
To and fro tassel-strings.

The creeper's leaves also swing;
The youth wears archer's ring.
An archer's ring he wears;
For us he no longer cares.
He puts on airs and swings
To and fro tassel-strings.

The River Wide**

Who says the River's wide?
A reed could reach the other side.
Who says Song's far-off? Lo!
I could see it on tiptoe.

Who says the River's wide?

---

* It was said that the conceited youth alluded to Duke Hui of Wei who murdered his elder brother and succeeded to the State in 718 B.C. (see Poem "A Farewell Song")
** This song was said to be written by a daughter of Xuan Jiang who longed to see her son, Duke Xiang of Song.

A boat could reach the other side.
Who says Song's far away?
I could reach it within a day.

My Lord*

My lord is brave and bright,
A hero in our land,
A vanguard in King's fight,
With a lance in his hand.

Since my lord eastward went,
Like thistle looks my hair.
Have I no anointment?
For whom should I look fair?

Let it rain, let it rain!
The sun shines bright instead.
I miss my lord in vain,
Heedless of aching head.

Where's the Herb to Forget?
To plant it north I'd start.
Missing my lord, I fret:
It makes me sick at heart.

---

* A wife mourned over the protracted absence of her lord on the King's service around 706 B.C.. This was considered as the earliest song of a wife longing for her husband in service.

A Lonely Husband*

Like lonely fox he goes
On the bridge over there.
My heart sad and drear grows:
He has no underwear.

Like lonely fox he goes
At the ford over there.
My heart sad and drear grows:
He has no belt to wear.

Like lonely fox he goes
By riverside o'er there.
My heart sad and drear grows:
He has no dress whate'er.

Gifts**

She throws a quince to me;
I give her a green jade
Not in return, you see,
But to show acquaintance made.

---

* It was said that in this song a woman expressed her desire for a husband, for through the misery and desolation of the State of Wei, many, both men and women, were left unmarried or had lost their partners.

** This song referred to an interchange of courtesies between a lover and his mistress.

She throws a peach to me;
I give her a white jade
Not in return, you see,
But to show friendship made.

She throws a plum to me;
I give her jasper fair
Not in return, you see,
But to show love fore'er.

Songs Collected around the Capital, Modern Henan

The Ruined Capital*

The millet drops its head;
The sorghum is in sprout.
Slowly I trudge and tread;
My heart is tossed about.
Those who know me will say
My heart is sad and bleak;
Those who don't know me may
Ask me for what I seek.
O boundless azure sky,
Who's ruined the land and why?

The millet drops its head;
The sorghum in the ear.
Slowly I trudge and tread;
My heart seems drunk and drear
Those who know me will say
My heart is sad and bleak;
Those who don't know me may

---

* In 769 B.C. King Ping of the Zhou Dynasty removed the capital to the east and from this time the kings of Zhou sank nearly to the level of the princes of the States. An official seeing the desolation of the old capital wrote this song expressing his melancholy.

Ask me for what I seek.
O boundless azure sky,
Who's ruined the land and why?

The millet drops its head;
The sorghum is in grain.
Slowly I trudge and tread;
My heart seems choked with pain.
Those who know me will say
My heart is sad and bleak;
Those who don't know me may
Ask me for what I seek.
O boundless azure sky,
Who's ruined the land and why?

My Man Is Away*

My man's away to serve the State;
I can't anticipate
How long he will there stay
Or when he'll be on homeward way.
The sun is setting in the west;
The fowls are roosting in their nest;
The sheep and cattle come to rest.
To serve the state my man's away.

---

* This song expressed the feeling of a wife on the prolonged absence of her husband on service and her longing for his return.

How can I not think of him night and day?

My man's away to serve the state;
I can't anticipate
When we'll again have met.
The sun's already set;
The fowls are roosting in their nest;
The sheep and cattle come to rest.
To serve the state my man's away.
Keep him from hunger and thirst, I pray.

What Joy*

My man sings with delight;
In his left hand a flute of reed,
He calls me to sing with his right,
What joy indeed!

My man dances in delight;
In his left hand a feather-screen,
He calls me to dance with his right.
What joy foreseen!

---

* It was said that this song showed the husband's satisfaction and his wife's joy on his return.

In Garrison*

Slowly the water flows;
Firewood can't be carried away.
You're afraid of your foes;
Why don't you in garrison stay?
How much for home I yearn!
O when may I return?

Slowly the water flows;
No thorn can be carried away.
You're afraid of your foes;
Why don't you in army camps stay?
How much for home I yearn!
O when may I return?

Slowly the water flows;
Rushes can't be carried away.
You're afraid of your foes;
Why don't you in army tents stay?
How much for home I yearn?
O when may I return?

---

* The troops of Zhou murmured against the lords who kept them on duty in the State of Shen, modern Nanyang. The water which flows so slowly and whose power is too weak to carry away firewood or thorn or rushes may allude to the Kingdom of Zhou, too weak to defend its frontiers.

Grief of a Deserted Wife*

Amid the vale grow mother-worts;
They are withered and dry.
There's a woman her lord deserts.
O hear her sigh!
O hear her sigh!
Her lord's a faithless guy.

Amid the vale grow mother-worts;
They are scorched and dry.
There's a woman her lord deserts.
O hear her cry!
O hear her cry!
She has met a bad guy.

Amid the vale grow mother-worts;
They are now drowned and wet.
There's a woman her lord deserts.
See her tears jet!
See her tears jet!
It's too late to regret.

---

* This song was expressive of pity for a deserted wife.

Past and Present*

The rabbit runs away,
The pheasant in the net.
In my earliest day
For nothing did I fret;
In later years of care
All evils have I met.
O I would sleep fore'er.

The rabbit runs away,
The pheasant in the snare.
In my earliest day
For nothing did I care;
In later years of ache
I'm in grief and despair.
I'd sleep and never wake.

The rabbit runs away,
The pheasant in the trap.
In my earliest day
I lived without mishap;
But in my later year
All miseries appear.
I'd sleep and never hear.

---

* The present referred to the time of King Ping (718–696 B.C.). The rabbit was said to be of a crafty nature while the pheasant to be bold and determined and easily snared.

A Refugee*

Creepers spread all the way
Along the river clear,
From brothers far away,
I call a stranger "father dear."
Though called "dear father," he
Seems not to care for me.

Creepers spread all the way
Beside the river clear.
From brothers far away,
I call a stranger "mother dear."
Though called "dear mother," she
Seems not to cherish me.

Creepers spread all the way
Beyond the river clear.
From brothers far away,
I call a stranger "brother dear."
Though called "dear brother," he
Seems not to pity me.

---

* A refugee mourned over his lot, unpitied by man and woman, old and young. The growth of creepers on the soil proper to them was presented by the refugee in contrast to his own position, torn from his family and proper soil.

One Day When I See Her Not*

To gather vine goes she.
I miss her whom I do not see,
One day seems longer than months three.

To gather reed goes she.
I miss her whom I do not see,
One day seems long as seasons three.

To gather herbs goes she.
I miss her whom I do not see,
One day seems longer than years three.

To Her Captive Lord **

Rumbling your cart,
Reedlike your gown,
I miss you in my heart.
How dare I make it known?

Rattling your cart,
Reddish your gown,
I miss you in my heart.
How dare I have it shown?

---

* It has become proverbial that a short absence from the lover seems to be long, and longer the more she is dwelt upon.
** This song was said to be written by the beautiful Lady of Peach Blossom, whose lord became a captive of the prince of Chu.

Living, we dwell apart;
Dead, the same grave we'll share.
Am I not true at heart?
By the bright sun I swear.

To Her Lover*

Hemp on the mound I see.
Who's there detaining thee?
Who's there detaining thee?
From coming jauntily to me?

Wheat on the mound I'm thinking of.
Who detains thee above?
Who detains thee above
From coming with me to make love?

On the mound stands plum tree.
Who's there detaining thee?
Who's there detaining thee
From giving girdle gems to me?

---

* A woman longed for the presence of her lover who, she thought, was detained from her by another woman.

Songs Collected in Zheng, Modern Henan

A Good Wife*

The black-dyed robe befits you well;
When it's worn out, I'll make another new.
You go to work in your hotel;
Come back, I'll make a meal for you.

The black-dyed robe becomes you well;
When it's worn out, I'll get another new.
You go to work in your hotel;
Come back, I'll make a meal for you.

The black-dyed robe does suit you well;
When it's worn out, you'll have another new.
You go to work in your hotel;
Come back, I'll make a meal for you.

Cadet My Dear**

Cadet my dear,
Don't leap into my hamlet, please,
Nor break my willow trees!
Not that I care for these;

---

* It was said that this song was expressive of the wife's regard that was due to the virtue and ability of her lord.

** A woman begged her lover not to excite the suspicions and remarks of her parents and others.

It is my parents that I fear.
Much as I love you, dear,
How can I not be afraid
Of what my parents might have said!

Cadet my dear,
Don't leap over my wall, please,
Nor break my mulberries!
Not that I care for these;
It is my brothers that I fear.
Much as I love you, dear,
How can I not be afraid
Of what my brothers might have said!

Cadet my dear,
Don't leap into my garden, please,
Nor break my sandal trees!
Not that I care for these;
It is my neighbors that I fear.
Much as I love you, dear,
How can I not be afraid
of what my neighbors might have said!

The Young Cadet*

The young cadet to chase has gone;

---

* It was said that the young cadet referred to the younger brother of Duke Zhuang of Zheng who succeeded Duke Wu in 742 B.C..

It seems there's no man in the town.
Is it true there's none in the town?
It's only that I cannot find
Another hunter so handsome and kind.
The young cadet's gone hunting in the wood.
In the town there's no drinker good.
Is it true there's no drinker good?
In the town no drinker of wine
Looks so handsome and fine.

The young cadet has gone to countryside;
In the town there's none who can ride.
Is it true there's none who can ride?
I cannot find among the young and old
Another rider so handsome and bold.

Hunting*

Our lord goes hunting in the land,
Mounted in his cab with four steeds.
He waves and weaves the reins in hand;
Two outside horses dance with speed.
Our lord goes hunting in grass land;
The hunters' torches flame in a ring.
He seizes a tiger with bared hand
And then presents it to the king.

---

* This was the earliest description of hunting in Chinese poetry.

BOOK OF POETRY

Don't try, my lord, to do it again
For fear you may get hurt with pain!

Mounted in his chariot and four,
Hunting afield our lord does go.
The inside horses run before;
Two on the outside follow in a row.
Our lord goes to the waterside;
The hunters' torches blaze up high.
He knows not only how to ride
But also shoot with his sharp eye.
He runs and stops his steeds at will
And shoots his arrows with great skill.

Mounted in cab and four steeds fine,
Our lord goes hunting in the lands.
Two on the inside have their heads in a line;
Two on the outside follow like two hands.
To waterside our lord does go;
The hunters' fire spreads everywhere.
His grey and yellow steeds go slow;
The arrows he shoots become rare.
Aside his quiver now he lays
And returns his bow to the case.

Qing Warriors*

Qing warriors stationed out,
Four mailed steeds run about.
Two spears adorned with feathers red,
Along the stream they roam ahead.

Qing warriors stationed on the shore
Look martial in their cab and four.
Two spears with pheasant's feathers red,
Along the stream they stroll ahead.

Qing warriors stationed on the stream
Look proud in their cab and mailed team.
Driver at left, spearsman at right,
The general shows his great delight.

Officer in Lamb's Fur**

His fur of lamb is white
As the man is upright.
The officer arises
Unchanged in a crisis.

With cuffs of leopard-skin,

---

* This was a satire against Duke Wen who ruled in the State of Zheng (662–627 B.C.) but maneuvered uselessly an army of Qing on the frontier.
** This song celebrated some officer of Zheng for his elegant appearance and integrity.

The fur of lamb he's in
Makes him look strong and bold;
To the right he will hold.

His fur of lamb is bright
With three stripes left and right.
The officer stands straight,
A hero of the State.

Leave Me Not*

I hold you by the sleeve
Along the public way.
O do not hate and leave
A mate of olden day!

I hold you by the hand
Along the public road.
Don't think me ugly and
Leave your former abode!

A Hunter's Domestic Life**

The wife says, "Cocks crow, hark!"
The man says, "It's still dark."
"Rise and see if it's night;

---

* A woman entreated her lover not to cast her off.
** A wife sent her husband from her side to his hunting and expressed her affection for him.

The morning star shines bright."
"Wild geese and ducks will fly;
I'll shoot them down from high."

"At shooting you are good;
I'll dress the game as food.
Together we'll drink wine
And live to ninety-nine.
With zither by our side,
In peace we shall abide."

"I know your wifely care;
I'll give you pearls to wear.
I know you will obey;
Can pearls and jade repay?
I know your steadfast love;
I value nothing above."

Lady Jiang*

A lady in the cab with me
Looks like a flower from a hedge-tree.
She goes about as if in flight;
Her girdle-pendants look so bright.
O Lady Jiang with pretty face,
So elegant and full of grace!

---

* It was said that this was a praise of the newly-wed Lady Jiang.

The lady together with me
Walks like a blossoming hedge-tree.
She moves about as if in flight;
Her girdle-pendants tinkle light.
O Lady Jiang with pretty face,
Can I forget you so full of grace?

A Joke*

Uphill stands mulberry
And lotus in the pool.
The handsome I don't see;
Instead I see a fool.

Uphill stands a pine-tree
And in the pool leaves red.
The pretty I don't see;
I see the sly instead.

Sing Together**

Leaves sear, leaves sear,
The wind blows you away.
Sing, cousins dear,
And I'll join in your lay.

---

* A woman mocked her lover as a sly fool.
** When leaves wafted in the wind after harvest, a songstress asked her companions to sing and dance together like wafting leaves.

Leaves sear, leaves sear,
The wind wafts you away.
Sing, cousins dear,
And I'll complete your lay.

A Handsome Guy*

You handsome guy
Won't speak to me words sweet.
For you I sigh
And can not drink nor eat.

You handsome guy
Won't eat with me at my request.
For you I sigh
And cannot take my rest.

Lift up Your Robe**

If you think of me as you seem,
Lift up your robe and cross that stream!
If you don't love me as you seem,
Can I not find another one?
Your foolishness is second to none.

---

* Some misunderstanding seemed to have arisen between the poetess and her handsome lover.
** A woman sang to her lover who would not lift up his robe and cross the stream to meet her.

If you think of me as you seem,
Lift up your gown and cross this stream!
If you don't love me as you seem,
Can I not find another mate?
Your foolishness is really great.

Lost Opportunity*

You looked plump and plain
And waited for me in the lane.
Why did I not go with you? I complain.

You looked strong and tall
And waited for me in the hall.
I regret I did not return your call.

Over my broidered skirt
I put on simple shirt.
O Sir, to you I say;
Come in your cab and let us drive away!

I put on simple shirt
Over my broidered skirt.
O Sir, I say anew:
Come in your cab and take me home with you!

---

* A woman regretted that she had not kept her promise and wished that her lover would come again.

A Lover's Monologue*

At eastern gate on level ground
There are madder plants all around.
My lover's house is very near,
But far away he does appear.

'Neath chestnut tree at eastern gate
Within my house in vain I wait.
How can I not think of my dear?
Why won't he come to see me here?

Wind and Rain**

The wind and rain are chill;
The crow of cocks is shrill.
When I've seen my man best,
Should I not feel at rest?

The wind whistles with showers;
The cocks crow dreary hours.
When I've seen my dear one,
With my ill could I not have done?
Gloomy wind and rain blend;

---

* A woman thought of her lover and complained that he did not come to her though his house was very near, at the eastern gate of the capital of Zheng.
** This described the joy of a lonely wife on seeing her husband's return in wind and rain.

The cocks crow without end.
When I have seen my dear,
How full I feel of cheer!

To a Scholar*

Student with collar blue,
How much I long for you!
Though to see you I am not free,
O why don't you send word to me?

Scholar with belt-stone blue,
How long I think of you!
Though to see you I am not free,
O why don't you come to see me?

I'm pacing up and down
On the wall of the town.
When to see you I am not free,
One day seems like three months to me.

Believe Me**

Wood bound together may
Not be carried away.

---

* A woman longed for her lover.
** A woman asserted good faith to her husband and protested against people who would make them doubt each other. A bundle of firewood might allude to a couple well united.

We have but brethren few;
There're only I and you.
What others say can't be believed,
Or you will be deceived.

A bundle of wood may
Not be carried away.
We have but brethren few;
There are only we two.
Do not believe what others say!
Untrustworthy are they.

My Lover in White*

Outside the eastern gate
Like clouds fair maidens date.
Though they are fair as cloud,
My love's not in the crowd.
Dressed in light green and white,
Alone she's my delight.

Outside the outer gate
Like blooms fair maidens date.
Though like blooms they are fair,
The one I love's not there.

---

* A man praised his lover in white, contrasted with beautiful maidens dating outside the eastern gate of the capital of Zheng.

Dressed in scarlet and white,
Alone she gives me delight.

The Creeping Grass*

Afield the creeping grass
With crystal dew o'erspread,
There's a beautiful lass
With clear eyes and fine forehead,
When I meet the clear-eyed,
My desire's satisfied.

Afield the creeping grass
With round dewdrops o'erspread,
There's a beautiful lass
With clear eyes and fine forehead.
When I meet the clear-eyed,
Amid the grass let's hide!

Riverside Rendezvous**

The Rivers Zhen and Wei
Overflow on their way.

---

* This song described the love-making of a young man and a beautiful lass amid the creeping grass o'erspread with morning dew.
** It was the custom of the State of Zheng for young people to meet and make love by the riverside on the festive day of the third lunar month in spring.

The lovely lad and lass
Hold in hand fragrant grass.
"Let's look around," says she;
"I've already," says he.
"Let us go there again!
Beyond the River Wei
The ground is large and people gay."
Playing together then,
They have a happy hour;
Each gives the other peony flower.

The Rivers Zhen and Wei
Flow crystal-clear;
Lad and lass squeeze their way
Through the crowd full of cheer.
"Let's look around," says she;
"I've already," says he
"Let us go there again!
Beyond the River Wei
The ground is large and people gay."
Playing together then,
They have a happy hour;
Each gives the other peony flower.

Songs Collected in Qi, Modern Shandong

A Courtier and His Wife*

"Wake up!" she says, "Cocks crow.
The court is on the go."
"It's not the cock that cries,"
He says, "but humming flies."

"The east is brightening;
The court is in full swing."
"It's not the east that's bright
But the moon shedding light."

"See buzzing insects fly.
It's sweet in bed to lie.
But courtiers will not wait;
None likes you to be late."

Two Hunters**

How agile you appear!
Amid the hills we meet.

---

* This was a dialogue between a courtier and his wife. It was said that the dialogue might refer to the marquess of Qi (934–894 B.C.) and the marchioness.

** This was the compliments interchanged by two hunters of Qi. Some critics said that this was a specimen of admirable satire, through which the boastful manners of the people of Qi were clearly exhibited.

Pursuing two boars, compeer,
You bow and say I'm fleet.

How skilful you appear!
We meet halfway uphill.
Driving after two males, compeer,
You bow and praise my skill.

How artful you appear!
South of the hill we meet.
Pursuing two wolves, compeer!
You bow and say my art's complete.

The Bridegroom*

He waits for me between the door and screen,
His crown adorned with ribbons green
Ended with gems of beautiful sheen.

He waits for me in the court with delight,
His crown adorned with ribbons white
Ended with gems and rubies bright.

He waits for me in inner hall,
His crown adorned with yellow ribbons all
Ended with gems like golden ball.

---

* A bride described her first meeting with the bridegroom who should wait for her arrival first at the door, then in the court and at last in the inner hall, according to ancient nuptial ceremony.

Nocturnal Tryst*

The eastern sun is red;
The maiden like a bloom
Follows me to my room.
The maiden in my room
Follows me to the bed.

The eastern moon is bright;
The maiden I adore
Follows me out of door.
The maiden out of door
Leaves me and goes out of sight.

A Tryst before Dawn**

Before the east sees dawn,
You put on clothes upside down.
O upside down you put them on,
For orders come from ducal crown.

Before the east is bright,
You take the left sleeve for the right
You put in left sleeve your right arm,
For orders bring disorder and alarm.

---

* The maiden came to the tryst like the eastern sun and left her lover like the eastern moon.
** A toiler complained of the early rise before dawn and the disorder brought by the order of the duke and the supervisor.

Don't leave my garden fence with willow tree;
Do not stare at my naked body, please.
You either come too late at night,
Or leave me early in twilight.

Incest*

To Duke Xiang of Qi

The southern hill is great;
A male fox seeks his mate.
The way to Lu is plain;
Your sister with her train
Goes to wed Duke of Lu.
Why should you go there too?

The shoes are made in pairs

---

* This was a satire against Duke Xiang of Qi and Duke Huan of Lu. In 708 B.C. Duke Huan rnarried a daughter of Qi, known as Wen Jiang. There was an improper affection between her and her brother, Duke Xiang; and on his succession to Qi, the couple visited him. The consequences were incest between the brother and sister, the murder of the husband and a disgraceful connection, long continued, between the guilty pair. In the first stanza, the great southern hill alluded to the great State of Qi and the male fox seeking his mate alluded contemptuously to Duke Xiang seeking his sister who was going to wed Duke Huan of Lu. In the second stanza, the shoes and strings of gems made in pairs alluded to the union of man and wife. In the third stanza, the ground well prepared for hemp alluded to the preparations for marriage between Duke Huan and Wen Jiang. In the last stanza, the splitting of firewood was a formality in contracting a marriage during the Zhou Dynasty.

And strings of gems she wears.
The way to Lu is plain;
Your sister goes to reign
And wed with Duke of Lu.
Why should you follow her too?

To Duke Huan of Lu

For hemp the ground is ploughed and dressed
From north to south, from east to west.
When a wife comes to your household,
Your parents should be told.
If you told your father and mother,
Should your wife go back to her brother?

How is the firewood split?
An axe can sever it.
How can a wife be won?
With go-between it's done.
To be your wife she's vowed;
No incest is allowed.

Missing Her Son*

Don't till too large a ground,
Or weed will spread around.

---

* It was said that song was written for Wen Jiang of Qi (see the preceding poem) missing her son who became Duke Zhuang of Lu at the age of thirteen.

Don't miss one far away,
Or you'll grieve night and day.

Don't till too large a ground,
Or weed overgrows around.
Don't miss the far-off one,
Or your grief won't be done.

My son was young and fair
With his two tufts of hair.
Not seen for a short time,
He's grown up to his prime.

Hunter and Hounds*

The bells of hound
Give ringing sound;
Its master's mind
Is good and kind.

The good hound brings
Its double rings;
Its master's hair
Is curled and fair.
The good hound brings
Its triple rings;

---

* This was a description of a handsome hunter. It was said that this was a satire against Duke Xiang's wild addiction to hunting to the detriment of public interest.

Its master's beard
Is deep revered.

Duchess Wen Jiang of Qi*

The basket is worn out
And fishes swim about.
The duchess comes with crowd,
Capricious like the cloud.

The basket is worn out;
Bream and tench swim about.
The duchess comes like flower,
Inconstant like the shower.

The basket is worn out;
Fish swim freely about.
Here comes Duke of Qi's daughter,
Changeable like water.

Duke of Qi and Duchess of Lu**

The duke's cab drives ahead

---

* The worn-out basket unable to catch fish alluded to Duke Huan of Lu unable to control the bold licentious conduct of his wife Wen Jiang in returning to the State of Qi (see note on Poem "Incest").
** This was a satire against the open shamelessness of Duchess of Wen Jiang of Lu in her meeting with her brother, Duke Xiang of Qi. The merry-making might allude to their love-making (see note on Poem "Incest").

With screens of leather red;
The duchess starts her way
Before the break of day.

The duke's steeds run amain;
Soft looks their hanging rein.
The duchess speeds her way
At the break of the day.

The river flows along;
Travellers come in throng.
Duke and duchess meet by day
And make merry all the way.

The river's overflowed
With travellers in crowd.
Duke and duchess all day
Make merry all the way.

The Archer Duke*

Fairest of all,
He's grand and tall,
His forehead high
With sparkling eye;
He's fleet of foot

---

* This song referred to Duke Zhuang of Lu, son of Duchess Wen Jiang and nephew of Duke Xiang of Qi.

And skilled to shoot.

His fame is high
With crystal eye;
In brave array
He shoots all day;
Each shot a hit,
No son's so fit.

He's fair and bright
With keenest sight;
He dances well;
Each shot will tell;
Four shots right go;
He'll quell the foe.

Songs Collected in Wei, Modern Shanxi

A Well-drest Lady and Her Maid*

In summer shoes with silken lace,
A maid walks on frost at quick pace.
By slender fingers of the maid
Her mistress' beautiful attire is made.
The waistband and the collar fair
Are ready now for her mistress to wear.

The lady moves with pride;
She turns her head aside
With ivory pins in her hair.
Against her narrow mind
I'll use satire unkind.

A Scholar Unknown**

By riverside, alas!
A scholar gathers grass.
He gathers grass at leisure,
Careful beyond measure,
Beyond measure his grace,

---

* This was a satire against a well-dressed lady and a praise of her sewing maid.
** This was a criticism of the State of Wei where only wealthy lords could be high officials while brilliant scholars could only gather grass and leaves without any official duty.

Why not in a high place?

By riverside picks he
The leaves of mulberry.
Amid the leaves he towers
As brilliant as flowers.
Such brilliancy and beauty,
Why not on official duty?

By riverside he trips
To gather the ox-tips.
His virtue not displayed
Like deeply buried jade.
His virtue once appears,
He would surpass his peers.

A Scholar Misunderstood*

Fruit of peach tree
Is used as food.
It saddens me
To sing and brood.
Who knows me not
Says I am proud.
He's right in what?
Tell me aloud.

---

* This was another criticism of the State of Wei where unemployed poor scholars used peach and date as food.

I'm full of woes
My heart would sink,
But no one knows,
For none will think,

Of garden tree
I eat the date.
It saddens me
To roam the state.
Who knows me not
Says I am queer.
He's right in what?
O let me hear!
I'm full of woes;
My heart would sink.
But no one knows,
For none will think.

A Homesick Soldier*

I climb the hill covered with grass
And look towards where my parents stay.
My father would say, "Alas!
My son's on service far away;
He cannot rest night and day.

---

* A young soldier on service solaced himself with the thought of home.

O may he take good care
To come back and not remain there!"

I climb the hill devoid of grass
And look towards where my parents stay.
My mother would say, "Alas!
My youngest son's on service far away;
He cannot sleep well night and day.
O may he take good care
To come back and not be captive there!"

I climb the hilltop green with grass
And look towards where my brothers stay.
My eldest brother would say, "Alas!
My youngest brother is on service far away;
He stays with comrades night and day.
O may he take good care
To come back and not be killed there!"

Gathering Mulberry*

Among ten acres of mulberry
All the planters are free.
Why not come back with me?

Beyond ten acres of mulberry

---

* This was a song sung by a planter of mulberry trees to a lass after the gathering of mulberries.

All the lasses are free.
O come away with me!

The Woodcutter's Song*

Chop, chop our blows on elm-trees go;
On rivershore we pile the wood.
The clear and rippling waters flow.
How can those who nor reap nor sow
Have three hundred sheaves of corn in their place?
How can those who nor hunt nor chase
Have in their courtyard badgers of each race?
Those lords are good
Who do not need work for food!

Chop, chop, our blows for wheel-spokes go;
By riverside we pile the wood.
The clear and even waters flow.
How can those who nor reap nor sow
Have three millions of sheaves in their place?
How can those who nor hunt nor chase
Have in their courtyard games of each race?
Those lords are good
Who need no work to eat their food!

Chop, chop our blows for the wheels go;

---

* This was a satire against those idle and greedy lords of the state.

At river brink we pile the wood.
The clear and dimpling waters flow.
How can those who nor reap nor sow
Have three hundred ricks of corn in their place?
How can those who nor hunt nor chase
Have in their courtyard winged games of each race?
Those lords are good
Who do not have to work for food!

Large Rat*

Large rat, large rat,
Eat no more millet we grow!
Three years you have grown fat;
No care for us you show.
We'll leave you now, I swear,
For a happier land,
A happier land where
We may have a free hand.

Large rat, large rat,
Eat no more wheat we grow!
Three years you have grown fat;
No kindness to us you show.
We'll leave you now, I swear,

---

* The large rat was symbolic of the corrupt official and the happier land or state was a Utopia of the peasants.

For a happier state,
A happier land where
We can decide our fate.

Large rat, large rat,
Eat no more rice we grow!
Three years you have grown fat;
No rewards to our labor go.
We'll leave you now, I swear,
For a happier plain,
A happier plain where
None will groan or complain.

Songs Collected in Tang, Modern Shanxi

The Cricket*

The cricket chirping in the hall,
The year will pass away.
The present not enjoyed at all,
We'll miss the passing day.
Do not enjoy to excess
But do our duty with delight!
We'll enjoy ourselves none the less
If we see those at left and right

The cricket chirping in the hall,
The year will go away.
The present not enjoyed at all,
We'll miss the bygone day.
Do not enjoy to excess
But only to the full extent!
We'll enjoy ourselves none the less
If we are diligent.

The cricket chirping by the door,
Our cart stands unemployed.
The year will be no more
With the days unenjoyed.

---

* We might see in this song the cheerfulness and discretion of the people of Jin and their tempered enjoyment at fitting seasons.

Do not enjoy to excess
But think of hidden sorrow!
We'll enjoy ourselves none the less
If we think of tomorrow.

Why Not Enjoy? *

Uphill you have elm-trees;
Downhill you have elms white.
You have dress as you please.
Why not wear it with delight?
You have horses and car.
Why don't you take a ride?
One day when dead you are,
Others will drive them with pride.

Uphill you have varnish trees;
Downhill trees rooted deep.
You have rooms as you please.
Why not clean them and sweep?
You have your drum and bell.
Why don't you beat and ring?
One day when tolls your knell,
Joy to others they'll bring.

Uphill you have chestnut trees;

---

* This was a satire on the folly of not enjoying the good things and letting death put them into the hands of others.

Downhill trees with deep root.
You have wine as you please.
Why not play lyre and lute
To be cheerful and gay
And to prolong your bloom?
When you are dead one day,
Others will enter your room.

Our Prince*

The clear stream flows ahead
And the white rocks out stand.
In our plain dress with collars red,
We follow you to eastern land.
Shall we not rejoice since
We have seen our dear prince?

The clear stream flows ahead
And naked rocks out stand.
In plain dress with sleeves broidered red,
We follow you to northern land.
How can we feel sad since
We have seen our dear prince?

---

* The prince referred to the uncle of Marquis Zhao of Jin, who was raised by a rebellious party to displace the Marquis in 73 B.C.. The rocks were symbolic of the conspirators and the speaker was an adherent of the conspiracy who bad heard the secret order to conspire against Marquis Zhao of Jin.

The clear stream flows along the border;
Wave-beaten rocks stand out.
We've heard the secret order,
But nothing should be talked about.

The Pepper Plant*

The fruit of pepper plant
Is so luxuriant.
The woman there
Is large beyond compare.
O pepper plant, extend
Your shoots without end!

The pepper plant there stands;
Its fruit will fill our hands.
The woman here
Is large without a peer.
O pepper plant, extend
Your shoots without end!

A Wedding Song**

The firewood's tightly bound

---

* The productive pepper plant referred to a reproductive or fertile woman. That is the reason why a woman's bedroom was called pepper chamber in Chinese.
** The firewood or hay or thorns tightly bound alluded to husband and wife well united. The first stanza should be sung by the bride, the second by the guests and the third by the bridegroom.

When in the sky three stars appear.
What evening's coming round
For me to find my bridegroom here!
O he is here! O he is here!
What shall I not do with my dear!

The hay is tightly bound
When o'er the house three stars appear.
What night is coming round
To find this couple here!
O they are here! O they are here!
How lucky to see this couple dear!

The thorns are tightly bound
When o'er the door three stars appear.
What midnight's coming round
For me to find my beauty here!
O she is here! O she is here!
What shall I not do with my dear?

A Wanderer*

A tree of russet pear
Has leaves so thickly grown.
Alone I wander there
With no friends of my own.

---

* This was the lament of a beggar deprived of his brothers and relatives or forsaken by them.

Is there no one
Who would of me take care?
But there is none
Like my own father's son.
O wanderer, why are there few
To sympathize with you?
Can yon not find another
To help you like a brother?

A tree of russet pear
Has leaves so lushly grown.
Alone I loiter there
Without a kinsman of my own.
Is there no one
Who would take care of me?
But there is none
Like my own family.
O loiterer, why are there few
To sympathize with you?
Can you not find another
To help you like a brother?

An Unkind Lord in Lamb's Fur*

Lamb's fur and leopard's cuff,
To us you are so rough.

---

* The people of some lord complained of his hard treatment of them.

Can't we find another chief
Who would cause us no grief?

Lamb's fur and leopard's cuff,
You ne'er give us enough.
Can't we find another chief
Who would assuage our grief?

The Peasants' Complaint*

Swish, swish sound the plumes of wild geese;
They can't alight on bushy trees.
We must discharge the king's affair.
How can we plant our millet with care?
On what can our parents rely?
O gods in boundless, endless sky,
When can we live in peace? I sigh.

Swish, swish flap the wings of wild geese;
They can't alight on jujube trees.
We must discharge the king's affair.
How can we plant our maize with care?
On what can our parents live and rely?
O gods in boundless, endless sky,
Can all this end before I die?

---

* The men of Jin called out to warfare by the king's order mourned over the consequent suffering of their parents and longed for their return to their ordinary agricultural pursuits.

Swish, swish come the rows of wild geese;
They can't alight on mulberries.
We must discharge the king's affair.
How can we plant our rice with care?
What can our parents have for food?
O Heaven good, O Heaven good!
When can we gain a livelihood?

To His Deceased Wife*

Have I no dress?
You made me seven.
I'm comfortless,
Now you're in heaven.

Have I no dress?
You made me six.
I'm comfortless
As if on pricks.

The Russet Pear Tree**

A lonely tree of russet pear
Stands still on the left of the way.
O you for whom I care,

---

* The speaker was thinking of his deceased wife who had made his dress for him.
** The russet pear tree was said to be symbolic of a lonely woman longing for her lover.

Won't you come as I pray?
In my heart you're so sweet.
When may I give you food to eat?

A lonely tree of russet pear
Stands still on the road's right-hand side.
O you for whom I care,
Won't you come for a ride?
In my heart you're so sweet.
When may I give you food to eat?

An Elegy*

Vine grows o'er the thorn tree;
Weeds in the field o'erspread.
The man I love is dead.
Who'd dwell alone with thee?

Vine grows o'er jujube tree;
Weeds o'er the graveyard spread.
The man I love is dead.
Who'd stay alone with thee?

How fair the pillow of horn

---

* This was the first elegy in Chinese poetry. A widow mourned the death of her husband killed in the war waged by Duke Xian of Jin (reigned 675–650 B.C.). The vine supported by the tree might be suggestive of the widow's own desolate, unsupported condition or descriptive of the battleground where her husband had met his death.

And the embroidered bed!
The man I love is dead.
Who'd stay with thee till morn?

Long is the summer day;
Cold winter night appears.
After a hundred years
In the same tomb we'd stay.

The winter night is cold;
Long is the summer day.
When I have passed away,
We'll be in same household.

Rumor*

Could the sweet water plant be found
On the top of the mountain high?
The rumor going round,
If not believed can't fly.
Put it aside, put it aside
So that it can't prevail.
The rumor spreading far and wide
Will be of no avail.
Could bitter water plant be found

---

* This was directed against Duke Xian of Jin who killed his son on believing rumors. Rumors should no more be believed than water plants could be found on the top of the mountain.

At the foot of the mountain high?
The rumor going round
Is what we should deny.
Put it aside, put it aside
So that it can't prevail.
The rumor spreading far and wide
Will be of no avail.

Could water plants be found
East of the mountain high?
The rumor going round,
If disregarded, will die.
Put it aside, put it aside
So that it can't prevail.
The rumor spreading far and wide
Will be of no avail.

Songs Collected in Qin, Modern Shaanxi

Lord Zhong of Qin*

The cab bells ring;
Dappled steeds neigh.
"Let ushers bring
In friends so gay!"

There're varnish trees uphill
And chestnuts in lowland.
Friends see Lord Zhong sit still
Beside lute-playing band.
"If we do not enjoy today,
At eighty joy will pass away."

There're mulberries uphill
And willows in lowland.
Friends see Lord Zhong sit still
Beside his music band.
"If we do not enjoy today,
We'll regret when life ebbs away."

---

* This song celebrated the pleasures of Lord Zhong of Qin, who, made a great officer of the court by King Xuan in 826 B.C., began to turn Qin from a barbarian state to a music-loving civilized one, which unified China and founded the Empire of Qin in 221 B.C..

Winter Hunting*

Holding in hand six reins
Of four iron-black steeds,
Our lord hunts on the plains
With good hunters he leads.

The male and female preys
Have grown to sizes fit.
"Shoot at the left!" he says;
Their arrows go and hit.

He comes to northern park
With his four steeds at leisure;
Long-and short-mouthed hounds bark
In the carriage of pleasure.

A Lord on Expedition**

His chariot finely bound,
Crisscrossed with straps around,
Covered with tiger's skin,
Driven by horses twin;

---

* This song celebrated the growing opulence of Duke Xiang, grandson of Lord Zhong of Qin, as seen in his hunting in 769 B.C..
** The wife of a Qin lord absent on an expedition against the western tribes who killed King You of Zhou in 771 B.C., gave a glowing description of his chariot, steeds and weapons and expressed her regret at his absence.

His steeds controlled with reins
Through slip rings like gilt chains;
I think of my lord dear
Far-off on the frontier;
He's pure as jade and plain.
O my heart throbs with pain.

His four fine steeds there stand;
He holds six reins in hand.
The insides have black mane,
Yellow the outside twain.
Dragon shields on two wings,
Buckled up as with strings.
I think of my lord dear
So good on the frontier.
When will he come to me?
Can I be yearning-free?

How fine his team appears!
How bright his trident spears!
His shield bears a carved face;
In tiger's skin bow-case
With bamboo frames and bound;
With strings, two bows are found.
I think of my dear mate,
Rise early and sleep late.
My dear, dear one,
Can I forget the good you've done?

Where Is She?*

Green, green the reed,
Frost and dew gleam.
Where's she I need?
Beyond the stream.
Upstream I go;
The way's so long.
And downstream, lo!
She's thereamong.

White, white the reed,
Dew not yet dried.
Where's she I need?
On the other side.
Upstream I go;
Hard is the way.
And downstream, lo!
She's far away.

Bright, bright the reed,
With frost dews blend.
Where's she I need?
At river's end.
Upstream I go;
The way does wind.

---

* This was said to be the first symbolic love song in Chinese poetry.

And downstream, lo!
She's far behind.

Duke Xiang of Qin*

What's on the southern hill?
There're mume trees and white firs.
Our lord comes and stands still,
Wearing a robe and furs.
Vermillion is his face.
O what majestic grace!

What's on the southern hill?
There are trees of white pears.
Our lord comes and stands still;
A broidered robe he wears.
His gems give tinkling sound,
Long live our lord black-gowned!

---

* This song celebrated the dignity of Duke Xiang of Qin, the first of Qin lords recognized as a prince of the kingdom, who, wearing the black ducal robe conferred by King Ping in 769 B.C. after his victory over the western tribes who had killed King You in 771 B.C., passed by the Southern Mountain 25 kilometers south of the capital (modern Xi'an) on his homeward way to Qin.

Burial of Three Worthies*

The golden orioles flew
And lit on jujube tree.
Who's buried with Duke Mu?
The eldest of the three.
This eldest worthy son
Could be rivaled by none.
Coming to the graveside,
Who'd not be terrified?
O good Heavens on high,
Why should the worthy die?
If he could live again,
Who not have been slain?

The golden oriole flew
And lit on mulberry.
Who's buried with Duke Mu?
The second of the three.
The second worthy son
Could be equalled by none.
Coming to the graveside,
Who'd not be terrified?
O good Heavens on high,

---

* The three worthies were buried alive together with 174 others in the same grave with Duke Mu of Qin in 620 B.C.. They were not so free as the golden oriole.

Why should the worthy die?
If he could live again,
Who would not have been slain?

The golden oriole flew
And lit on the thorn tree.
Who's buried with Duke Mu?
The youngest of the three.
The youngest worthy son
Could be surpassed by none.
Coming to the graveside,
Who'd not be terrified?
O good Heavens on high,
Why should the worthy die?
If he could live again,
Who would not have been slain?

The Forgotten*

The falcon flies above
To the thick northern wood.
While I see not my love,
I'm in a gloomy mood.
How can it be my lot
To be so much forgot?

---

* A wife told her grief because of the absence of her husband and his forgetfulness of her.

The bushy oaks above
And six elm-trees below.
While I see not my love,
There is no joy I know.
How can it be my lot
To be so much forgot?

The sparrow-plums above
Below trees without leaf.
While I see not my love,
My heart is drunk with grief.
How can it be my lot
To be so much forgot?

Comradeship*

Are you not battle-drest?
Let's share the plate for breast!
We shall go up the line.
Let's make our lances shine!
Your foe is mine.

Are you not battle-drest?
Let's share the coat and vest!

---

* This was the song sung by Duke Ai of Qin when he dispatched five hundred chariots to the rescue of the State of Chu besieged by Wu in 505 B.C..

We shall go up the line.
Let's make our halberds shine!
Your job is mine.

Are you not battle-drest?
Let's share the kilt and the rest!
We shall go up the line.
Let's make our armour shine!
We'll march your hand in mine.

Farewell to Duke Wen of Jin*

I see my uncle dear
Off north of River Wei.
What's the gift for one I revere?
Golden cab on the way.

I see my uncle dear
Off and think of my mother.
What's the gift for one she and I revere?
Jewels and gems for her brother.

---

* This song was sung by Duke Kang of Qin in 635 B.C. while, heir-apparent of Qin, he escorted his uncle into the State of Jin where he became the famous Duke Wen after nineteen years' refuge in Qin.

Not As Before*

Ah me!
Where is my house of yore?
Now I've not a great deal
To eat at every meal.
Alas!
I can't live as before.

Ah me!
Where are my dishes four?
Now hungry I feel at every meal.
Alas!
I can't eat as before.

---

* This song was said to be a complaint against Duke Kang of Qin who was not so hospitable as Lord Zhong (in Poem "Lord Zhong of Qin") and Duke Mu of Qin.

Songs Collected in Chen, Modern Henan

A Religious Dancer*

In the highland above
A witch dances with swing.
With her I fall in love;
Hopeless, I sing.

She beats the drum
At the foot of highland.
Winter and summer come,
She dances plume in hand.

She beats a vessel round
On the way to highland.
Spring or fall comes around,
She dances fan in hand.

Secular Dancers**

From white elms at east gate
To oak-trees on the mound
Lad and lass have a date;

---

* This song described the pleasure-seeking of the people of Chen in the capital where there was a mound in the highland, favorite resort of pleasure-seekers.
** This song described wanton associations of the young people of Chen. The mound at the eastern gate was a favorite resort of pleasure-seekers.

They dance gaily around.

A good morning is chosen
To go to the south where,
Leaving the hemp unwoven,
They dance at country fair.

They go at morning hours
Together to highland.
Lasses look like sunflowers,
A token of love in hand.

Contentment*

Beneath the door of single beam,
You can sit and rest at your leisure.
Beside the gently flowing stream,
You may drink to stay hunger with pleasure.

If you want to eat fish,
Why must you have bream as you wish?
If you want to be wed,
Why must you have Qi the nobly bred?

If you want to eat fish,
Why must you have carp as you wish?

---

* This showed that one might enjoy oneself and forget one's hunger, be satisfied with fish of smaller note and be happy with a wife though she were not of a noble family.

If you want to be wed,
Why must you have Song the highly bred?

To a Weaving Maiden*

At eastern gate we could
Steep hemp in river long.
O maiden fair and good,
To you I'll sing a song.

At eastern gate we could
Steep nettle in the creek.
O maiden fair and good,
To you I wish to speak.

At eastern gate we could
Steep in the moat rush-rope.
O maiden fair and good,
On you I hang my hope.

A Date**

On poplars by east gate

---

* The stalks of the hemp had to be steeped, preparatory to getting the threads or filaments from them so that the maiden might weave clothes.

** The rustling poplar leaves and the evening star hinted at the lovers before their love making and the shivering leaves and the morning star at the couple after their love making.

The leaves are rustling light.
At dusk we have a date;
The evening star shines bright.

On poplars by east gate
The leaves are shivering.
At dusk we have a date;
The morning star is quivering.

The Evil-doing Usurper*

The thorn at burial gate
Should soon be cut away;
The usurper of the State
Should be exposed to the day;
If he's exposed too late,
He'll still do what he may.

At burial gate there's jujube tree,
On which owls perch all the day long;
The usurper from evil is not free.

---

* This was a satirical song directed against Tuo of Chen, a brother of Duke Huan (743-706 B.C.), upon whose death Tuo killed his eldest son and got possession of the State of Chen, but was killed by its neighboring state the year after. The thorn and the owl were both things of evil omen, and were employed here to introduce the evil-doing usurper. The legend went that this song was sung by a mulberry-gathering woman to ward off an official's attempt to rape her.

Let's warn him by a song!
But he won't listen to our plea,
For he takes right for wrong.

Riverside Magpies*

By riverside magpies appear;
On hillock water grasses grow.
Believe none who deceives, my dear,
Or my heart will be full of woe.

How can the court be paved with tiles
Or hillock spread with water grass?
Believe, my dear, none who beguiles,
Or I'll worry for you, alas!

The Moon**

The moon shines bright;
My love's snow-white.
She looks so cute.
Can I be mute?

---

* This song might speak of the separation between lovers effected by evil tongues or refer to Duke Xuan of Chen (691–647 B.C.) who believed slanderers.
** This was the first song in Chinese poetry describing the poet's love for a beauty in moonlight.

The bright moon gleams;
My dear love beams.
Her face so fair,
Can I not care?

The bright moon turns;
With love she burns.
Her hands so fine,
Can I not pine?

The Duke's Mistress*

"Why are you going to the Wood?
To see the fair lady's son?"
"I'm going to its neighborhood
To see the son of the fair one."

"I'll drive to the countryside
And take a short rest there;
I'll change my horse and ride
To breakfast with the fair."

---

* This song was directed against the intrigue of Duke Ling of Chen (reigned 612–598 B.C.) with the beautiful Lady Xia. The duke went to the wood in the countryside to tryst with her under the pretext of visiting her son Xia Nan, by whom he was killed in 598 B.C..

A Bewitching Lady*

By poolside over there
Grow reed and lotus bloom.
There is a lady fair
Whose heart is full of gloom.
She does nothing in bed;
Like streams her tears are shed.

By poolside over there
Grow reed and orchid bloom.
There is a lady fair
Heart-broken, full of gloom.
Tall and with a curled head,
She does nothing in bed.

By poolside over there
Grow reed and lotus thin.
There is a lady fair
Tall and with double chin.
She does nothing in bed,
Tossing about her head.

---

* It was said that this song described the bewitching Lady Xia mourning over the death of Duke Ling of Chen and her son Xia Nan killed by King Zhuang of Chu in 598 B.C. (See Poem "The Duke's Mistress").

Songs Collected in Kuai, Modern Henan

The Last Lord of Kuai*

You seek amusement in official dress;
You hold your court in sacrificial gown.
How can we not think of you in distress?
O how can our heavy heart not sink down?

You find amusement in your lamb's fur dress;
In your fox's fur at court you appear.
How can we not think of you in distress?
O how can our heart not feel sad and drear?

You appear in your greasy dress
Which glistens in the sun.
How can we not think of you in distress?
We are heart-broken at the wrong you've done.

The Mourning Wife**

The deceased's white cap seen,
His worn-out face so lean,

---

* The lamb's fur was used for official dress, but the lord of Kuai wore it while seeking amusement; the fox's fur was used for sacrificial dress, but the lord wore it at court. This showed that the lord neglected state affairs and that was the reason why the State of Kuai was extinguished by the State of Zheng in 769 B.C..

** It was said that mourners should wear white cap, white dress and white cover-knee since then.

I feel a sorrow keen.

Seeing my lord's white dress,
I become comfortless;
I would share his distress.

I see his white cover-knee,
Sorrow is knotted on me,
One with him I would be!

The Unconscious Tree*

In lowland grows the cherry
With branches swaying in high glee.
Why do you look so merry?
I envy you, unconscious tree.

In lowland grows the cherry
With flowers blooming in the breeze.
Why do you look so merry?
I envy you quite at your ease.

In lowland grows the cherry
With fruit overloading the tree.
Why do you look so merry?
I envy you from cares so free.

---

* The speaker, groaning under the oppression of the government, wished he were an unconscious tree.

Nostalgia*

The wind blows a strong blast;
The carriage's running fast.
I look to homeward, way.
Who can my grief allay?

The whirlwind blows a blast;
The cab runs wild and fast.
Looking to backward way,
Can I not pine away?

Who can boil fish?
I'll wash their boiler as they wish.
Who's going west?
Will he bring words at my request?

---

* This song spoke of King Ping's removal to the east as a result of the barbarian invasion in 769 B.C. when the State of Kuai, the poet's homeland, was extinguished by Duke Wu of Zheng (770–743 B.C.).

BOOK OF SONGS

Songs Collected in Cao, Modern Shandong

The Ephemera*

The ephemera's wings
Like morning robes are bright.
Grief to my heart it brings;
Where will it be at night?

The ephemera's wings
Like rainbow robes are bright.
Grief to my heart it brings;
Where will it rest by night?

The ephemera's hole
Like robe of hemp snow-white.
It brings grief to my soul:
Where may I go tonight?

Poor Attendants**

Holding halberds and spears,
The attendants escort

---

* This was directed against Duke Zhao of Cao (reigned 661–651 B.C.) occupied with frivolous pleasures and oblivious of important matters. The small State of Cao was extinguished by Duke Jing of Song in 487 B.C.
** This was directed against Duke Gong of Cao who had three hundred worthless peers but only one hundred diligent attendants in his court and who was impolite to Duke Wen of Jin in 641 B.C..

The rich three hundred peers,
Wearing red cover-knee in court.

The pelicans catch fish
Without wetting their wings;
The peers have what they wish,
But they're unworthy things.

The pelicans catch fish
Without wetting their beak;
The peers do what they wish,
Unworthy of favor they seek.

At sunrise on south hill
he attendants still wait;
Their hungry daughters feel ill,
Weeping their bitter fate.

An Ideal Ruler*

The cuckoo in the mulberries
Breeds seven fledglings with ease.
An ideal ruler should take care
To deal with all men fair and square.
If he treats all men fair and square,
He would be good beyond compare.

---

* An ideal ruler was celebrated by way of contrast with the rulers of the State of Cao.

The cuckoo in the mulberries
Breeds fledglings in mume trees.
An ideal ruler should be fair and bright,
His girdle hemmed with silk white.
If he's as bright as silken hems,
He'd be adorned with jade and gems.

The cuckoo in the mulberries
Breeds fledglings in the jujube trees.
An ideal ruler should be polite;
Whatever he does should be right.
If he is right as magistrate,
He'd be a model for the state.

The cuckoo in the mulberries
Breeds fledglings in the hazel trees.
Ruler should be a good magistrate
To help the people of the state.
If he helps people to right the wrong,
May he live ten thousand years long!

The Capital*

The bushy grass drowned by
Cold water flowing down,

---

* The bushy grass and plants drowned in cold water might allude to the small State of Cao drowned in misery which made the writer think of the capital of Zhou and of its prosperity.

When I awake, I sigh
For our capital town.

The southernwood drowned by
Cold water flowing down,
When I awake, I sigh
For our municipal town.

The bushy plants drowned by
Cold water flowing down,
When I awake, I sigh
For our old royal town.

Where millet grew in spring,
Enriched by happy rain;
The state ruled by the wise king,
The toilers had their grain.

Songs Collected in Bin, Modern Shaanxi

Life of Peasants*

In seventh moon Fire Star west goes;
In ninth to make dress we are told.
In eleventh moon the wind blows;
In twelfth the weather is cold.
We have no warm garments to wear.
How can we get through the year?
In the first moon we mend our plough with care;
In the second our way afield we steer.
Our wives and children take the food
To southern fields; the overseer says, "Good!"

In seventh moon Fire Star west goes;
In ninth we make dress all day long.
By and by warm spring grows
And golden orioles sing their song.
The lasses take their baskets deep
And go along the small pathways
To gather tender mulberry leaves in heap.
When lengthen vernal days,
They pile in heaps the southernwood.

---

* This was a description of the life of the peasants in Bin, where the first settlers of the House of Zhou dwelt for nearly five centuries from 1796 to 1325 B.C..

They are in gloomy mood.
For they will say adieu to maidenhood.

In seventh moon Fire Star west goes;
In eighth we gather rush and reed.
In silkworm month with axe's blow
We cut mulberry sprigs with speed.
We lop off branches long and high
And bring young tender leaves in.
In seventh moon we hear shrikes cry;
In eighth moon we begin to spin.
We use a bright red dye
And a dark yellow one
To color robes of our lord's son.

In fourth moon grass begins to seed;
In fifth cicadas cry.
In eighth moon to reap we proceed;
In tenth down come leaves dry.
In eleventh moon we go in chase
For wild cats and foxes fleet.
To make furs for the sons of noble race.

In the twelfth moon we meet
And manoeuvre with lance and sword.
We keep the smaller boars for our reward
And offer larger ones o'er to our lord.
In fifth moon locusts move their legs;

In sixth the spinner shakes its wings.
In seventh the cricket lays its eggs;
In eighth under the eaves it sings.
In ninth it moves indoors when chilled;
In tenth it enters under the bed.
We clear the corners, chinks are filled,
We smoke the house and rats run in dread.
We plaster northern window and door
And tell our wives and lad and lass;
The old year will soon be no more.
Let's dwell inside, alas!

In sixth moon we've wild plums and grapes to eat;
In seventh we cook beans and mallows nice.
In eighth moon down the dates we beat;
In tenth we reap the rice
And brew the vernal wine,
A cordial for the oldest-grown.
In seventh moon we eat melon fine;
In eighth moon the gourds are cut down.
In ninth we gather the hemp-seed;
Of fetid tree we make firewood;
We gather lettuce to feed
Our husbandmen as food.

In ninth moon we repair the threshing-floor;
In tenth we bring in harvest clean;

The millet sown early and late are put in store,
And wheat and hemp, paddy and bean.
There is no rest for husbandmen:
Once harvesting is done, alas!
We're sent to work in lord's house then.
By day for thatch we gather reed and grass;
At night we twist them into ropes,
Then hurry to mend the roofs again,
For we should not abandon the hopes
Of sowing in time our fields with grain.

In the twelfth moon we hew out ice;
In the first moon we store it deep.
In the second we offer early sacrifice
Of garlic, lamb and sheep.
In ninth moon frosty is the weather;
In tenth we sweep and clear the threshing-floor.
We drink two bottles of wine to-gether
And kill a lamb before the door.
Then we go up to the hall where
We raise our buffalo-horn cup
And wish our lord to live fore'er.

A Mother Bird*

Owl, owl, you've taken my young ones away.

---

* This was the first fable in Chinese poetry.

Do not destroy my nest!
With love and pain I toiled all day
To hatch them without rest.
Before it is going to rain,
I gather roots of mulberry
And mend my nest with might and main
Lest others bully me.

My claws feel sore
From gathering reeds without rest;
I put them up in store
Until my beak feels pain to mend my nest.

Sparse is my feather
And torn my tail;
My nest is tossed in stormy weather;
I cry and wail to no avail.

Coming Back from the Eastern Hills*

To east hills sent away,
Long did I there remain.
Now on my westward way,
There falls a drizzling rain.
Knowing I'll be back from the east,
My heart yearns for the west.

---

* The Duke of Zhou put down a rebellion in the east after 1125 B.C..

Book of Poetry

Fighting no more at least,
I'll wear a farmer's vest.
Curled up as silkworm crept
On the mulberry tree,
Beneath my cart alone I slept.
O how it saddened me!

To east hills sent away,
Long did I there remain.
Now on my westward way,
There falls a drizzling rain.
The vine of gourd may clamber
The wall and eave all o'er;
I may find woodlice in my chamber
And cobwebs across the door;
I may see in paddock deer-track
And glow-worms' fitful light.
Still I long to be back
To see such sorry sight.

To east hills sent away,
Long did I there remain.
Now on my westward way,
There falls a drizzling rain.
The cranes on ant-hill cry;
My wife in cottage room
May sprinkle, sweep and sigh
For my returning home.

The gourd may still hang high
Beside the chestnut tree.
O three years have gone by
Since last she was with me.

To east hills sent away,
Long did I there remain.
Now on my westward way,
There falls a drizzling rain.
The oriole takes flight
With glinting wings outspread.
I remember on horse bright
My bride came to be wed.
Her sash by her mother tied,
She should observe the rite.
Happy was I to meet my bride;
How happy when my wife's in sight!

With Broken Axe*

With broken axe in hand
And hatchet, our poor mates

---

* In 1125 B.C. the Duke of Zhou undertook an expedition against the four eastern states ruled by his own brothers Guan and Cai and Yan and the son of the last king of Shang. The battles were so fierce that many axes and hatchets were broken, and it took him three years to put down the rebellion.

Follow our duke from eastern land;
We've conquered the four states.
Alas! those who are not strong
Cannot come along.

With broken axe in hand
And chisel, our poor mates
Follow our duke from eastern land;
We've controlled the four states.
Alas! those who do not survive!
Lucky those still alive.

With broken axe in hand
And halberd, our poor mates
Follow our duke from eastern land
We've ruled o'er the four states.
Alas! those who are dead!
Lucky, let's go ahead.

An Axe-handle*

Do you know how to make
An axe-handle? With an axe keen.
Do you know how to take

---

* It was said that this song was sung by a bridegroom to his unmarried friends. That was the reason why a go-between was called a handlemaker in China.

A wife? Just ask a go-between,
When a handle is hewed,
The pattern should not be far.
When a maiden is wooed,
See how many betrothal gifts there are.

The Duke's Return*

In a nine-bagged net
There are breams and red-eyes.
See ducal coronet
And gown on which the broidered dragon flies.

Along the shore the swan's in flight.
Where will our duke alight?
He stops with us only tonight.
The swan's in flight along the track.
Our duke, once gone, will not come back.
His soldiers pass the night in bivouac.
Let's keep his broidered gown.
May he not leave our town
Lest in regret our heart will drown!

---

* The people of the eastern states expressed their admiration of the Duke of Zhou and sorrow at his return to the capital in 1122 B.C..

Like an Old Wolf *

The duke can't go ahead
Nor at his ease retreat.
He's good to put on slippers red
And leave the regent's seat.

The duke cannot retreat
Nor with ease forward go.
He's good to leave his seat
And keep his fame aglow.

---

* The Duke of Zhou was regent, in 1115 B.C., but he could neither advance nor retreat, for if he should advance, the rumor would spread that he would seize the throne; if he should retreat, the young king would be dethroned. He was like an old wolf which would be hindered by its dewlap in advancing and would tread on its own tail in retreating. The Duke left the regent's seat and restored King Cheng to the throne in 1109 B.C..

BOOK OF ODES

First Decade of Odes

To Guests*

How gaily call the deer
While grazing in the shade!
I have welcome guests here.
Let lute and pipe be played.
Let offerings appear
And lute and strings vibrate.
If you love me, friends dear,
Help me to rule the state.

How gaily call the deer
While eating southernwood!
I have welcome guests here
Who give advices good.
My people are benign;
My lords will learn from you.
I have delicious wine;
You may enjoy my brew.

How gaily call the deer
Eating grass in the shade!
I have welcome guests here.

---

* This was a festal ode sung at entertainments to the king's guests from the feudal states. It referred to the time of King Wen (1184–1134 B.C.).

Let lute and flute be played.
Play lute and zither fine;
We may enjoy our best.
I have delicious wine
To delight the heart of my guest.

Loyalty and Filial Piety*

Four horses forward go
Along a winding way.
How can my homesickness not grow?
But the king's affairs bear no delay.
My heart is full of woe.

Four horses forward go;
They pant and snort and neigh.
How can my homesickness not grow?
But the king's affairs bear no delay.
I can't rest nor drive slow.

Doves fly from far and near
Up and down on their way.
They may rest on oaks with their peer.
But the king's affairs bear no delay,
And I can't serve my father dear.

---

* This was a festal ode complimentary to an officer on his return from an expedition, celebrating the union in him of loyal duty and filial feeling.

Doves fly from far and near
High and low on their way.
They may perch on trees with their peer.
But the king's affairs bear no delay,
And I can't serve my mother dear.
I drive black-maned white steed
And hurry on my way.
Don't I wish to go home with speed?
I can't but sing this lay
Though I have my mother to feed.

The Envoy*

The flowers look so bright
On lowland and on height.
The envoy takes good care
To visit people here and there.

"My ponies have brown manes
And smooth are the six reins.
I ride them here and there,
Making inquiries everywhere."

"My horses have white manes:
Silken are the six reins.

---

* This was an ode appropriate to the despatch of an envoy, complimentary to him and suggesting instructions as to the discharge of his duties.

I ride them here and there,
Seeking counsel everywhere."

"My horses have black manes;
Glossy are the six reins.
I ride them here and there,
Seeking advice everywhere."

"My horses have grey manes;
Shiny are the six reins.
I ride them here and there,
Visiting people everywhere."

Brotherhood*

The blooms of cherry tree,
How gorgeous they appear!
Great as the world may be,
As brother none's so dear.

A dead man will be brought
To brother's mind with woe.
A lost man will be sought
By brothers high and low.

When a man is in need,
Like wagtails flying high

---

* This ode came into use at entertainments given at the court to the princes of the same surname as the Royal House.

To help him brothers speed,
While good friends only sigh.

Brothers quarrel within;
They fight the foe outside.
Good friends are not akin;
They only stand aside.

When war comes to an end,
Peace and rest reappear.
Some may think a good friend
Better than brothers dear.

But you may drink your fill
With dishes in array
And feel happier still
To drink with brothers gay.

Your union with your wife
Is like music of lutes
And with brothers your life
Has longer, deeper roots.

Delight your family
Your wife and children dear.
If farther you can see,
Happiness will be near.

Friendship and Kinship*

The blows on brushwood go
While the songs of the bird
From the deep vale below
To lofty trees are heard.
Long, long the bird will sing
And for an echo wait;
Even though on the wing,
It tries to seek a mate.
We're more than what it is.
Can we not seek a friend?
If gods listen to this,
There is peace in the end.

Heigh-ho, they fell the wood;
I have strained off my wine.
My fatted lamb is good;
I'll ask kinsmen to dine.
Send them my best regards
Lest they resist my wishes.
Sprinkle and sweep the yards
And arrange eight round dishes.
Since I have fatted meat,
I'll invite kinsmen dear.

---

* This was a festal ode sung at the entertainment of friends, intended to celebrate the duty and value of friendship.

Why won't they come to eat?
Can't they find pleasure here?

On brushwood go the blows;
I have strained off my wine.
The dishes stand in rows;
All brethren come to dine.
Men may quarrel o'er food,
O'er late or early brew.
Drink good wine if you could,
Or o'ernight brew will do.
Let us beat drums with pleasure
And dance to music fine.
Whenever we have leisure,
Let's drink delicious wine.

The Royalty*

May Heaven bless our king
With great security,
Give him favor and bring
Him great felicity
That he may do more good

---

* This was an ode responsive to any of the five preceding. The guests feasted by the king celebrated his praises and desired for him the blessing of Heaven and his ancestors, whose souls were supposed to appear in the witch.

And people have more food.

May Heaven bless our king
With perfect happiness,
Make him do everything
Right and with great success
That he may have his will
And we enjoy our fill.

May Heaven bless our king
With great prosperity
Like hills and plains in spring
Grown to immensity
Or the o'erbrimming river
Flowing forever and ever.

Offer your wine and rice
From summer, fall to spring
As filial sacrifice
To your ancestral king
Whose soul in the witch appears:
"May you live long, long years!"

The spirit comes and confers
Many blessings on you
And on simple laborers
But daily food and brew.
The common people raise

Their voice to sing your praise:

"Like the moon in the sky
Or sunrise o'er the plain,
Like southern mountains high
Which never fall or wane
Or like luxuriant pines,
May such be your succeeding lines!"

A Homesick Warrior*

We gather fern
Which springs up here.
Why not return
Now ends the year?
We left dear ones
To fight the Huns.
We wake all night:
The Huns cause fright.

We gather fern
So tender here.
Why not return?
My heart feels drear.

---

* This and the next two epic odes formed a triad, having reference to the same expedition undertaken in the time of King Wen when he was only Duke of Zhou discharging his duty as chief of the region of the west, to the last king of Shang.

Book of Odes

Hard pressed by thirst
And hunger worst,
My heart is burning
For home I'm yearning.
Far from home, how
To send word now?

We gather fern
Which grows tough here.
Why not return?
The tenth month's near.
The war not won,
We cannot rest.
Consoled by none,
We feel distressed.

How gorgeous are
The cherry flowers!
How great the car
Of lord of ours!
It's driven by
Four horses nice.
We can't but hie
In one month thrice.

Driven by four
Horses aligned,
Our lord before,

We march behind.
Four horses neigh,
Quiver and bow
Ready each day
To fight the foe.

When I left here,
Willows shed tear.
I come hack now,
Snow bends the bough.
Long, long the way;
Hard, hard the day.
Hunger and thirst
Press me the worst.
My grief o'erflows.
Who knows? Who knows?

General Nan Zhong and His Wife*

Our chariots run
To pasture land.
The Heaven's Son
Gives me command.
Let our men make
Haste to load cart!

---

* General Nan Zhong was the speaker in the first four stanzas and his wife in the last two.

The state at stake,
Let's do our part!

Out goes my car
Far from the town.
Adorned flags are
With falcons brown,
Turtles and snakes.
They fly in flurry.
O my heart aches
And my men worry.

Ordered am I
To build north wall.
Cars seem to fly;
Flags rise and fall.
I'm going forth,
Leading brave sons,
To wall the north
And beat the Huns.

On parting day
Millet in flower.
On westward way
It snows in shower.
The state at stake,
Can I leave borders?
My heart would ache

At royal orders.

Hear insects sing;
See hoppers spring!
My lord not seen,
My grief is keen.
I see him now;
Grief leaves my brow.
With feats aglow,
He's beat the foe.

Long, long this spring,
Green, green the grasses.
Hear orioles sing;
See busy lasses!
With captive crowd,
Still battle-drest,
My lord looks proud:
He's quelled the west.

A Soldier's Wife*

Lonely stands the pear tree
With rich fruit on display.
From the king's affairs not free,

---

* This ode was a description of the anxiety and longing of a soldier's wife for his return, the first stanza in autumn, the second in spring and the last two in another autumn.

He's busy day by day.
The tenth moon's drawing near,
A soldier's wife, I feel drear,
My husband is not here.

Lonely stands the peat tree;
So lush its leaves appear.
From the king's affairs he's not free;
My heart feels sad and drear.
So lush the plants appear;
A soldier's wife, I feel drear,
Where is my husband dear?

I gather fruit from medlar tree
Upon the northern hill.
From the king's affairs he's not free;
Our parents rue their fill.
See shabby car appear
With horses weary and drear:
My soldier must be near.

Nor man nor car appear;
My heart feels sad and drear.
Alas! you're overdue.
Can I not long for you?
The fortune-tellers say.
You must be on your way.
But why should you delay?

Fish and Wine*

How fish in the basket are fine!
Sand-blowers and yellow-jaws as food.
Our host has wine
So abundant and good.

How fish in the basket are fine!
So many tenches and breams.
Our host has wine
So good and abundant it seems.

How fish in the basket are fine!
So many carps and mud-fish.
Our host has wine
As abundant as you wish.

How abundant the food
So delicious and good!
How delicious the food at hand
From the sea and the land!
We love the food with reason
For it is all in season.

---

* This was an ode used at district entertainments. The domain of the king was divided into six districts of which the more trusted and able officers were presented every third year to the king and feasted. The same thing took place in the states which were divided into three districts. At the former of those entertainments this ode was sung in the first place.

Second Decade of Odes

Southern Fish Fine*

Southern fish fine
Swim to and fro.
Our host has wine;
Guests drink and glow.

Southern fish fine
Swim all so free.
Our host has wine;
Guests drink with glee.

South wood is fine
And gourds are sweet.
Our host has wine;
With cheer guests meet.

Birds fly in line
O'er dale and hill.
Our host has wine;
Guests drink their fill.

Longevity**

Plants grow on southern hill

---

* This was a festal ode appropriate to the entertainment of worthy guests, celebrating the generous sympathy of the entertainer.
** This was a festal ode where the host proclaimed his complacence in the guests and then supplicated blessings on them one by one.

And on northern grows grass.
Enjoy your fill,
Men of first class.
May you live long
Among the throng!

In south grow mulberries
And in north poplars straight.
Enjoy if you please,
Glory of the State.
May you live long
Among the throng!

Plums grow on southern hill;
On northern medlar trees.
Enjoy your fill,
Lord, as you please.
You're people's friend;
Your fame's no end.

Plants grow on southern hill;
On northern tree on tree.
Enjoy your fill
Of longevity.
You're a good mate
Of our good state.

Trees grow on southern hill

And on northern hill cold.
Enjoy your fill
And live till old.
O may felicity
Fall to posterity!

Southernwood*

How long grows southernwood
With dew on it so bright!
Now I see my men good,
My heart is glad and light.
We talk and laugh and feast;
Of our care we are eased.

How high grows southernwood
With heavy dew so bright!
Now we see our lord good
Like dragon and sunlight.
With impartiality
He'll enjoy longevity.

How green grows southernwood
Wet with fallen dew bright!
Now I see my men good.

---

* The host was the speaker in the first and third stanzas and the guests in the second and last. This ode was sung on occasion of the king's entertaining the feudal princes who had come to his court.

Let us feast with delight
And enjoy brotherhood,
Be happy day and night.

How sweet the southernwood
In heavy dew does stand!
Now we see our lord good,
Holding the reins in hand.
Bells ringing far and near,
We're happy without peer.

The Heavy Dew*

The heavy dew so bright
Is dried up on the trunk.
Feasting long all the night,
None will retire till drunk.

The heavy dew is bright
On lush grass in the dell.
We feast long all the night
Till rings the temple bell.

Bright is the heavy dew
On date and willow trees.
Our noble guests are true

---

* This festal ode was proper to the night entertainment of the feudal princes at the royal court.

And good at perfect ease.

The plane and jujube trees
Have their fruits hanging down.
Our noble guests will please
In manner and renown.

The Red Bow*

Receive the red bow unbent
And have it stored.
It's a gift I present
To guest adored.
Drums beat and bells ring soon.
Let's feast till noon.

Receive the red bow unbent
Fitted on its frame.
It's a gift I present
To guest of fame.
Drums beat and bells ring soon.
Let's drink till noon.

Receive the red bow unbent

---

* This festal ode was sung on occasion of a feast given by the king to some prince for the merit he had achieved, and the conferring on him of a red bow, which was the highest testimonial of merit, for red was the color of honor with the dynasty of Zhou.

Placed in its case.
It's a gift I present
To guest with grace.
Drums beat and bells ring soon.
Let's eat till noon.

Our Lord Visiting the School*

Lush, lush grows southernwood
In the midst of the height.
Now we see our lord good,
We greet him with delight.

Lush, lush grows southernwood
In the midst of the isle.
Now we see our lord good,
Our faces beam with smile.

Lush, lush grows southernwood
In the midst of the hill.
Now we see our lord good,
He gives us shells at will.

---

* It was said that this ode celebrated the attention paid by the king to the education of talent. The lush southernwood and the boats were metaphorical of the talented youth of the kingdom, without aim or means of culture until the king provided for their training and furnished them with offices and salary thereafter.

The boats of willow wood
Sink or swim east or west.
Now we see our lord good,
Our heart can be at rest.

General Ji Fu*

Days in sixth moon are long,
Chariots ready to fight.
All our horses are strong,
Flags and banners in flight.
The Huns come in wild band;
The danger's imminent.
To save our royal land
An expedition's sent.

My four black steeds are strong,
Trained with skill and address.
Days in sixth moon are long;
We've made our battle dress.

---

* This epic ode and the thirteen odes which followed were all referred to the time of King Xuan (826–781 B.C.). After Kings Cheng and Kang, the House of Zhou fell into decay. Li, the eighth king from Kang, was so oppressive that the people drove him from the capital. The Huns took advantage of this internal disorder and invaded and ravaged the country till King Xuan succeeded to the throne and dispatched against them General Ji Fu, whose successful operations in 826 B.C. were sung by Zhang Zhong, writer of this ode.

Nice battle dress is made;
Each day thirty li's done.
Our forces make a raid,
Ordered by Heaven's Son.

My four steeds are strong ones,
With their heads in harness.
We fight against the Huns
In view of great success.
Careful and strict we'd be;
In battle dress we stand.
In battle dress stand we
To defend the king's land.

The Huns cross the frontier;
Our riverside towns fall.
The invaders come near
North of our capital.
Like flying birds we speed,
With silken flags aglow.
Ten large chariots lead
The way against the foe.

The chariots move along
And proceed high and low.
The four horses are strong
And at high speed they go.
We fight against the huns.

BOOK OF ODES

As far as northern border.

Wise Ji Fu leads brave sons
And puts the State in order.

Ji Fu is feasted here
With his gifts on display.
He's back from the frontier,
Having come a long way.
He entertains his friends
With roast turtles and fish.
The filial Zhang Zhong spends
His time there by Ji's wish.

General Fang*

Let's gather millet white
In newly broken land.
General Fang will alight
Here to take the command.
Three thousand cars arrive
With his great well trained forces.
The general takes a drive
On four black and white horses.
Four piebalds in a row

---

* This epic ode celebrated General Fang who conducted this grand expedition against the tribes of the south in 825 B.C..

Draw chariot red and green,
With reins and hooks aglow
Seal skin and bamboo screen.

Let's gather millet white
In newly broken land.
General Fang will alight
On the field rein in hand.
Three thousand cars arrive
With flags and banners spread.
The general leads the drive
In chariot painted red.
Hear eight bells' tinkling sound
And gems of pendant ring.
See golden girdle round
His robe conferred by the king.

Rapid is the hawks' flight:
They soar up to the sky
And then here they alight.
General Fang comes nigh;
Three thousand cars arrive;
His well-trained soldiers come.
Men ingle and beat drum
His forces in array,
The general has good fame,
Drums rolling on display

And flags streaming in flame.

You southern savages dare
To invade our great land.
Our General Fang is there;
At war he's good hand.
The general leads his forces
To make captives of the crowd.
His chariot drawn by horses
Now rumbles now rolls loud
Like clap or roll thunder
General Fang in command.
Puts the Huns down and under
And southern savage band.

Great Hunting*

Our chariots strong
Have well-matched steeds.
Our train is long;
Eastward it seeds.

Our chariots good,

---

* This epic ode celebrated a great hunting presided over by King Xuan (reigned 826–781B.C.) on occasion of his giving audience to the feudal princes at the eastern capital of Luo after the two victories won by General Ji Fu over the northern tribes in 826 B.C. and by General Fang over the southern tribes in 825 B.C..

Four steeds in front,
Drive to east wood
Where we shall hunt.

Our king afield,
Flags on display,
With archers skilled
Pursues his prey.

He drives four steeds
Strong and aglow.
Red-shoed, he leads
His lords in row.

Strings fit, they choose
Arrows and bows.
Archers in twos
Reap games in rows.

Four yellow steeds
Run straight and fit.
Our chariot speeds,
Each shot a hit.

Long, long steeds neigh;
Flags float and stream.
Footmen look gay;
With smiles cooks beam.
On backward way

We hear no noise.
What happy day!
How we rejoice!

Royal Hunting*

On lucky vernal day
We pray to Steed Divine.
Our chariots in array,
Four horses stand in line.
We come to wooded height
And chase the herds in flight.

Three days after we pray,
Our chosen steeds appear.
We chase all kinds of prey:
Roebucks, does, stags and deer.
We come to riverside.
Where Heavens' Son may ride.

Look to the plain we choose:
There are all kinds of prey,
Here in threes, there in twos,
Now they rush, now they stay.
We chase from left and right
To the royal delight.

---

* This ode celebrated a hunting expedition by King Xuan on a smaller scale, attended by his own officers and within the royal domain.

See the king bend his bow,
Put arrow on the string,
On a boar let it go;
A rhino's killed by the king.
He invites guests to dine,
With cups brimful of wine.

Third Decade of Odes

The Toilers*

Wild geese fly high
With wings a rustling.
We toilers hie
Afield a-bustling.
Some mourn their fate:
They've lost their mate.

Wild geese in flight
In marsh alight.
We build town wall
From spring to fall.
We've done our best
But have no rest.

Wild geese fly high;
They mourn and cry.
The wise may know
Our toil and pain.
The fool says, "No,
Do not complain!"

---

* This was a folk song collected in the countryside and not a festal ode sung in th court.

Early Audience*

How goes the night?
It's at its height.
In royal court a hundred torches blaze bright.
Before my lords appear,
Their ringing bells I'll hear.

How goes the night?
It's passed its height.
In royal court the torches shed a lambent light.
Before my lords appear,
Their tinkling bells will come near.

How goes the night?
Morning is near.
In royal court is blown out torches' light.
Now all my lords appear;
I see their banners from here.

Water Flows**

The waters flow
Towards the ocean.

---

* This was a soliloquy of King Xuan, waking now and again in his anxiety not to be late at his morning levee.
** This ode bewailed the disorder of the times and the general indifference to it, and traced it to the slanderers encouraged by men in power. The first two lines of the last stanza, missing in the original, are supplanted by the translator.

Hawks fly in slow
Or rapid motion.
My friends and brothers,
Alas! don't care
For their fathers and mothers
Nor state affair.

The waters flow
In current strong.
Hawks fly now low
Now high and long.
None play their part
But hatch their plot.
What breaks my heart
Can't be forgot.

The waters flow
At rising tide.
Hawks fly so low
Along hillside.
Let's put an end
To talks ill bred,
Respectful friend,
Lest slanders spread.

The Crane Cries*

In the marsh the crane cries;
Her voice is heard for miles.
Hid in the deep fish lies
Or it swims by the isles.
Pleasant a garden's made
By sandal trees standing still
And small trees in their shade.
Stones from another hill
May be used to polish jade.

In the marsh the crane cries;
Her voice is heard on high.
By the isle the fish lies
Or in tile deep near-by.
Pleasant the garden in our eyes
Where sandal trees stand still
And paper mulberries 'neath them.
Stones from another hill
May be used to polish gem.

---

* The garden described in this ode alluded to a state, the crane and sandal trees to manifested talents, the fish and small trees and paper mulberries to undiscovered talents, and stones from another hill to unpolished talents from other states. It was important for a state to discover and employ different talents.

To the Minister of War*

O minister of war!
We're soldiers of the crown.
Why send us to an expeditionary corps
So that we cannot settle down?

O minister of war!
We're guardians' of this land.
Why send us to an expeditionary corps
So that we're under endless command?

O minister of war!
Why don't you listen to others?
Why send us to an expeditionary corps
So that we cannot feed out mothers?

The White Pony**

The pony white
Feeds on the hay.
Tether it tight,
Lengthen the joy of the day

---

* The soldiers of the Royal Guard complained of the service imposed on them by the minister of war in 787 B.C. when the royal army had sustained a great defeat from some of the northern tribes and the royal guards were ordered to join the expeditionary force, a duty which did not belong to them.

** The host tried to detain the white pony so as to have its master always with him and expressed his regret on the guest's departure.

So that its master may
At ease here stay.

The pony white
Feeds on bean leaves.
Tether it tight;
Lengthen the joy of the eves
So that its master may
As guest here stay.

The pony white
Brings pleasure here.
My noble guest so bright,
Be in good cheer.
Enjoy at ease.
Don't take leave, please!

The pony white
Feeds on fresh grass.
My guest gem-bright.
Leaves, me, alas!
O from you let me hear.
So that to me you're near.

Yellow Birds*

O yellow birds, hear phrase.

---

* The speaker who had withdrawn to another state found his expectations of the people there disappointed and proposed to return to his homeland.

Don't settle on the trees.
Don't eat my paddy grain.
The people here won't deign
To treat foreigners well.
I will go back and dwell
In my family cell.

O yellow birds, hear please.
Don't perch on mulberries.
Don't eat my sorghum grain.
The people here won't deign
To come and understand.
I will go back offhand
To my dear brethren's land.

O yellow birds, hear please.
Don't settle on oak-trees.
Don't eat my millet grain.
The people here won't deign
To let me live at ease.
So I'll go back again
To my dear uncles' plain.

A Rejected Husband*

I go by countryside
With withered trees o'erspread.

---

* A husband rejected by his wife returned to his own homeland.

BOOK OF POETRY

With you I would reside
For to you I was wed.
Now you reject my hand,
I'll go back to my land.

I go by countryside
with sheep's foot overspread.
I'll sleep by your bedside
For to you I was wed.
Now you reject my hand,
I'll go back to homeland.

I go by countryside
With pokeweed overspread.
You drove husband outside,
To another you'll wed.
I can't bear your disdain,
So I go back with pain.

Installation*

The stream so clean,
Mountains so long,
Bamboo so green,
Lush pines so strong.

---

* This ode was probably made for a festival on the completion and dedication of a palace, of which there was a description with good wishes for the builder and his posterity.

O brothers dear,
Do love each other.
Make no scheme here
Against your brother.

Inherit all from fathers' tombs,
Build solid wall
And hundred rooms
North, south, east, west,
Where you may walk,
And sit and rest,
And laugh and talk.
The frames' well bound
For earth they pound.
Nor wind nor rain,
Nor bird nor mouse
Could spoil in vain
Your noble house.

As man stands right,
As arrow's straight,
As birds in flight
Spread wings so great,
'Tis the abode
Fit for our lord.

Square is the hall
With pillars tall.

The chamber's bright,
The bedroom's deep.
Our lord at night
May rest and sleep.

Bamboo outspread
On rush-mat bed
Where one may rest
Or lie awake
Or have dreams blest
Of bear or snake.
Witches divine
The bear's a sign
Of newborn son
And the snake's one
Of daughter fine.

When a son's blest,
In bed he's laid,
In robe he's drest
And plays with jade.
Of crown he's proud,
He'll lord o'er crowd.

When daughter's blest,
She's put aground,
In wrappers drest,
She'll play with spindle round.

She'd do nor wrong nor good
But care for wine and food;
She'd cause her parents dear
Nor woe nor fear.

The Herdsmen's Song*

Who says you have no sheep?
There're three hundred in herd.
Have you no cows to keep?
Ninety cattle's low is heard.
Your sheep don't strive for corn;
They're at peace horn to horn.
When your cattle appears,
You see their frapping ears.

Some cattle go downhill;
Others drink water clear.
Some move; others lie still.
When your herdsmen appear,
They bear hats of bamboos
And carry food and rice.
Cattle of thirty hues
Are fit for sacrifice.

---

* This ode was supposed to celebrate the largeness and condition of King Xuan's flocks and herds, with an auspice of the prosperity of the kingdom.

Then come your men of herds
With large and small firewood
And male and female birds.
Your sheep appear so good;
Fat, they don't run away;
Tame, they don't go astray.
At wave of arms, behold!
They come back to the fold.

Then dreams the man of herds
Of locusts turned to fishes.
Tortoise and snake to birds.
The witch divines our wishes;
The locust turned to fish
Foretells a bumper year;
The snakes turned, as we wish,
To greater household dear.

Fourth Decade of Odes

To Grand Master Yin*

South Mountain's high;
Crags and jags tower.
Our people's eye
Looks to your power.
We're in distress
For state affair.
It's in a mess.
Why don't you care?

South Mountain's high,
Rugged here and there.
In people's eye:
You're as unfair.
Distress and woes
Fall without end.
Our grievance grows;
But you won't mend.

Master Yin stands
Pillar of state.

---

* This was a lamentation over the miserable state of the kingdom caused by Grand-Master Yin and King You who reigned 780–770 B.C. and after whose death there took place the removal of the royal residence to the eastern capital—the great event in the history of the Zhou Dynasty.

With power in hands
You rule our fate.
On you rely
People and crown.
Heaven on high!
You've false renown.

Is what you do
Worthy of trust?
We don't think you
Have used men just.
You put the mean
In a high place.
Let all your kin
Fall in disgrace!

Heaven unfair
And pitiless
Sends man to scare;
We're in distress.
Send us men just
To bring us rest,
Worthy of trust;
We're not distressed.

Great Heaven, lo!
Troubles ne'er cease.
Each month they grow;

We have no peace.
We're grieved at heart.
Who rule and reign,
Distress and woes
State set apart?
We toil with pain.

I drive my four
Steeds in harness.
I look before
And see distress.

On evil day.
You wield your spear.
When you are gay,
You drink with cheer.

Heaven's unjust;
Our king's no rest.
To our disgust
Alone you're blest.

I sing to lay
Evil deeds bare
So that you may
Mind state affair.

Lamentation*

In frosty moon
My heart is grieved.
Rumors spread soon
Can't be believed.
I stand alone;
My grief won't go.
With cares I groan
And ill I grow.

Why wasn't I born
Before or after?
I suffer scorn
From people's laughter.
Good words or bad
Are what they say.
My heart feels sad,
Filled with dismay.

My heart feels grieved;
Unlucky am I.
People deceived,
Slaves and maids cry.
Alas for me!

---

* This was a lamentation over the miseries of the kingdom caused by King You's employment of worthless men and his indulgence of his favorite Lady Shi of Bao.

Can I be blest?
The crow I see,
Where can it rest?

See in the wood
Branch large or small.
For livelihood
We suffer all.
Dark is the sky.
Who'll make it clear.
Heavens on high
Cause hate and fear.

The hills said low
Are mountains high.
Why don't we go
Against the lie?
About our dream,
What do they know?
Though wise they seem
They can't tell male
From female crow.
To what avail?

High are the skies;
Down I must bow.
Thick the earth lies;
I must walk slow.

Though what I say
Has no mistakes,
Men of today
Bite me like snakes.
See rugged field
Where lush grows grain.
How can I yield
To might and main?
I was sought after
But couldn't be got.
With pride and laughter
They use me not.

Laden with cares,
My heart seems bound.
The state affairs
In woe are drowned.
The flames though high
May be put out,
The world's lost by
Fair Lady Bao.

Long grieved my heart,
I meet hard rain.
Loaded your cart,
No wheels remain.
O'erturned 'twill lie;
For help you'd cry.

BOOK OF ODES

Keep your wheel-aid
And spoke well-made.
Show oft concern
For driver good
Lest he o'erturn
Your cart of wood.
You may get o'er
Difficulties,
But not before
You thought of this.

Fish in the pool
Knows no delight.
Deep in water cool
They're still in sight.
Saddened, I hate
Evils of the state.

They have' wine sweet
And viands good,
So they can treat
Their kin and neighborhood.
In loneliness I feel distress.
The poor have houses small;
Their food is coarse.
Woes on them fall;
They've no resource.
Happy the rich class;
But the poor, alas!

President Huang Fu*

In the tenth month the sun and moon
Cross each other on the first day.
The sun was then eclipsed at noon,
An evil omen, people say.
The moon became then small;
The sun became not bright.
The people one and all
Are in a wretched plight.

Bad omen, moon and sun
Don't keep their proper way.
In the states evil's done;
The good are kept away.
The eclipse of the moon
Is not uncommon thing;
That of the sun at noon
Will dire disaster bring.

Lightning flashes, rolls thunder,
There is nor peace nor rest.
The streams bubble from under;
Crags fall from mountain-crest.

---

* This political ode was the lamentation of an officer over the prodigies, celestial and terrestrial, betokening the ruin of Zhou. He expounded the true causes of these and named the chief culprit Huang Fu.

The heights become deep vale;
Deep vales turn into height.
Men of this time bewail;
What to do with such plight?

Huang Fu presides over the state;
Fan the interior,
Jia Bo is magistrates;
Zhong Yong is minister.
Zou records worthy deeds;
Of stable Qui takes care.
Yu is captain of steeds;
All flatter Lady Bao the fair.

Oh, this Huang Fu would say
He's done all by decree,
But why drive me away
Without consulting me?
Why move my house along
And devastate my land?
Has he done nothing wrong?
The law is in his hand.

Huang Fu says he is wise
And builds the capital.
He chooses men we despise,
Corrupt and greedy all.
No men of worthy deeds

Are left to guard the crown;
Those who have cars and steeds
Are removed to his town.

I work hard all day long;
Of my toil I'm not proud.
I have done nothing wrong;
Against me slander's loud.
Distress of any kind
Does not come from on high.
Good words or bad behind
Would raise a hue and cry.

My homeland's far away;
I feel so sad and drear.
Other people are gay;
Alone I am grieved here.
When all people are free,
Why can't I take my ease?
I dread Heaven's decree;
I can't as my friends do what I please.

Untimely Rain*

The heaven high,
Not kind for long,

---

* The speaker was a groom of the chambers.

Spreads far and nigh
Famine on throng.
Heaven unfair,
You have no care
Nor have you thought.
Sinners are freed;
Those who sin not,
Why should, they bleed?

Where can I go after the fall
Of Zhou's capital?
Ministers gone,
None knows my toil
Nor serves the throne
But all recoil.
Of the lords none
At court appear.
No good is done
But evil here.

Why isn't just word
Believed when heard?
Travelers know
Nowhere to go.
O lord, be good
And show manhood!
Don't you revere
Heaven you fear?

After the war
Famine's not o'er.
I, a mere groom,
Am full of gloom.
Among lords who
Will speak the true?
They like good word;
Bad one's not heard.

Alas! What's true
Cannot be said,
Or woe on you,
Your tongue and head.
If you speak well
Like stream ne'er dry,
You will excel
And soon rise high.

It's hard to be
An officer.
The wrongs you see
Make you incur
Displeasure great
Of Heaven's Son,
Or in the state
Friends you have none.

Go back to capital!

You say your home's not there.
My bitter tears would fall
To say what you can't bear:
"When you left, who
Built house for you?"

Counselors*

The Heaven's ire
On earth descends.
The counsels dire
Go without ends.
They follow one
Not good but bad.
The good not done,
I feel so sad.

Controversy
Is to be rued.
They disagree
On what is good.
On what is bad
They will depend.
I feel not glad;
How will this end?

---

* This was a lamentation over the recklessness and incapacity of the king's plans and of his counselors.

The tortoise bored,
Nothing's foretold.
Men on the board
No right uphold.
The more they say;
The less they do.
They won't start on their way.
How can we ask them to?

Alas! formers of plan
Won't follow those of yore.
No principles they can
Formulate as before.
They follow counselors
Who can nothing good yield.
They ask the wayfarers
About houses to build.

Though bounded is our state,
Our men may be wise or not.
Our numbers are not great;
Some know to plan and plot;
Others are able to think
Like stream from spring will flow.
Together they will sink
In common weal and woe.

Don't fight a tiger with bare hand,

Nor cross without a boat the stream.
You may know one thing in your land,
But not another as you deem.
Be careful as if you did stand
On the brink of the gulf of vice
Or tread upon thin ice!

Reflections*

Small is the cooing dove,
But it can fly above.
My heart feels sad and drear,
Missing my parents dear.
Till daybreak I can't sleep,
Lost so long in thoughts deep.

Those who are grave and wise,
In drinking won't get drunk;
But those who have dull eyes
In drinking will be sunk.
From drinking be restrained.
What's lost can't be regained.

There are beans in the plain;
People gather their grain.

---

* Some officer, in a time of disorder and misgovernment, urges on his brothers the duty of maintaining their own virtue and of observing the greatest caution.

The insect has young ones;
The sphex bears them away.
So teach and train your sons
Lest they should go astray.

The wagtails wing their ways
And twittering they're gone.
Advancing are my days;
Your months are going on.
Early to rise and late to bed!
Don't disgrace those by whom you're bred!

The greenbeaks on their tour
Peck grain in the stack-yard.
I am lonely and poor,
Unfit for working hard.
I go out to divine
How can I not decline,

Precarious, ill at ease,
As if perched on trees;
Careful lest I should ail
On the brink of a vale;
I tremble twice or thrice
As treading on thin ice.

The Banished Prince*

With flapping wings the crows
Come back, flying in rows.
All people gay appear;
Alone I'm sad and drear.
O what crime have I even
Committed against Heaven?
With pain my heart's pierced through.
Alas! what can I do?

The highway should be plain,
But it's o'ergrown with grass.
My heart is wound'd with pain
As if I'm pound'd, alas!
Sighing, I lie still dressed;
My grief makes me grow old.
I feel deeply distressed,
Gnawed by headache untold.

The mulberry and other
Trees planted by our mother

---

* The eldest son and heir-apparent of King You of Zhou bewailed his banishment because the king, enamoured of Lady Shi of Bao and led away by slanderers, announced that a child by Lady Shi should be his successor. When King You was killed in 770 B.C., the banished prince was recalled and became King Ping who removed the capital to the east.

And father are protected
As our parents are respected.
Without the fur outside
And the lining inside,
Can we live at a time
Without reason or rhyme?

Lush grow the willow trees;
Cicadas trill at ease.
In water deep and clear
Rushes and reeds appear.
Adrift I'm like a boat;
I know not where I float.
My heart deeply distressed,
In haste I lie down dressed.

The stag off goes
At a fast gait;
The pheasant crows,
Seeking his mate.
The ruined tree
Stript of its leaves
Has saddened me.
Who knows what grieves?

The captured hare
May be released;
The dead o'er there

Buried at least.
The king can't bear
The sight of me;
Laden with care,
My tears flow free.

Slanders believed
As a toast drunk,
The king's deceived,
In thoughts not sunk.
The branch cut down,
They leave the tree.
The guilty let alone,
They impute guilt to me.

Though higher than a mountain
And deeper than a fountain,
The king ne'er speaks light word or jeers,
For even walls have ears.
"Do not remove my dam
And my basket for fish!"
I can't preserve what I am.
What care I for my wish?

Disorder and Slander*

O great Heaven on high,
You're called our parent dear.
Why make the guiltless cry
And spread turmoil far and near?
You cause our terror great;
We're worried for the guiltless.
You rule our hapless fate;
We're worried in distress.

Sad disorder comes then
When untruth is received.
Disorder comes again
When slanders are believed.
If we but blame falsehood,
Disorder will decrease.
If we but praise the good,
Disorder soon will cease.

If we make frequent vows,
Disorder will still grow.
If we to thieves make bows,
They will bring greater woe.

---

* The speaker, suffering from the king through slander, appealed to Heaven, dwelled on the nature and evil of slander and expressed his detestation of and contempt for the slanderers.

Book of Odes

What they say may be sweet;
The woe grows none the less.
The disorder complete
Will cause the king's distress.

The temple's grand,
Erected for ages.
Great work is planned
By kings and sages.
Judge others' mind
But by your own.
The hound can find
Hares running down.

The supple tree
Plant'd by the good,
From slander free,
You can tell truth from falsehood.
Grandiose word
Should not be heard.
Sweet sounding one
Like organ-tongue.
Can deceive none
Except the young.

Who is that knave
On river's border,
Nor strong nor brave,

Root of disorder?
You look uncanny.
How bold are you?
Your plans seem many;
Your followers are few.

Friend or Foe?*

Who's the man coming here
So deep and full of hate?
My dame he's coming near.
But enters not my gate.
Is he a follower
Of the tyrant? Yes, sir.

Two friends we did appear;
Alone I am in woes.
My dam he's coming near,
But past my gate he goes.
He is different now;
He has broken his vow.

Who's the man coming here,
Passing before my door?

---

* The speaker, suffering from slander and suspecting that the slanderer was an old friend, intimated the grounds of his suspicion and lamented his case, while he would welcome the restoration of their former relations.

His voice I only hear,
But see no man of yore.
How can he not fear then
Neither heaven nor men?

Who's the man coming forth
Like a whirlwind which roars?
Why does he not go north
Nor to the southern shores?
Why comes he near my dam
And disturbs what I am?

Even when you walk slow,
You won't stop where you are.
And then when fast you go,
How can you grease your car?
You will not come to see,
Let alone comfort me.

If you should but come in,
Then I would feel at ease.
But you do not come in,
I know you're hard to please.
You won't come to see me,
Nor will set my heart free.

Earthen whistle you blew;
I played bamboo flute long.

When I was friend with you,
We had sung the same song.
Before offerings now,
Can you forget your vow?

I curse you as a ghost,
For you have left no trace.
I will not be your host
I see your ugly face.
But I sing in distress
For you are pitiless.

A Eunuch's Complaint

A few lines made to be
Fair shell embroidery,
You slanderers in dress
Have gone to great excess.

The Sieve Stars in the south
Opening wide their mouth,
You vile slanderers, who
Devise the schemes for you?

You talk so much, o well;
In slander you excel.
Take care of what you say.
Will it be believed? Nay.

You may think you are clever,
Slandering people ever.
But deceived, they will learn
You'll be punished in turn.

The proud are in delight,
The crowd in sorry plight.
Heaven bright, heaven bright!
Look on the proud;
Pity the crowd!

O you vile slanderers,
Who are your counselors?
I would throw you to feed
The wolf's or tiger's greed.
If they refuse to eat,
I'd tread you down my feet
Or cast you to north land
Or throw to Heave's hand.

The eunuch Mengzi, I
Go to the Garden High
By a willowy road long
And make this plaintive song.
Officials on your way,
Hearken to it, I pray.

Fifth Decade of Odes

Weal and Woe*

Strong winds hard blow,
Followed by rain.
In times of woe
Firm we'd remain;
Cast off in weal,
Lonely I feel.

Strong winds hard blow
From morn till night.
In times of woe
You held me tight;
Cast off in weal,
How sad I feel!

Strong winds blow high,
But mountains stand.
No grass but die,
Nor trees in land.
Much good's forgot;
Small faults ale not.

---

* A woman complained of the alienation produced by the change for the better in the circumstances.

The Parents' Death*

Long and large grows sweet grass,
Not wild weed of no worth.
My parents died, alas!
With toil they gave me birth.

Long and large grows sweet grass,
Not shorter weed on earth,
My parents died, alas!
With pain they gave me birth.

When the pitcher is void,
Empty will be the jar.
Our parents' life destroyed,
How sad we orphans are!

On whom can I rely,
Now fatherless and motherless?
Outdoors, with grief I sigh;
Indoors, I seem homeless.

My father gave me birth;
By mother I was fed.
They cherished me with mirth,
And by them I was bred.

---

* A son deplored his hard fate in being prevented from rendering the last services to his parents and enlarged on the parental claim.

They looked after me
And bore me out and in.
Boundless as sky should be
The kindness of our kin.

The southern mountain's high;
The wind soughs without cheer.
Happy are those near by;
Alone I'm sad and drear.

The southern mountain's cold;
The wind blows a strong blast.
Happy are young and old;
My grief fore'er will last.

East and West*

The tripod's full of food;
They eat with spoons of wood.
The road's smooth like whetstone
For lords to go alone.
Like arrow it is straight,
On which no people circulate.

---

* The descendents of Shang in the East complained of the inequality between the East and the West ruled by the government of Zhou, and vented their indignation by showing the deceit in Heaven where stars did not live up to their fine names: the Winnowing Fan could not winnow and the Dipper could not hold wine.

Recalling bygone years,
In streams run down my tears.

In east states, large and small,
The looms are empty all.
In summer shoes we go
On winter frost or snow.
Even the noble sons
Walk on foot like poor ones.
Seeing them come and go,
My heart is full of woe.

Cold water passing by,
Do not soak our firewood!
Woeful we wake and sigh
For scanty livelihood.
If our firewood is dry,
We may carry it west.
If wet, we can but sigh.
O when may we have rest?

We toilers of the east
Are not paid as those of the West;
The western nobles at least
Are all splendidly drest.
The rich and noble sons
Don't care about their furs,
But as slaves the poor ones

Serve all the officers.

If we present them wine,
They do not think it fine.
If we present them jade,
They don't think it well-made.
The Silver River bright
Looks down on us in light.
The Weaving Stars are three;
All day long they are free.

Though all day long they move,
They weave nothing above.
Bright is the Cowherd Star,
But it won't draw our car.
Morning Star in the east,
Eight Net Stars catch no beast,
Evening Star in the west,
What use though they don't rest?

In south the Winnowing Fan
Cannot sift grain for man.
In north the Dipper fine
Cannot ladle good wine.
The Sieve shines in the south,
Idly showing its mouth.
In the north shines the Plough
With handle like a bow.

Banishment to the South*

From fourth to sixth moon when
The summer heat remains,
Our fathers are kind men;
Can they leave me in pains?

The autumn days are chill;
All plants and grass decay.
In distress I am ill.
Where can I go? Which way?

In winter days severe
The vehement wind blows.
No one feels sad and drear.
Why am I alone in woes?

Trees on the hill were good
And mume trees far and nigh.
Who has destroyed the wood?
Who knows the reason why?

Water from fountain flows
Now muddy and now clear.
But I'm each day in woes.

---

* An officer banished to the south deplored the misery he had suffered in summer, autumn and winter, compared himself to destroyed tree and muddy water and complained that he was not so free as hawk and fish and that he could not grow like ferns and medlars.

How can I not be drear?

The rivers east and west
Crisscross in southern land.
In work I did my best.
Who'd give me helping hand?

Like hawk or eagle why
Cannot I skyward' go?
Like fish why cannot I
Go to hide down below?

Above grow ferns in throng,
And medlars spread below.
Alas! I've made this song
To ease my heart of woe.

Injustice*

To gather medlars long,
I go up northern height.
Being an officer strong,
I'm busy day and night
For the royal affairs.

---

* A petty officer complained of the arduous and continual duties unequally imposed upon him and keeping him away from his duty to his parents, while others were left to enjoy their ease.

Who for my parents cares?
The land under the sky
Is all the king's domain;
The people far and nigh
Are under royal reign.
But ministers unfair
Load me with heavy care.

Four steeds run without rest
For state affairs all day long.
They say I'm at my best
And few like me are strong.
I have a robust chest
And may go east and west.

Some enjoy rest and ease;
Others worn out for the state.
Some march on without cease;
Others lie in bed early and late.

Some know not people's pain;
Others toil for state affairs.
Some long in bed remain;
Others laden with great cares.

Some drink all the day long;
Others worry for woe.
Some only say all's wrong;
To hard work others go.

Don't Trouble*

Don't push an ox-drawn cart
Or you'll raise dust about.
Do not trouble your heart
Or you'll be ill, no doubt.

Don't push an ox-drawn cart
Or dust will dim your sight.
Do not trouble your heart
Or you can't see the light.

Don't push an ox-drawn cart
Or dust will darken the way.
Do not trouble your heart
Or you will pine away.

A Nostalgic Official**

O Heaven high and bright,
On lower world shed light!
Westward I came by order
As far as this wild border
Of second month then on the first day;

---

* This ode read like the song of a driver who advised people not to do anything beyond human power lest it should get them into trouble.
** An official kept long abroad on distant service deplored the hardships of his lot and tendered good advice to those officials in power at court.

Now cold and heat have passed away.
Alas! my heart is sad
As poison drives me mad.
I think of those in power;
My tears fall down in shower.
Will I not homeward go?
I fear traps high and low.

When I left home for here
Sun and moon ushered in new year.
Now when may I go home?
Another year will come.
I sigh for I am lonely.
Why am I busy only?
O how can I feel pleasure?
I toil without leisure.
Thinking of those in power,
Can I have happy hour?
Don't I long for parental roof?
I'm afraid of reproof.

When I left for the west,
With warmth the sun and moon were blest.
When can I go home without cares,
Busy on state affairs?
It is late in the year;
They reap beans there and here.

I feel sad and cast down;
I eat the fruit I've sown.
Thinking of those in power,
I rise at early hour.
Will I not homeward go?
I fear returning blow.

Ah! officials in power,
There's no e'er-blooming flower.
When you're on duty long,
You should know right from wrong.
If Heaven should have ear,
Justice would then appear.

Ah! officials in power,
There's no e'er-resting hour,
Should you do duty well,
You'd know heaven from hell.
If Heaven should know you,
Blessings would come to view.

Bells and Drums*

The bells ring deep and low;

---

* This ode was supposed to refer to the expedition of King You to the country of the Huai, where he abandoned himself to the delights of music in 771 B.C., one year before he was killed by the western tribes.

The vast river waves flow.
My heart is full of woe.
How can I forget then
Those music-making men?

The bells sound shrill and high;
The river waves flow by,
My heart heaves long, long sigh.
How can I forget then
Those music-loving men?

The bells and drums resound;
Three isles emerged, once drowned.
My heart feels grief profound.
How can I forget then
Those music-playing men?

They beat drum and ring bell,
Play lute and zither well,
In flute or pipe excel,
Sing odes and southern song
And dance with nothing wrong.

Winter Sacrifice*

O let us clear away

---

* The "spirit" was a representative or personator of the worthy dead or great fathers who were sacrificed to; the "grandson" was the name given to the sacrificer or the king of the Zhou Dynasty.

All the overgrown thorns!
Just as in olden days
We plant millet and corns.
Our millet overgrows
And our barns stand in rows;
Our sorghum overgrows
And our stacks stand in rows.
We prepare wine and meat
For temple sacrifice;
We urge spirits to eat
And invoke blessings thrice.

We clean the oxen nice
And offer them in heap
For winter sacrifice.
We flay and broil the sheep
And cut and carve the meat.
The priest's at the temple gate
Till service is complete.
Then come our fathers great.
They enjoy food and wine
And to their grandson say,
"Receive blessings divine,
Live long and be e'er gay!"

The cooks work with great skill
And prepare all the trays.

They roast or broil at will;
Women help them always.
Smaller dishes abound
For the guests left and right.
They raise cups and drink round
According to the rite.
They laugh and talk at will
When witches come and say,
"Receive more blessings still;
Live long with glee for aye!"

With respect we fulfil
The due rites one by one.
The priests announce the will
Of spirits to grandson:
"Fragrant's the sacrifice;
They enjoy meat and wine.
They confer blessings thrice
On you for rites divine.
You have done what is due
Correctly with good care.
Favors conferred on you
Will be found everywhere."

The ceremonies done,
Drums beaten and bells rung,
In his place the grandson,

The priest then gives his tongue:
"The spirits drunken well,
The dead ready to go."
Let's beat drum and ring bell
For them to go below!
Cooks and women, come here.
Remove trays without delay.
Uncles and cousins dear,
At private feast let's stay.

Music played in the hall,
We eat when spirits go.
Enjoying dishes, all
Forget their former woe.
They drink their fill and eat,
Bowing the head, old and young.
"The spirits love your meat
And will make you live long.
Your rites are duly done;
You are pious and nice.
Let nor son nor grandson
Forget the sacrifice!"

Spring sacrifice at the Foot of the Southern Mountain*

The Southern Mountain stands,

---

* This sacrificial ode traced husbandry to its first author, King Yu of Xia (2205–2197 B.C.).

Exploited by Yu's hands.
The plains spread high and low
Tilled by grandsons, crops grow.
Of southeast fields we find
The boundaries defined.

Clouds cover winter sky;
Snowflakes fall from on high.
In spring comes drizzling rain;
It moists and wets the plain.
Fertile grow all the fields;
Abundant are their yields.

Their acres lie in row;
Millet and sorghum grow.
Grandsons reap harvest fine
And make spirits and wine.
They feast their guests with food
That they may live for good.

Gourds grow amid the field
And melons have gross yield.
They are, pickled in slices,
Offered in sacrifices,
That we may receive love
And long life from Heaven above.

We offer purest wine
To ancestors divine;

Kill a bull with red hair
By a knife in hand bare;
We rid it of hair red
And take fat from the bled.

During the sacrifice
The fat burned gives smell nice.
Our ancestors delight
In the service and rite.
We grandsons will be blest
With longest life and best.

Sixth Decade of Odes

Harvest*

"Endless extend my boundless fields;
A tenth is levied of their yields.
I take grain from old store
To feed the peasants' mouth.
We've good years as of yore;
I go to acres south.
They gather roots and weed;
Lush grow millets I see.
Collected by those who lead,
They are presented to me.

"I offer millets nice
And rams in sacrifice
To spirits of the land
That lush my fields become.
Joyful my peasants stand;
They play lute and beat drum.
We pray to God of Fields
That rain and sunshine thrives
To increase our millet yields
And bless my men and their wives."

---

* This ode described husbandry and sacrifices connected with it, and happy under standing between the peasants and their lord, who was the speaker in the first two stanzas.

Our lord's grandson comes near.
Our wives and children dear
Bring food to acres south,
The o'erseer opens mouth,
From left to right takes food
And tastes whether it's good.
Abundant millets grow
Over acres high and low.
Our lord's grandson is glad;
His peasants are not bad.

The grandson's crops in piles
Stand high as the roof tiles.
His stacks upon the ground
Look like hillock and mound.
He seeks stores in all parts
And conveys crops in carts,
We peasants sing in praise
Of millet, paddy, maize.
He'll be blessed night and day
And live happy for aye.

Farm Work*

Busy with peasants' cares,

---

* The first stanza described the farm work in spring, the second that in summer, the third harvest in autumn and the last sacrifice in winter.

Seed selected, tools repaired,
We take our sharp plough-shares
When all is well prepared.
We begin from south field
And sow grain far and wide.
Gross and high grows our yield;
Our lord's grandson's satisfied.

The grain's soft in the ear
And then grows hard and good.
Let nor grass nor weed appear;
Let no insects eat it as food.
All vermins must expire
Lest they should do much harm.
Pray gods to put them in fire
To preserve our good farm,

Clouds gather in the sky;
Rain on public fields come down,
It drizzles from on high
On private fields of our own.
There are unreaped young grain
And some ungathered sheaves,
Handfuls left on the plain
And ears a widow perceives.
And gleans and makes a gain.

Our lord's grandson comes here.

Our wives bring food to acres south
Together with their children dear;
The overseer opens mouth.
We offer sacrifice
With victims black and red,
With millet and with rice.
We pray to fathers dead
That we may be blessed thrice.

Grand Review*

See River Luo in spring
With water deep and wide.
Thither has come the king,
Happy and dignified,
In red knee-covers new,
Six armies in review.

See River Luo in spring;
Deep and wide flows its stream.
Thither has come the king;
Gems on his scabbard gleam.
May he live long and gay,
His house preserved for aye!

See River Luo in spring;

---

* This ode read like a hymn sung by feudal princes met at some gathering in praise of the king as he appeared among them.

Its stream flows deep and wide.
Thither has come the king;
He's blessed and dignified.
May he live long and great
And long preserve his state!

A Noble Lord*

Flowers give splendid sight
With lush leaves by the side.
I see the lord so bright;
My heart is satisfied.
My heart is satisfied,
I praise him with delight.

Flowers give splendid sight;
They're deep yellow and red.
I see the lord so bright,
Elegant and well-bred.
Elegant and well-bred,
I bless him with delight.

Flowers give splendid sight;
They are yellow and white.
I see the lord so bright
With four steeds left and right.

---

* This ode was said to be responsive to the former: the king celebrated the praises of the chief among the feudal princes.

With four steeds left and right,
He holds six reins with delight.

He goes left if he will,
Driving the steeds with skill.
If he will he goes right,
Driving with main and might.
As he has true manhood,
At what he does he's good.

The Royal Toast*

Hear the green-beaks' sweet voice
And see their variegated wings fly.
Let all my lords rejoice
And be blessed from on high.

Hear the green-beaks' sweet voice
And see their feather delicate.
Let all my lords rejoice
And be buttress to the state.

Be a buttress or screen,
Set an example fine,
Be self-restrained and keen,
Receive blessings divine.

---

* The king, celebrating his feudal princes, expressed his admiration of them and good wishes for them.

The cup of rhino horn
Is filled with spirits soft.
Do not feel pride nor scorn,
And blessings will come oft.

The Love-birds*

Flying love-birds need rest
When large and small nets spread.
May you live long and blest,
Wealthy and happily wed!

On the dam love-birds stay,
In left wing hid the head.
May you live safe for aye,
Duly and happily wed!

Four horses in the stable
With grain and forage fed.
May you live long and stable,
For you're happily wed.

Four horses in the stable
With forage and grain fed.
May you live comfortable,
For you're happily wed.

---

* The love-birds flying in pairs alluded to the newly-wed and the four horses were used to draw the carriage of the bride.

The Royal Banquet*

Who are those lords so fine
In leather cap or hood,
Coming to drink your wine
And eat your viands good?
Can they be others?
They are your brothers.
They are like mistletoe
That o'er cypress does grow.
When they see you not, how
Can their hearts not be sad?
When they do see you now,
They are happy and glad.

Who are those lords so fine
In deer skin cap or hood,
Coming to drink your wine
And eat your seasonable food?
Can they be others?
They are your brothers.
They are like mistletoe
That o'er the pine does grow.
When they see you not, how
Can their hearts not feel sad?

---

* This ode celebrated the King You feasting with his relatives.

When they do see you now,
They feel all right and glad.

Who are those lords so fine
With leather cap on head,
Coming to drink your wine,
With food the table spread?
O how can they be others?
They are our cousins and brothers.
We are like snow or rain;
Nothing will long remain.
Death may come any day;
We can enjoy tonight at least.
Drink and rejoice as you may;
Let us enjoy the feast!

On the Way to the Bride's House*

Having prepared my creaking cart,
I go to fetch my bride.
Nor hungry nor thirsty at heart,
I'll take her as good guide,
Nor good friends come nor priest;
We'll rejoice in our feast.

---

* This ode was said to be sung at a wedding and the wood-splitting might allude to love-making in ancient Chinese songs.

BOOK OF POETRY

In the plain there's dense wood
And pheasants with long tail.
I love my young bride good;
She'll help me without fail.
I'll praise her when we feast,
Never tired in the least.

Though we have no good wine,
We'll drink, avoiding waste.
Though our viands are not fine,
We may give them a taste.
Though no good to you can I bring,
Still we may dance and sing.

I climb the mountain green
To split oak for firewood.
Amid leaves lush and green
I split oak for firewood.
Seeing my matchless bride,
I will be satisfied.

You're good like mountains high;
Like the road you go long.
My four steeds run and hie;
Six reins like lute-strings weave a song.
When I'm wed to my bride,
How my heart will be satisfied!

Blue Flies*

Hear the buzzing blue flies;
On the fence they alight.
Lord, don't believe their lies;
Friend, don't take wrong for right.

Hear blue flies buzzing, friend;
They light on jujube trees.
The slander without end
Spreads in the state disease.

Hear blue flies buzzing, friend;
They light on hazel tree.
The slander without end
Sets you at odds with me.

Revelry**

The guests come with delight
And take place left and right.
In rows arranged the dishes,
Displayed viands and fishes.
The wine is mild and good;
Guests drink and eat the food.

---

* It was said that this ode was directed against King You who lent a ready ear to slander and blue flies became symbolic of slanderers.
** Directed against drunkenness, this ode was a lively picture of the license of the time of King You.

Bells and drums in their place,
They raise their cups with grace.
The target set on foot,
With bows for them to shoot,
The archers stand in row,
Ready their skill to show.
If the target is hit,
You'll drink a cup for it.

They dance to music sweet
Of flute and to drumbeat.
Rites are performed to please
Our ancestors with ease.
The offerings on hand
Are so full and so grand.
You will be richly blessed,
Sons, grandsons and the rest.
Happy is every man.
Let each do what he can.
Each guest shoots with his bow;
The host joins in the row.
Let's fill an empty cup.
When one hits, all cheer up.

When guests begin to feast,
They are gentle at least.
When they've not drunk too much,
They would observe the rite;

When they have drunk too much,
Their deportment is light.
They leave their seats and go
Capering to and fro.
When they've not drunk too much,
They are in a good mood;
When they have drunk too much,
They're indecent and rude.
When they are deeply drunk,
They know not where they're sunk.

When they've drunk their cups dry,
They shout out, brawl and cry.
They put plates upside down;
They dance like funny clown.
When they have drunk wine strong,
They know not right from wrong.
With their cups on one side,
They dance and slip and slide.
If drunk they went away,
The host would happy stay.
But drunk they will not go;
The host is full of woe.
We may drink with delight
If we observe the rite.

Whenever people drink,
In drunkenness some sink.

Appoint an inspector
And keep a register.
But drunkards feel no shame;
On others they'll lay blame.
Don't drink any more toast,
Or they will wrong the host.
Do not speak if you could;
Say only what you should.
Don't say like drunkard born.
You're a ram without horn.
With three cups you've lost head;
With more you'd be drunk dead.

Seventh Decade of Odes

The Fish among the Weed*

The fish among the weed,
Showing large head, swims with speed
The king in the capital
Drinks happy in the hall.

The fish swims thereamong,
Showing its tail so long.
The king in the capital
Drinks cheerful in the hall.

The fish among the weed
Sheltered by rush and reed,
The king in the capital
Dwells carefree in the hall.

Royal Favours**

Gather beans long and short
In baskets round and square.

---

* This ode celebrated the praise of King Wu after his triumph over the last king of the Shang Dynasty. The fish was in its proper place, enjoying what happiness it could, and so it served to introduce King Wu enjoying himself in his capital.

** This ode was responsive to the former, celebrating the appearance of the feudal princes at the court, the splendor of their array, the propriety of their demeanor and the favors conferred on them by the king.

The lords come to the court.
What suitable things there
Can be given to meet their needs?
A state cab and horses four.
What else besides the steeds?
Dragon robes they adore.

Gather cress long and short
Around the spring near by.
The lords come to the court;
I see dragon flags fly.
Flags flutter in the breeze,
Three or four horses run,
Bells ringing without cease,
The lords come one by one.

Red covers on their knees
And their buskins below,
They go with perfect ease
In what the king bestows.
They receive with delight
High favours from the king;
They receive with delight
Good fortune in a string.

On branches of oak-tree,
What riot lush leaves run!
The lords guard with high glee

The land of Heaven's Son,
They receive with delight
Blessings from high and low.
Attendants left and right
Follow them where they go.

The boat of willow wood
Fastened by band and rope,
Of happy lords and good
The king scans the full scope.
They receive with high glee
All blessings from the king.
They're happy and carefree;
Fortune comes on the wing.

Admonition*

Tighten the string of the bow,
Its recoil will be swift.
If brothers alien go,
Their affection will shift.

If you alienate
Your relatives and brothers,
People will imitate

---

* This ode was directed against the king's cold treatment of his relatives and his encouragement to calumniators.

BOOK OF POETRY

You when you deal with others.

When there is brotherhood,
Good feeling is displayed.
When brothers are not good,
Much trouble will be made.

The people have no grace,
They blame the other side;
They fight to get high place
And come to fratricide.

Old steeds think themselves good;
Of the young they don't think.
They want plenty of food
And an excess of drink.

Don't teach apes to climb trees
Nor add mud to the wall.
If you do good with ease,
They'll follow you one and all.

Flake on flake falls the snow;
It dissolves in the sun.
Don't despise those below.
The proud will be undone.

The snow falls flake on flake;
It will melt in sunlight.
Let no barbarians make

You fall into a sad plight.

The Unjust Lord*

Lush is the willow tree.
Who won't rest under it?
The lord's to punish free.
Don t fall into the pit.
You lend him hand and arm,
But he will do you harm.

Lush is the willow tree.
Who won't shelter 'neath it?
The lord's to punish free;
His ire bursts in a fit.
You lend him arm and hand;
He'll ban you from the land.

The bird flies as it can
Even up to the sky.
The heart of such a man
Will go up far and high.
Whate'er for him you do,
He's free to punish you.

---

* This ode was directed against King Li (877–841 B.C.), tyrannical and oppressive, punishing where punishment was not due, whose court was not frequented by the princes of the states.

Men of the Old Capital*

Men of the old capital
In yellow fox-fur dress,
With face unmoved at all,
Spoke with pleasing address.
At the old capital
They were admired by all.

Men of the old capital
Wore their hat up-to-date;
The noble ladies tall
Had hair so thick and straight.
Although I see them not,
Could their face be forgot?

Men of the old capital
Wore pendant from the ear;
The noble ladies tall
Were fair without a peer.
Although I see them not,
Could their dress be forgot?

Men of the old capital
With girdles hanging down;
And noble ladies tall

---

* This was an ode praise of the lords and ladies of the old capital, written after King Ping removed the capital to the east in 770 B.C..

With hair like tail of scorpion,
Of them could I see one,
After them I would run.

His girdle hanging there
Suited so well his gown;
Her natural curled hair
Was wavy up and down.
I see not their return.
How much for them I yearn!

My Lord Not Back*

I gather all the morn king-grass,
But get not a handful, alas!
In a wisp is my hair,
I'll go home and wash it with care.

I gather all the morn plants blue,
But get not an apronful for you.
You should be back on the fifth day.
Now it's the sixth, why the delay?

If you should hunting go,
I would put in its case your bow.

---

* A wife told her sorrow and incapability of attending to anything in the prolonged absence of her husband to whom she was fondly attached.

If you should go to fish,
I'd arrange your line as you wish.

What might we take out of the stream?
O tench and bream.
O tench and bream,
With what wild joy my face would beam!

On Homeward Way after Construction*

Young millet grows tall and strong,
Fattened by genial rain.
Our southward journey's long;
The Lord of Shao cheers the train.

Our carts go one by one;
Our oxen follow the track.
Our construction is done,
So we are going back.

We go on foot or run;
Our host goes in a throng.
Our construction is done,
So we are going along.

---

* This ode celebrated the service of Duke Mu of Shao in building the city of Xie (modem Tang County in Henan Province) for the marquisate of Shen established by King Xuan (826–781 B.C.) as a bulwark against the encroachments of wild tribes.

The town of Xie stands strong,
Built by our lord with might and main.
Our expedition's long
And our lord leads the train.

Lowland becomes a plain;
Streams are cleared east and west.
Our lord leads the campaign;
The king's heart is at rest.

The Mulberry Tree*

The lowland mulberry tree's fair;
Its leaves are lush and bright.
When I see my love there,
How great will be my delight!

The lowland mulberry tree's fair;
Its leaves shed glossy light,
When I see my love there,
How can I not feel delight?

The lowland mulberry tree's fair;
Its leaves darken each day.
When I see my love there,
How much have I to say?

---

* This ode read like a song in which a woman spoke of her admiration and love for a man fair as the mulberry tree and bright as its leaves.

I love him in my heart,
Why won't I tell him so?
Better keep it apart
That sweeter it will grow.

The Degraded Queen*

White flowered rushes sway
Together with white grass,
My lord sends me away
And leaves me alone, alas!

White clouds with dewdrops spray
Rushes and grass all o'er.
Hard is heavenly way;

---

* The queen of King You (reigned 780–770 B.C.) complained of being degraded and forsaken for the sake of his fair mistress Lady Shi of Bao. The first stanza suggested the idea of the close connection between rushes and grass as it should be between king and queen. The idea in Stanza 2 seemed to be that the clouds bestowed their dewy influences on rushes and grass while the king neglected the queen. The flooding in Stanza 3 was the greatest benefit to the ricefields, not so did the king deal with the queen. The idea in Stanza 4 seemed to be that the queen had a smaller stove than the king's mistress. Stanza 5 suggested that the king's angry shout was heard without the palace. In Stanza 6 the crane was a clean bird and the heron an unclean one. The idea in Stanza 7 was that the lovebirds were more faithful than the lang. Stanza 8 compared the queen to the stone King You trod underfoot.

My lord loves me no more.

Northward the stream goes by,
Flooding the rice fields there.
With wounded heart I sigh,
Thinking of his mistress fair.

Wood's cut from mulberry tree
To make fire in the stove.
His mistress fair makes me
Lose the heart of my love.

When rings the palace bell,
Its sound is heard without.
When I think of him well,
I hear but angry shout.

The heron may eat fish
While the crane hungry goes.
His mistress has her wish
While I am full of woes,

The lovebirds on the dam
Hide their beaks 'neath left wings.
The woe in which I am
Is what my unkind lord brings.

The stone becomes less thick
On which our feet oft tread.

My heart becomes love-sick
For my lord's left my bed.

Hard Journey*

O hear the oriole's song!
It rests on mountain slope.
The journey's hard and long.
How can a tired man cope?
Give me food and be kind,
Help me, encourage me,
Tell the carriage behind
To stop and carry me!

O hear the oriole's song!
It rests at mountain yon.
Do I fear journey long?
I fear I can't go on.
Give me food and be kind,
Help me, encourage me,
Tell the carriage behind
To stop and carry me!

O hear the oriole's song!
It rests at mountain's bend.
Do I fear journey long?

---

* Some inferior complained of his toil in an expedition and the neglect with which he was treated by his superiors.

I can't get to its end.
Give me food and be kind,
Help me, encourage me,
Tell the carriage behind
To stop and carry me!

Frugal Hospitality*

The gourd's waving leaves are fine,
Taken and boiled in haste.
Our good friend has sweet wine;
He pours it out for a taste.

The rabbit's meat is fine
When baked or roasted up.
Our good friend has sweet wine;
He presents us a cup.

The rabbit's meat is fine
When broiled or roasted up,
Our good friend has sweet wine;
We present him a cup.

The rabbit's meat is fine
When baked or roasted up.
Our good friend has sweet wine;
We fill each other's cup.

---

* This ode described the simple manners and decency of an earlier time.

Eastern Expedition*

The mountain frowns
With rocky crowns.
Peaks high, streams long,
Toilsome the throng.
Warriors east go;
No rest they know.

The mountain frowns
With craggy crowns.
Peaks high, streams bend.
When is the end?
Warriors go east.
When be released?

White-legged swines wade
Through streams and fade.
In Hyades the moon
Foretells hard rain soon.
Warriors east go;
No plaint they show.

---

* This ode commemorated the hardships of a long and difficult expedition to the east, undertaken in the time of King Li (877–841 B.C.).

Famine*

The bignonia blooms
Yellow and fade.
My heart is full of gloom;
I feel the wound grief's made.

The bignonia blooms
Have left the green leaves dry.
Could I foretell what looms,
I would not live but die.

The ewe's lean; large its head.
In fish-trap there's no fish.
Some people may be fed;
Few can get what they wish.

Nowhere but Yellow Grass**

Nowhere but yellow grass,
Not a day when we've rest,
No soldier but should pass
Here and there, east or west.

---

* The speaker lamented the famine and misery in consequence of the general decay of the kingdom.

** This was the last ode which read like a song describing the misery of the soldiers constantly employed on expeditionary service and treated without any consideration in the time of King You (780–770 B.C.).

Nowhere but rotten grass,
None but has left his wife,
We poor soldiers, alas!
Lead an inhuman life.

We're not tigers nor beast.
Why in the wilds do we stay?
Alas! we're men at least.
Why toil we night and day?

Unlike the long-tailed foxes
Deep hidden in the grass,
In our carts with our boxes
We toil our way, alas!

BOOK OF EPICS

First Decade of Epics

Heaven's Decree*

King Wen rests in the sky;
His spirit shines on high.
Though Zhou is an old state,
It's destined to be great.
The House of Zhou is bright;
God brings it to the height.
King Wen will e'er abide
At God's left or right side.

King Wen was good and strong;
His fame lasts wide and long.
God's gifts to Zhou will run
From his son to grandson.

---

* This was the first epic ode celebrating King Wen (1184–1134 B.C.), dead and alive, as the founder of the Zhou Dynasty. It was attributed to the Duke of Zhou for the benefit of the young King Cheng (1114–1076 B.C.). It showed how King Wen's virtue drew to him the favoring regard of Heaven and made him a bright pattern to his descendants and their ministers. Stanza 5 carried on the subject of the descendants of the previous dynasty, called first Shang and then Yin. When they appeared at the court of Zhou, they assisted at the sacrifices of the king in his ancestral temple, which began with a libation of fragrant spirits to bring down the spirits of the departed. The libation was poured out by the representative of the dead and the cup with the spirits was handed to him by Yin officers.

Descendants of his line
Will receive gifts divine;
So will talents and sage
Be blessed from age to age;

From age to age they're blest;
They work with care and zest.
Brilliant, they dedicate
Their lives to royal state.
Born in this royal land,
They'll support the house grand.
With talents standing by,
King Wen may rest on high.

King Wen was dignified,
Respected far and wide.
At Heaven's holy call
The sons of Shang come all.
Those sons of the noblesse
Of Shang are numberless.
As Heaven orders it,
They cannot but submit.

Submission's nothing strange;
Heaven's decree may change.
They were Shang's officers;
They're now Zhou's servitors.
They serve wine in distress

In Shang cap and Yin dress.
You loyal ministers,
Don't miss your ancestors!

Miss no ancestors dear;
Cultivate virtue here!
Obey Heaven's decree
And you'll live in high glee.
Ere it lost people's heart,
Yin played its ordained part.
From Yin's example we see
It's hard to keep decree.

O keep Heaven's decree
Or you will cease to be.
Let virtue radiate;
Profit from Yin's sad fate.
All grow under the sky
Silently far and nigh.
Take pattern from King Wen.
All states will obey you then.

Three Kings of Zhou*

Gods know on high

---

* This epic ode celebrated King Ji who married Princess Ren of Yin; King Wen who married Xin; and King Wu who overthrew the dynasty of Shang in 1121 B.C..

Book of Epics

What's done below.
We can't rely
On grace they show.
It's hard to retain
The royal crown.
Yin-Shang did reign;
It's overthrown.

Ren, Princess Yin,
Left Shang's town-wall
To marry in Zhou's capital.
She wed King Ji,
The best of men.

Then pregnant, she
Gave birth to Wen.
When he was crowned,
Wen served with care
The gods around,
Blessed here and there.
His virtue's great,
Fit head of the state.

Heaven above
Ruled o'er our fate.
It chose with love
For Wen a mate.
On sunny side

Of River Wei
Wen found his bride
In rich array.

Born in a large state,
The celestial bride
And auspicious mate
Stood by riverside.
On bridge of boats they met,
Splendor ne'er to forget.

At Heaven's call
Wen again wed In capital
Xin nobly-bred.
She bore a son
Who should take down,
When victory's won,
The royal crown.

Shang troops did wield
Stones on hard wood.
Wu vowed afield;
"To us kinghood!
Gods are behind.
Keep your strongmind!"

The field is wide;
War chariots strong.

The steeds we ride
Gallop along.
Our Master Jiang
Assists the king
To overthrow the Shang
Like eagle on the wing.
A morning bright
Displaced the night.

The Migration in 1325 B.C.*

Gourds grow in long, long trains;
Our people grew in the plains.
They moved to Qi from Tu,
Led by old Duke Tan Fu,
And built kilnlike hut and cave
For house they did not have.

Tan Fu took morning ride;
Along the western side
Of River Wei came he
To the foot of Mount Qi;
His wife Jiang came at his right

---

* This epic ode narrated the beginning and subsequent growth of the House of Zhou, its removal from Bin to the foot of Mount Qi under Duke Tan Fu in 1325 B.C. and its settlement in the plain of Zhou, down to the time of King Wen.

BOOK OF POETRY

To find a housing site.

Zhou plain spread at his feet
With plants and violets sweet.
He asked his men their mind,
And by tortoise shell divined.
He was told there to stay
And build homes right away.

They settled at the site
And planned to build left and right.
They divided the ground
And dug ditches around.
From west to east there was no land
But Tan Fu took in hand.

He named two officers
In charge of laborers
To build their houses fine.
They made walls straight with the line
And bound the frame-boards tight.
A temple rose in sight.

They brought basketfuls of earth
And cast it in frames with mirth.
Then they beat it with blows
And pared the walls in rows.
A hundred walls did rise;

Drums were drowned in their cries.

They set up city gate;
It stood so high and straight.
They set up palace door
They'd never seen before.
They reared an altar grand
To spirits of the land.

The angry foe not tame
Feared our Duke Tan Fu's name.
Oaks and thorns cleared away,
People might go their way.
The savage hordes in flight
Panted and ran out of sight.

The lords no longer strove;
King Wen taught them to love.
E'en strangers became kind;
They followed him behind.
He let all people speak
And defended the weak.

King Wen and Talents*

Oak trees and shrubs lush grow;

---

* This epic ode celebrated King Wen using talents in war and in the pre-war sacrifice and breeding or cultivating them after the war.

They'll make firewood in row.
King Wen has talents bright
To serve him left and right.

King Wen has talents bright
To hold cups left and right
To offer sacrifice
And pour libations nice.
On River Jin afloat
Many a ship and boat,
The king orders to fight
Six hosts of warriors bright.

The Milky Way on high
Makes figures in the sky.
The king of Zhou lives long
And breeds talents in throng.

Figures by chisels made
Look like metal or jade.
With them our good king reigns
Over his four domains.

Sacrifice and Blessing*

At the mountain's foot, lo!
How lush the hazels grow!

---

* The prince referred to King Wen blessed by his ancestors.

Our prince is self-possessed,
And he prays to be blessed.

The cup of jade is fine,
O'erflowed with yellow wine.
Our prince is self-possessed;
He prays and he is blessed.

The hawks fly in the sky;
The fish leap in the deep.
Our prince is self-possessed;
He prays his men be blessed.

Jade cups of wine are full;
Ready is the red bull.
He pays the sacred rite
To increase blessings bright.

Oaks grow in neighborhood,
And are used for firewood.
Our prince is self-possessed;
By gods he's cheered and blessed.

How the creeper and vine
Around the branches twine!
Our prince is self-possessed;
He prays right and is blessed.

King Wen's Reign*

Reverent Lady Ren
Was mother of King Wen.
She loved grandmother dear,
A good wife without peer.
Si inherited her fame;
From her a hundred sons came.

Good done to fathers dead,
Nowhere complaint was spread,
They reposed as they could.
King Wen set example good
To his dear wife and brothers,
His countrymen and others.

At home benevolent,
In temple reverent,
He had gods e'er in view;
No wrong would he e'er do.

All evils rectified,
No ill done far and wide.
Untaught, he knew the right;
Advised, he saw the light.

---

* This was an ode sung in praise of the virtue of King Wen and the excellent character of his grandmother Jiang, his mother Ren and his wife Si.

The grown-up became good;
E'en the young showed manhood.
All talents sang in praise
Of King Wen's olden days.

The Rise of Zhou*

O God is great!
He saw our state,
Surveyed our land,
Saw how people did stand.
Dissatisfied
With Yin-Shang's side,
Then He would fain
Find out again.
Another state
To rule its fate
His eyes turned west;
Our state was blessed.

Tai cut the head
Off the trunk dead
And hewed with blows

---

* This epic ode showed the rise of the House of Zhou to the sovereignty of the kingdom and the achievement of King Tai, his son King Ji and his grandson King Wen who conquered the Mi tribe and the Chong State in 1135 B.C..

The bushy rows.
The rotten trees
And mulberries
Were cleared away
Or put in array.
God made the road
For men's abode.
King Tai was made
Heaven's sure aide.

God visited Mount Qi
And thinned oak tree on tree.
Cypress and pines stood straight;
God founded the Zhou State.
He chose Tai as its head,
And Ji when Tai was dead.
Ji loved his brothers dear;
His heart was full of cheer.
When Ji was head of state,
He made its glory great.
The House of Zhou was blest
North to south, east to west.

God gave King Ji
The power to see
Clearly right from wrong
That he might rule for long.

With intelligence great
He could lead the whole state;
He ruled with wisdom high,
Thus obeyed far and nigh.
In his son King Wen's days
People still sang his praise.
For God's blessings would run
To his son and grandson.

To our King Wen God said,
"Don't let the foe invade
Your holy land with might;
First occupy the height."
The Mi tribe disobeyed,
On our land made a raid,
Attacked Yuan and Gong State;
King Wen's anger was great.
He sent his troops in rows
To stop invading foes
That the Zhou House might stand
And rule over the land.

The capital gave order
To attack from Yuan border
And occupy the height.
Let no foe come with might
Near our hill or our mountain

Nor to drink from our fountain
Nor our pools filled by rain.
King Wen surveyed the plain,
Settled and occupied
Hillside and riverside.
As great king he would stand
For people and the land.

To our King Wen God said,
"High virtue you've displayed.
You're ever lenient
To deal out punishment.
Making no effort on your part,
You follow me at heart."
To our King Wen God said,
"Consult allied brigade,
Attack with brethren strong,
Use scaling ladders long
And engines of assault
To punish Chong tribe's fault."

The engines of on-fall
Attacked the Chong State wall.
Many captives were ta'en
And left ears of the slain.
Sacrifice made afield,
We called the foe to yield.

The engines of on-fall
Destroyed the Chong State wall.
The foe filled with dismay,
Their forces swept away.
None dared insult Zhou State;
All obeyed our king great.

The Wondrous Park*

When the tower began
To be built, every man
Took part as if up-heated,
The work was soon completed.
"No hurry," said the king,
But they worked as his offspring.

In Wondrous Park the king
Saw the deer in the ring
Lie at his left and right;
How sweet sang the birds white.
The king by Wondrous Pond
Saw fishes leap and bound.

In water-girded hall .
Beams were long and posts tall.

---

* This ode showed the joy of the people in the growing opulence of King Wen who moved his capital to Feng after the overthrow of the State of Chong in 1135 B.C., only one year before his death.

Drums would beat and bells ring
To amuse our great king.

Drums would beat and bells ring
To amuse our great king.
The lizard-skin drums beat;
Blind musicians sang sweet.

King Wu*

In Zhou successors rise;
All of them are kings wise.
To the three kings in heaven
King Wu in Hao is given.

King Wu in Hao is given
To the orders of Heaven.
He would seek virtue good
To attain true kinghood.

To attain true kinghood,
Be filial a man should.
He'd be pattern for all;
"Be filial" is his call.

All people love King Wu;

---

* This ode was sung in praise of King Wu (reigned 1121–1113B.C.), walking in the ways of his forefathers and by his filial piety securing the throne to himself and his posterity.

What they are told, they do.
Be filial a man should;
The bright successor's good.

All bright successor's good
Follow their fatherhood.
For long they will be given
The blessings of good Heaven.

The blessings of good Heaven
And good Earth will be given
For long yea's without end
To the people's great friend.

Kings Wen and Wu*

King Wen had a great fame
And famous he became.
He sought peace in the land
And saw it peaceful stand.

---

* This epic ode was sung in praise of King Wen and King Wu. The first four stanzas showed how King Wen displayed his military prowess only to secure the tranquility of the people and how this appeared in the building of Feng as his capital city. In Stanza 5 King Yu (reigned 2205–2197 B.C.) referred to the founder of the Xia Dynasty. The last four stanzas showed how King Wu entered, in his capital of Hao, into the sovereignty of the kingdom with the sincere good will of all the people.

O King Wen was so grand!

King Wen whom gods did bless
Achieved martial success.
Having overthrown Chong,
He fixed his town at Feng.
O may King Wen live long!

King Wen built moat and wall
Around the capital
Not for his own desire
But for those of his sire.
O our prince we admire!

King Wen at capital
Strong as the city wall,
The lords from state to state
Paid homage to prince great.
Our royal prince was great.

The River Feng east flowed;
Our thanks to Yu we owed.
The lords from land to land
Paid homage to king grand.
How great did King Wu stand!

He built water-girt hall
At Hao the capital.
North to south, east to west,

By people he was blest.
King Wu was at his crest.

The king divined the site;
The tortoise-shell foretold it right
To build the palace hall
At Hao the capital,
King Wu was admired by all.

By River Feng white millet grew.
How could talents not serve King Wu?
All that he'd planned and done
Was for the son and grandson.
King Wu was second to none.

Second Decade of Epics

Hou Ji, the Lord of Corn*

Who gave birth to the Lord of Corn?
By Lady Jiang Yuan he was born,
How gave she birth to her son nice?
She went afield for sacrifice.
Childless, she prayed for a son, so
She trod on the print of God's toe.
She stood there long and took a rest,
And she was magnified and blessed.
Then she conceived, then she gave birth,
It was the Lord of Corn on earth.

When her carrying time was done,
Like a lamb slipped down her first son.
Of labor she suffered no pain;
She was not hurt, nor did she strain.
How could his birth so wonderful be?
Was it against Heaven's 'decree?
Was God displeased with her sacrifice.
To give a virgin a son nice?

The son abandoned in a lane
Was milked by the cow or sheep.

---

* This epic ode was sung in praise of Hou Ji, the Lord of Corn, legendary founder of the House of Zhou.

Abandoned in a wooded plain,
He's fed by men in forest deep.
Abandoned on the coldest ice,
He was warmed by birds with their wings.
When flew away those birds so nice,
The cry was heard of the nursling's.
He cried and wailed so long and loud
The road with his voice was o'erflowed.

He was able to crawl aground
And then rose to his feet.
When he sought food around,
He learned to plant large beans and wheat.
The beans he planted grew tall;
His millet grew in rows;
His gourds teemed large and small;
His hemp grew thick and close.

The Lord of Corn knew well the way
To help the growing of the grain.
He cleared the grasses rank away
And sowed with yellow seed the plain.
The new buds began to appear;
They sprang up, grew under the feet.
They flowered and came into ear;
They drooped down, each grain complete.
They became so good and so strong,

Our Lord would live at Tai for long.

Heaven gave them the lucky grains
Of double-kernelled millet black
And red and white ones on the plains,
Black millet reaped was piled in stack
Or carried back on shoulders bare.
Red and white millet growing nice
And reaped far and wide, here and there,
Was brought home for the sacrifice.

What is our sacrifice?
We hull and ladle rice,
We sift and tread the grain,
Swill and scour it again.
It's steamed and then distilled;
We see the rites fulfilled.
We offer fat with southern wood
And a skinned ram as food.
Flesh roast or broiled with cheer
Brings good harvest next year.

We load the stands with food,
The stands of earthenware or wood.
God smells its fragrance rise;
He's well pleased in the skies.
What smell is this, so nice?
It's Lord of Corn's sacrifice.

This is a winning way;
It's come down to this day.

Banquet*

Let no cattle and sheep
Trample on roadside rush
Which bursts up with root deep
And with leaves soft and lush.
We're closely related brothers.
Let us be seated near.
Spread mats for some; for others
Stools will be given here.

Mats spread one on another,
Servants come down and up.
Host and guests pledge each other;
They rinse and fill their cup.
Sauce brought with prickles ripe
And roast or broiled meat,
There are provisions of tripe,
All sing to music sweet.

The bow prepared is strong
And the four arrows long.

---

* This ode celebrated some entertainment given by the king to his relatives, with the trial of archery after the banquet; it also celebrated the honor done on such occasions to the aged.

The guests all try to hit
And stand in order fit.
They fully draw the bow
And four arrows straight go.
They hit like planting trees;
Those who miss stand at ease.

The grandson is the host;
With sweet or strong Wine they toast.
They drink the cups they hold
And pray for all the old.
The hoary old may lead
And help the young in need.
May their old age be blessed;
May they enjoy their best!

Sacrificial Ode*

We've drunk wine strong
And thank your grace.
May you live long!
Long live your race!

---

* It was said that this ode was responsive to the previous one. The king's relatives expressed their sense of his kindness and their wishes for his happiness, mostly in the words in which the personator of the dead had conveyed the satisfaction of his ancestors with the sacrifice offered to them and promised to him their blessing.

We've drunk wine strong
And eaten food.
May you live long!
Be wise and good!

Be good and wise!
By God you're led.
See spirit rise
And speak for our dead.

What does he say?
Your food is fine,
Constant friends stay
At the service divine.

With constant friends
And filial sons
There won't be end
For pious ones.

To you belong
The pious race.
May you live long!
Be blessed with grace!

Your race appears
By Heaven blessed.
You'll live long years,
Served east and west.

Who will serve you?
You will have maids and men.
Their sons will renew
Their service again.

The Ancestor's Spirit*

On the stream waterbirds appear;
On earth descends the spirit good.
Your wine is sweet and clear,
And fragrant is your food.
The spirit comes to drink and eat;
Your blessing will be sweet.

On the sand waterbirds appear;
On earth enjoys the spirit good.
Abundant is your wine clear;
Delicious is your food.
The spirit comes to drink and eat;
Your blessing will be complete.

On the isle waterbirds appear;
In his place sits the spirit good.
Your wine is pure and clear;
In slices are your meat and food.

---

* This ode was appropriate to the feast given to the personator of the departed on the day after the sacrifice in the ancestral temple.

The spirit eats and drinks sweet wine;
You will receive blessing divine.

Waterbirds swim where waters meet;
The spirit sits in a high place.
In his high place he drinks wine sweet;
You will receive blessing and grace.
The spirit drinks and eats his food;
You'll receive blessing doubly good.

In the gorge waterbirds appear;
Drunken on earth the spirit good.

Delicious is your wine clear;
Broiled or roast your meat and food.
The spirit comes to drink and feast;
You'll have no trouble in the least.

King Cheng*

Happy and good our king,
Of his virtue all sing.
He's good to people all;
On him all blessings fall
And favor from on high
Is renewed far and nigh.

---

* This ode was probably sung in praise of King Cheng (1114–1076 B.C.), who succeeded King Wu at the age of thirteen with the Duke of Zhou as regent.

They are blessed, everyone
Of his sons and grandsons.
He's majestic and great,
Fit ruler of the state.
Blameless and dutiful,
He follows father's rule.

His bearing dignified,
His virtue spreads far and wide.
From prejudice he's free,
Revered by all with glee.
He receives blessings great,
Modeled on from state to state.

He's modeled on without end;
Each state becomes his friend.
Ministers all and one
Admire the Heaven's Son.
Dutiful, he is blessed;
In him people find rest.

Duke Liu*

Duke Liu was blessed;
He took nor ease nor rest.
He divided the fields

---

* This epic ode told the story of Duke Liu, the second legendary hero of the House of Zhou, who moved from Tai to Bin in 1796 B.C..

And stored in barns the yields.
In bags and sacks he tied
Up grain and meat when dried.
He led people in rows,
With arrows and drawn bows.
With axes, shields and spears,
They marched on new frontiers.

Duke Liu would fain
Survey a fertile plain
For his people to stay.
On that victorious day
No one would sigh nor rest.
He came up mountain-crest
And descended again.
We saw his girdle then
Adorned with gems and jade,
His precious sword displayed.

Duke Liu crossed the mountains
And saw a hundred fountains.
He surveyed the plain wide
By the southern hillside.
He found a new capital
Wide for his people all.
Some thought it good for the throng;
Others would not dwell there for long.

There was discussion free;
They talked in high glee.

Duke Liu was blessed;
At capital he took rest,
Put stools on mats he spread
For officers he led.
They leant on stools and sat
On the ornamented mat.
A penned pig was killed;
Their gourds with wine were filled.
They were well drunk and fed;
All hailed him as state head.

Duke Liu would fain
Measure the hill and plain
Broad and long; he surveyed
Streams and springs, light and shade;
His three armies were placed
By the hillside terraced;
He measured plains anew
And fixed the revenue.
Fields were tilled in the west;
The land of Bin was blessed.

Duke Liu who wore the crown
At Bin had settled down.
He crossed the River Wei

To gather stones by day.
All boundaries defined,
People worked with one mind
On the Huang Riverside
Towards Guo River wide.
The people dense would stay
On the shore of the Ney.

Take Water from Far Away*

Take water from pools far away,
Pour it in vessels that it may
Be used to steam millet and rice.
A prince should give fraternal advice
Like parent to his people nice.

Take water from pools far away,
Pour it in vessels that it may
Be used to wash the spirit-vase.
A prince should give fraternal praise
To his people for better days.

Take water from pools far away,
Pour it in vessels that it may
Be used to cleanse everything.

---

* This ode was attributed to Duke Kang of Shao for the admonition to King Cheng to fulfill his duties like a parent to his people so that his people may cling to him.

To our fraternal prince or king
Like water his people will cling.

King Cheng's Progress*

The mountain undulates;
The southern breeze vibrates.
Here our fraternal king
Comes crooning and wandering;
In praise of him I sing.

You're wandering with pleasure
Or taking rest at leisure.
O fraternal king, hear!
May you pursue the career
Of your ancestors dear!

Your territory's great
And secure is your state.
O fraternal king, hear!
May you pursue your career
As host of gods whom you revere!

For long you're Heaven-blessed;
You enjoy peace and rest.

---

* This was another ode addressed by Duke Kang of Shao to King Cheng, desiring for him long prosperity and congratulating him in order to admonish him on the happiness of his people.

O fraternal king, hear!
May you pursue your career
And be blessed far and near!

You've supporters and aides
Virtuous of all grades
To lead or act as wing.
O our fraternal king,
Of your pattern all sing.

Majestic you appear,
Like jade-mace without peer;
You're praised from side to side.
O fraternal king, hear!
Of the state you're the guide.

Phoenixes fly
With rustling wings
And settle high.
Officers of the king's
Employed each one
To please the Heaven's Son.

Phoenixes fly
With rustling wings
To azure sky.
Officers of the king's
At your command

Please people of the land.

Phoenixes sing
On lofty height;
Planes grow in spring
On morning bright.
Lush are plane-trees;
Phoenixes sing at ease.

O many are
Your cars and steed;
Your steed and car
Run at high speed.
I sing but to prolong
Your holy song.

The People Are Hard Pressed*

The people are hard pressed;
They need a little rest.
Do the Central Plain good,
You'll reign o'er neighborhood.
Of the wily beware;
Against the vice take care!
Put the oppressors down
Lest they fear not the crown.

---

* This ode was made by Duke Mu of Shao to reprehend King Li (877–841 B.C.), notorious for his tyranny.

Show kindness far and near;
Consolidate your sphere.

The people are hard pressed;
They need repose and rest.
Do the Central Plain good,
People will come from neighborhood.
Of the wily beware;
Against bad men take care!
Repress those who oppress;
Relive those in distress.
Through loyal service done
The royal quiet is won.

The people are hard pressed;
They need relief and rest.
Do good in the capital,
You'll please your people all.
Of the wily beware;
Against wicked men take care!
Repress those who oppress
Lest they go to excess.
In manner dignified
You'll have good men at your side.

The people are hard pressed;
They need some ease and rest.
Do good in Central Plain

To relieve people's pain.
Of the wily beware;
Against evil take care!
Put the oppressors down
Lest your rule be o'erthrown.
Though still young in the state,
What you can do is great,

The people are hard pressed;
They need quiet and rest.
Do good in Central Plain
Lest people suffer pain.
Of the wily beware;
Of flattery take care!
Put the oppressors down
Lest the state be o'erthrown.
O king, as jade you're nice.
Please take my frank frank advice!

Censure*

God won't our kingdom bless;
People are in distress.
Your words incorrect are,
Your plans cannot reach far.

---

* This was a censure made by Count of Fan (modern Hui County, Henan Province) on the prevailing misery in the times of King Li.

Book of Epics

You care not what sages do;
What you say is not true.
Your plans are far from nice;
So I give you advice.

Heaven sends troubles down.
O how can you not frown?
It makes turmoil prevail;
You talk to no avail.
If what you say is right,
'Twill be heard with delight.
If what you say is not,
It will soon be forgot.

Our duties different,
We serve the government.
I give you advice good;
Your attitude is rude,
My advice is sought after;
It's no matter for laughter.
Ancient saying is good;
"Consult cutters of wood!"

Heaven is doing wrong.
How can you get along?
I'm an old lord sincere.
How can you proud appear?
I'm not proud of my age.

Book of Poetry

How can you tease a sage?
Trouble will grow like fire,
Beyond remedy when higher.

Heaven's anger displayed,
Don't cajole nor upbraid!
The good and dignified
Are mute as men who died.
The people groan and sigh,
But none dare to ask why,
Wild disorder renewed,
Who'd help our multitude?

Heaven helps people mute
By whistle as by flute,
As two maces form one,
As something brought when done.
Bring anything you please,
You'll help people with ease.
They've troubles to deplore.
Don't give them any more!

Good men a fence install;
The people form a wall.
Screens are formed by each state
And each family great.
Virtue secures repose,
Walled up by kinsmen close.

BOOK OF EPICS

Do not destroy the wall;
Be not lonely after all!

Revere great Heaven's ire
And do not play with fire!
Revere great Heaven gay
And don't drive your own way.
There's nought but Heaven knows;
It's with you where you go,
Great Heaven sees all clear;
It's with you where you appear.

BOOK OF POETRY

Third Decade of Epics

Warnings*

God's influence spreads vast
Over people below.
God's terror strikes so fast;
He deals them blow on blow.
Heaven gives people birth,
On whom he'd not depend.
At first they're good on earth,
But few last to the end.

"Alas!" said King Wen of the west,
"You king of Yin-Shang, lo!
How could you have oppressed
And exploited people so?
Why put those in high place
Who did everything wrong?
Why are those who love grace

---

* This was a warning addressed to King Li who brought the Zhou Dynasty into imminent peril by his violent oppressions, his neglect of good men, his employment of mean creatures, his disannulling the old statutes and laws, his drunkenness and the fierceness of his will, but it was put in the mouth of King Wen delivering his warnings to the last king of the Shang Dynasty, in the hope that King Li would transfer the figure to himself and alter his course so as to avoid a similar ruin.

Book of Epics

Oppressed e'er by the strong?"

"Alas!" said King Wen of the west,
"You king of Yin-Shang, lo!
Why not help the oppressed
And give the strong a blow?
Why let rumors wide spread
And robbers be your friend?
Let curse fall on your head
And troubles without end!"

"Alas!" said King Wen of the west,
"You king of Yin-Shang, lo!
You do wrong without rest.
Can good out of wrong grow?
You know not what is good;
You've no good men behind.
Good men not understood,
To you none will be kind."

"Alas!" said King Wen of the west,
"You king of Yin-Shang, lo!
You drink wine without rest;
On a wrong way you go.
You know not what's about,
Nor tell darkness from light.
Amid clamour and shout
You turn day into night."

"Alas!" said King Wen of the west,
"You king of Yin-Shang, lo!
Cicadas cry without rest
As bubbling waters flow.
Things great and small go wrong
But heedless still you stand.
Indignation grows strong
In and out of the land."

"Alas!" said King Wen of the west,
"You king of Yin-Shang's days!
Not that you're not God-blessed,
Why don't you use old ways?
You've no experienced men,
But the laws have come down,
Why won't you listen then?
Your state will be o'erthrown."

"Alas!" said King Wen of the west,
"You who wear Yin-Shang's crown!
Know what say people blessed:
When a tree's fallen down,
Its leaves may still be green
But roots exposed to view.
Let Xia's downfall be seen
As a warning to you!"

Admonition by Duke Wu of Wei*

What appears dignified
Reveals a good inside.
You know as people say:
There're no sages but stray.
When people have done wrong,
It shows their sight not long,
When sages make mistakes,
It shows their wisdom breaks.
If a leader is good,
He'll tame the neighborhood.
If his virtue is great,
He'll rule o'er every state.
When he gives orders,
They'll reach the borders.
As he is dignified,
He's obeyed far and wide.

Look at the present state;
Political chaos' great.
Subverted the virtue fine,
You are besotted by wine.

---

* This ode was made by Duke Wu of Wei at ninety to admonish himself and King Ping who was still young. It was the earliest proverbial ode in Chinese poetry.

You wish your pleasure last
And think not of the past.
Enforce the laws laid down
By kings who wore a crown!

Or Heaven won't bless you
Like water lost to view,
Till you're ruined and dead.
Rise early, late to bed!

Try to sweep the floor clean;
Let your pattern be seen.
Keep cars and steeds in rows
And your arrows and bows.
If on alert you stand,
None dare invade your land.

Do people real good;
Make laws against falsehood.
Beware of what's unforeseen;
Say rightly what you mean.
Try to be dignified;
Be kind and mild outside.
A flaw in white jade found,
Away it may be ground;
A flaw in what you say
Will leave its influence to stay.

Don't lightly say a word
Nor think it won't be heard.
Your tongue is held by none;
Your uttered words will run.
Each word will answered be;
No deed is done for free.
If you do good to friend
And people without end,
You'll have sons in a string
And people will obey you as king,

Treat your friends with good grace;
Show them a kindly face.
You should do nothing wrong
E'en when far from the throng.
Be good when you're alone;
No wrong is done but known.
Think not you are unseen;
The sight of God is keen.
You know not what is in his mind,
Let alone what's behind.

When you do what is good,
Be worthy of manhood.
With people get along;
In manners do no wrong.
Making no mistakes small,

Book of Poetry

You'll be pattern for all,
For a peach thrown on you,
Return a plum as due,
Seeking horns where there's none,
You make a childish fun.
The soft, elastic wood
For stringed lute is good.
A mild, respectful man
Will do good when he can.
If you meet a man wise,
At what you say he tries
To do what he thinks good.
But a foolish man would
Think what you say untrue:
Different is his view.

Alas! young man, how could
You tell evil from good?
I'll lead you by the hand
And show you where you stand.
I'll teach you face to face
So that you can keep pace.
I'll hold you by the ear,
You too have a son dear.
If you are not content,
In vain your youth is spent.

Great Heaven fair and bright,
I live without delight.
Seeing you dream all day,
My heart will pine away.
I tell you now and again,
But I advise you in vain.
You think me useless one;
Of my words you make fun.
Can you say you don't know
How old today you grow?

Alas! young man, I pray,
Don't you know ancient way?
Listen to my advice,
And you'll be free from vice.
If Heaven's ire come down,
Our state would be o'erthrown.
Just take example near by,
You'll see justice on high.
If far astray you go,
You'll plunge people in woe.

Misery and Disorder*

Lush are mulberry trees;
Their shade affords good ease.
When they're stript of their leaves,
The people deeply grieves,
They're so deeply distressed
That sorrow fills their breast.
O Heaven great and bright,
Why not pity our plight?

The steeds run far and nigh;
The falcon banners fly.
The disorder is great;
There's ruin in the state.
So many killed in clashes,
Houses reduced to ashes.
Alas! we're full of gloom;
The state is near its doom.

Nothing can change our fate;
Heaven won't help our state.
Where to stop we don't know;
We have nowhere to go.

---

* The Earl of Rui mourned over the misery and disorder of the times, with a view to reprehend the misgovernment of King Li, especially his oppressions and listening to bad counselors. Their shade affords good ease.

BOOK OF EPICS

Good men may think and brood;
They strive not for their good.
Who is the man who sows
The dire distress and woes?

With heavy heart I stand,
Thinking of my homeland.
Born at unlucky hour,
I meet God's angry power,
From the east to the west,
I have nowhere to rest.
I see only disorder;
In danger is our border.

If you follow advice,
You may lessen the vice.
Let's gain a livelihood;
Put things in order good,
Who can hold something hot
If he waters it not?
Can remedy be found
If the people are drowned?

Standing against the breeze,
How can you breathe at ease?
Could people forward go
Should an adverse wind blow?
Love cultivated soil;

Let people live on toil.
The grain to them is dear;
They toil from year to year.

Heaven sends turmoil down
To ruin the royal crown.
Injurious insects reign
And devour crop and grain.
Alas! in Central State
Devastation is great.
What can I do but cry
To the boundless great sky?

If the king's good and wise,
He's revered in our eyes.
He'll make his plans with care
And choose ministers fair and square.
If he has no kinghood,
He'll think alone he's good.
His thoughts are hard to guess,
His people in distress.

Behold! among the trees
The deer may roam at ease.
Among friends insincere
You cannot roam with cheer,
Nor advance nor retreat
As in a strait you meet.

How wise these sages are!
Their views and words reach far.
How foolish those men bad!
They rejoice as if mad.
We can't tell them what we know
For fear of coming woe.

These good men you avoid,
They are never employed.
Those cruel men in power
Are courted from hour to hour.
So disorder is bred
And evil deeds wide spread.

The big wind blows a gale
From the large, empty vale.
What can a good man say?
It is of no avail!
In the court bad men stay;
What they say will prevail.

The big wind blows its way;
In the court bad men stay.
When praised, they're overjoyed;
When blamed, they play the drunk.
Good men are not employed;
In distress they are sunk.

Alas! alas! my friend,

Can I write to no end?
Like a bird on the wing,
Hit, you may be brought down.
Good to you I will bring,
But at me you will frown.

Don't do wrong to excess;
People fall in distress.
If you do people wrong,
How can they get along?
If they take a wrong course,
It's because you use force.

People live in unrest,
For robbers spread like pest.
I say that will not do;
You say that is not true.
Though you think I am wrong,
I've made for you this song.

Great Drought*

The Silver River shines on high,

---

* On occasion of a great drought in 821 B.C. King Xuan expostulated with God and the spirits who might he expected to succour him and his people, asked them wherefore they were contending with him and detailed the measures he had taken and was still taking for the removal of the calamity. The Silver River in Stanza 1 was the Chinese name for the Milky Way.

Revolving in the sky.
The king heaves sigh on sigh;
"O what wrong have we done?
What riot has death run!
Why have famines come one by one?
What sacrifice have we not made?
We have burned all maces of jade.
Have we not killed victims in herd?
How is it that we are not heard?

"The drought has gone to excess;
The heat has caused distress.
There's no sacrifice we've not made;
For gods above we've buried jade.
There are no souls we don't revere
In temples far and near.
The Lord of Corn can't stop the drought;
Ruin falls on our land all about.
The Almighty God won't come down.
Why should the drought fall on my crown!

"Excessive is the drought;
I am to blame, no doubt.
I palpitate with fear
As if thunder I hear.
Of people I'm bereft;
How many will be left?

The Almighty on high
Does not care if we die.
O my ancestors dear,
Don't you extinction fear?
"Excessive is the drought;
No one can put it out.
The sun burns far and wide;
I have nowhere to hide.
Our end is coming near;
I see no help appear.
Dukes and ministers dead
All turn away the head.
O my ancestors dear,
How can you not appear?

"The drought spreads far and nigh;
Hills are parched and streams dry.
The demon vents his ire;
He spreads wide flame and fire.
My heart's afraid of heat;
Burned with grief, it can't beat.
Why don't the souls appear?
Won't they my prayer hear?
Almighty in the sky,
Why put on me such pressure high?

"The drought holds excessive sway,

But I dare not go away.
Why has it come from on high?
I know not the reason why.
Early I prayed for a good year,
Sacrifice offered there and here.
God in heaven, be kind!
Why won't you bear this in mind?
O my reverend sire,
Why vent on me your ire?

"The drought has spread far and near;
People dispersed there and here.
Officials toil in vain;
The premier brings no rain.
The master of my horses
And leaders of my forces,
There's none but does his best;
There's none who takes a rest.
I look up to the sky.
What to do with soil dry?

"I look up to the sky;
The stars shine bright on high.
My officers have done their best;
With rain our land's not blessed.
Our course of life is run,
But don't give up what's done.

Pray for rain not for me
But for officials on the knee.
I look up to the sky;
Will rain and rest come from on high?"

Count of Shen*

The four mountains are high;
Their summits touch the sky.
Their spirits come on earth
To Fu and Shen gave birth.
The Shen State and Fu State
Are Zhou House's bulwarks great.
They screen it from attack
On the front and the back.

Count Shen was diligent
In royal government.
At Xie he set up capital,
A pattern for southern states all.

---

* This epic ode celebrated the appointment by King Xuan of the brother of his mother to be the Count of Shen and defender of the southern border of the kingdom, with the arrangements made for his entering on his charge. The writer was General Ji Fu who appeared in Poem "General Fang" as the commander of an expedition against the tribes of the Huns in the commencement of King Xuan's reign.

Count Shao was ordered by the king
To take charge of the house-building.
Of southern States Shen's made the head,
Where his great influence will spread.

The king ordered Shen's chief
To be pattern to southern fief,
And employ men of capital
To build the city wall.
The king gave Count Shao his command
To define Count Shen's land.
The king ordered his steward old
To remove Shen's household.

The construction of State of Shen
Was done by Count Shao and his men.
They built first city walls
And then the temple halls.
The great works done by the lord,
The king gave Count Shen as reward
Four noble steeds at left and right
With breasthooks amid trappings bright.

The king told Count Shen to speed
To his state in cab and steed.
"I've thought of your town beforehand;
Nowhere's better than southern land.
I confer on you this mace,

Symbol of dignity and grace.
Go, my dear uncle, go
And protect the south from the foe."

Count Shen set out for Xie;
The king feasted him at Mei.
Count Shen would take command
At Xie in southern land.
Count Shao was ordered to define
Shen's land and border line,
And provide him with food
That he might find his journey good.

Count Shen with flags and banners
Came to Xie, grand in manners.
His footmen and charioteers
Were greeted by the town with cheers.
The state will be guarded by men
Under the command of Count Shen,
Royal uncle people adore
And pattern in peace as in war.

Count Shen with virtue bright
Is mild, kind and upright.
He'll keep all states in order,
With fame spread to the border.
I, Ji Fu, make this song

In praise of the count strong.
I present this beautiful air
To the count bright and fair.

Premier Shan Fu*

Heaven who made mankind
Endowed him with body and mind.
The people loved manhood.
Could they not love the good?
Heaven beheld our crown
And shed light up and down.
To help his son on earth,
To Shan Fu he gave birth.

Cadet Shan Fu is good,
Endowed with mild manhood.
Dignified is his air;
He behaves with great care,
He follows lessons old;
He is as strong as bold.
He follows Heaven's Son
That his orders may be done.

---

* This epic ode celebrated the virtue of Premier Shan Fu and his despatch to the east to fortify the capital of the State of Qi (modern Shandong Province). Like the preceding ode, this was also made by General Ji Fu to present to his friend on his departure from the court.

The king orders him to appear
As pattern to each peer;
To serve as his ancestors dear
And protect the king here;
To give orders to old and young
And be the king's throat and tongue;
To spread decrees and orders
That they be obeyed on four borders.

The orders dignified
Are spread out far and wide.
Premier Shan Fu does know
The kingdom's weal and woe.
He's wise and free from blame,
To guard his life and fame.
He's busy night and day
To serve the king for aye.

As people have said oft,
"We choose to eat the soft;
The hard will be cast out."
On this Shan Fu cast doubt.
He won't devour the soft;
Nor is the hard cast oft.
He'll do the weak no wrong,
Nor will he fear the strong.

People say everywhere,

BOOK OF EPICS

"Virtue is light as air;
But few can hold it high."
I ponder with a sigh:
Only Shan Fu can hold it high
And needs no help from the sky.
When the king has defect,
Shan Fu helps him correct.

Where Shan Fu goes along,
Run his four horses strong.
His men alert would find
They often lag behind.
His four steeds run east-bound
To eight bells' tinkling sound.
The king orders him to go down
To fortify the eastern town.

His four steeds galloping,
His eight bells gaily ring.
Shan Fu goes to Qi State;
His return won't be late.
I, Ji Fu, make this song
To blow like breeze for long.
O Shan Fu, though we part,
My song will soothe your heart.

BOOK OF POETRY

The Marquis of Han*

The Liang Mountains are grand;
Yu of Xia cultivated the land.
The Marquis of Han came his way
To be invested in array.
"Serve as your fathers had done,"
In person said the Heaven's Son,
"Do not belie our trust;
Show active zeal you must.
Let things be well arranged;
Let no order be changed.
Assist us to extort
Lords who won't come to court."

His cab was drawn by four steeds
Long and large, running high speeds.
The marquis at court did stand,
His mace of rank in hand.
He bowed to Heaven's Son,
Who showed him his gifts one by one.
The dragon flags all new
And screens made of bamboo,

---

* This epic ode celebrated the Marquis of Han, his investiture and King Xuan's charge to him; the gifts he received and the parting feast; his marriage; the excellence of his territory and his sway over the region of the north.

Black robes and slippers red,
Carved hooks for horse's head,
A tiger's skin aboard
And golden rings for the lord.

The marquis went on homeward way
At Tu for the night he did stay.
Xian Fu invited him to dine,
Drinking a hundred vases of wine.
What were the viands in the dishes?
Roast turtles and fresh fishes.
And what was the ragout?
Tender shoots of bamboo.
What were the gifts furthermore?
A cab of state and horses four.
So many were the dishes fine,
The marquis with delight did dine.

The marquis was to wed
The king's niece in nuptial bed.
It was the daughter of Gui Fu
The marquis came to woo.
A hundred cabs came on the way
To Gui's house in array.
Eight bells made tinkling sound,
Shedding glory around.
Virgins followed the bride in crowd

As beautiful as cloud.
The marquis looked round
The house in splendor drowned.

Gui Fu in war had fame.
Among the states whence he came,
He liked Han by the water,
Where he married his daughter.
In Han there are large streams
Full of tenches and breams;
The deer and doe are mild
And tigers and cats wild;
The bears or black or brown
Roam the land up and down.
His daughter Ji lived there;
She found no state more fair.

The city wall of Han
Was built by people of Yan.
Han ancestors got orders
To rule o'er tribes on borders.
The marquis has below.
Him tribes of Zhai and Mo.
He should preside as chief
Of northern states and fief;
Lay out fields, make walls strong
And dig deep moats along;

Present skins of bears brown
And fox white to the crown.

Duke Mu of Shao*

Onward the rivers roared;
Forward our warriors poured.
There was no rest far and nigh;
We marched on River Huai.
Our cars drove on the way
Our flags flew on display.
There was no peace far and nigh;
We marched on tribes of Huai.

Onward the rivers flow;
Backward our warriors go.
The State reduced to order,
We come back from the border.
There is peace east and west;
North and south there is rest.
An end is put to the strife;
The king may live a peaceful life.

On the two rivers' borders

---

* This epic ode celebrated an expedition in 825 B.C. against the southern tribes of the Huai and the work done for King Xuan by Shao Hu, Duke Mu of Shao, with the manner in which the king rewarded him and he responded to the royal favor.

The king gives Shao Hu orders:
"Open up countryside
And land and fields divide.
Let people rule their fate
And conform to our state.
Define lands by decree
As far as southern sea."

The king gives Shao Hu orders
To inspect southern borders;
"When Wen and Wu were kings,
Your ancestors were their wings.
Say not young you appear;
Do as your fathers dear.
You have well served the state;
I'll give you favor great."

"Here is a cup of jade
And wine of millet made
Tell your ancestors grand
I'll confer on you more land.
I'll gratify your desires
As my sire did your sire's."
Hu bows aground to say:
"May Heaven's Son live for aye!"

Hu bows aground again
In praise of royal reign.

He engraves Duke Shao's song,
Wishing the king live long.
The Heaven's Son is wise;
His endless fame will rise.
His virtue is so great
That he'll rule o'er every state.

Expedition against Xu*

Grand and wise is the sovereign who
Gave charge to Minister
And Grand-master Huang Fu,
Of whom Nan Zhong was ancestor.
"Put my six armies in order
And ready for warfare.
Set out for southern border
With vigilance and care!"

The king told Yin to assign
The task to Count Xiu Fu

---

* This epic ode celebrated an expedition of King Xuan against the State of Xu, a northern tribe of the Huai. The commander-in-chief was Huang Fu, a descendant of General Nan Zhong who had done good service to the state against the Huns in the times of King Wen (see Poem "General Nan Zhong and His wife"), and not President Huang Fu who was mentioned in Poem "President Huang Fu" as a very bad and dangerous man in the times of King You, King Xuan's son and successor.

To march his troops in line
And in vigilance too;

To go along the river shore
Until they reach the land of Xu;
And not to stay there any more
When the three tasks get through.

How dignified and grand
Did the Son of Heaven show!
He advanced on the land
Nor too fast nor too slow.
The land of Xu was stirred
And greatly terrified
As if a thunder heard
Shook the land far and wide.

The king in brave array
Struck the foe with dismay.
His chariots went before;
Like tigers did men roar.
Along the riverside
They captured the foes terrified.
They advanced to the rear
And occupied their sphere.

The legions of the king's
Are swift as birds on wings.

Like rivers they are long;
Like mountains they are strong.
They roll on like the stream;
Boundless and endless they seem.
Invincible, unfathomable, great,
They've conquered the Xu State.

The king has wisely planned
How to conquer Xu's land.
Xu's chiefs come to submit
All through the king's merit.
The country pacified,
Xu's chiefs come to the king's side,
They won't again rebel;
The king says, "All is well."

Complaint against King You*

I look up to the sky;
Great Heaven is not kind.
Restless for long am I;
Down fall disasters blind.
Unsettled is the state;
We're distressed high and low.

---

* The speaker deplored the misery and oppression that prevailed in the time of King You (780–770B.C.) and intimated that they were caused by the interference of Lady Shi of Bao in the government.

Book of Poetry

Insects raise havoc great,
Where's the end to our woe?
The net of crime spreads wide.
Alas! where can we hide!

People had fields and lands,
But you take them away.
People had their farm hands;
On them your hands you lay.
This man has done no wrong;
You say guilty is he.
That man's guilty for long;
You say from guilt he's free.

A wise man builds a city wall;
A fair woman brings its downfall.
Alas! such a woman young
Is no better than an owl;
Such a woman with a long tongue
Will turn everything foul.
Disaster comes not from the sky
But from a woman fair.
You can't teach nor rely
On woman and eunuch for e'er.

They slander, cheat and bluff,
Tell lies before and behind.
Is it not bad enough?

Book of Epics

How can you love a woman unkind?
They are like men of trade
For whom wise men won't care.
Wise women are not made
For state but household affair.

Why does Heaven's blame to you go?
Why won't gods bless your state?
You neglect your great foe
And regard me with hate.
For omens you don't care;
Good men are not employed.
You've no dignified air;
The state will be destroyed.

Heaven extends its sway
Over our weal and woe.
Good men have gone away;
My heart feels sorrow grow.
Heaven extends its sway
O'er good and evil deeds.
Good men have gone away;
My heart feels sad and bleeds.

The bubbling waters show
How deep the spring's below.
Alas! the evil sway
Begins not from today.

Why came it not before
Or after I'm no more?
O boundless Heaven bright,
Nothing is beyond your might,
Bring to our fathers no disgrace
But save our future race!

King You's Times*

Formidable Heaven on high
Sends down big famine and disorder.
Fugitives wander far and nigh;
Disaster spreads as far as the border.

Heaven sends down its net of crime;
Officials fall in civil strife.
Calamitous is the hard time;
The state can't lead a peaceful life.

Deceit and slander here and there,
Wrong-doers win the royal grace.
Restless, cautious and full of care,
We are afraid to lose our place.

---

* The speaker bemoaned the misery and ruin which were going on, showing they were owing to King You's employment of mean and worthless men, and he wished he king would use such ministers as the Duke of Shao.

As in a year of drought
There can be no lush grass,
No withered leaves can sprout.
This state will perish, alas!

We had no greater wealth
In bygone years;
We're not in better health
Than our former compeers.
They were like paddy fine;
We're like coarse rice.
Why not give up your wine
But indulge in your vice!
A pool will become dry
When no rain falls from the skies;
A spring will become dry
When no water from below rise.
The evil you have done will spread.
Won't it fall on my head?

In the days of Duke Shao
Our land ever increased.
Alas! alas! but now
Each day our land decreased.
Men of today, behold!
Don't you know anything of old?

BOOK OF HYMNS

Hymns of Zhou

First Decade of Hymns of Zhou

King Wen's Temple*

Solemn's the temple still;
Princes their duties fulfil.
Numerous officers,
Virtuous King Wen's followers,
Worship his soul on high,
Whom they hurry to glorify.
There are none but revere
Tirelessly their ancestor dear.

King Wen Deified**

Great Heaven goes its way
Without cease and for aye.
O King Wen's virtue great
Will likewise circulate.
His virtue overflows
And in his descendants grows.

---

* This was the first hymn celebrating the reverential manner in which a sacrifice to King Wen (1184–1134 B.C.) was performed.
** This hymn celebrating King Wen's virtue as comparable to that of Heaven was sung when King Cheng performed a sacrifice to his grandfather in 1110 B.C..

Whatever King Wen has done
Will profit his grandson.

King Wen's Statutes*

The world is clear and bright;
King Wen's statutes shed light,
Begin by sacrificial rite
And end by victory great.
God, bless Zhou's State!

King Cheng's Inaugural Address**

O princes bright and brave
Favored by former kings!
Boundless blessings we have
Will pass to our offsprings.
Don't sin against your state
And you'll be honored as before.
Think of your service great

---

* This was the third hymn appropriate at some sacrifice to King Wen and celebrating his statutes, It was sung to accompany the performance of the dance of King Wen, which consisted in going through a number of bodily movements and evolutions, intending to illustrate the style of fighting introduced by Wen in his various wars.

** This hymn was made on the occasion of King Cheng's accession to the government in 1109 B.C. when he thus addressed the princes who had assisted him in the ancestral temple.

You may enlarge still more.
Try to employ wise men,
Your influence will spread from land to land.
Try to practise virtue then
Your good example will forever stand.
O of all things,
Forget not former kings!

Mount Qi*

Heaven made lofty hill
For former kings to till.
King Tai worked the land
For King Wen to expand.
The former kings are gone;
The mountain path is good to travel on.
O ye son and grandson,
Pursue what your forefathers have begun!

King Cheng's Hymn**

By great Heaven's decrees
Two kings with power were blessed,
King Cheng dare not live at ease

---

* This hymn was appropriate to a sacrifice to King Tai who labored the land at the foot of Mount Qi (Poem "The Rise of Zhou").
** This hymn was appropriate to a sacrifice to King Cheng (reigned 1109–1076 B.C.), son of King Wu and grandson of King Wen.

But day and night does his best

To rule the State in peace
And pacify east and west.

King Wu's Sacrificial Hymn*

I offer sacrifice
Of ram and bull so nice.
May Heaven bless my state!
I observe King Wen's statutes great;
I'll pacify the land.
O King Wen grand!
Come down and eat, I pray.
Do I not night and day
Revere Almighty Heaven?
May your favor to me be given!

King Wu's Progress**

A progress through the state is done.
O Heaven, bless your son!
O bless the Zhou House up and down!

---

* This hymn was appropriate to a sacrifice to King Wen in the hall of audience where King Wu assembled all the princes to undertake an expedition against the last king of Shang in 1121 B.C..

** This hymn was appropriate to King Wu's sacrifice to Heaven and to the spirits of the Mountains and Rivers on a progress through the kingdom after the overthrow of the Shang Dynasty in 1121 B.C..

Our victory is so great
That it shakes state on state.
We revere gods for ever
Of mountain and of river.
Our king is worthy of the crown.
Zhou's House is bright and full of grace:
Each lord is in his proper place,
With spears and shields stored up in rows,
And in their cases arrows and bows.
The king will do his best
To rule the kingdom east and west.
O may our king be blessed!

Kings Cheng and Kang*

King Wu was full of might;
He built a career bright.
God gives Cheng and Kang charge
This glory to enlarge.
Kings Cheng and Kang are blessed
To rule from east to west.
How splendid is their reign!
Hear drums' and bells' refrain.
Hear stones and flutes resound.

---

* This hymn was appropriate to a sacrifice to Kings Wu, Cheng and Kang.

With blessings we are crowned.
Blessings come to our side;
Our lords look dignified.
We are drunk and well fed;
Blessings come on our head.

Hymn to the Lord of Corn*

O Lord of Corn so bright,
You're at God's left or right.
You gave people grain-food;
None could do us more good.
God makes us live and eat;
You told us to plant wheat,
Not to define our border
But to live in good order.

---

* This hymn was appropriate to the border sacrifice when Hou Ji, the Lord of Corn, was worshipped as the correlate of God (Poem "Hou Ji, the Lord of Corn").

Second Decade of Hymns of Zhou

Husbandry*

Ah! ye ministers dear,
Attend to duties here.
The king's set down the rule,
You should know to the full.
Ah! ye officers dear,
It is now late spring here.
What do you seek to do?
Tend the fields old and new.
Wheat grows lush in the field.
What an enormous yield!
Ah! Heaven bright and clear
Will give us a good year.
Men, get ready to wield
Your sickles, spuds and hoes
And reap harvest in rows.

King Kang's Prayer**

O King Cheng in the sky,
Please come down from on high.

---

* This was instructions given to the officers of husbandry, probably after the sacrifice in spring for a good year.
** This hymn was said to be King Kang's prayer to King Cheng for a good year.

See us lead the campaign
To sow all kinds of grain,
And till our fields with glee
All over thirty li!
Ten thousand men in pairs
Plough the land with the shares.

The Guest Assisting at Sacrifice*

Rows of egrets in flight
Over the marsh in the west.
Like those birds dressed in white,
Here comes our noble guest.
He's loved in his own State;
He is welcome in ours.
Be it early or late,
His fame for ever towers.

Thanksgiving**

Millet and rice abound this year;
High granaries stand far and near.

---

* This hymn celebrated the representative of the former dynasty who had come to court to assist at sacrifice. It might have been sung when the king was dismissing the guest in the ancestral temple.

** This ode of thanksgiving for a plentiful year was used at the sacrifice in autumn and winter.

There are millions of measures fine;
We make from them spirits and wine
And offer them to ancestors dear.
Then we perform all kinds of rite
And call down blessings from Heaven bright.

Temple Music*

Musicians blind, musicians blind,
Come to the temple court behind.
The plume-adorned posts stand
With teeth-like frames used by the band;
From them suspend drums large and small,
And sounding stones withal.
Music is played when all's complete;
We hear pan-pipe, flute and drumbeat.
What sacred melody
And solemn harmony!
Dear ancestors, give ear;
Dear visitors, come here!
You will enjoy our song
And wish it to last long.

---

* This hymn was made on the occasion of the Duke of Zhou's completing his instruments of music and announcing the fact in a grand performance in the temple of King Wen.

Sacrifice of Fish*

In Rivers Ju and Qi
Fish in warrens we see.
There're sturgeons large and small,
Mudfish, carp we enthral
For temple sacrifice
That we may be blessed twice.

King Wu's Prayer to King Wen**

We come in harmony;
We stop in gravity,
The princes at the side
Of the king dignified.
"I present this bull nice
And set forth sacrifice
To royal father great.
Bless your filial son and his state!

"You're a sage we adore,
A king in peace and war.

---

* This hymn was sung in the last month of winter and in spring when the king presented a fish in the ancestral temple as an act of duty and an acknowledgement that it was to his ancestors favor that the king and the people were indebted for the supplies of food which they received from the waters.

** This prayer was said to be appropriate at a sacrifice by King Wu to his father Wen.

O give prosperity
To Heaven and posterity!

"Bless me with a life long,
With a state rich and strong!
I pray to father I revere
And to my mother dear."

King Cheng's Sacrifice to King Wu*

The lords appear before the king
To learn the rules he ordains.
The dragon flags are bright
And the carriage bells ring.
Glitter the golden reins,
His splendor at its height.
The filial king leads the throng
Before his father's shrine.
He prays to be granted life long
And to maintain his rights divine.
May Heaven bless his state!
The princes brave and bright
Be given favors great
That they may serve at left and right.

---

* This hymn was appropriate to an occasion when the feudal princes were assisting King Cheng at a sacrifice to King Wu in 1113 B.C..

Guests at the Sacrifice*

Our guests alight
From horses white.
Their train is long,
A noble throng.

Stay here one night;
Fasten their horses tight.
Stay here three nights or four;
Let no horse leave the door!

Escort guests on their way;
Say left and right, "Good day!"
Say "Good day" left and right
Till day turns into night.

Hymn to King Wu Great and Bright**

O King Wu great and bright,
Matchless in main and might.
King Wen beyond compare
Opened the way for his heir.

---

* This ode celebrated the Viscount of Wei on one of his appearances at the capital and assisting at the sacrifice in the ancestral temple of Zhou. Uncle of the last king of the Shang Dynasty, he was made Duke of Song to continue the sacrifices of the House of Shang.

** This hymn was sung in the ancestral temple to the music regulating the dance in honor of the achievements of King Wu.

King Wu after his sire
Quelled Yin's tyrannic fire.
His fame grows higher and higher.

Third Decade of Hymns of Zhou

Elegy on King Wu*

Alas! how sad am I!
Over my deceased father I cry.
Lonely, I'm in distress
To lose my father whom gods bless.
Filial all your life long,
You loved grandfather strong
As if he were ever in courtyard.
Fatherless, I am thinking hard
Of you both night and day.
O kings to be remembered for aye!

King Cheng's Ascension to the Throne**

I take counsel on early days;
How to follow my father's ways?
Ah! but he is far above me
And to reach him I am not free.
Please help me to get to his side,

---

* This elegy was appropriate to the young King Cheng, declaring his sentiments in the temple of his father.
** This seemed to be a sequel to the former hymn. The young king told of his difficulties and incompetencies, asked for counsel to help to follow the example of his father, stated how he meant to do so and concluded with an appeal to King Wu.

To learn on what I should decide.
I am a young king not so great
To shoulder hard tasks of the state.
I will follow him up and down,
Take counsel to secure the crown.
Rest in peace, royal father dear,
O help me to be bright and clear!

King Cheng's Consultation*

Be reverent, be reverent!
The Heaven's way is evident.
Do not let its favor pass by
Nor say Heaven's remote on high.

It rules over our rise and fall
And daily watches over all.
"I am a young king of our state,
But I will show reverence great.
As sun and moon shine day and night,
I will learn to be fair and bright.
Assist me to fulfill my duty
And show me high virtue and beauty!"

---

* This dialogue might be a portion of the consultation which took place in the temple, between King Cheng and his ministers. The first half was the admonition of the ministers and the second the reply of the king.

King Cheng's Self-criticism*

I blame myself for woes gone by
And guard against those of future nigh.
A wasp is a dangerous thing.
Why should I seek its painful sting?
At first only a wren is heard;
When it takes wing, it becomes a bird.
Unequal to hard tasks of the state,
I am again in a narrow strait.

Cultivation of the Ground**

The grass and bushes cleared away,
The ground is ploughed at break of day.
A thousand pairs weed, hoe in hand;
They toil in old or new-tilled land.
The master comes with all his sons,
The older and the younger ones.
They are all strong and stout;

---

* King Cheng acknowledged that he had erred and stated his purpose to be careful in the future; he would guard against the slightest beginning of evil and was penetrated with a sense of his own incompetencies. This piece might be considered as the conclusion of the service in the ancestral temple with which it and the previous three were connected.

** This piece was an accompaniment of some royal sacrifice.

At noon they take meals out.

They love their women fair
Who take of them good care.
With the sharp plough they wield,
They break the southern field.
All kinds of grain they sow
Burst into life and grow,
Young shoots without end rise;
The longest strike the eyes.
The grain grows lush here and there;
The toilers weed with care.
The reapers come around;
The grain's piled up aground.
There're millions of stacks fine
To be made food or wine
For our ancestors' shrine
And for the rites divine.
The delicious food
Is glory of kinghood.
The fragrant wine, behold!
Gives comfort to the old.
We reap not only here
But always in good cheer.
We reap not only for today
But always in our fathers' way.

Hymn of Thanksgiving*

Sharp are plough-shares we wield;
We plough the southern field.
All kinds of grain we sow
Burst into life and grow.
Our wives come to the ground
With baskets square and round
Of millet and steamed bread,
With straw-hat on the head.
We weed with hoe in hand
On the dry and wet land.
When weeds fall in decay,
Luxuriant millets sway.

When millets rustling fall,
We reap and pile them up all
High and thick as a wall.

Like comb teeth stacks are close;
Stores are opened in rows.
Wives and children repose
When all the stores are full.

We kill a tawny bull,

---

* This hymn was made for the thanksgiving to the spirits of the land and the grain in autumn and it was proper therefore that it should set forth the beginning and the end of the labors of husbandry.

Whose horns crooked appear.
We follow fathers dear
To perform rites with cheer.

Supplementary Sacrifice*

In silken robes clean and bright,
In temple caps for the rite,
The officers come from the hall
To inspect tripods large and small,
To see the sheep and oxen down and up
And rhino horns used as cup,
To see if mild is wine,
If there is noise before the shrine
In sacrifice to lords divine.

The Martial King**

The royal army brave and bright
Was led by King Wu in dark days

---

* This piece belonged to the entertainment of the personator of the dead in connection with the supplementary sacrifice on the day after one of the great sacrifices in the ancestral temple.

** This was King Cheng's hymn in praise of King Wu or the Martial King who reigned 1121–1115 B.C. It was made to announce in the temple of King Wu the completion of the dance intended to represent the achievements of the king in the overthrow of the Shang and the establishment of the Zhou Dynasty. Poem "Hymn to King Wu" and the three that followed this were also sung in connection with that dance.

To overthrow Shang and bring back light
And establish the Zhou House's sway.
Favored by Heaven, I
Succeed the Martial King.
I'll follow him as nigh
As summer follows spring.

Hymn to King Wu*

All the states pacified,
Heaven favors Zhou far and wide,
Rich harvest from year to year.
How mighty did king Wu appear
With his warriors and cavaliers
Guarding his four frontiers
And securing his state!
Favored by Heaven great,
Zhou replaced Shang by fate.

King Wu's Hymn to King Wen**

King Wen's career is done;
I will follow him as son,

---

* This hymn was considered as a portion of the larger piece sung to the dance celebrating the merit and success of King Wu.

** This hymn celebrating the praise of King Wen was said to be the third of the pieces sung to the dance mentioned in the note on Poem "The Martial King."

Thinking of him without cease.
We have conquered Shang to seek peace.
O our royal decree
Should be done in high glee.

The King's Progress*

O great is the Zhou State!
I climb up mountains high
To see hills undulate
And two rivers flow by.
Gods are worshipped, I see,
Under the boundless sky,
All by royal decree.

---

* This hymn was said to be the fourth of the six pieces sung to the dance celebrating the greatness of Zhou and its firm possession of the kingdom, as seen in King Wu's progress.

Hymns of Lu

Horses*

How sleek and large the horses are
Upon the plain of borders far!
What color are these horses bright?
Some black and white, some yellow light,
Some are pure black, others are bay.
What splendid chariot steeds are they!
The Duke of Lu has clear fore-sight;
He has prepared his steeds to fight.

How sleek and large the horses are
Upon the plain of borders far!
What color are these horses bright?
Some piebald, others green and white;
Some brownish red, others dapple grey.

What fiery chariot steeds are they!
The Duke of Lu has good fore-sight:
He will employ his steeds in fight.

How sleek and large the horses are
Upon the plain of borders far!

---

* This was an ode celebrating Duke Xi of Lu (658–626 B.C.) for his constant and admirable thoughtfulness, especially as seen in the number and quality of his horses.

What color are these steeds well trained?
Some flecked, some white and black-maned,
Some black and white-maned, others red.
They are chariot horses well-bred.
The Duke of Lu has fine fore-sight,
He has bred and trained his steeds to fight.

How sleek and large the horses are
Upon the plain of borders far!
What color are these horses bright?
Some cream-like, others red and white;
Some white-legged, others fishlike eyed.
They drive war chariots side by side.
The Duke of Lu has grand fore-sight:
He will drive his brave steeds to fight.

The Ducal Feast*

Sleek and strong, sleek and strong,
Four brown steeds come along.
The officers are wise,
Stay late but early rise.
Like egrets white
Dancers alight.

---

* This piece related how Duke Xi of Lu feasted together with his officers and how the officers expressed their good wishes.

Book of Poetry

The drums resound;
Tipsy, they dance aground
In happiness they are drowned.

Sleek and strong, sleek and strong,
Four stallions come along.
The officers drink wine;
Early and late they are fine.
Like egrets white
Dancers in flight.
The drums resound;
Drunk, they go round;
In happiness they are drowned.

Sleek and strong, sleek and strong,
Four grey steeds come along.
The officers eat food
Early and late they are good.
From now and here,
Abundant be each year!
The duke has well done,
So will his son and grandson,
They will be happy everyone.

The Poolside Hall*

Pleasant is the pool half-round
Where plants of cress abound.
The Marquis of Lu comes nigh;
His dragon banners fly,
His flags wave on the wing
And his carriage bells ring.
Officers old and young
Follow him all along.

Pleasant is the pool half-round
Where water-weeds abound.
The Marquis of Lu comes near;
His horses grand appear.
His horses appear strong;
His carriage bells ring long.
With smiles and with looks bland,
He will instruct and command.

Pleasant is the pool half-round
Where mallow plants abound.
The Marquis pays a call

---

* This was an ode in praise of Marquis or Duke Xi of Lu, celebrating his interest in the state college built by the poolside and his exaggerated triumph over the tribes of the Huai, celebrated in the poolside hall.

And drinks wine in the hall.
After wine, it is foretold,
"You will never grow old.
If along the way you go,
You will overcome the foe."

The Marquis' virtue high
Is well-known far and nigh.
His manner dignified,
He is ever people's guide.
He is bright as well as brave,
Worthy son of ancestors grave.
He is full of filial love
And seeks blessings from above.

The Marquis of Lu bright
Sheds his virtuous light.
He has built the poolside hall;
Huai tribes pay him homage all.
His tiger-like compeers
Presents the foe's left ears.
His judges wisdom show;
They bring the captive foe.

His officers aligned
With their forces combined
Drove in martial array
Southeastern tribes away.

They came on backward way
Without noise or display.
At poolside hall they show
What they have done with the foe.

They notch their arrows long
On bows with bone made strong.
Their chariots show no fears,
With tireless charioteers.
The tribes of Huai they quell
Dare no longer rebel.
As the Marquis would have it,
The tribes of Huai submit.

The owls flying at ease
Settle on poolside trees.
They eat our mulberries
And sing sweet melodies.
The chief of Huai tribes brings
All rare and precious things:
Ivory tusks, tortoise old,
Southern metals and gold.

Hymn to Marquis of Lu*

Solemn the temples stand,
Well-built, well-furnished, grand.
There we find Jiang Yuan's shrine:
Her virtue was divine.
On God she did depend
And safely by the end
Of her ten months was born
Hou Ji, our Lord of Grain or Corn.
Blessed by Heaven, he knew
When sowing time was due
For wheat and millet early or late.
Invested with a state,
He taught people to sow
The millet and to grow
The sorghum and the rice.
All over the country nice
He followed Yu of Xia's advice.

The grandson of Hou Ji
King Tai came to install
Himself south of mount Qi,

---

* This was the longest epic ode or hymn in praise of Marquis or Duke Xi of Lu, celebrating his magnificent career of success. It was written by Xi Si on an occasion when the Marquis had repaired on a large scale the temple of the State of Lu.

Nearer to Shang capital.
Then came Kings Wen and Wu;
They both followed King Tai.
King Wu beat Shang in Mu,
Decreed by Heaven high.
"You should have nor fear nor doubt
For great God is with you.
You'll wipe Shang forces out,
With victory in view."
King Cheng said to his uncle great,
"I will set up your eldest son
As Marquis of Lu State
And enlarge the land you have won
To protect the Zhou State."

The Duke of Lu was made
Marquis in the east obeyed,
And given land to cultivate,
Hills, rivers and attached state.
He was Duke of Zhou's grandson
And Duke Zhuang's eldest son.
With dragon banners at command,
He came six reins in hand.
He made his offering
In autumn as in spring
To God in Heaven great
And Hou Ji of Zhou State.

He offered victims nice
For the great sacrifice
And received blessings twice
From his ancestors dear;
Even the Duke of Zhou did appear.

In summer came the rite;
In autumn horns were capped of bull.
There were bulls red and white,
Bull-figured goblets full,
Roast pig, soup and minced meat,
And dishes of bamboo and wood,
And dancers all-complete.
Blessed be ye grandsons good!
May you live in prosperity
And protect the eastern land!
May you have longevity
And may the land of Lu long stand!
Unwaning moon, unsunken sun,
Nor flood nor earthquake far and nigh.
In long life you are second to none,
And firm as mountain high.
A thousand war chariots were seen;
Each had two spears with tassels red
And two bows bound by bands green.
Thirty thousand men the duke led
In shell-adorned helmets were dressed.

They marched in numbers great
To quell the tribes of north and west
And punish southern state.
None of them could stand your attack.

May you enjoy prosperity!
With hoary hair and wrinkled back,
May you enjoy longevity!
Age will give you advice.
May you live great and prosperous
To a thousand years old or twice!
May you live long and vigorous
As eyebrows long unharmed by vice!

Lofty is Mountain Tai
Looked up to from Lu State.
Mounts Gui and Meng stand nigh
And eastward undulate
As far as eastern sea.
Huai tribes make no ado
But go down on their knee
Before the Marquis of Lu.

We have Mounts Fu and Yi
And till at Xu the ground
Which extends to the sea
Where barbarians are found.
No southern tribe dare disobey

The Marquis of Lu's command;
None but would homage pay
To the Marquis of Lu grand.

Heaven gives Marquis blessings great
And a long life to rule over Lu.
He shall restore Duke of Zhou's State
And dwell at Chang and Xu.
The Marquis feasted his ministers
With his fair wife and mother old
And other officers
For the state he shall hold.
He shall be blessed with golden hairs
And juvenile teeth like his heir's.

The hillside cypress and pine
Are cut down from the root;
Some as long as eight feet or nine,
Others as short as one foot.
They are used to build temples new
With inner chambers large and long.
Behold! the temples stand in view.
It is Xi Si who makes this song
Which reads so pleasant to the ear
That people will greet him with cheer.

Hymns of Shang

Hymn to King Tang*

How splendid! how complete!
Let us put drums in place.
Listen to their loud beat,
Ancestor of our race.

Your descendants invite
Your spirit to alight
By resounding drumbeat
And by flute's music sweet.
In harmony with them
Chimes the sonorous gem.

The descendants with cheer
Listen to music bright.
Bells and drums fill the ear
And dancers seem in flight.
Our visitors appear
Also full of delight.
Our sires since olden days
Showed us the proper ways

---

* This hymn was appropriate to a sacrifice to King Tang the successful who overthrew the dynasty of Xia and founded that of Shang in 1765 B.C. It dwelt on the music and the reverence with which the service was performed.

To be meek and polite
And mild from morn to night.
May you accept the rite
Your filial grandson pays!

Hymn to Ancestor*

Ah! ah! ancestor dear,
Shower down blessings here.
Let your blessings descend
On your sons without end.
Our wine is clear and sweet.
Make our happiness complete.
Our soup is tempered well,
Good in flavor and smell.
We pray but silently:
Bless us with longevity,
White hair and wrinkled brow.

We have no contention now.
In cars with wheels leather-bound,
At eight bells' tinkling sound,
The princes come to pray

---

* This was another hymn appropriate to sacrifice to King Tang of Shang, Shang dwelling on the spirits, the soup and the gravity of the service and assisting princes.

We might be blessed for aye.
O give us far and near
Rich harvest year by year!
O ancestor, alight!
May you accept the rite
Your filial grandsons pay
And bless us as we pray!

The Swallow*

Heaven sent Swallow down
To give birth to the sire
Of Shang who wore the crown
Of land of Yin entire.
God ordered Martial Tang,
To conquer four frontiers,
To appoint lords of Shang
To rule over nine spheres.
The forefathers of Shang
Reigned by Heaven's decree.
King Wu Ding, descendant of Tang.

---

* This hymn was appropriate to a sacrifice in the ancestral temple of Shang. The Sire of Shang was said to be born around 2300 B.C. when his mother bathing in some open place took and swallowed an egg dropped by a swallow. The Martial Tang founded the dynasty and his grandson moved the capital to Yin. This hymn was intended to do honor to King Wu Ding (1328–1263B.C.).

Now rules over land and sea.
Wu Ding is a martial king,
Victor second to none.
Ten dragon chariots bring
Sacrifice on the run.
His land extends a thousand *lis*
Where people live and rest.
He reigns as far as the four seas;
Lords come from east and west.
They gather at the capital
To pay homage in numbers great.
O good Heaven, bless all
The kings of the Yin State!

The Rise of Shang*

The sire of Shang was wise;
Good omens had appeared for long.
Seeing the deluge rise,
He helped Yu stem the current strong,

---

* This epic ode celebrated Qi the sire of Shang who helped King Yu of the Xia Dynasty to stem the deluge around 2200 B.C.; Xiang Tu his grandson; Tang the Martial King who founded the Shang Dynasty; and Yi Yin or A Heng, Tang's chief minister, on occasion of a great sacrifice when all the previous kings of the dynasty and the lords of Shang and their famous ministers were honored in the service, probably in the year 1713 B.C..

Extend the state's frontier
And domain far and wide.
He was son born from Swallow queer
And Princess of Rong, its bride.

He held successful sway
Over states large and small.
He followed his proper way
To inspect all and instruct all.
Xiang Tu, his martial grandson,
Ruled over land and sea he had won.
Heaven's favor divine
Lasted down to the Martial King.
Toward his lords benign,
In praise of God he'd often sing.
His virtue grows day by day;
It is God he reveres.
God orders him to hold sway
And be model to the nine spheres.

He received ensigns large and small
From subordinate princes far and nigh.
He received blessings from gods all
For which he did nor seek nor vie.
To lords he was nor hard nor soft;
His royal rule was gentle oft.
He received favors from aloft.

He received tributes large and small
From princes subordinate.
He received favors from gods all;
He showed his valor great.
Unshaken, he was fortified,
Unscared, unterrified.
All blessings came to his side.

His banners flying higher,
His battle-ax in his fist,
The Martial King came like fire
Whom no foe could resist.
Xie Jie was like the roots
Which could no longer grow
When he lost his three shoots,
Wei, Gu, Kun Wu, Tang's former foe.
The Martial King destroyed the brutes
And he ruled high and low.

In times when ruled King Tang,
There was prosperity for Shang.
Heaven favored his son
With Premier A Heng to run
The government and state
At left and right of the prince great.

Hymn to King Wu Ding*

How rapid did Yin troops appear!
They attacked Chu State without fear.
They penetrated into its rear
And brought back many a captive's ear.
Wu Ding conquered Chu land.
What an achievement grand!

The king gave Chu command,
"South of our state you stand.
In the time of King Tang
Even the tribes of Jiang
Dared not but come to pay
Homage under his sway.
Such was the rule of Shang."

Heaven gave lords its orders
To build their capitals within Yu's borders,
To pay homage each year,
To do their duties, not to fear
Its punishment severe
If farmwork is well done far and near.

---

* This was an epic ode celebrating the war of King Wu Ding against the southern tribe of Chu, its success and the general happiness and virtue of his reign. This hymn was probably made when a special temple was built for him in 1256 B.C..

Heaven ordered the lords to know
The reverent people below.
They should do no wrong nor be
Indolent and carefree.
To each subordinate state
May be brought blessings great!

The capital was full of order,
A model for states on the border.
The king had great renown
And brilliance up and down.
He enjoyed longevity.
May he bless his posterity!

We climbed the mountain high
Where pine and cypress pierced the sky.

We felled them to the ground
And hewed them square and round.
We built with beams of pine
And pillars large and fine
The temple for Wu Ding's shrine.

许译中国经典诗文集

诗经

许渊冲　英译
周振甫　中文译注

五洲传播出版社　中华书局

序

欧美国家很少有人知道,世界上最早的诗集是中国的《诗经》。《诗经》包括三百零五篇诗歌,大约产生于两千五百年前。最早的一篇据陈子展《诗经直解》,是《商颂》中的《长发》,约作于公元前1713年。最晚的一篇,一说是《秦风》中的《无衣》,公元前505年申包胥哭秦庭时,秦哀公为代赋《无衣》之诗;一说是《陈风》中的《株林》,是刺陈灵公"淫乎夏姬"之诗,据《诗经直解》,约作于公元前599年。两说都是公元前6世纪。

《诗经》按照音乐类型分为《国风》、《小雅》、《大雅》和《颂》四个部分。《国风》一百六十篇包括周王室的乐官在十五个诸侯国的封地采集到的民歌民谣。《小雅》七十四篇多是西周贵族宴会用的乐章,《大雅》三十一篇多用于朝廷庆典。《颂》四十篇是用于宗庙祭祀的赞歌,又分为《周颂》三十一篇,《鲁颂》四篇,《商颂》五篇。《商颂》最早,约作于公元前17世纪至12世纪,相传是西周后期宋国大夫正考甫从周太师处得到的;一说是正考甫所作,商王室的后人宋襄公祭祀祖先所用,但是证据不足。

西周早期的诗篇约作于公元前11世纪至9世纪,包括全部《周颂》,一部分《大雅》和一小部分《国风》。大部分诗篇都是"赋"(叙事诗)或史诗,最出色的是《大雅》中的《生民》《公刘》《绵》《皇矣》和《大明》,这些史诗描写了周王朝是如何建立,商王朝是如何灭亡的。西周后期的诗篇约作于公元前9至8世纪，包括大部分《大雅》，几乎全部《小雅》，还有一小部分《国风》。有些雅歌赞颂了中兴的周宣王（公元前9世纪末至8世纪初在位）南征北战的赫赫武功，如《大雅·常武》描写了宣王东征徐国的胜利；《小雅·六月》记载了尹吉甫北伐狎狁的史实；《小雅·采芑》叙述了方叔南征荆楚的武功。这些意气风发、斗志昂扬、威震四方的赞歌颂词的作者，有的是朝廷的史官，有的却是统率三军的大将，如《六月》的作者是"张仲孝友"，而《大雅》中的《崧高》和《烝民》却是"文武吉甫"赠别申伯和仲山甫时所作。这些诗篇虽然极尽了赞颂之能事，但是比起《小雅》中描述士兵亲身经历的《采薇》来，却又显得稍逊一筹；《采薇》中的"昔我往矣，杨柳依依；今我来思，雨雪霏霏"传诵千古，被誉为"《诗》三百中最佳之句"。

《诗经》中最好的作品还是《国风》，包括东周时期采集到的民歌民谣，大部分作于公元前8至6世纪。民歌大都纯朴自然，反映了古代人民各方面的生活、劳动斗争、思想感情、喜怒哀乐。如《豳风·七月》描写了农民一年的劳动生活，他们耕地、织布、打猎，为主人酿酒、修建房屋，自己却不得温饱。《魏风·伐檀》讽刺了不劳而获、贪得无厌的贵族；《周南·芣苢》是农村妇女采集车前子的劳动之歌。《召南·野有死麕》描写猎人如何爱上了一个美丽的少女。《周南·关雎》叙述一对青年男女如何在春天钟情、在夏天求爱、在秋天定亲、在冬天结合的过程。《唐风·鸨羽》表达了农民在外服役的辛苦；《邶风·日月》写出了弃妇的不幸。《击鼓》抒发了士兵思家之情，而《燕燕》和《绿衣》却描写了生离死别的痛苦。

孔子说过："诗可以兴,可以观,可以群,可以怨。"用今天的话来说,就是诗可以启发,可以反映,可以交流,可以讥讽。在我看来,《国风》主要反映了劳动人民的生活,启发他们去做好事,讽刺了统治者的丑恶行为。如《周南》《召南》反映了古代人民的家庭生活;《卫风》《邶风》讽刺了贵族腐化堕落的习俗;《郑风》《陈风》反映了民间的爱情生活;《豳风》启发了人民对周公的拥戴。

《小雅》主要用于贵族之间交流,反映了贵族的生活,也指责了他们的错误。如《鹿鸣之什》中有六篇用于王家宴会;《南有嘉鱼之什》中有两篇用于诸侯宴会,两篇描写王家狩猎;《鸿雁之什》中第一篇发泄了对乱世的不满,《祈父》却是士兵对大臣的怨言;《节南山之什》都是对周幽王宠爱褒姒的批评;《谷风之什》中有被压迫贵族的呼声;《甫田之什》中有收获时贵族祭神求福的乐歌,其中《宾之初筵》写贵族酗酒的醉态,栩栩如生,是不可多得的佳作;《鱼藻之什》则多是对周厉王暴虐无道的批评。不过《小雅》有些诗篇可以收入《国风》或《大雅》中,如《采薇》《出车》记载西伯、南仲西征的事,可以算是《大雅》。

《大雅》记载史实,反映统治者的生活。如《文王之什》中有六篇记文王事,两篇记武王事,《绵》记古公亶父自豳迁岐,《皇矣》记太王、王季及文王伐密伐崇的事,都是史诗;《生民之什》中第一篇叙述周民族始祖后稷的神话,《假乐》《泂酌》《卷阿》是写成王的诗,《民劳》《板》是刺厉王的诗;《荡之什》中有三篇讽刺厉王,《云汉》等三篇赞美宣王,《崧高》赞美申伯,《烝民》赞美仲山甫,《韩奕》赞美韩侯,《瞻卬》《召旻》讽刺幽王。所以《大雅》可以算是西周王室的兴衰史。

《颂》主要用来赞美王室祖先的丰功伟绩,启发后人对祖先的崇拜,达到齐家治国的目的。《周颂·清庙之什》中歌颂文王、武王、成王的各有三篇,《思文》一篇歌颂后稷。《臣工之什》第一篇是农事诗,第十篇《武》是宗庙舞歌,其他八篇都是祭祀诗。《闵予小子之什》据说是周公摄政时所作,前七篇都与成王有关;《访落》是成王登基的赞歌,《敬之》写成王君臣关系,《小毖》写成王自我批评,《载芟》是农事诗,《良耜》《丝衣》是祭祀诗,《酌》等四篇和《武》一样是宗庙舞歌。《鲁颂》只有四篇,都是赞美鲁僖公的。僖公其实是个平庸之辈,但是作为周公的后裔,享受了王室祭典的特权,受到过孔子的批评。《商颂》是《诗经》中最古的诗篇。《长发》是商王朝的开国史;《那》等三篇歌颂汤武开国之君,《殷武》赞美武丁中兴之举。从内容看,说《商颂》是宋人祭祖乐章,似乎不能令人信服。大致说来,《颂》可以兴,《大雅》可以观,《小雅》可以群,《国风》可以怨。

《诗经》中常用的三种修辞手法是"赋""比""兴","赋"是直叙其事,"比"包括明喻、暗喻,"兴"是"先言他物以引起所咏之辞也"。《魏风·硕鼠》就是以动物比人的一个好例子。在这首诗中,硕鼠的形象和全诗主题有关;有时,"先言他物"和"所咏之辞"并无直接关系,只有作者感情上的联系,也就是说,同为作者爱憎的对象,如《鄘风·墙有茨》，"茨"与"中冓之言"并无关系，只是同为作者所憎。有时，"先言他物"不过是为了押韵顺口的缘故，如《召南·草虫》。

《诗经》的另一个特点是重调叠咏很多，可以增强诗歌的情韵，加深读者的印象。有时一行只变换一两个字，韵也变了，诗情也发展了；有时整行重复，有时整段重复，如《周南·芣苢》和《召南·摽有梅》。中国古诗的句式大致可以分为四言体、五言体、七言体和杂言体。四言诗出现最早，在《诗经》中也最多，可以说是已臻成熟了。四言体每行只有两个音步，比起五、七言体来，节奏更加干脆利落。《诗经》中的绝大部分诗歌都押韵，韵式多种多样：有的每行押韵，有的隔行押韵，有的整段一韵到底，有的行内有韵，有的还用双声加强音乐效果。

《诗经》中的词汇丰富，尤其是叠字、双声、韵语等的运用变化多端，使得诗歌描写生动，声调悦耳。此外还有叠句、合唱等等，也是民间歌谣常用的手法。

《诗经》的"风、雅、颂、赋、比、兴"叫作六艺，受到后世高度评价，对历代诗人产生了重要的影响。试比较下列引文，可见一斑。

1. 《周颂·桓》：保有厥士，于以四方。

    刘邦《大风歌》：安得猛士兮守四方？

2. 《唐风·蟋蟀》：今我不乐，日月其除！

    《古诗十九首》：为乐当及时，何能待来兹？

3. 《邶风·燕燕》：瞻望弗及，伫立以泣。

    苏武《别妻》：握手一长叹，泪为生别滋。

诗经

4. 《卫风•氓》：三岁为妇，靡室劳矣。
夙兴夜寐，靡有朝矣。
《孔雀东南飞》：鸡鸣入机织，夜夜不得息。
三日断五匹，大人故嫌迟。

5. 《陈风•衡门》：衡门之下，可以栖迟。
泌之洋洋，可以乐饥。
陶潜《归园田居》：户庭无尘杂，虚室有余闲。
久在樊笼里，复得返自然。

6. 《陈风•月出》：月出皎兮！佼人僚兮！
李白《越女词》：镜湖水如月，耶溪女如雪。

7. 《鲁颂•闷宫》：泰山岩岩，鲁邦所詹。
杜甫《望岳》：岱宗夫如何？齐鲁青未了。

8. 《齐风•东方之日》：东方之日兮，
彼姝者子，在我室兮。
在我室兮，履我即兮。
李商隐《无题》：金蟾啮锁烧香入，
玉虎牵丝汲井回。

9. 《魏风•硕鼠》：硕鼠硕鼠，无食我黍！
三岁贯女，莫我肯顾。
曹邺《官仓鼠》：官仓老鼠大如斗，
见人开仓亦不走。
健儿无粮百姓饥，
谁遣朝朝入君口？

10. 《陈风•东门之杨》：东门之杨，其叶牂牂。
昏以为期，明星煌煌。

序

欧阳修《生查子》：去年元夜时，花市灯如昼。

月上柳梢头，人约黄昏后。

从以上十例可以看出《诗经》对历代诗人影响多大。《诗经》在国内虽然非常重要，但在国外并不广为人知，直到18世纪威廉·琼斯爵士才把部分诗篇译成英文散体和韵体，据说对英国19世纪诗人拜伦、雪莱、丁尼生等产生了巨大影响（见《外国语》总15期8页）。到了19世纪60年代，英国理雅各才把全部《诗经》译成散体英文，在香港出版；到1871年，他又在伦敦出版了《诗经》三百零五篇的韵体译本，此书于1967年在纽约重印。他的译本注释丰富，是学者的译文，但不如原文简朴。1891年伦敦又出版了艾伦和詹宁斯的《诗经》英译本。艾本押韵，译文随意改动原文，有增有删，与其说是翻译，不如说是改写。吕叔湘编《中诗英译比录》选了几篇艾译。詹译本则没有见到，不好妄评。

到了20世纪，1906年伦敦出版了克拉默宾的韵体译本，他译的《玉笛集》（中国诗选）十年之内重印十次，可算畅销；从《中诗英译比录》中选的《氓》来看，他的译文不像艾译那样自由，而且格律也不如艾严谨。1913年在波士顿出版了海伦·华德尔的韵体译本，从她译的《氓》来看，删节太多，而且重新组织。她的译本销路较好，二十年内重印六次。和她相反，路易丝·哈芒德走了另外一个极端，她试图把一个中文字译成一个英文音节，毫不增减，而且保持原诗韵律。她的《邶风·式微》译得很成功，但不知道她译了多少篇《诗》。

《诗经》的早期译者都用韵体。庞德是在理雅各之后第一个把《诗经》译成自由体的诗人。他的译本于1915年在剑桥出版，1954年在哈佛大学出版社重印。他认为译诗是个创造性的问题，他的译文经常被当成创作而选入近代英美诗选，影响很大，但译文错误很多，不能算是佳译。另外一个把《诗经》译成自由诗的是韦理，他的译本于1937年在伦敦出版。他在《译自中文》的序中说：中国的旧诗句句都有一定的字数，必须用韵，很像英国的传统诗，而不像欧美今天的自由诗。但他译诗却不用韵，因为他认为用韵不可能不因声损义；他用一个重读音节来代表一个汉字，并将这种格律比之为英诗的无韵体。庞德和韦理都不知道：译诗如不传达原诗的音美，就不能保存原诗的意美。《诗经》总的说来是用韵的，译诗如不用韵，绝不可能产生和原诗相似的效果。恰恰相反，用韵的音美有时反而有助于传达原诗的意美。这就是说，用韵固然可能因声损义，不用韵则一定因声损义，用韵损义的程度反比不用韵小。试比较韦理《周南·关雎》和本书的译文，韦译"关关雎鸠"，无论意美、音美，都远不如本书。

诗无达诂，就以《关雎》而论，"雎鸠"到底是什么鸟？"君子"到底是什么人？"荇菜"到底是什么菜？众说纷纭。而"左右流之"，有人说"流"是"求"或"采"，韦理就是这样译的，但读来觉得牵强。我认为译诗要博采众家之长，而对《关雎》解释得最好的，是《诗经鉴赏集》王气中的文章。他说"关关"两句表示时令，夏历二月春分季节，鸟兽开始交配。"荇菜"开春发芽，入夏才浮出水面；"左右流之"，是说明荇菜在水面或左或右浮动的样子。"左右采之"，是说荇菜到了夏秋之间长大可采，比兴新郎新娘双方的恋爱已经达到成熟阶段；"琴瑟友之"说明还举行过订婚的仪式。"左右芼之"说明他们的结婚季节,是在秋冬农事生活闲隙荇菜成熟的时候,人们要把它采食了。总之,《关雎》歌唱新婚夫妇在一年内由相识、求爱、热恋、订盟以至结婚的全过程。这样一讲,才会明白孔子为什么把《关雎》列为《诗经》之首,因为这篇诗概括了中国礼乐治国的哲学。由此可见,外国译者对中国传统文化没有深刻的了解,是不大可能译好《诗经》的。一些诗有不同的解释,难分高下。如《周南·卷耳》,余冠英说"这是女子怀念征夫的诗。她在采卷耳的时候想起了远行的丈夫,幻想他在上山了,过冈了,马病了,人疲了,又幻想他在饮酒自宽"。钱锺书认为这不是幻想,而是实事:"作诗之人不必即诗中所咏之人,妇与夫皆诗中人,诗人代言其情事,故各曰'我'……夫为一篇之主而妇为宾也。男女两人处两地而情事一时,批尾家谓之'双管齐下',章回小说谓之'话分两头'。"从真的观点看来,钱说更高;但从美的观点来看,则又以余说为上,因为"不言己之怀人,而愈见怀人情笃"。因此,我在一个译本中采用余说,而在本书中则采用钱说;这样更可以看出《诗经》内涵的丰富。又如《召南·小星》,传统的解释是指小妾,以致"小星"成了妾的代称;今天一般认为是写小臣出差;我也是在一个译本中用前说,在本书中用后说。但如《唐风·无衣》,一般认为是览衣感旧,睹物思人;《诗经楚辞鉴赏辞典》却认为是伤逝,情真意切,不胜依依,我就两本都按伤逝译了。总而言之,我的英译希望尽可能传达《诗经》的意美、音美和形美,并且与以往的各种语体译文也不尽相同。

《诗经》是中国古代的教科书,对建立及维护中国几千年的传统文化起了非常重大的作用。概括起来，儒家治国之道就是"礼乐"二字。"礼"模仿自然外在的秩序，"乐"模仿自然内在的和谐；"礼"可以养性，"乐"可以怡情；"礼"是"义"的外化，"乐"是"仁"的外化。做人要重"仁义"，治国要重"礼乐"，这就是中国文化几千年不衰的原因。世界各国，希腊、罗马有古无今，英、美、法、德、俄有今无古，印度、埃及都曾遭受亡国之痛，只有中国屹立世界东方，几千年如一日，对世界文明作出了独一无二的贡献。因此，把中国文化的瑰宝《诗经》译成具有意美、音美和形美的韵文，对东西文化的交流，对21世纪世界文化的建立，一定会有不可低估的意义。

许渊冲
1993年4月18日
北京大学畅春园舞山楼

卷一

国 风

周 南

其说不一，或认为周是古国名，后来周王以为周公、召公采邑；南是南方诸侯之国。或说周、召是地名，周南即周以南之地，召南即召以南之地。

关 雎

关关雎鸠①，在河之洲。窈窕淑女②，君子好逑③。
参差荇菜④，左右流之⑤。窈窕淑女，寤寐求之⑥。
求之不得，寤寐思服⑦。悠哉悠哉⑧，辗转反侧⑨。
参差荇菜，左右采之。窈窕淑女，琴瑟友之⑩。
参差荇菜，左右芼之⑪。窈窕淑女，钟鼓乐之⑫。

【注释】

①关关：雌雄两鸟的和鸣声。雎鸠（jū jiū 居究）：一种水鸟。　②窈窕（yǎo tiǎo 咬挑）：娴静漂亮。淑女：贤德的女子。③好：男女相悦。逑（qiú 求）：通"仇"，配偶。　④参差（cēn cī 岑刺）：高低不齐。荇（xìng 杏）菜：水中植物，叶浮在水面上，根茎可吃。　⑤流：择取。　⑥寤寐（wù mèi 物妹）：犹言日夜。睡醒为"寤"，睡着为"寐"。　⑦思：语助词。服：思念。

⑧悠:长久。　⑨辗转反侧:翻来覆去,睡不着觉。　⑩友:亲爱。
⑪芼(mào 冒):采。　⑫乐:娱悦。

【译文】

鱼鹰关关对着唱,停在河中沙洲上。漂亮善良好姑娘,该是君子好对象。

或长或短的荇菜,或左或右把它采。漂亮善良好姑娘,睡里梦里求怎样。

求她总是得不到,睡里梦里想更牢。长啊长啊长想念,翻来覆去睡不好。

或长或短的荇菜,或左或右把它采。漂亮善良好姑娘,弹琴鼓瑟把她爱。

或长或短的荇菜,或左或右把它采。漂亮善良好姑娘,敲钟鼓使她开怀。

葛　覃

葛之覃兮①,施于中谷②,维叶萋萋③。黄鸟于飞④,集于灌木⑤,其鸣喈喈⑥。

葛之覃兮,施于中谷,维叶莫莫⑦。是刈是濩⑧,为絺为绤⑨,服之无斁⑩。

言告师氏⑪,言告言归⑫。薄污我私⑬,薄澣我衣⑭。害澣害否⑮?归宁父母⑯。

【注释】

①葛:一种多年生蔓草,纤维可织布。覃(tán 弹):延长。

②施（yì 义）：蔓延。中谷：山谷中。　③维：发语词。萋萋：茂盛貌。　④黄鸟：黄莺，一说黄雀。于：语助词。　⑤集：群鸟栖息在树上。　⑥喈喈（jiē 皆）：鸟鸣声。　⑦莫莫：茂盛貌。　⑧刈（yì 义）：割。濩（huò 获）：煮。　⑨绤（chī 吃）：细葛布。绤（xì 细）：粗葛布。　⑩服：服用，指穿。斁（yì 译）：厌恶。　⑪言：语助词。下同。师氏：女师。《传》："师，女师也。古者女师教以妇德、妇言、妇容、妇功。"　⑫告归：告假回父母家。　⑬薄：语助词。污：洗去污垢。私：内衣。一说指日常所穿的衣服。　⑭澣（huàn 患）：同"浣"，洗。衣：外衣。一说礼服。　⑮害（hé 何）：通"何"。　⑯归宁：归问父母安。

【译文】

葛藤长又长，山沟里延伸，叶儿密密层层。黄莺飞成群，聚集在灌木丛中，叽叽叽叽叫不停。

葛藤长又长，山沟里延伸，叶儿密密层层。割啊煮啊忙不停，织成粗布和细布，穿上了它多舒服。

我向女师告个假，要回娘家。脏了的内衣搓一搓，脏了的外衣涮一涮。哪件该洗哪件不该洗？急着要见爹妈。

卷 耳

采采卷耳①，不盈顷筐②。嗟我怀人③，寘彼周行④。
陟彼崔嵬⑤，我马虺隤⑥。我姑酌彼金罍⑦，维以不永怀⑧。
陟彼高冈，我马玄黄⑨。我姑酌彼兕觥⑩，维以不永伤⑪。
陟彼砠矣⑫，我马瘏矣⑬，我仆痡矣⑭，云何吁矣⑮！

【注释】

①卷耳：草本植物名，嫩苗可食，也可药用。　②盈：满。顷筐：斜口筐，后高前倾。　③我：采者女子自称。怀：思念。　④寘：同"置"。周行（háng 杭）：大道。　⑤陟（zhì 治）：登。崔嵬：山高峻。　⑥我：思妇代远行丈夫的自称。下同。虺隤（huī tuí 灰颓）：马疲不能升高之病。　⑦姑：姑且。金罍（léi 雷）：饰金的酒器，大肚小口。　⑧维：发语词。永怀：常想念。　⑨玄黄：马生病而变色。闻一多《诗经通义》："眼花亦谓之玄黄。"　⑩兕觥（sì gōng 四宫）：用犀牛角做的酒器。　⑪永伤：永久伤痛。　⑫砠（jū 居）：有土的石山。　⑬瘏（tú 涂）：劳累过度致病。　⑭痡（pū 铺）：疲困不能行走。　⑮云：语助词。吁（xū 需）：忧叹。

【译文】

采啊采啊采卷耳，卷耳装不满浅筐。一心思念出门人，搁下浅筐大路旁。

登上高高的峻岭，我的马儿腿发软。且把壶酒来斟满，喝上一杯心稍安。

登上高高的山岗，我的马儿眼花昏。且把壶酒来斟满，宽慰自己不忧伤。

登上高高的石山，我的马儿要趴下，我的仆人快累垮，这份忧伤何时了啊！

樛 木

南有樛木①，葛藟累之②。乐只君子③，福履绥之④。
南有樛木，葛藟荒之⑤。乐只君子，福履将之⑥。

南有樛木,葛藟萦之⑦。乐只君子,福履成之⑧。

【注释】

①樛(jiū 鸠)木:树木向下弯曲。 ②葛藟(lěi 垒):藟似葛,有茎可以缠树。累:缠,挂。 ③只:语助词。 ④福履:犹福禄。绥:安。 ⑤荒:掩盖。 ⑥将:扶助。 ⑦萦:缠绕。 ⑧成:成就。

【译文】

南山有棵弯腰树,野葛到来缠住它。有这快乐的君子,幸福到来安定他。

南山有棵弯腰树,野葛到来掩盖它。有这快乐的君子,幸福到来扶助他。

南山有棵弯腰树,野葛到来萦绕它。有这快乐的君子,幸福到来成就他。

螽 斯

螽斯羽①,诜诜兮②。宜尔子孙,振振兮③。
螽斯羽,薨薨兮④。宜尔子孙,绳绳兮⑤。
螽斯羽,揖揖兮⑥。宜尔子孙,蛰蛰兮⑦。

【注释】

①螽(zhōng 终):蝗虫的一种,身长色青,叫声从翅膀里发出。斯:的。羽:翅膀。 ②诜诜(shēn shēn 深深):和顺的响声。 ③振振(zhēn zhēn 真真):众盛貌。 ④薨薨(hōng hōng 轰轰):

众多。　⑤绳绳：不绝貌。　⑥揖揖（jī jī 积积）：聚集。　⑦蛰蛰（zhí zhí 执执）：和集。

【译文】

　　螽儿的翅膀，发出沙沙响。应该您的子孙，多得无可量。
　　螽儿的翅膀，飞得翁翁响。应该您的子孙，相继无可量。
　　螽儿的羽翼，发出响唧唧。应该你的子孙，多得称密集。

桃　夭

桃之夭夭①，灼灼其华②。之子于归③，宜其室家④。
桃之夭夭，有蕡其实⑤。之子于归，宜其家室。
桃之夭夭，其叶蓁蓁⑥。之子于归，宜其家人。

【注释】

　　①夭夭：指树还年轻长得好。　②灼灼（zhuó 酌）：指红红。③之子：这个姑娘。子也可指女的。于归：出嫁。归指嫁。　④室家：家庭。　⑤蕡（fén 坟）：大。　⑥蓁蓁（zhēn zhēn 真真）：茂盛。

【译文】

　　桃树年轻枝正好，花开红红开得妙。这个姑娘来出嫁，适宜恰好成了家。
　　桃树年轻枝正好，结的果儿大得妙。这个姑娘来出嫁，适宜恰好成一家。
　　桃树年轻长得好，叶儿茂密密得妙。这个姑娘来出嫁，适宜一家人都好。

兔 罝

肃肃兔罝①,椓之丁丁②。赳赳武夫③,公侯干城④。
肃肃兔罝,施于中逵⑤。赳赳武夫,公侯好仇⑥。
肃肃兔罝,施于中林。赳赳武夫,公侯腹心。

【注释】

①肃肃:严肃认真。兔:野兔。罝(jū 居):网。 ②椓(zhuó 酌):敲击。丁丁(zhēng zhēng 争争):伐木声。 ③赳赳(jiū jiū 纠纠):健壮威武。 ④干城:垣城,城墙,犹屏障。 ⑤施:加到。中逵:逵中,九达之道,四通八达的大路。 ⑥仇:同"逑",配偶,这里指伴当、帮手。

【译文】

严肃认真结兔网,柱子敲打响丁当。赳赳武夫真勇猛,公侯要他做屏障。

严肃认真结兔网,放在大路的中央。赳赳武夫真勇猛,公侯用做好伴当。

严肃认真结兔网,放在树林的中央。赳赳武夫真勇猛,公侯认做腹心样。

芣 苢

采采芣苢①,薄言采之②。采采芣苢,薄言有之。
采采芣苢,薄言掇之③。采采芣苢,薄言捋之④。
采采芣苢,薄言袺之⑤。采采芣苢,薄言襭之⑥。

诗经

【注释】

① 采采：采了又采。芣苢（fú yǐ 浮以）：车前子，多年生草本，叶自根际丛生，广椭圆形。开淡紫小花，结果。诗称捋之，当指捋果实。叶可供食用，实可供药用。 ②薄言：发语词。 ③掇（duō 多）：拾取。 ④捋（luō 啰）：用手握物而脱取。 ⑤袺（jié 结）：手执衣襟以承物。 ⑥襭（xié 协）：翻动衣襟插于腰带以承物。

【译文】

采呀采呀车前子，赶些快快来采它。采呀采呀车前子，赶些快快占有它。

采呀采呀车前子，赶些快快拾取它。采呀采呀车前子，赶些快快捋取它。

采呀采呀车前子，翻过衣襟装着它。采呀采呀车前子，插好衣襟藏着它。

汉 广

南有乔木①，不可休思②。汉有游女③，不可求思。汉之广矣，不可泳思。江之永矣④，不可方思⑤。

翘翘错薪⑥，言刈其楚⑦。之子于归，言秣其马⑧。汉之广矣，不可泳思。江之永矣，不可方思。

翘翘错薪，言刈其蒌⑨。之子于归，言秣其驹。汉之广矣，不可泳思。江之永矣，不可方思。

【注释】

①乔木：高树。树高则树荫少。 ②思：语助词。 ③汉：汉水。游女：爱游的女子，不必指为仙女。 ④江：指长江。永：水流

长。　⑤方：《鲁诗》方作舫，小舟。　⑥翘翘（qiáo qiáo 桥桥）：如鸟尾上长羽的高起。错薪：错杂为薪。　⑦楚：牡荆。　⑧秣（mò 末）：用草喂马。　⑨蒌（lóu 楼）：蒌蒿，多年生草本，多生水滨，高四五尺，叶互生，羽状深裂。叶嫩时可食，老则为薪。

【译文】

南方有棵高高树，树下少荫不可休。汉水之上有游女，女虽好游不可求。汉水太广太直流，汉水上面不可游。长江的水长又长，航行不用小船舫。

高高杂草做柴好，割草首要割荆条。这个姑娘要出嫁，喂她的马为了她。汉水太广太直流，汉水之上不可游。长江之水长又长，航行不用小船舫。

高高杂草做柴好，割草先要割芦蒿。这个姑娘要出嫁，喂饱马驹为了她。汉水太广太直流，汉水上面不可游。长江之水长又长，航行不用小船舫。

汝　坟

遵彼汝坟①，伐其条枚②。未见君子，惄如调饥③。
遵彼汝坟，伐其条肄④。既见君子，不我遐弃⑤。
鲂鱼赪尾⑥，王室如燬⑦。虽则如燬，父母孔迩⑧。

【注释】

①遵：沿着。汝：汝水，源出河南嵩县西南天息山，东南流入淮水。坟：河堤。　②条：树枝。枚：树干。　③惄（nì 匿）如：饥困貌。调：通"朝"，早晨。　④条肄（yì 异）：新生的枝条。　⑤遐：远。　⑥鲂（fáng 房）鱼：一名鳊鱼，细鳞，鱼之美者。赪（chēng 称）：赤色。　⑦燬（huǐ

毁）：火。　⑧孔迩：很近。

【译文】

顺那汝水走上大堤岸，砍那树枝再砍树干。没有看见那位君子，如同早上没吃饭。

顺那汝水上大堤，砍那新生的树枝。既然看到那君子，还好不把我抛弃。

鲂鱼劳累尾巴红，王朝像火烧相同。虽则像火烧那样，父母很近要供奉。

麟 之 趾

麟之趾①，振振公子②。于嗟麟兮！
麟之定③，振振公姓④。于嗟麟兮！
麟之角，振振公族⑤。于嗟麟兮！

【注释】

①麟：《广雅·释兽》："麒麟步行中规，折还中矩，不履生虫，不折生草。"　②振振（zhēn zhēn 真真）：仁厚貌。　③定：额。严粲《诗缉》："有额者宜抵，唯麟之额，可以抵而不抵。""有角者宜触，唯麟之角，可以触而不触。"　④公姓：公孙。　⑤公族：族人。

【译文】

不踏生物的麟脚趾，好比仁厚的公子。值得赞美的麟啊！
不顶人的麟额头，好比公孙多仁厚。值得赞美的麟啊！
不触人的麟头角，好比仁厚的公族。值得赞美的麟啊！

召 南

见《周南》。

鹊 巢

维鹊有巢,维鸠居之①。之子于归,百两御之②。
维鹊有巢,维鸠方之③。之子于归,百两将之④。
维鹊有巢,维鸠盈之⑤。之子于归,百两成之⑥。

【注释】

①鸠:斑鸠,布谷鸟,占有其它的鸟巢。 ②御:侍候。 ③方:占有。 ④将:送。 ⑤盈:满。古时诸侯嫁女,有陪嫁的媵女,以侄娣陪嫁,所以诸侯一娶九女。 ⑥成:成就,即成礼。

【译文】

喜鹊树上有个窠,斑鸠飞来居住它。这个姑娘要出嫁,百辆车子侍候她。

喜鹊树上有个窠,斑鸠飞来占有它。这个姑娘要出嫁,百辆车子来送她。

喜鹊树上有个窠,斑鸠飞来占满它。这个姑娘要出嫁,百辆车子成就她。

诗经

采蘩

于以采蘩①,于沼于沚②。于以用之,公侯之事。
于以采蘩,于涧之中。于以用之,公侯之宫。
被之僮僮③,夙夜在公。被之祁祁④,薄言还归。

【注释】

①于以:问词。蘩:白蒿,生陂泽中,叶似嫩艾,茎或赤或白。②沼:沼泽。沚:小洲。 ③被:通"髲(bì币)",首饰。僮僮:盛。 ④祁祁(qí qí 其其):繁盛。

【译文】

什么地方采白蒿,水边洲上和湖沼。什么地方能用到,公侯的事祭祖考。

什么地方采白蒿,山涧中间能找到。什么地方能用到,公侯宫里祭祖庙。

首饰佩戴得丰崇,早夜祭祀在从公。首饰佩戴得多众,祭祀完毕回家中。

草虫

喓喓草虫①,趯趯阜螽②。未见君子,忧心忡忡③。亦既见止④,亦既觏止⑤,我心则降。

陟彼南山,言采其蕨⑥。未见君子,忧心惙惙⑦。亦既见止,亦既觏止,我心则说⑧。

陟彼南山,言采其薇⑨。未见君子,我心伤悲。亦既见止,亦既觏止,我心则夷⑩。

【注释】

①喓喓（yāo yāo 腰腰）：虫声。　②趯趯（tì tì 惕惕）：跳跃。阜螽：蚱蜢。　③忡忡（chōng chōng 冲冲）：心跳。　④止：语助词。　⑤觏（gòu 构）：相会。　⑥蕨（jué 厥）：羊齿类植物，地下茎很长，春季长嫩叶，可吃。　⑦惙惙（chuò chuò 绰绰）：惶惑。⑧说：同"悦"。　⑨薇（wēi 微）：野菜，叶子一种绿色，一种褐色，嫩的可吃。　⑩夷：平。

【译文】

喓喓只听草虫叫，蚱蜢只会拍拍跳。没有看见君子人，心里忧愁咚咚跳。既然看见他，既然交好他，我的心平不再跳。

登那南山路不缺，为采山中那个蕨。没有看见君子人，心里忧愁好惶惑。既然看见他，既然会见他，我的心儿才喜悦。

登那南山路不奇，为采山中那个薇。没有看见君子人，我的心里又悲凄。既然看见他，既然会见他，我心才能得欣喜。

采 蘋

于以采蘋①，南涧之滨。于以采藻②，于彼行潦③。
于以盛之，维筐及筥④。于以湘之⑤，维锜及釜⑥。
于以奠之，宗室牖下⑦。谁其尸之⑧，有齐季女⑨。

【注释】

①蘋：浮萍，蕨类植物，生浅水中。　②藻（zǎo 早）：藻类植物，没有根茎叶的区分，用细胞分裂繁殖，生浅水中。　③行潦（háng lǎo 杭老）：流的水沟，流的积水。　④筥（jǔ 举）：圆竹器。　⑤湘：烹煮。

⑥锜（qí 其）：三足釜。釜：炊具。　⑦牖（yǒu 有）：窗子。　⑧尸：主持。古代祭祀用人作神，称尸。　⑨齐：同"斋"，沐浴视敬。季：排行第四。

【译文】

什么地方采浮萍，在那南涧的水滨。什么地方采浮藻，在那流水的沟边好。

什么东西装得好，只有方筐圆篓好。什么器具能煮好，三足釜和釜煮得好。

什么地方祭献它，宗室里头南窗下。什么人来主这事，有个斋戒的少女娃。

甘　棠

蔽芾甘棠①，勿翦勿伐，召伯所茇②。
蔽芾甘棠，勿翦勿败③，召伯所憩。
蔽芾甘棠，勿翦勿拜④，召伯所说⑤。

【注释】

①蔽芾（fèi 费）：茂盛。甘棠：棠梨树，落叶乔木，开花白的叫甘棠，果实圆而小，味甜。　②召伯：召公奭为诸侯的长，称伯。茇（bá 拔）：草舍，止于其下以自蔽，犹草舍。　③败：败坏。　④拜：弯，弯枝向下如人拜。　⑤说：通"税"，舍，休憩。

【译文】

茂盛的棠梨树，不剪不砍它，召伯曾留在树下。

茂盛的棠梨树，不剪不坏它，召伯曾休息在树下。
茂盛的棠梨树，不剪不弯它，召伯曾经住过夜。

行 露

厌浥行露①，岂不夙夜②，谓行多露③。

谁谓雀无角，何以穿我屋？谁谓女无家，何以速我狱④？虽速我狱，室家不足⑤！

谁谓鼠无牙⑥，何以穿我墉？谁谓女无家，何以速我讼？虽速我讼，亦不女从！

【注释】

①厌浥（yè yì 夜义）：沾湿。行：路。 ②夙夜：早夜，夜未尽天未明时。 ③谓：通"畏"。 ④速：催，加快。 ⑤室家：成室成家，即婚姻。 ⑥牙：牙比齿长。说鼠只有齿无牙。

【译文】

沾湿是路上的露，难道清早不走路，怕的是路上多露。

谁说雀儿没有角，怎么啄穿我的屋？谁说女儿没婆家，怎么催我进牢狱？虽然催我进牢狱，成室的道理还不足。

谁说老鼠没长牙，怎么穿透我的墙？谁说女儿没婆家，怎么催迫告我状？虽然催迫告我状，也不从你告我状！

羔 羊

羔羊之皮，素丝五紽①。退食自公②，委蛇委蛇③。
羔羊之革④，素丝五緎⑤。委蛇委蛇，自公退食。

羔羊之缝⑥，素丝五总⑦。委蛇委蛇，退食自公。

【注释】

①五纰（tuó 驼）：陈奂《传疏》：五当读为交午之午。严粲《诗缉》："纰，缝也。"闻一多《通义》："缝之义亦交午也。""五纰"即"午纰"，丝线交午缝制的意思。　②退食自公：退朝进食出自公家，是公家供食。　③委蛇（yí 夷）：委曲自得之貌。　④革：犹皮。　⑤五绒：犹五纰。　⑥缝：革。　⑦五总：犹五纰。

【译文】

羔羊的皮需要缝，白丝交错来细缝。退朝进食亦自公，委曲前进态从容。

羔羊的革需要缝，白丝交错来细缝。委曲前进态从容，退朝进食亦自公。

羔羊的皮需要缝，白丝交错来细缝。委曲前进态从容，朝朝进食亦自公。

殷其雷

殷其雷①，在南山之阳②。何斯违斯③？莫敢或遑④。振振君子，归哉归哉！

殷其雷，在南山之侧。何斯违斯？莫敢遑息。振振君子，归哉归哉！

殷其雷，在南山之下。何斯违斯？莫或遑处⑤。振振君子，归哉归哉！

【注释】

①殷（yīn 引）：雷声。 ②阳：指山的南方。 ③何斯：斯指此人。违斯：违，离开；斯，指此地。 ④或：有。遑（huáng 皇）：暇。 ⑤处：居。

【译文】

殷殷的雷声，在南山的南边啊。何以在此又离开此呀？没有敢休息啊。诚厚的君子，归来啊归来啊！

殷殷的雷声，在南山的旁边啊。何以在此又离开此呀？没有敢休息啊。诚厚的君子，归来啊归来啊！

殷殷的雷声，在南山的下边啊。何以在此又离开此呀？没有敢闲暇呀。诚厚的君子，归来啊归来啊！

摽 有 梅

摽有梅①，其实七兮。求我庶士②，迨其吉兮③。
摽有梅，其实三兮。求我庶士，迨其今兮。
摽有梅，顷筐墍之④。求我庶士，迨其谓之⑤。

【注释】

①摽（biào 俵）：落下。 ②求：追求。庶：众。 ③迨：及。 ④顷筐：同"倾筐"。墍（jì 既）：取。 ⑤谓：说话。

【译文】

落下的有梅子，枝头留下梅子七成。追求我的众士人，及到这是好时辰。

诗经

　　落下的有梅子,枝头梅子三成。追求我的众士人,及到今朝是好时辰。

　　落下的有梅子,尽这筐来取它。追求我的众士人,及时说话就得成。

小　星

　　嘒彼小星①,三五在东②。肃肃宵征③,夙夜在公,寔命不同④。

　　嘒彼小星,维参与昴⑤。肃肃宵征,抱衾与裯⑥,寔命不犹⑦。

【注释】

　　①嘒(huì 诲):微光。　②三五:参宿三星,昴宿五星。　③肃肃:急忙。征:行。　④寔:实。　⑤参(shēn 申)昴(mǎo 卯):二十八宿中的二宿。　⑥衾(qīn 亲):被子。裯(chóu 稠):床帐。　⑦犹:如。

【译文】

　　微光的是那小星,三颗五颗在东方的是大星。急急忙忙夜里行,从早到夜都从公,实在命运各不同。

　　微光的是那小星,参宿与昴宿是大星。急急忙忙夜里行,被子帐子自己抱,实在命运不如人。

江有汜

　　江有汜①,之子归。不我以②,不我以,其后也悔。

江有渚③，之子归。不我与，不我与，其后也处④。
江有沱⑤，之子归。不我过⑥，不我过，其啸也歌。

【注释】

①汜（sì 四）：由主流分出而复汇合的河流。 ②以：用。 ③渚：水中的小洲。 ④处：闻一多《诗经新义》：训忧。 ⑤沱（tuó 驼）：江的支流。 ⑥不我过：不至我处。

【译文】

大江也有水倒流，这个男人归来正时候。他不用我，他不用我，他的懊悔在后头。

大江也有小的洲，这个男人归来正时候。他不同我好，他不同我好，他的发愁在后头。

大江也会有支流，这个男人归来正时候。他不到我处，他不到我处，他把哭当歌在后头。

野有死麕

野有死麕①，白茅包之。有女怀春，吉士诱之②。
林有朴樕③，野有死鹿。白茅纯束④，有女如玉。
舒而脱脱兮⑤，无感我帨兮⑥，无使尨也吠⑦。

【注释】

①麕（jūn 军）：獐子。 ②吉士：男子的美称，当指青年猎人。 ③朴樕（sù 速）：小树。 ④纯束：捆扎。 ⑤舒：缓缓。脱脱（duì duì 兑兑）：慢慢。 ⑥感：通"撼"。帨（shuì 税）：围裙。 ⑦尨（máng 忙）：多毛狗。

【译文】

野地里有死獐子,用白茅草包裹它。有个姑娘动了心,吉祥的人引诱她。

树林里有小树,野地里有死鹿。白茅草搓纯来捆着它,有个女儿美如玉。

缓缓地慢慢来啊,不要动我的围裙啊,不要使狗叫啊。

何彼秾矣

何彼秾矣①?唐棣之华②。曷不肃雍③?王姬之车。

何彼秾矣?华如桃李。平王之孙④,齐侯之子。

其钓维何?维丝伊缗⑤。齐侯之子,平王之孙。

【注释】

①秾(nóng 农):繁盛。 ②唐棣(dì 第):郁李,落叶灌木,高五六尺,春开花,夏结实。 ③曷:何。肃雍:严肃雍容。 ④平王:东周第一代君主,名宜臼。 ⑤缗(mín 民):纶,捻丝成纶,即钓丝。

【译文】

怎么那么繁盛?郁李开的花。何以不严肃雍容?那是王姬的车。

怎么那么繁盛?花像桃和李。那是平王的外孙,是齐侯的好女。

她的钓鱼用什么?用丝线做钓绳。是齐侯的好女,是平王的外孙。

驺 虞

彼茁者葭①,壹发五豝②,于嗟乎驺虞③。
彼茁者蓬④,壹发五豵⑤,于嗟乎驺虞。

【注释】

①茁(zhuó 浊):壮实。葭(jiā 家):芦苇。 ②豝(bā 巴):牝猪。 ③驺(zōu 邹)虞:天子掌鸟兽之官,即官家的猎人。 ④蓬:蓬蒿。 ⑤豵(zōng 宗):小猪。

【译文】

那茁壮的芦苇做箭干,一箭发射到五母猪啊,正好样的猎人啊。

那茁壮的蓬蒿做箭干,一箭发射到五小猪啊,正好样的猎人啊。

卷 二

国 风

邶 风

邶、鄘、卫：三国名。周武王克商以后，夺商王纣都朝歌(在今河南淇县)，将朝歌一带分为邶、鄘、卫三地。后卫占有邶、鄘。

柏 舟

汎彼柏舟①，亦汎其流②。耿耿不寐③，如有隐忧④。微我无酒⑤，以敖以游⑥。

我心匪鉴⑦，不可以茹⑧。亦有兄弟，不可以据。薄言往愬⑨，逢彼之怒。

我心匪石，不可转也。我心匪席，不可卷也。威仪棣棣⑩，不可选也⑪。

忧心悄悄⑫，愠于群小⑬。觏闵既多⑭，受侮不少。静言思之，寤辟有摽⑮。

日居月诸⑯，胡迭而微⑰。心之忧矣，如匪澣衣。静言思之，不能奋飞。

【注释】

①汎（fàn 泛）：随水流动。 ②流：中流。 ③耿耿（gěng gěng 梗梗）：不安貌。 ④隐：深。 ⑤微：非。 ⑥敖：游。 ⑦鉴：

镜子。　⑧茹（rú 如）：容纳。　⑨愬：同"诉"。　⑩威仪：庄严容止。棣棣：雍容闲雅。　⑪选：屈挠退让。　⑫悄悄：忧貌。　⑬愠（yùn 运）：怨恨。　⑭闵（mǐn 敏）：忧伤。　⑮寤：交互。辟（pì 僻）：捶击。摽（piào 票）：抚心。　⑯居、诸：语助。　⑰迭：更动。微：隐微，无光。

【译文】

柏木船儿随水流，也是随波顺着流。心内不安难入睡，像有深切的忧愁。不是我没有酒，用来到处游。

我的心不是镜子，不可以照。也有兄弟，不可以靠。说是去诉苦，碰上他们在发怒。

我的心不是磨石，不可以转。我的心不是席子，不可以卷。我的尊严面子，不可退让自止。

心内忧愁不了，成群小人憎恨不少。遭到痛苦既已多，受的侮辱也不少。静静地想它，交互抚心只扰扰。

太阳啊月亮啊，为啥轮流不放光。心内的忧愁除不了，好像没洗脏内衣。静静地想想它，不能奋翅起高飞。

绿 衣

绿兮衣兮①，绿衣黄里②。心之忧矣，曷维其已③。
绿兮衣兮，绿衣黄裳④。心之忧矣，曷维其亡⑤。
绿兮丝兮，女所治兮。我思古人⑥，俾无訧兮⑦。
絺兮绤兮⑧，凄其以风。我思古人，实获我心。

【注释】

①衣：指上衣。 ②里：指上衣的衬里，黄布来衬里。 ③曷：何时。 ④裳：下衣，即裤子。 ⑤亡：止。 ⑥古人：一说"古人"即"故人"，改字，不从。 ⑦俾：使。讹：同"尤"，过错。 ⑧绪（chī 痴）：细葛布。绤（xì 隙）：粗葛布。

【译文】

绿啊上衣啊，绿上衣啊黄里衣。心里的忧啊，何时它才止哩。

绿啊上衣啊，绿上衣啊黄下衣。心里的忧啊，何时它才消失哩。

绿啊丝呀，女人所做的呀。我想念古代人，使我没有过错啊。

葛布不论粗或细，穿上身凉风凄凄。我想念古代人，实在获得我心意。

燕 燕

燕燕于飞，差池其羽①。之子于归，远送于野。瞻望弗及，泣涕如雨。

燕燕于飞，颉之颃之②。之子于归，远于将之。瞻望弗及，伫立以泣③。

燕燕于飞，下上其音。之子于归，远送于南④。瞻望弗及，实劳我心。

仲氏任只⑤，其心塞渊。终温且惠，淑慎其身。先君之思⑥，以勖寡人⑦。

【注释】

①差（cī）池：不整齐。　②颉颃（jié háng 杰杭）：飞而上下。　③伫（zhù 住）：久。　④南：南方。　⑤仲：第二。氏：姓氏。任：姓任。　⑥先君：已死的君主。　⑦寡人：寡德之人，庄姜自称。

【译文】

燕子展开翅膀飞，翅膀展开不整齐。这个妇人要大归，远远送她到郊区。睁眼望她望不见，哭泣眼泪落如雨。

燕子展开翅膀飞，忽上忽下望见它。这个妇人要大归，远远出来往送她。睁眼望她望不见，久立哭泣想着她。

燕子展开翅膀飞，下下上上发呢喃。这个妇人要大归，远远送她去向南。睁眼望她望不见，实在劳我心不安。

仲氏你姓任，你心想得远又深。终于温柔又惠爱，善良谨慎及你身。你还想念到先君，用来勉励我寡人。

日　月

日居月诸①，照临下土。乃如之人兮，逝不古处②。胡能有定，宁不我顾③。

日居月诸，下土是冒④。乃如之人兮，逝不相好。胡能有定，宁不我报⑤。

日居月诸，出自东方。乃如之人兮，德音无良⑥。胡能有定，俾也可忘⑦。

日居月诸，东方自出。父兮母兮，畜我不卒⑧。胡能有定，报我不述。

【注释】

①居、诸：语助辞。 ②逝：语助辞。古：古道。 ③宁：岂。 ④冒：覆盖。 ⑤报：回答。 ⑥德音：好话。 ⑦俾：使。 ⑧畜：养育。

【译文】

太阳啊月亮啊，照亮下面的疆土。是这样的人啊，不用古道和我相处。怎么能够有一定，岂有不把我照顾。

太阳啊月亮啊，下面的土地是光照。是这样的人啊，不和我相好。怎么能够有一定，岂有不向我回报。

太阳啊月亮啊，出来从东方。是这样的人啊，好话完全变样。怎么能有一定，使我也可以把他忘。

太阳啊月亮啊，出来从东方。父亲啊母亲啊，对我为啥不终养。怎么能够有一定，回报我的话不好讲。

终 风

终风且暴①，顾我则笑。谑浪笑敖，中心是悼。
终风且霾②，惠然肯来。莫往莫来，悠悠我思。
终风且曀③，不日有曀。寤言不寐④，愿言则嚏⑤。
曀曀其阴，虺虺其雷⑥。寤言不寐，愿言则怀。

【注释】

①终风：整天刮风。 ②霾（mái 埋）：阴尘。 ③曀（yì 翳）：阴沉。 ④寤（wù 悟）：睡醒。 ⑤嚏（tì 替）：打喷嚏。 ⑥虺虺（huǐ huǐ 毁毁）：打雷声。

【译文】

整天刮风又狂暴,看见了我就好笑。戏谑狂浪又讪笑,我的心中是伤悼。

整天刮风又扬土,惠爱那样肯光顾。如果不去不来问,老是令我把他想。

整天刮风又阴沉,不定那天有天阴。卧时醒着不能睡,愿他想我打喷嚏。

黑沉沉是天阴,豂轰轰是天打雷。卧着不能入睡,愿他能对我长怀。

击 鼓

击鼓其镗①,踊跃用兵②。土国城漕③,我独南行。
从孙子仲,平陈与宋④。不我以归,忧心有忡⑤。
爰居爰处⑥,爰丧其马。于以求之,于林之下。
死生契阔⑦,与子成说⑧。执子之手,与子偕老。
于嗟阔兮,不我活兮。于嗟洵兮⑨,不我信兮⑩。

【注释】

①镗(tāng 汤):堂堂;击鼓声。　②踊跃:跳跃,表高兴。兵:兵器。　③土国:为国家兴土功。城漕:在漕地筑城。一说漕在河南滑县东。　④平:和好。陈与宋:陈国和宋国。　⑤忡(chōng 冲):状忧愁。　⑥爰(yuán 元):于何。　⑦契阔:契合疏阔。　⑧成说:成约,约定。　⑨洵(xún 旬):信用。　⑩信:古伸字。

【译文】

敲击大鼓堂堂响,士兵跳跃弄刀枪。为国土功,为漕建城墙,我独向南走一趟。

跟从统帅公孙子仲,交好与国陈和宋。不许我归来,心里忧苦有忡忡。

在哪里定我的住处,在哪里失掉他的马。在哪里去找它,在树林的下面。

死活和契合远隔,同您成功相说。握着您的手,同您到老不脱。

可叹啊如今远隔啊,不许我还活啊。可叹我的信用啊,不能使我伸说啊。

凯 风

凯风自南①,吹彼棘心②。棘心夭夭③,母氏劬劳④。
凯风自南,吹彼棘薪。母氏圣善,我无令人⑤。
爰有寒泉,在浚之下⑥。有子七人,母氏劳苦。
睍睆黄鸟⑦,载好其音。有子七人,莫慰母心。

【注释】

①凯风:和风。 ②棘心:酸枣小树,酸枣树枝上多刺,初生即有刺,心指刺,棘心指小酸枣。酸枣为落叶灌木,开黄绿色小花,结枣味酸。 ③夭夭:指树小小,未长大。 ④劬(qú 渠):辛勤。 ⑤令人:善人。 ⑥浚(jùn 俊):卫国地名。 ⑦睍睆(xiàn huǎn 现缓):好看。

【译文】

和风来从南方了，吹那酸枣树还小。酸枣树小小，母亲勤累又辛劳。

和风来从南方了，吹那酸枣成柴篠。母亲圣明又善良，我们没有善人怎么好。

有寒冷的泉水，在浚城下面围绕。有儿子七个人，母亲还是勤苦辛劳。

好看的黄鸟，传来好听的叫声。有儿子七个人，没有能安慰母亲的心。

雄 雉

雄雉于飞，泄泄其羽①。我之怀矣，自诒伊阻②。
雄雉于飞，下上其音。展矣君子③，实劳我心。
瞻彼日月，悠悠我思。道之云远，曷云能来。
百尔君子④，不知德行。不忮不求⑤，何用不臧⑥。

【注释】

①泄泄（yì yì 意意）：慢慢。《传》："雄雉见雌雉飞，而鼓其翼泄泄然。"比喻丈夫想念她，精神萎靡。 ②诒（yí 夷）：留。伊：语辞。阻：忧。 ③展：诚实。 ④百尔：指众多。 ⑤忮（zhì 至）：害。 ⑥臧（zāng 赃）：善。

【译文】

雄的野鸡展翅飞，展开翅膀慢慢飞。我的怀念啊，独留阻隔忧伤啊。

雄的野鸡展翅飞，或下或上传它的音。诚实的君子啊，确实劳苦我的心。

眼看日月向人催，长长思念积成堆。道路又说这么远，何时说他能回来。

众多的君子们，不知什么叫德行。不去害人不贪富，怎么不善都可行。

匏有苦叶

匏有苦叶①，济有深涉②，深则厉③，浅则揭④。
有弥济盈⑤，有鷕雉鸣⑥。济盈不濡轨⑦，雉鸣求其牡。
雝雝鸣雁⑧，旭日始旦。士如归妻，迨冰未泮⑨。
招招舟子，人涉卬否⑩。人涉卬否，卬须我友。

【注释】

①匏（páo 袍）：葫芦。 ②济：水名，源出河南济源县王屋山，古时与黄河并入海，今下游古道为黄河所夺。 ③厉：以衣涉水。 ④揭（qì 气）：提起衣裳渡水。 ⑤弥：水满。 ⑥鷕（wěi 尾）：此野鸡叫声。 ⑦轨：车轴头。 ⑧雝雝（yōng yōng 拥拥）：雁鸣声。 ⑨泮（pàn 判）：冰解。 ⑩卬（áng 昂）：我。

【译文】

葫芦叶子味道苦，济水深处也得渡。水深连带衣裳过，水浅提起衣裳过。

茫茫水满济河充，雌野鸡叫声不穷。济河水不浸车轴头，雌野鸡叫着求那雄。

和谐叶声是雁子,初升太阳东方红。你如有心来娶妻,过河切莫解冰封。

船夫招招开渡船,人来摆渡我则否。人来摆渡我则否,我是须要我的友。

谷 风

习习谷风①,以阴以雨。黾勉同心②,不宜有怒。采葑采菲③,无以下体。德音莫违,及尔同死。

行行迟迟,中心有违④。不远伊迩⑤,薄送我畿⑥。谁谓荼苦⑦,其甘如荠⑧。宴尔新婚,如兄如弟。

泾以渭浊,湜湜其沚⑨。宴尔新婚,不我屑以。毋逝我梁⑩,毋发我笱⑪。我躬不阅⑫,遑恤我后⑬。

就其深矣,方之舟之⑭。就其浅矣,泳之游之。何有何亡,黾勉求之。凡民有丧,匍匐救之⑮。

不我能慉⑯,反以我为雠⑰。既阻我德,贾用不售⑱。昔育恐育鞫⑲,及尔颠覆。既生既育,比予于毒。

我有旨蓄,亦以御冬。宴尔新婚,以我御穷。有洸有溃⑳,既诒我肄。不念昔者,伊余来塈㉑。

【注释】

①习习:风声。谷风:山谷里来的风。 ②黾(mǐn 敏)勉:勉力。 ③葑菲(fēng fēi 封非):萝卜蔓菁。 ④违:恨。 ⑤迩:近。 ⑥畿(jī 机):门槛; ⑦荼(tú 途):苦菜。 ⑧荠(jì 祭):荠菜。 ⑨湜湜(shí shí 食食):水清。沚(zhǐ 止):水停止。 ⑩梁:鱼梁,筑堤以捕鱼。开梁则鱼皆游去。 ⑪笱(gǒu

狗）：捕鱼竹笼，鱼能进不能出。 ⑫阅：容纳。 ⑬恤（xù 序）：忧。 ⑭方：并船。 ⑮匍匐（pú fú 蒲服）：爬行。 ⑯慉（xù 畜）：好，爱。 ⑰雠：同"仇"。 ⑱贾（gǔ 古）：经商。 ⑲鞫（jū 居）：穷困。 ⑳洸（guāng 光）：武貌。溃（kuì 愧）：怒貌。 ㉑塈（xì 戏）：爱。

【译文】

豁啦啦吹来山里风，又是阴天又下雨。同心合意来生活，不该对我来发怒。采了萝卜采萝菁，不要因为它是根。好话不要来违反，说是同你一同死。

出门走走走得慢，心中有恨走不快。不远很近难回去，你只送我大门坎。谁说荼菜味道苦，它的甜味像荠菜。你的新婚多快乐，像兄像弟加成对。

泾水因为渭水浑，泾水停下也清澄。你的新婚多快乐，不屑与我来相亲。不要放开我鱼梁，不要打开我鱼筐。我身尚且不相容，难忧我后终无穷。

就它的水深啊，用并船或船来渡它。就它的水浅啊，用游泳来渡它。什么有什么没有，没有的勉力去相求。凡是人家有丧亡，走不动也要爬着去救。

不再爱我，反而以我为仇。既然掩盖我的好处，好比卖货不能售。从前生活恐惧又潦倒，同你一起倾覆颠倒。现在生活过得好，你却把我比做毒蟊。

我有好的积蓄，也可用来抵御过冬。你新婚很快乐，用我来抵御困穷。又动武又发怒，既已让我劳苦。从前的恩情你不眯，我昔来时曾相爱。

式 微

式微式微①，胡不归？微君之故②，胡为乎中露③？
式微式微，胡不归？微君之躬，胡为乎泥中？

【注释】

①式：发语辞。微：衰落。 ②微：非，不是。 ③中露：露户。

【译文】

衰微啊衰微，为什么不归？不是君主的缘故，为什么身上受露？

衰微啊衰微，为什么不归？不是为了您的身体，为什么滚在泥巴里？

旄 丘

旄丘之葛兮①，何诞之节兮②？叔兮伯兮，何多日也？
何其处也？必有与也。何其久也？必有以也。
狐裘蒙戎③，匪车不东④。叔兮伯兮，靡所与同⑤。
琐兮尾兮⑥，流离之子⑦。叔兮伯兮，褎如充耳⑧。

【注释】

①旄（máo 毛）丘：前高后低的土山。 ②诞之节：长的茎，葛茎较长。 ③蒙戎：龙茸，多毛。 ④匪：同"非"。 ⑤靡：无。同：同情。 ⑥琐：小。尾：微。 ⑦流离：流亡。 ⑧褎（xiù 袖）如：多笑貌。充耳：耳旁挂的塞物，持在帽上。

诗经

【译文】

土山上的葛茎啊，怎么长的茎啊？叔啊伯啊，怎么多天不来行？

怎么安处啊？一定有相与的人。怎么这样久啊？一定有它的原因。

狐皮的毛乱纷纷，不是车子不东行。叔啊伯啊，没有同情结成群。

小啊微啊，流亡的人。叔啊伯啊，微笑着充耳不闻。

简 兮

简兮简兮①，方将万舞②。日之方中，在前上处。
硕人俣俣③，公庭万舞。有力如虎，执辔如组④。
左手执籥⑤，右手秉翟⑥。赫如渥赭⑦，公言锡爵⑧。
山有榛⑨，隰有苓⑩。云谁之思，西方美人。彼美人兮，西方之人兮。

【注释】

①简：选择。 ②将：大。万舞，一种舞名。合武舞与文舞称万舞，武舞用干（盾牌），文舞用野鸡尾。诗里讲执籥，不讲执干，可能又改了。 ③硕（shuò 朔）：高大。俣俣（yǔ yǔ 与与）：大而美。 ④辔：马缰绳。驾车的，一车四马，一马两绳，四马八绳，两绳系车上，六绳执驾车人手。组：丝带。 ⑤籥（yuè 跃）：乐器，可吹。 ⑥翟（dí 敌）：野鸡尾。 ⑦赫：红色。渥（wò 沃）：厚。赭（zhě 者）：赤褐色。 ⑧锡：赐。爵：酒器。 ⑨榛（zhēn 真）：榛树所结的果，称榛子。 ⑩隰（xí 席）：湿地。苓（líng 伶）：一种苦的药。

【译文】

选择啊选择啊,刚要开场的《万舞》。太阳刚在中间,他在前面的上处。

高大的人身体魁梧,在公的院子内跳《万舞》。有力量像老虎,拿着缰绳像柔轻的带组。

拿笛吹奏指挥的靠左手,拿野鸡尾舞蹈的靠右手。脸红得像深色的赭石,公说赐他一杯酒。

山上有榛栗,湿地长苦苓。说在想哪一个,想西方来的漂亮人。那个漂亮人啊,是西方来的人啊。

泉 水

毖彼泉水①,亦流于淇②。有怀于卫,靡日不思。娈彼诸姬③,聊与之谋。

出宿于泲④,饮饯于祢。女子有行⑤,远父母兄弟。问我诸姑,遂及伯姊。

出宿于干,饮饯于言。载脂载舝⑥,还车言迈⑦。遄臻于卫⑧,不瑕有害⑨。

我思肥泉⑩,兹之永叹。思须与漕,我心悠悠。驾言出游,以写我忧。

【注释】

①毖(bì 必):水流貌。 ②淇:水名,源出河南林县,流至淇县入卫河。 ③诸姬:卫姓姬,卫女出嫁时有娣侄陪嫁亦姓姬。 ④泲(jì 际)、祢(nǐ 你)、干、言:皆卫国地名。 ⑤行:嫁。 ⑥舝(xiá 侠):车轴两头的金属键。 ⑦迈:远。 ⑧遄(chuán 传):

速。臻（zhēn 真）：到。 ⑨瑕：何。 ⑩肥泉：卫地名。

【译文】

涓涓流的那泉水，也流到淇水。有心想到卫国，没有一天不想念。诸位姓姬的好女，姑且和她们商议。

出门住宿在泲，亲朋饯行在祢。姑娘要出嫁，远远离开父母兄弟。回家问候众位姑姑，还连到大姊。

出门住宿在干，亲朋饯行在言。油脂涂车安好轴，调转车行远又快。直到卫国多么快，何不问有什么害。

我想到肥泉，对此不免长叹息。想到须邑和曹邑，我的心里长想念。驾车去出游，用来书写我的忧。

北 门

出自北门，忧心殷殷①。终窭且贫②，莫知我艰。已焉哉！天实为之，谓之何哉！

王事适我③，政事一埤益我④。我入自外，室人交遍谪我。已焉哉！天实谓之，谓之何哉！

王事敦我⑤，政事一埤遗我。我入自外，室人交遍摧我⑥。已焉哉！天实为之，谓之何哉！

【注释】

①殷殷：状忧貌。 ②窭（jù 巨）：鄙陋不能备礼。 ③适：派给。 ④埤（pí 皮）：加。 ⑤敦：逼迫。 ⑥摧：挫折，讥刺。

【译文】

我从北门出来，心里忧愁意漫漫。既鄙陋又贫困，没人知道我艰难。算了吧！天实在这样安排，说它什么啊！

周王的事派给我，公差一发加给我。我从外面回家，家人交互地责备我。算了吧！天实在这样安排，说它什么啊！

周王的事逼迫我，公差一发加给我。我从外面回家，家人交相讽刺我。算了吧！天实在这样安排，说它什么啊！

北 风

北风其凉，雨雪其雱①。惠而好我②，携手同行。其虚其邪③，既亟只且④。

北风其喈，雨雪其霏。惠而好我，携手同归。其虚其邪，既亟只且。

莫赤匪狐，莫黑匪乌。惠而好我，携手同车。其虚其邪，既亟只且。

【注释】

①雱（páng 旁）：雪盛貌。 ②惠而：惠然，爱好貌。 ③虚：慢。邪：通"徐"，也是慢意。 ④亟（jí 急）：急迫。只且（jū 居）：语助词。

【译文】

北风吹得冷，下雪下得猛。惠然爱好我，握手一同走。慢慢又慢走，既然急迫宜快走。

北风吹得响，下雪下得猛。惠然爱好我，握手同回一起走。

慢慢又慢走,既然急迫宜快走。

没有赤的不是狐,没有黑的不是乌。惠然爱好我,握手同趁一车走。慢慢又慢走,既然急迫宜快走。

静 女

静女其姝①,俟我于城隅②。爱(薆)而不见③,搔首踟蹰④。

静女其娈⑤,贻我彤管⑥。彤管有炜⑦,说(悦)怿女(汝)美⑧。

自牧归(馈)荑⑨,洵美且异⑩。匪女(汝)之为美,美人之贻。

【注释】

①静:幽雅。姝(shū 殊):美。 ②城隅:城边隐蔽处。 ③爱:隐。 ④踟蹰(chí chú 池除):徘徊不定。 ⑤娈(luán 鸾):美丽。 ⑥彤(tóng 同)管:红管草。 ⑦炜(wěi 伟):光彩。 ⑧说(悦)怿(yì 亦):喜悦。 ⑨牧:野外。荑(tí 提):初生的茅。 ⑩洵(xún 旬):实在。

【译文】

幽静姑娘长得美,等我在城角里。隐蔽着看不见,搔着头立在那里。

幽静姑娘真美丽,送我彤管有用意。彤管有着红艳艳,我是喜爱你的美。

自从野外归来送我荑,确实美丽又怪异。不是认为你美丽,因为是美人的赠贻。

新 台

新台有泚①，河水弥弥②。燕婉之求③，蘧篨不鲜④。
新台有洒⑤，河水浼浼⑥。燕婉之求，蘧篨不殄。
鱼网之设，鸿则离之⑦。燕婉之求，得此戚施⑧。

【注释】

①新台：卫宣公替世子伋（jí 级）娶齐女，听说齐女美，在河边造了一座新台，把齐女给自己娶来，称为宣姜。泚（cǐ 此）：鲜明貌。 ②弥弥（mǐ mǐ 米米）：盛满貌。 ③燕婉：安顺。 ④蘧篨（qú chú 渠除）：蛤蟆。鲜：善。 ⑤洒（cuǐ 璀）：高峻貌。 ⑥浼浼（měi měi 每每）：水盛貌。 ⑦鸿：指蛤蟆。离：通"罹"。 ⑧戚施：指蛤蟆。

【译文】

新台照水倒影明，河水涨得与岸平。求的安顺夫婿好，嫁个蛤蟆不像人。

新台靠水造得高，河水涨满浪滔滔。求的安顺夫婿好，嫁个蛤蟆不得了。

鱼网设备为捕鱼，蛤蟆入网空怜渠。求的安顺夫婿好，得这蛤蟆怎么了。

二子乘舟

二子乘舟①，泛泛其景②。愿言思子，中心养养③。
二子乘舟，泛泛其逝。愿言思子，不瑕有害。

【注释】

①二子乘舟：卫宣公夺娶了世子伋的妻，生了寿和朔，想杀死伋，立寿做世子，派伋去坐船，叫船夫翻船淹死伋。寿知道了，就同伋一起去乘船，船夫因此不敢翻船。　②泛泛：浮水。景：同"憬"，远行貌。③养养：忧貌。

【译文】

两位公子去坐船，飘浮河上去得远。思念啊思念两公子，心里很是忧愁。

两位公子趁船来，飘浮河上去不还。思念啊思念两公子，该不会有危害。

鄘 风

见《邶风》。

柏 舟

泛彼柏舟,在彼中河。髧彼两髦①,实维我仪②。之死矢靡它③!母也天只,不谅人只④!

泛彼柏舟,在彼河侧。髧彼两髦,实维我特⑤。之死矢靡慝⑥!母也天只,不谅人只!

【注释】

①髧(dàn 淡):发垂貌。当时头发上戴帽,帽上挂两块耳塞,头发也分成两股。两髦(máo 毛):即把头发分成两股。 ②仪:配偶,对象。 ③之:到。矢:誓。靡:无。 ④只:语助词。 ⑤特:同"仪"。 ⑥慝(tè 特):邪恶。

【译文】

浮荡水中柏木船,浮在河中水泱泱。那人头发分两边,实是我的好对象。到死发誓没他心!母亲也像天那样,不体谅人呀怎么样!

浮荡水中柏木船,在那河边好浮荡。那人头发分两边,实是我的好对象。到死发誓不变心!母亲也像天那样,不体谅人啊怎么样!

诗经

墙 有 茨

墙有茨①，不可扫也。中冓之言②，不可道也。所可道也，言之丑也。

墙有茨，不可襄也③。中冓之言，不可详也。所可详也，言之长也。

墙有茨，不可束也。中冓之言，不可读也。所可读也，言之辱也。

【注释】

①茨（cí 词）：蒺藜，一年生草本植物，果实有刺。 ②中冓（gòu 构）：宫中。 ③襄：除去。

【译文】

墙上有蒺藜草，不可以来扫。宫中的话，不可以向外传道。如可以向外传道，说了使人害臊。

墙上有蒺藜草，不可以除掉。宫中的话，不可以详细讲。如可以详细讲，说的内容也太长。

墙上有蒺藜草，不可以捆束。宫中的话，不可以接触。如可以接触，说来都是耻辱。

君子偕老

君子偕老①，副笄六珈②。委委佗佗③，如山如河。象服是宜④，子之不淑，云如之何。

玼兮玼兮⑤，其之翟也。鬒发如云⑥，不屑髢也⑦。玉之瑱也⑧，象之揥也⑨，扬且之晳也⑩。胡然而天也，胡然而帝也。

瑳兮瑳兮⑪，其之展也⑫。蒙彼绉绤，是绁袢也⑬。子之清扬⑭，扬且之颜也⑮。展如之人兮⑯，邦之媛也⑰。

【注释】

①君子：指卫宣公。 ②副：指首饰。笄（jī 鸡）：簪子，插在发中的。六珈（jiā 家）：加在簪子上的珠宝。 ③委委佗佗（tuó 驮）：庄重又雍容。 ④象服：绘画的衣服。 ⑤玼（cǐ 此）：鲜明。 ⑥鬒（zhěn 诊）：黑发。 ⑦髢（dí 狄）：假发。 ⑧瑱（tiàn 掭）：垂在两耳旁的玉。 ⑨揥（tì 替）：发钗类首饰。 ⑩扬：眉上广。皙（xī 析）：白。 ⑪瑳（cuō 搓）：鲜白。 ⑫展：礼服。 ⑬绁袢（xiè fán 屑烦）：夏天穿的白色内衣。 ⑭扬：视清明。 ⑮扬：额角。 ⑯展：诚。 ⑰媛：美女。

【译文】

宣公和你同到老，首饰玉簪加六宝。行走庄重态雍容，思如河深貌山崇。华服上身真充融，你的为人不善良，说的又是怎么样。

衣鲜艳啊真鲜艳，绣上雉毛真是艳。黑发如云何等美，不屑用那假发佩。美玉耳环垂两边，象牙发插发最妍，额头宽广又白皙，怎么好像个天仙，怎么好像天帝升上乾。

美丽啊真美丽，她的礼服真美丽。罩上她的薄纹衣，是夏天穿的白内衣。你的眉清目秀，额角丰满是天授。诚像你这人啊，是国中的美人。

桑 中

爰采唐矣①，沬之乡矣②。云谁之思？美孟姜矣③。期我乎桑中④，要我乎上宫⑤，送我乎淇之上矣⑥。

爰采麦矣，沬之北矣。云谁之思？美孟弋矣。期我乎桑中，要我乎上宫，送我乎淇之上矣。

爰采葑矣⑦，沬之东矣。云谁之思？美孟庸矣。期我乎桑中，要我乎上宫，送我乎淇之上矣。

【注释】

①爰：于何，在什么地方。唐：菟丝子，寄生蔓草，比喻女方依靠男方。　②沬（mèi 妹）：卫邑名。　③孟：兄弟姊妹中排行最长的。姜是齐国女；弋（yì 亦），杞女；庸在沬东，孟庸，指庸族的长女，嫁给卫国的。　④桑中：地名。　⑤要（yāo 腰）：邀。上宫：地名。⑥淇：水名，源出河南林县，流至淇县入卫河。　⑦葑：芜菁。

【译文】

在什么地方采菟丝子，在那个沬乡。说是想那个呢？想的是美丽的孟姜，她约我在桑中，她邀我在上宫，她在淇水上把我送。

在什么地方采麦，在沬邑的北乡。说是想那个呢？想美丽的弋家大姑娘。她约我在桑中，她邀我在上宫，她在淇水上把我送。

在什么地方采芜菁，在沬邑的沬乡东。说想什么人呢？想美丽的孟庸。她约我在桑中，她邀我到上宫，她在淇水上把我送。

鹑之奔奔

鹑之奔奔①，鹊之彊彊②。人之无良，我以为兄。鹊之彊彊，鹑之奔奔。人之无良，我以为君。

【注释】

①鹑(chún 淳)：鹑鹑。奔奔：指居有常匹，飞则相随貌。　②彊彊（jiāng jiāng 江江）：与"奔奔"相似。

【译文】

雌鹑跟着雄鹑飞，雌鹊跟着雄鹊飞。男人却是不良善，我为什么当作兄长看。雌鹊跟着雄鹊飞，雌鹑跟着雄鹑飞。男人却是不良善，我为什么当作君主看。

定之方中

定之方中①，作于楚宫②。揆之以日③，作于楚室④。树之榛栗，椅桐梓漆⑤，爰伐琴瑟。

升彼虚矣⑥，以望楚矣。望楚与堂⑦，景山与京⑧。降观于桑，卜云其吉，终然允臧⑨。

灵雨既零⑩，命彼倌人⑪，星言夙驾⑫，说于桑田⑬。匪直也人⑭，秉心塞渊，騋牝三千⑮。

【注释】

①定：星名，叫营室。此星认为在夏历十月可以营造宫室。　②楚宫：楚丘的宫。　③揆（kuí 葵）：度量太阳的出来和没落来定方向。　④楚室：整齐的房室，楚指整齐。　⑤榛、栗、椅、桐、梓、漆：皆树名。　⑥虚：指漕邑为墟，即荒废了。　⑦楚与堂：楚丘与堂邑。　⑧景山与京：大山与高丘。　⑨臧（zāng 赃）：善，好。　⑩灵雨：好雨。零：落下。　⑪倌（guān 官）人：驾车的人。　⑫星：晴。《韩诗》："星，精

也。"精,晴明。夙:早。 ⑬说(shuì 税):通"税",停止。 ⑭匪直:不特。 ⑮骒(lái 来):七尺以上的马。牝(pìn 聘):母马。

【译文】

营室星儿正当中,十月造筑楚丘宫。按照太阳定方向,后造居室兴冲冲。种的榛树兼有栗,还种椅桐和梓漆,于是好伐作琴瑟。

登那漕邑已成墟,望见楚丘可定居。再望楚丘与堂邑,大山高丘相和集。下来观察那种桑,占卜都说这里吉,终于是善好居地。

好雨既下水涓涓,命令那个驾车员,天晴早早把车驾,把车停在种桑田。不特劝农耕好田,用心充实又深远,七尺雌马繁殖到三千。

蝃 蝀

蝃蝀在东①,莫之敢指。女子有行②,远父母兄弟。
朝隮于西③,崇朝其雨④。女子有行,远兄弟父母。
乃如之人也,怀昏姻也。大无信也⑤,不知命也⑥。

【注释】

①蝃蝀(dì dōng 帝东):彩虹。 ②行:指出嫁。 ③隮(jī 鸡):彩云。 ④崇朝:终朝。 ⑤无信:无媒妁之言。 ⑥不知命:不知父母之命。

【译文】

彩虹出在东方啊,没有人敢指点它。姑娘要出嫁,远远离开父母兄弟家。

早上彩云出在西,整个早晨在下雨。姑娘要出嫁,远远离开兄弟父母家。

是这样的人呀,想念婚嫁呀。太没有信,不知道父母的命。

相 鼠

相鼠有皮,人而无仪①。人而无仪,不死何为?
相鼠有齿,人而无止②。人而无止,不死何俟?
相鼠有体,人而无礼。人而无礼,胡不遄死③?

【注释】

①仪:威仪,使人尊敬的仪表。 ②止:容止,行动的所止,指遵守礼法。 ③遄(chuán 船):快。

【译文】

观察老鼠有皮,人却没有威仪。人而没有威仪,不死还干什么呢?

观察老鼠有齿,人却没有行止。人而没有行止,等待什么还不死?

观察老鼠有体,人却没有礼。人而没有礼,何不赶快死去?

干 旄

孑孑干旄①,在浚之郊②。素丝纰之③,良马四之。彼姝者子,何以畀之④。

孑孑干旟⑤,在浚之都。素丝组之,良马五之。彼姝者子，何以予之。

孑孑干旌⑥，在浚之城。素丝祝之⑦，良马六之。彼姝者子，何以告之。

【注释】

①孑孑（jié jié 杰杰）：特出貌。干：旗杆。旄（máo 毛）：旄牛尾做旗，旄牛即为氂牛。　②浚（jùn 峻）：卫地名。　③纰（pí 皮）：把旗的边上用线缝好。　④畀（bì 闭）：给与。　⑤旟（yú 鱼）：画有鹰隼的旗。　⑥旌（jīng 精）：上用野鸡毛装饰的旗。　⑦祝：连结。

【译文】

特出的干挂氂牛尾旗，走在浚邑的郊区。用白丝线把旗边缝好，用好马四匹做前驱。那个美好的人呀，拿什么来送给他呀。

特出的干挂画隼鸟旗，走在浚邑的都市里。用白丝线把旗边缝好，用好马五匹做前驱。那个美好的人呀，拿什么来送给他呀。

特出的干挂鸟羽旗，走在浚邑的城区。用白丝线把旗边缝好，用好马六匹做前驱。那个美好的人呀，拿什么来告诉这个人呀。

载　驰

载驰载驱，归唁卫侯①。驱马悠悠②，言至于漕。大夫跋涉，我心则忧。

既不我嘉③，不能旋反④。视尔不臧，我思不远。

既不我嘉，不能旋济⑤。视尔不臧，我思不閟⑥。

陟彼阿丘⑦，言采其蝱⑧。女子善怀，亦各有行⑨。许人尤之⑩，众稚且狂⑪。

我行其野，芃芃其麦⑫。控于大邦，谁因谁极⑬？大夫君子，无我有尤。百尔所思，不如我所之。

【注释】

①唁（yàn 厌）：吊问失国。 ②悠悠：遥远。 ③嘉：好。 ④旋：转车。 ⑤济：止。 ⑥閟（bì 必）：同"毖"，慎。 ⑦阿丘：有一边高的山丘。 ⑧蝱（méng 萌）：贝母药。 ⑨行：道路，指主张。 ⑩尤：指过错。 ⑪众：通"终"，既是。 ⑫芃芃（péng péng 蓬蓬）：茂盛。 ⑬极：急。

【译文】

赶车赶马快些走，回来吊问失国的卫侯。赶着马儿走远路，走到漕邑还不留。大夫赶来阻止我，使我心里发忧愁。

既然对我不赞成，要我回去我不能。看你想法都不好，我的想法岂不深。

既然对我不赞成，要我转回我不能。看你想法都不好，我的想法岂不慎。

登上那个阿丘，采点贝母来解忧。女人善于怀想，也各有主张。许国大夫责备我，既是幼稚又发狂。

我走到卫国的原野，看见麦子正猛长。我求大国来相帮，靠谁谁能急着来帮？大夫君子们，不要指责我有过错。百种法子是你们所想，不如我亲自所往。

卫 风

见《邶风》注。

淇 奥

瞻彼淇奥①,绿竹猗猗②。有匪君子③,如切如磋④,如琢如磨⑤。瑟兮僩兮⑥,赫兮咺兮⑦。有匪君子,终不可谖兮⑧。

瞻彼淇奥,绿竹青青。有匪君子,充耳琇莹⑨,会弁如星⑩。瑟兮僩兮,赫兮咺兮。有匪君子,终不可谖兮。

瞻彼淇奥,绿竹如箦⑪。有匪君子,如金如锡,如圭如璧。宽兮绰兮⑫。猗重较兮⑬。善戏谑兮⑭,不为虐兮。

【注释】

①奥:弯曲处。 ②猗猗:长而美。 ③匪:通"斐",文采。 ④切磋:治骨曰切,治象牙曰磋。 ⑤琢磨:治玉曰琢,治石曰磨。 ⑥瑟:庄严貌。僩(xiàn 现):宽大貌。 ⑦赫:威严貌。咺(xuān 喧):威仪。 ⑧谖(xuān 宣):忘。 ⑨琇(xiù 秀):宝石。莹:光彩。 ⑩会弁(biàn 便):鹿皮帽接合处。如星:会合处缀上宝石如星。 ⑪箦(zé 则):积,郁积。 ⑫绰:旷达。 ⑬猗:通"倚"。重较:相重复的车厢横木。 ⑭戏谑:开玩笑。

【译文】

看那淇水弯曲处,绿竹美盛有秩序。这个文雅的君子人,如切如磋治骨器,如雕玉石美如许。庄严啊宽大啊,烜赫啊威仪啊。这个文雅的君子人,终于教人不可忘掉他。

看那淇水湾曲处,绿竹青青有秩序。这个文雅的君子人,耳瑱美玉光莹莹,帽缝宝玉有如星。庄严啊宽大啊,烜赫啊威仪啊。这个文雅的君子人,终于不可忘掉他。

看那淇水湾曲处,绿竹郁积有秩序。这个文雅的君子人,像金像锡般贵重,像圭像璧美如许。宽广啊阔绰啊,像依靠车子重较啊。善于对人们作戏谑,不去对人们作暴虐。

考 槃

考槃在涧①,硕人之宽②。独寐寤言③,永矢弗谖。
考槃在阿④,硕人之薖⑤。独寐寤歌,永矢弗过。
考槃在陆,硕人之轴⑥。独寐寤宿,永矢弗告。

【注释】

①考:成就。槃(pán 盘):快乐。 ②宽:放松。 ③寐:睡。寤:睡醒。 ④阿:山的曲隅。 ⑤薖(kē 科):快活。 ⑥轴:宽舒。

【译文】

快乐成就在涧中,高大人儿心宽松。独睡独醒独自语,永远发誓不忘记。

快乐成就在山阿,高大人儿快活多。独睡独醒独唱歌,永远发誓不错过。

诗经

快乐成就在平陆,高大人儿心快乐。独睡独醒独自卧,永远发誓弗告诉。

硕 人

硕人其颀①,衣锦褧衣②。齐侯之子,卫侯之妻,东宫之妹③,邢侯之姨,谭公维私④。

手如柔荑⑤,肤如凝脂,领如蝤蛴⑥,齿如瓠犀⑦,螓首蛾眉⑧。巧笑倩兮⑨,美目盼兮⑩。

硕人敖敖⑪,说于农郊。四牡有骄,朱幩镳镳⑫,翟茀以朝⑬。大夫夙退,无使君劳。

河水洋洋,北流活活⑭,施罛濊濊⑮,鳣鲔发发⑯,葭菼揭揭⑰。庶姜孽孽⑱,庶士有朅⑲。

【注释】

①硕人:高大的美人。颀(qí 其):指高。 ②褧(jiǒng 炯):布罩衣。穿锦衣的人,要穿布罩衣。 ③东宫:指齐国的太子宫。 ④私:古时女子称姊妹之丈夫为私。 ⑤荑:茅草芽。 ⑥蝤蛴(qiú qí 囚齐):天牛红虫,色白身长。 ⑦瓠犀:瓠瓜的子,白而整齐。 ⑧螓(qín 秦):以蝉而小,头宽广正方。蛾眉:蚕蛾的触角,细长而曲。 ⑨倩:笑靥美好貌。 ⑩盼:望,指眼波流动。 ⑪敖敖:身高貌。 ⑫幩(fén 坟):帛绢,用在马口上,使不汗。镳镳(biāo biāo 标标):马嚼子。马衔两旁的铁饰称镳。镳镳,盛美貌。 ⑬翟茀(fú 弗):野鸡毛羽作车后的装饰。 ⑭活活(guō guō 郭郭):水流声。 ⑮罛(gū 孤):大鱼网。濊濊(huò huò 或或):撒网入水声。 ⑯鳣(zhān 毡):鲤鱼。鲔(wěi 委):鲟鱼。发发(bō bō 波波):

鱼跳跃声。　⑰葭菼（jiā tǎn　家坦）：初生芦苇和荻。揭揭（jiē jiē　孑孑）：长貌。　⑱孽孽（niè niè　聂聂）：盛饰貌。　⑲朅（qiè　怯）：勇武貌。

【译文】

　　高大美人实在高，身穿锦衣布衣罩。是齐侯的女儿，又是卫侯的妻，是齐太子的亲妹妹，邢国侯的小姨，谭公是她的妹婿。

　　手指像初生的柔荑，皮肤像凝结的白脂，头颈像白而长的蝤蛴，牙齿整齐得像那瓠瓜子，方正前额细弯眉。巧妙笑时酒窝好，美目盼时眼波俏。

　　高大美人面貌妙，车子停止在近郊。四匹雄马气势骄，红色带子马勒飘，手拿雉羽来上朝。大夫可以早退朝，不要使君主多辛劳。

　　黄河流水满洋洋，向北流势波浟浟，鱼网撒在水中央，鳣鱼鲔鱼忙乱跳，芦苇荻梗正猛长。庶姜陪嫁盛饰忙，庶士护送也逞强。

氓

　　氓之蚩蚩①，抱布贸丝。匪来贸丝，来即我谋。送子涉淇，至于顿丘②。匪我愆期③，子无良媒。将子无怒④，秋以为期。

　　乘彼垝垣⑤，以望复关⑥。不见复关，泣涕涟涟⑦。既见复关，载笑载言⑧。尔卜尔筮⑨，体无咎言⑩。以尔车来，以我贿迁⑪。

　　桑之未落，其叶沃若⑫。于嗟鸠兮，无食桑葚⑬。于嗟女兮，无与士耽⑭。士之耽兮，犹可说也⑮。女之耽兮，不可说也。

桑之落兮,其黄而陨⑯。自我徂尔⑰,三岁食贫。淇水汤汤⑱,渐车帷裳⑲。女也不爽⑳,士贰其行㉑。士也罔极㉒,二三其德。

三岁为妇,靡室劳矣。夙兴夜寐,靡有朝矣。言既遂矣,至于暴矣。兄弟不知,咥其笑矣㉓。静言思之,躬自悼矣。

及尔偕老,老使我怨。淇则有岸,隰则有泮㉔。总角之宴㉕,言笑晏晏㉖。信誓旦旦㉗,不思其反㉘。反是不思,亦已焉哉。

【注释】

①氓（méng）：民。蚩蚩（chī chī 吃吃）：戏笑貌。 ②顿丘：卫地名。 ③愆（qiān 千）：错过。 ④将：请。 ⑤垝（guǐ 诡）垣：毁坏的墙。 ⑥复关：地名,氓所居地。 ⑦涟涟（lián lián 连连）：眼泪连接貌。 ⑧载：则。 ⑨筮（shì 是）：用蓍草占吉凶。 ⑩体：卜卦的征兆。咎言：不吉的话。 ⑪贿（huǐ 悔）：财物,指嫁妆。 ⑫沃若：润泽貌。 ⑬葚（shèn 慎）：桑树所结果实。 ⑭耽（dān 单）：乐过其节,极爱。 ⑮说：通"脱",摆脱。 ⑯陨（yǔn 允）：落下。 ⑰徂（cú 殂）：往。 ⑱汤汤（shāng shāng 商商）：水多貌。 ⑲渐（jiān 尖）：沾湿。 ⑳爽：失,差。 ㉑贰：有二心。 ㉒罔极：不可测。 ㉓咥（xì 戏）：大笑貌。 ㉔隰（xí 席）：水名,即漯（luò 洛）河。泮（pàn 判）：岸。 ㉕总角：古时儿童两边梳辫,如双角,指童年。宴：欢乐。 ㉖晏晏：和柔。 ㉗旦旦：诚恳貌。 ㉘反：反覆。已：止。

【译文】

那人前来笑嘻嘻,抱着布匹来换丝。不是真的来换丝,来前找我谈婚辞。送你渡过淇水去,到了顿丘分别伊。不是我误了婚期,是你没有请好媒。请你不要生怒气,清秋时节是佳期。

登上那坏墙头,用来望那复关。没有看见复关,哭泣得眼泪接连。既然看见复关,又是笑来又发言。你已卜吉又请筮,卦上没有不祥话。用你的车子来,把我嫁妆运一回。

桑叶没有落下时,叶儿润泽又繁盛。可叹那小斑鸠啊,不要吃那桑葚。可叹那姑娘啊,不要同男人爱过分。男人的爱过分,要摆脱还可以讲。姑娘的爱过分,要摆脱不可以讲。

桑树的叶儿落了啊,叶儿枯黄往下掉。自从我到你家来,三年贫困过不少。当年淇水满洋洋,打湿车里帷子和下裳。我的心思不变样,你的行为却两样。男人心思不可测,三心两意也算德。

三年做个媳妇了,没有家事不辛劳。早起晚睡过惯了,没有一天息过朝。说是既经遂心了,你的态度变凶暴。兄弟对此不知道,看见我时只是笑。静静地细细想一回,自身独个儿自伤悼。

原想和你同到老,老使我怨终不断。淇水洋洋有个岸,湿水长长也有岸。我们小时的快乐,说说笑笑是一贯。山盟海誓岂不算,不想从前多灿烂。从前灿烂你不想,也是罢了莫再讲。

竹 竿

籊籊竹竿①,以钓于淇。岂不尔思,远莫致之。
泉源在左②,淇水在右。女子有行,远兄弟父母。
淇水在右,泉源在左。巧笑之瑳③,佩玉之傩④。
淇水滺滺⑤,桧楫松舟。驾言出游,以写我忧。

【注释】

①簜簜（dí dí 狄）：长而尖貌。 ②泉：指百泉，在卫的西北，东南流入淇水。 ③瑳（cuō 磋）：玉色鲜白。 ④傩（nuó 挪）：有节奏。 ⑤滺滺（yóu yóu 由由）：水流貌。

【译文】

钓鱼竹竿长又尖，用来垂钓淇水边。岂有不是这样想，莫能达到道路长。

泉水源头在左边，淇水河流在右边。姑娘自从出嫁后，远离兄弟父母前。

淇河水流在右边，泉水源头在左边。巧妙笑时齿鲜白，佩玉行动声接连。

淇河之水长长流，桧树做楫松做舟。坐着轻舟来出游，用来舒写心中忧。

芄 兰

芄兰之支①，童子佩觿②。虽则佩觿，能不我知。容兮遂兮③，垂带悸兮④。

芄兰之叶，童子佩韘⑤。虽则佩韘，能不我甲⑥。容兮遂兮，垂带悸兮。

【注释】

①芄（wán 丸）兰：植物名，一名萝藦，蔓生。支：枝条。②觿（xī 希）：解结的用具，用象骨制，形如锥。 ③容：容仪。遂：成就。 ④悸：带下垂貌。 ⑤韘（shè 涉）：钩弦用具，射

箭时用，象骨制。　⑥甲：一作"狎"。

【译文】

芄兰的枝，像童子佩带的象锥。虽则像象锥，能够不同我相知。有容仪啊有成就啊，带子下垂都有样啊。

芄兰的叶子，像童子佩带的象钩。虽则像象钩，能够不同我亲狎。有容仪啊有成就啊，带子下垂都有样啊。

河 广

谁谓河广①，一苇杭之②。谁谓宋远，跂余望之③。
谁谓河广，曾不容刀④。谁谓宋远，曾不崇朝⑤。

【注释】

①河：指黄河。　②一苇：指黄河的广，一束芦苇可以航行，杭：通"航"。　③跂（qì 气）：踮起脚尖。　④刀：通"舠"，指小船。　⑤崇朝：终朝，来回不过一个早晨。

【译文】

谁说黄河太宽广，一束芦苇可以航。谁说宋国太遥远，踮起脚来可以望。

谁说黄河太宽广，竟然容不下一小舠。谁说宋国太遥远，竟然不到一终朝。

伯 兮

伯兮朅兮①，邦之杰兮。伯也执殳②，为王前驱。

自伯之东③,首如飞蓬④。岂无膏沐⑤,谁适为容⑥?
其雨其雨,杲杲日出⑦。愿言思伯,甘心首疾。
焉得谖草⑧,言树之背⑨。愿言思伯,使我心痗⑩。

【注释】

①伯:老大。朅(qiè 妾):威武。 ②殳(shū 书):古兵器,杖类,长丈二而无刃。 ③之:往。 ④飞蓬:乱飞的蓬草。 ⑤膏沐:化妆用的油脂。 ⑥谁适为容:为谁修饰打扮。 ⑦杲杲(gǎo gǎo 搞搞):阳光强烈貌。 ⑧谖(xuān 萱)草:即萱草,亦称忘忧草。 ⑨背:指北堂。 ⑩痗(mèi 妹):病。

【译文】

老大啊,勇武啊,是国内的英杰啊。老大拿着丈二棒,为了周王当前锋。

自从老大亲往东,我的头发像飞蓬。难道没有脂和油,为谁修饰为谁容?

该下雨该下雨,一轮红日高高出。愿意说是念老大,头脑发病甘受害。

怎么得到忘忧草,说是种在北堂好。愿意说是念老大,使我心里受病害。

有 狐

有狐绥绥①,在彼淇梁②。心之忧矣,之子无裳③。
有狐绥绥,在彼淇厉④。心之忧矣,之子无带。
有狐绥绥,在彼淇侧。心之忧矣,之子无服。

【注释】

①狐:一说狐比喻男性。绥绥:指独自行走。 ②梁:桥。 ③裳:下裳,指裤子。 ④厉:河水深,摆渡处。

【译文】

有只狐狸独自走,在那淇水桥边头。我的心里直发愁,这人裤儿也没有。

有只狐狸独自走,在那淇水摆渡口。我的心里直发愁,这人带子也没有。

有只狐狸独自走,在那淇水旁边头。我的心里直发愁,这人衣服也没有。

木 瓜

投我以木瓜①,报之以琼琚②。匪报也,永以为好也。
投我以木桃③,报之以琼瑶。匪报也,永以为好也。
投我以木李④,报之以琼玖。匪报也,永以为好也。

【注释】

①木瓜:植物名,落叶灌木或乔木,果实秋成熟,椭圆,有香气,经蒸煮或蜜渍后供食用。 ②琼琚(jū 居):指美玉。 ③木桃:指榠子。榠子似梨而酸涩。因此一说木桃即指榠子,因生于桃树,故称木。 ④木李:即榠楂,与木瓜相似,比木瓜大而色黄。因此有人即以木李为李子,因生在李树上,故加木。

【译文】

他送我用木瓜,用美玉报答他。不是答报,是永远作为相好。
他送我用木桃,报答他用琼瑶。不是答报,是永远作为相好。
他送我用木李,报答他用琼玖。不是答报,是永远作为相好。

王 风

周公建立洛邑,是谓东都。后来幽王失掉西周,他的儿子东迁洛邑,是谓东周。迁居洛邑王城的诗称为王风,即王国的诗。

黍 离

彼黍离离①,彼稷之苗②。行迈靡靡③,中心摇摇④。知我者谓我心忧,不知我者谓我何求。悠悠苍天,此何人哉!

彼黍离离,彼稷之穗。行迈靡靡,中心如醉。知我者谓我心忧,不知我者谓我何求。悠悠苍天,此何人哉!

彼黍离离,彼稷之实。行迈靡靡,中心如噎⑤。知我者谓我心忧,不知我者谓我何求。悠悠苍天,此何人哉!

【注释】

①黍(shǔ 暑):黍子,草本植物,子实淡黄色,去皮后叫黄米,煮熟后有黏性。离离:行列貌。 ②稷(jì 寂):高粱。 ③靡靡:行步迟缓貌。 ④摇摇:心神不安。 ⑤噎(yē 掖):气逆不顺。

【译文】

那个黍子长成行列,那个高粱正在长苗。走路慢慢地走,心里头不安地摇摇。知道我的人说我心在发愁,不知道我的人说我有什么要求。遥远的苍天啊,这是什么人造成的啊!

诗经

那个黍子长成行列,那个高粱正在抽穗。走路慢慢地走,心中像喝醉了酒。知道我的人说我心在发愁,不知道我的人说我有什么要求。遥远的苍天啊,这是什么人造成的啊!

那个黍子长成行列,那个高粱正在结实。走路慢慢地走,心中好像气逆发咽。知道我的人说我心发愁,不知道我的人说我有什么要求。遥远的苍天啊,这是什么人造成的啊!

君子于役

君子于役①,不知其期,曷至哉?鸡栖于埘②,日之夕矣,羊牛下来。君子于役,如之何勿思?

君子于役,不日不月,曷其有佸③?鸡栖于桀④,日之夕矣,羊牛下括⑤。君子于役,苟无饥渴!

【注释】

①役:服劳役。　②埘(shí 时):墙上挖洞做鸡窠。　③佸(huó 活):会合。　④桀:木桩。　⑤括(kuò 扩):来。

【译文】

先生在服劳役,不知他的期限,何时回来啊?鸡飞上窠,太阳下了山,羊牛下来。先生在服劳役,怎么不想一回?

先生在服劳役,不讲日子不讲月,怎么能够求会合?鸡栖息在小木桩,太阳下了山,牛羊下来。先生在服劳役,愿他没有饥和渴!

君子阳阳

君子阳阳①,左执簧②,右招我由房③。其乐只且!
君子陶陶④,左执翿⑤,右招我由敖。其乐只且!

【注释】

①阳阳:快乐。 ②簧:指笙,古代的乐器。笙以簧为舌。 ③由房:通"游敖",指游戏。 ④陶陶:和乐貌。 ⑤翿(dào 道):即纛,羽毛做的舞具。

【译文】

先生喜洋洋,左手拿着笙簧,右手招我去游逛。他的快乐无量!

先生乐陶陶,左手拿着羽毛舞纛,右手招我出游遨。他真快乐逍遥!

扬之水

扬之水①,不流束薪。彼其之子②,不与我戍申③。怀哉怀哉,曷月予还归哉?

扬之水,不流束楚。彼其之子,不与我戍甫。怀哉怀哉,曷月予还归哉?

扬之水,不流束蒲。彼其之子,不与我戍许。怀哉怀哉,曷月予还归哉?

【注释】

①扬：激扬。　②其：或作"己"，今按"己"译。　③戍：守卫。申、甫、许：皆地名。

【译文】

激扬翻腾的河水，一束薪不流去。那个自己乡里的人，不同我去守申。想念啊想念啊，哪月我还能回去啊？

激扬翻腾的河水，一捆柴不流去。那个自己乡里的人，不同我守甫。想念啊想念啊，哪月我还能回去。

激扬翻腾的河水，一捆蒲草不流去。那个自己乡里的人，不同我守许。怀念啊怀念啊，哪月我还能回去啊？

中谷有蓷

中谷有蓷①，暵其干矣②。有女仳离③，嘅其叹矣④。嘅其叹矣，遇人之艰难矣。

中谷有蓷，暵其脩矣⑤。有女仳离，条其歗矣⑥。条其歗矣，遇人之不淑矣。

中谷有蓷，暵其湿矣⑦。有女仳离，啜其泣矣⑧。啜其泣矣，何嗟及矣。

【注释】

①蓷（tuī 推）：益母草。　②暵（hàn 汉）：干燥。　③仳（pǐ 痞）离：离弃。　④嘅（kǎi 凯）：叹息。　⑤脩（xiū 休）：干肉，因指干。　⑥条：指长。歗（xiào 啸）：痛声。　⑦湿："曝（qì

泣)"的假借,干。 ⑧啜(chuò 辍):哭泣时抽噎。

【译文】

谷中长有益母草,干燥它又再求干。有女离弃伤心肝,感慨伤心又长叹。感慨伤心又长叹,嫁个男人真艰难。

谷中长有益母草,干燥它又长求干。有女离弃伤心肝,长长的有她的痛苦。长长的有她的痛苦,嫁了个人真不妥。

谷中长有益母草,干燥它变湿力求干。有女离弃伤心肝,呜咽哭泣伤心极。呜咽哭泣伤心极,怎么嗟叹来不及。

兔 爰

有兔爰爰①,雉离于罗②。我生之初,尚无为③,我生之后,逢此百罹。尚寐无吪④!

有兔爰爰,雉离于罦⑤。我生之初,尚无造⑥,我生之后,逢此百忧。尚寐无觉!

有兔爰爰,雉离于罿⑦。我生之初,尚无庸⑧,我生之后,逢此百凶。尚寐无聪!

【注释】

①爰爰:解网放纵。 ②离:同"罹",入网。罗:网。 ③无为:无所作为。 ④吪(é 俄):说话。 ⑤罦(fú 浮):捕鸟网。 ⑥造:造祸。 ⑦罿(tóng 童):捕鸟网。 ⑧庸:用,与"造"同。

【译文】

有兔脱网游不绝,野鸡入网网不裂。我的生活开始时,无所作为少磨折,我的生活到后来,碰到百种的磨折。还是睡着无可说!

有兔脱网好优游,野鸡入网无限愁。我的生活开始时,还是无事少闻祸,我的生活到后来,碰到这样百种忧。还是睡着才算休!

有兔脱网往前冲,野鸡陷在罗网中。我的生活开始时,还是无事天下同,我的生活到后来,碰到这样百种凶。还是睡着耳不聪!

葛藟

绵绵葛藟①,在河之浒②。终远兄弟,谓他人父。谓他人父,亦莫我顾。

绵绵葛藟,在河之涘③。终远兄弟,谓他人母。谓他人母,亦莫我有④。

绵绵葛藟,在河之漘⑤。终远兄弟,谓他人昆。谓他人昆,亦莫我闻⑥。

【注释】

①绵绵:长不断绝。葛藟(lěi 垒):蔓草名,见《诗·周南·樛木》。 ②浒(hǔ 虎):水边。 ③涘(sì 似):水边。 ④有:通"友"。 ⑤漘(chún 唇):水边。 ⑥闻:与"问"通。

【译文】

长长的野葛茎,在河的边上生。终于远离兄弟们,叫他人父。叫他人父,也没有对我照顾。

长长的野葛茎,在河的边上生。终于远离兄弟们,叫他人娘。叫他人娘,也没有对我抚养。

长长的野葛茎,在河的边上生。终于远离兄弟们,叫他人兄。叫他人兄,也没有对我问穷。

采 葛

彼采葛兮,一日不见,如三月兮。
彼采萧兮①,一日不见,如三秋兮②。
彼采艾兮,一日不见,如三岁兮。

【注释】

①萧:植物名,即青蒿,有香气。 ②三秋:三个秋天,一个秋天三个月,三个秋天即九个月。

【译文】

那个采葛啊,一天不见,好比隔了三个月啊。
那个采青蒿啊,一天不见,好比隔了三个秋啊。
那个采艾啊,一天不见,好比隔了三年啊。

大 车

大车槛槛①,毳衣如菼②。岂不尔思,畏子不敢。
大车啍啍③,毳衣如璊④。岂不尔思,畏子不奔。
穀则异室⑤,死则同穴。谓予不信,有如皦日⑥。

【注释】

①大车：姚际恒说是牛车。槛槛（kǎn kǎn 砍砍）：指车声。　②毳（cuì 脆）衣：车上蔽风雨的毡子。菼（tǎn 毯）：初生的芦苇花。　③啍啍（tūn tūn 吞吞）：指车慢而笨重的声音。　④璊（mén 门）：赤色的玉。⑤穀：活着。　⑥皦：同"皎"，光明。

【译文】

槛槛发声是牛车，车毡有似芦苇花。岂有我不想念你，怕你不敢成一家。

牛车开得慢又重，车毡颜色像玉红。岂有我不想念你，怕你出奔不相从。

活着住的不同房，死了同你在一坑。说我说话不可信，有这高高的太阳。

丘中有麻

丘中有麻，彼留子嗟①。彼留子嗟，将其来施施②。

丘中有麦，彼留国国。彼留子国，将其来食。

丘中有李，彼留之子。彼留之子，贻我佩玖。

【注释】

①彼留子嗟：彼是留子嗟，留子嗟是人名。　②将：请，愿。施施：高兴貌。

【译文】

土丘中间有苎麻,他是留子嗟。他是留子嗟,愿他高兴地来吧。
土丘中间有小麦,他是留子国。他是留子国,愿他快来谋吃食。
土丘中间有李树,他是留的子。他是留的子,他把美玉向我赠。

卷 三

国 风

郑 风

郑，国名。初本在今陕西西安附近，后徙封于新邑，即今河南新郑，成皋、荥阳虎牢之地，岩险闻天下。

缁 衣

缁衣之宜兮①，敝予又改为兮②。适子之馆兮③，还予授子之粲兮④。

缁衣之好兮，敝予又改造兮。适子之馆兮，还予授子之粲兮。

缁衣之席兮⑤，敝予又改作兮。适子之馆兮，还予授子之粲兮。

【注释】

①缁（zī 资）衣：黑衣。 ②敝：破坏。改为：改做。 ③馆：客舍。 ④粲：为"餐"之假借字。 ⑤席：宽，大。

【译文】

黑衣的适宜啊，破了我又替你改做啊。到你的客馆中啊，回来我送给你的饭啊。

黑衣的美好啊，破了我又替你改造啊。到你的客馆中啊，回来我送给你的饭啊。

黑衣的宽大啊，破了我又替你改做啊。到你的客馆中啊，回来我送给你的饭啊。

将 仲 子

将仲子兮①，无逾我里②，无折我树杞③。岂敢爱之，畏我父母。仲可怀也，父母之言，亦可畏也。

将仲子兮，无逾我墙，无折我树桑。岂敢爱之，畏我诸兄。仲可怀也，诸兄之言，亦可畏也。

将仲子兮，无逾我园，无折我树檀④。岂敢爱之，畏人之多言。仲可怀也，人之多言，亦可畏也。

【注释】

①将：请。　②逾：跨过。里：闾里。　③杞（qǐ 起）：杞柳，落叶乔木，像柳树，木质坚实。　④树杞、树桑、树檀：即杞树、桑树、檀树，倒文来押韵。

【译文】

请仲子啊，不要跨进我闾里，不要攀折我家的杞。难道我敢爱惜它，怕我爹娘要说话。仲子是可以怀念，爹娘的说话，也是可以害怕。

请仲子啊，不要跨过我家的墙，不要攀折我家的桑。难道我敢爱惜它，怕我的众兄长说话。仲子可以怀念，众位兄长的说话，也是可以害怕。

请仲子啊,不要跨进我家的园,不要攀折我家的檀。难道我敢爱惜它,怕旁人多说话。仲子可以怀念,旁人的多说话,也是可以害怕。

叔于田

叔于田①,巷无居人。岂无居人,不如叔也,洵美且仁。
叔于狩②,巷无饮酒。岂无饮酒,不如叔也,洵美且好。
叔适野,巷无服马③。岂无服马,不如叔也,洵美且武。

【注释】

①田:打猎。 ②狩:冬天打猎。 ③服马:用马驾车。

【译文】

叔在打猎,里巷内没有居住的人。难道没有居住的人,不像叔那样,确实美好并且慈仁。

叔去冬天打猎,闾巷没有人喝酒。难道没有人喝酒,不像叔那样,确实漂亮并且清秀。

叔在野外打猎,闾巷里没有人会驾马。难道没有人会驾马,不像叔那样,确实漂亮并且英武。

大叔于田

叔于田,乘乘马①。执辔如组,两骖如舞②。叔在薮③,火烈具举。襢裼暴虎④,献于公所。将叔无狃⑤,戒其伤女。

叔于田,乘乘黄。两服上襄⑥,两骖雁行。叔在薮,火烈具扬。叔善射忌,又良御忌,抑磬控忌⑦,抑纵送忌⑧。

叔于田，乘乘鸨⑨。两服齐首，两骖如手。叔在薮，火烈具阜。叔马慢忌，叔发罕忌，抑释掤忌⑩，抑鬯弓忌⑪。

【注释】

①乘乘：趁坐四匹马拉的车，后乘字指四匹马。 ②两骖（cān 参）：四匹马中外两匹叫骖马。 ③薮（sǒu 叟）：沼泽地，有水草处。 ④襢裼（tǎn xī 坦吸）：肉袒。暴虎：搏虎。 ⑤狃（niǔ 纽）：复。 ⑥两服：四匹马中间的两匹叫服马。上襄：并驾于前。 ⑦磬控：骋马曰磬，止马曰控。 ⑧纵送：发矢曰纵，从禽曰送。 ⑨鸨（bǎo 保）：黑白杂色马。 ⑩掤（bīng 兵）：箭筒盖。 ⑪鬯（chàng 唱）：弓囊。

【译文】

叔在打猎，趁着四匹马拉的车。手执缰绳像丝组，两匹旁马像在舞。叔在泽地边，猎火完全举起。赤膊空拳捉猛虎，献到公爷所。请叔不要再捉虎，谨戒它会害你真不妥。

叔在打猎，趁着拉车的四马毛色黄。两匹服马在中央，外面骖马像雁行。叔到草泽边，猎火都上扬。叔是善射的，又是好驾驶的，还是骋马止马的，还是发箭从禽的。

叔在打猎，趁的四匹驾车的马毛色杂。中间两匹服马齐头，旁边两匹骖马像两手。叔在薮泽上，猎火烧得旺。叔的马走得慢哩，叔的箭发少哩，还是把箭放进箭袋里，还是把弓放进弓袋里。

清 人

清人在彭，驷介旁旁①。二矛重英②，河上乎翱翔。

475

清人在消,驷介麃麃③。二矛重乔④,河上乎逍遥。
清人在轴,驷介陶陶。左旋右抽⑤,中军作好⑥。

【注释】

①驷介:四匹马披甲驾车。旁旁:强盛貌。 ②重英:以二重朱羽为矛饰。 ③麃麃(biāo biāo 标标):威武貌。 ④乔:雉羽。 ⑤旋:转车。抽:抽刀。 ⑥中军:指军中统帅。

【译文】

清地的兵在彭地,四匹马披甲很壮强。两支矛饰着二重红羽,在河上飞翔。

清地的兵在消地,四匹马披着甲极其骁骁。两个矛上挂着二重野鸡毛,在河上可以逍遥。

清地的兵在轴地,四匹马披着甲乐陶陶。左边转车右拔刀,将军头头做得好。

羔 裘

羔裘如濡①,洵直且侯②。彼其之子,舍命不渝③。
羔裘豹饰,孔武有力。彼其之子,邦之司直。
羔裘晏兮④,三英粲兮⑤。彼其之子,邦之彦兮⑥。

【注释】

①濡(rú 儒):润泽。 ②侯:美。 ③渝:变。 ④晏:鲜明貌。 ⑤三英:三次缝补。英指裘饰。 ⑥彦:士的美称。

【译文】

羔裘真是润泽,确是美好且顺直。那个是自己的人,舍弃性命不变实。

羔裘用豹皮装饰,显得勇武又有力。那个是自己的人,国中的主管是正直。

羔裘真是鲜明啊,三道镶边真美啊。那个自己的人,是国中的才彦啊。

遵大路

遵大路兮,掺执子之祛兮①。无我恶矣,不寁故也②。

遵大路兮,掺执子之手兮。无我魗兮③,不寁好也。

【注释】

①掺(shǎn 闪):执。祛(qū 区):袖口。 ②寁(jié 捷):速。 ③魗(chǒu 丑):丑。

【译文】

遵照大路走啊,拉着你的袖口啊。不要讨厌我,不要很快抛弃旧情啊。

遵照大路走啊,拉着你的手啊。不要嫌我丑啊,不要很快抛弃好朋友。

女曰鸡鸣

女曰鸡鸣,士曰昧旦①。子兴视夜,明星有烂②。将翱将翔③，弋凫与雁④。

　　弋言加之⑤，与子宜之⑥。宜言饮酒，与子偕老。琴瑟在御⑦，莫不静好。

　　知子之来之⑧，杂佩以赠之⑨。知子之顺之，杂佩以问之⑩。知子之好之，杂佩以报之。

【注释】

①昧旦：天将亮时。　②明星：启明星。　③翱翔：鸟飞貌。④弋（yì 亦）：用绳系在箭上射。　⑤加：射中。　⑥宜：《尔雅》："肴也。"作肴。　⑦御：奏。　⑧来：王引之《述闻》："读为劳来之来。"即慰劳。　⑨杂佩：各种佩玉，称杂佩。　⑩问：慰问。

【译文】

　　女人说鸡叫，男人说天刚刚亮。你起来看夜空，启明星有光亮。请你像飞那样，射野鸭与雁子不让。

　　射中了正好，给你烹饪从早。应该用来下酒，同你活到老。琴和瑟在弹奏，没有不安静和好。

　　知道你慰问我，送你杂佩不算宝。知道你顺着我，送你杂佩问你好。知道你恩爱我，送你杂佩用来报。

有女同车

　　有女同车，颜如舜华①。将翱将翔②，佩玉琼琚。彼美孟姜，洵美且都③。

　　有女同行，颜如舜英。将翱将翔，佩玉将将。彼美孟姜，德音不忘④。

【注释】

① 舜华、舜英：皆指木槿花。英指华。 ②将翱将翔：鸟飞貌，这里形容女子步态轻盈。 ③都：闲静。 ④德音：当指女子的德音。

【译文】

有个同车的姑娘，脸色美得像木槿花样。她将要飞翔，她的玉佩是宝玉优良。她是美丽的孟姜，确实美丽而且贤良。

有个姑娘同行，脸色真像开花的木槿。她将要飞行，玉佩锵锵发声。她是美丽的孟姜，她的德行不能忘。

山有扶苏

山有扶苏①，隰有荷华。不见子都，乃见狂且②。
山有乔松，隰有游龙③。不见子充，乃见狡童。

【注释】

①扶苏：一说同于扶疏，指枝叶茂盛的大树，一作桑树。 ②且（jū 拘）：指狂童。 ③游龙：红草，亦名水红。

【译文】

山上有桑树，洼地有荷花。没有看见漂亮的子都，却是看见丑陋的狂童。

山上有高松，洼地有水红。没有看见漂亮的子充，却是看见坏小童。

萚兮

萚兮萚兮①，风其吹(女)汝。叔兮伯兮，倡予和女②。
萚兮萚兮，风其漂女③。叔兮伯兮，倡予要女④。

【注释】

①萚(tuò 托)：树叶枯。 ②倡：唱。 ③漂：飘。 ④要：成也。凡乐节一终为一成，故要亦和。

【译文】

树叶枯啊树叶枯啊，风在把你吹破。老三啊老大啊，你来唱我来和。

树叶枯啊树叶枯啊，风在把你吹破。老三啊老大啊，你来唱我来和。

狡童

彼狡童兮，不与我言兮。维子之故①，使我不能餐兮。
彼狡童兮，不与我食兮。维子之故，使我不能息兮。

【注释】

①维：因为。

【译文】

那个狡猾的顽童啊，不同我言谈啊。因为你的缘故，使我不能吃饭啊。

那个狡猾的顽童啊，不同我吃饭啊。因为你的缘故，使我不能够安顿啊。

褰 裳

子惠思我，褰裳涉溱①。子不我思，岂无他人。狂童之狂也且②。

子惠思我，褰裳涉洧③。子不我思，岂无他士。狂童之狂也且。

【注释】

①褰（qiān 牵）：揭起。溱（zhēn 真）：水名，出密县境，东北流至新郑县，与洧水合。 ②且：语助词。 ③洧（wěi 委）：水名，出登封县北阳城山，东流至新郑县，合溱水为双泊河。

【译文】

你惠爱地想我，我提裤和你淌溱河。你不想我，难道没有别人。你这狂童也太狂妄么。

你惠爱地想我，我提裤同你淌洧河。你不想我，难道没有他人。你这狂童也太狂妄么。

丰

子之丰兮①，俟我乎巷兮。悔予不送兮②。
子之昌兮③，俟我乎堂兮。悔予不将兮④。
衣锦褧衣⑤，裳锦褧裳。叔兮伯兮⑥，驾予与行⑦。
裳锦褧裳，衣锦褧衣。叔兮伯兮，驾予与归⑧。

【注释】

①丰:丰满。 ②送:致女,即以女授婿。 ③昌:壮健。 ④将:送。 ⑤褧(jiǒng 窘):穿锦衣的罩单布衣。 ⑥叔、伯:古代女子对丈夫或情人的称呼。 ⑦行:指出嫁。 ⑧归:指出嫁。

【译文】

你的容貌丰满啊,等我在里巷啊。懊悔我不和你走啊。

你的体魄壮健啊,等我在堂屋啊。懊悔我不同你行啊。

穿着锦衣罩单衣,穿着锦裤罩单裤。叔啊伯啊,驾车和我走同路。

穿着锦裤罩单裤,穿着锦衣罩单衣。叔啊伯啊,驾车和我一同归。

东门之墠

东门之墠①,茹藘在阪②。其室则迩,其人甚远。
东门之栗,有践家室③。岂不尔思,子不我即④。

【注释】

①墠(shàn 扇):平坦。 ②茹藘(rú lú 如驴):茜草,可染红色。阪(bǎn 板):土坡。 ③践:成行列。 ④即:就。

【译文】

东门的地真平坦,茜草生长在山阪。她的房屋隔得近,她的人儿隔得远。

东门栗树真可嘉,栗下成列有室家。岂有我不想你透,你不前来把我就。

风 雨

风雨凄凄①,鸡鸣喈喈②。既见君子,云胡不夷③?
风雨潇潇④,鸡鸣胶胶。既见君子,云胡不瘳⑤?
风雨如晦,鸡鸣不已。既见君子,云胡不喜?

【注释】

①凄凄:寒凉。 ②喈喈(jiē jiē 皆皆):指鸡鸣声。 ③夷:同"怡",悦。 ④潇潇:猛烈。 ⑤瘳(chōu 抽):病愈。

【译文】

风雨寒冷地凄凄,鸡在喈喈地叫不已。既然看见君子人,说什么不喜?

风雨猛烈地潇潇,鸡在胶胶地叫。既然看见君子人,说什么病还不好。

风雨像黑暗,鸡叫还不已。既然看见君子人,说什么不欢喜。

子 衿

青青子衿①,悠悠我心。纵我不往,子宁不嗣音②?
青青子佩,悠悠我思。纵我不往,子宁不来?
挑兮达兮③,在城阙兮④。一日不见,如三月兮。

【注释】

①衿（jīn 今）：衣领。　②嗣：寄。　③挑达（tà 踏）：往来轻快貌。　④城阙：指城楼。

【译文】

青青是你的衣领，长长地挂在我的心。纵然我还不能去，你为什么不寄个音？

青青是你的佩带，长长地在我想念哉。纵然我不能去，你为什么不来？

你轻快地往来啊，登在城楼上啊。一天不看见你，如同隔了三个月啊。

扬之水

扬之水，不流束楚。终鲜兄弟，唯予与女。无信人之言，人实迋女①。

扬之水，不流束薪。终鲜兄弟，维予二人。无信人之言，人实不信。

【注释】

①迋（guàng 逛）：诳骗

【译文】

激扬的水，一捆荆条流不去。终于少个兄和弟，只有二人我和你。不要听信人家的言语，人家确实在骗你。

激扬的水，一捆柴都流不去。终于少个兄和弟，只有二人我和你。不要听信人家的言语，人家实在不说可信语。

出其东门

出其东门，有女如云。虽则如云，匪我思存。缟衣綦巾①，聊乐我员②。

出其闉阇③，有女如荼④。虽则如荼，匪我思且⑤。缟衣茹藘⑥，聊可与娱。

【注释】

①缟（gǎo 槁）衣：白色衣。綦（qí 脐）巾：青巾。 ②员：同"云"，语助词。 ③闉阇（yīn dū 因都）：城外曲城的重门。 ④荼：白茅花。 ⑤且：语助词。 ⑥茹藘（lú 驴）：茜草，可染绛色，指绛色围巾。

【译文】

走出那东门，有姑娘多得像云。虽则多得像云，不是我想念中人。只有那位白衣青巾，姑且是我喜爱的人。

走出曲城的重门，有姑娘多得像白茅花。虽则多得像白茅花，不是我牵挂中人。白衣红巾的那位，姑且可以同她相配。

野有蔓草

野有蔓草，零露漙兮①。有美一人，清扬婉兮②。邂逅相遇③，适我愿兮。

野有蔓草，零露瀼瀼④。有美一人，婉如清扬⑤。邂逅相遇，与子偕臧⑥。

【注释】

①漙（tuán 团）：露多。 ②婉：柔美。 ③邂逅：不约定而遇。 ④瀼瀼（ráng ráng 瓤瓤）：露多。 ⑤清扬：清明。 ⑥臧：善，好。

【译文】

野地里有蔓延的草，落下的露水密且浓啊。有美女一人，清明委婉啊。不约定而相遇，适合我的愿望啊。

野地里有蔓延的草，落下的露水多而清。有美女一人，委婉而清明。不约定而相遇，我与她相善。

溱洧

溱与洧，方涣涣兮①。士与女，方秉蕳兮②。女曰："观乎？"士曰："既且，且往观乎？"洧之外，洵訏且乐③。维士与女，伊其相谑，赠之以勺药④。

溱与洧，浏其清矣⑤。士与女，殷其盈矣⑥。女曰："观乎？"士曰："既且，且往观乎？"洧之外，洵訏且乐。维士与女，伊其将谑，赠之以勺药。

【注释】

①涣涣：水盛貌。 ②秉：拿着。蕳（jiān 肩）：兰草，与兰花有别。 ③訏（xū 虚）：大。 ④勺药：香草名，蘪芜类，一名耳离，非今之芍药花。 ⑤浏（liú 刘）：水清貌。 ⑥殷：众多。

【译文】

　　溱水和洧水,方才满满啊。小伙子和姑娘,方才拿了兰草啊。姑娘说:"去看看吧?"小伙子说:"已经看过,姑且去看看吧?"洧水的外面,确实地大而且快乐。只有男人和女人,他们互相戏谑,赠送的用勺药。

　　溱水和洧水,多么清啊。小伙子和姑娘,多得满满啊。姑娘说:"去看看吧?"小伙子说:"已经看过,姑且去看看吧?"洧水的外面,确实地大而且快乐。只有男人和女人,他们互相戏谑,赠送的用勺药。

诗经

齐　风

齐，国名，在今山东北部和中部。

鸡　鸣

"鸡既鸣矣，朝既盈矣①。""匪鸡则鸣，苍蝇之声。"

"东方明矣，朝既昌矣②。""匪东方则明，月出之光。"

"虫飞薨薨③，甘与子同梦④。""会且归矣，无庶予子憎⑤。"

【注释】

①朝：朝堂，朝廷。　②昌：盛，人多。　③薨薨（hōng hōng 烘烘）：虫群飞声。　④甘：甘心。　⑤无庶予子憎：庶无予子憎，庶几没有因我恨你。

【译文】

"鸡既然叫了，朝堂上既然人满了。""不是鸡叫，是苍蝇的声音。"

"东方亮了，朝堂上既然人多了。""不是东方亮，是月亮出来的光。"

"虫子薨薨地飞，甘心和你一同做梦。""朝会并且要回去了，庶几没有因我恨你。"

还

子之还矣①,遭我乎峱之间矣②。并驱从两肩兮③,揖我谓我儇兮④。

子之茂兮⑤,遭我乎峱之道兮。并驱从两牡兮,揖我谓我好兮。

子之昌兮⑥,遭我乎峱之阳兮。并驱从两狼兮,揖我谓我臧矣⑦。

【注释】

①还(xuán 旋):轻捷貌。 ②峱(náo 挠)山:泰山东临淄县南。 ③从:逐。肩:三岁的兽。 ④儇(xuān 喧):灵利。 ⑤茂:美满。 ⑥昌:盛壮貌. ⑦:臧:善,好。

【译文】

你的轻捷啊,遭逢我在峱山中间。并且赶走两只兽啊,向我作揖说我好转圜。

你的秀美啊,遭逢我在峱山的路上啊。并且赶走两只雄兽啊,对我作揖说我好猎啊。

你的剽悍啊,遭逢我在峱山的山南啊。并且驱赶两只狼啊,向我作揖说我善猎啊。

著

俟我于著乎而①,充耳以素乎而②,尚之以琼华乎而③。

俟我于庭乎而,充耳以青乎而,尚之以琼莹乎而。

俟我于堂乎而,充耳以黄乎而,尚之以琼英乎而④。

【注释】

①俟：等待。婿往女家亲迎，等待新人上车。著：门屏间。乎而：语助词。　②充耳：用瑱玉充耳。用线缝瑱玉，挂在帽子上，下垂两耳旁充耳。　③尚：通"上"，用玉加在帽上。　④琼华、琼莹、琼英：皆指美玉。华、莹、英皆指玉的光彩。

【译文】

他等我在门屏间，瑱玉用白丝线挂两边，上面以琼华加在帽沿。
他等我在院子间，瑱玉用青丝线挂两边，上面用琼莹加在帽沿。
他等我在堂屋间，瑱玉用黄丝线挂两边，上面用琼英加在帽沿。

东方之日

东方之日兮，彼姝者子①，在我室兮。在我室兮，履我即兮②。

东方之月兮，彼姝者子，在我闼兮③。在我闼兮，履我发兮④。

【注释】

①姝（shū 书）：美女。　②履我即：踩我就，踩我行。　③闼（tà 榻）：门内。　④履我发：踩我出发，踩我出发的足迹。

【译文】

东方的太阳啊，那个美丽的姑娘，在我的房啊。在我的房啊，踩着我的步子走啊。

东方的月亮啊,那个美丽的姑娘,在我的门旁啊。在我的门旁啊,踩我出发的脚步走啊。

东方未明

东方未明,颠倒衣裳。颠之倒之,自公召之。
东方未晞①,颠倒裳衣。倒之颠之,自公令之。
折柳樊圃②,狂夫瞿瞿③,不能辰夜④,不夙则莫。

【注释】

①晞(xī 希):破晓。 ②樊:樊篱。圃:菜园。 ③狂夫:狂妄的人。瞿瞿(jù jù 巨巨):惊顾貌。 ④辰夜:管夜里时刻。

【译文】

东方没有亮,颠去倒来穿衣裳。颠它倒它,从公爷召见他。
东方没有光,颠倒穿衣裳。倒它颠它,从公爷命令他。
攀折柳条作菜园的樊篱,狂妄的人睁眼看反。不能守住日夜,不是太早就太晚。

南 山

南山崔崔①,雄狐绥绥②。鲁道有荡③,齐子由归。既曰归止,曷又怀止④?
葛屦五两⑤,冠绥双止⑥。鲁道有荡,齐子庸止⑦。既曰庸止,曷又从止⑧?
芝麻如之何?衡从其亩⑨。取妻如之何?必告父母。既曰告止,曷又鞠止⑩?

析薪如之何?匪斧不克。取妻如之何?匪媒不得。既曰得止,曷又极止⑪?

【注释】

①崔崔:高貌。 ②绥绥:求偶貌。 ③荡:平坦。 ④怀:思念。 ⑤葛屦:用葛制成的鞋。五两:可以排列成双。 ⑥緌(ruí 蕤):帽带。双止:带是成双为止。 ⑦庸:用,用此道嫁给鲁侯。 ⑧从:从齐侯。 ⑨衡:横,东西为横。从:纵,南北为纵。 ⑩鞫(jú 菊):放任。 ⑪极:放纵到极点。

【译文】

南山高高的,雄的狐狸找伴罢。鲁国道路平坦,齐国女子从此出嫁。既然说是出嫁,怎么又想人过夜?

葛鞋排列成双,帽带打结成双。鲁国道路平坦,齐国女子用此出嫁。既然说用此出嫁,怎么又从人过夜?

种麻怎么样?或横或纵在田亩。娶妻怎么样?一定要告诉父母。既然说告诉父母,怎么又对她宽宥?

斫柴怎么样?不是斧头不能。娶妻怎么样?没有媒人不行。既然说娶了她,怎么又极端放行?

甫 田

无田甫田①,维莠骄骄②。无思远人,劳心忉忉③。
无田甫田,维莠桀桀④。无思远人,劳心怛怛⑤。
婉兮娈兮,总角丱兮⑥。未几见兮,突而弁兮⑦。

【注释】

①甫田：大田。 ②莠：狗尾草。骄骄：高大貌。 ③忉忉（dāo dāo 刀刀）：忧劳貌。 ④桀桀：高大貌。 ⑤怛怛（dá dá 达达）：悲伤。 ⑥丱（guàn 贯）：小孩梳两辫上翘，称总角。 ⑦弁（biàn 辨）：冠。古时二十岁称成人，戴冠。

【译文】

不要耕种那大田，只有狗尾草长得高。不要想念远去的人，想念起来心里忧劳。

不要耕种那大田，只有狗尾草长得长。不要想念远去的人，想念起来心里悲伤。

婉转啊漂亮啊，小时梳两小辫啊。几时没有看见啊，突然戴上帽子啊。

卢　令

卢令令①，其人美且仁。
卢重环②，其人美且鬈③。
卢重鋂④，其人美且偲⑤。

【注释】

①卢：猎狗。令令：猎狗头颈里铃的响声。 ②重环：子母环。 ③鬈（quán 拳）：头发弯曲。 ④鋂（méi 眉）：一大环贯二小环。 ⑤偲（cāi 猜）：多才。

【译文】

猎狗颈铃响令令,那人漂亮并慈仁。
猎狗颈铃是子母环,那人漂亮并头发弯。
猎狗颈铃两大铃,那人漂亮又多才。

敝 笱

敝笱在梁①,其鱼鲂鳏②。齐子归止,其从如云。
敝笱在梁,其鱼鲂鱮③。齐子归止,其从如雨。
敝笱在梁,其鱼唯唯④。齐子归止,其从如水。

【注释】

①笱(gǒu 狗):鱼篓,捕鱼具,鱼可入鱼篓而不能出。今坏了,已不能捕鱼。 ②鲂(fáng 防):鳊鱼。鳏(guān 关):黄颊鱼。这两种鱼都是大鱼,不能入笱。 ③鱮(xù 序):鲢鱼。这种鱼成群结队,也不入笱。 ④唯唯:鱼相随行之貌,也不入笱。

【译文】

坏的鱼篓在鱼梁,鲂鱼鳏鱼喜扬扬。齐国的女子回国去,她的跟从像云样。

坏的鱼篓在鱼梁,鲂鱼鲢鱼自游荡。齐国的女子回国去,她的跟从像雨样。

坏的鱼篓在鱼梁,鱼儿顺序自来往。齐国的女子回国去,她的跟从像水样。

载 驱

载驱薄薄^①,簟茀朱鞹^②。鲁道有荡,齐子发夕^③。
四骊济济^④,垂辔沵沵^⑤。鲁道有荡,齐子岂弟^⑥。
汶水汤汤^⑦,行人彭彭^⑧。鲁道有荡,齐子翱翔^⑨。
汶水滔滔^⑩,行人儦儦^⑪。鲁道有荡,齐子游敖。

【注释】

①薄薄:车快走声。 ②簟(diàn 电):竹席。茀(fú 扶):车帘。朱鞹(kuò 扩):染红的去毛兽皮,作为覆蔽。 ③发夕:晚上出发。 ④骊(lí 离):黑色马。济济:强壮。 ⑤沵沵(nǐ nǐ 你你):柔貌。指驾驶得好。 ⑥岂(kǎi 恺)弟:犹开明,始明。 ⑦汤汤(shāng shāng 伤伤):水大貌。 ⑧彭彭:多貌。 ⑨翱翔:鸟飞貌,这里形容遨游。 ⑩滔滔:水浩荡貌。 ⑪儦儦(biāo biāo 标标):众多貌。

【译文】

车马快走拍拍响,竹席红皮挂车厢。鲁国道路是平坦,齐女黄昏把车上。

四匹黑马多强壮,马缰下垂亦舒畅。鲁国道路是平坦,齐女乘车天初亮。

汶水流得自洋洋,走路人走得自嚷嚷。鲁国道路是平坦,齐国女子自遨翔。

汶水滔滔向前流,行人多得闹不休。鲁国道路是平坦,齐国女子自遨游。

诗经

猗 嗟

猗嗟昌兮①，颀而长兮②。抑若扬兮③。美目扬兮。巧趋跄兮④，射则臧兮。

猗嗟名兮⑤，美目清兮。仪既成兮⑥。终日射侯⑦，不出正兮⑧。展我甥兮⑨。

猗嗟娈兮，清扬婉兮。舞则选兮⑩，射则贯兮⑪，四矢反兮⑫，以御乱兮。

【注释】

①猗（yī 伊）嗟：赞美词。昌：盛。 ②颀（qí 其）：长貌。 ③抑：通"懿"，美貌。扬：额角丰满。 ④趋跄（qiāng 枪）：行走有节奏。 ⑤名：目上为名，指眉眼间。 ⑥仪：容仪。成：成就。 ⑦侯：箭靶。 ⑧正：箭靶中心。 ⑨展：诚。 ⑩选：正其舞位。 ⑪贯：中而穿革。 ⑫反：复也。指箭射中原处。

【译文】

阿呀壮盛啊，个子高而长啊。额角丰满而美啊，美的眼睛上扬啊。巧妙的行动有节度啊，箭射得好啊。

阿呀漂亮啊，美的眼睛清亮啊。仪容既经成就啊。整天射箭靶，不出红心啊。真是我的好外甥啊。

阿呀美好啊，眼睛清秀柔婉啊。舞蹈合节拍啊，射箭便中靶心啊，四支箭都中靶心啊，用来抵御叛乱啊。

魏 风

魏,国名,在今山西芮城东北,周初以封国姓,后为晋献公所灭。

葛 屦

纠纠葛屦①,可以履霜。掺掺女手②,可以缝裳。要之襋之③,好人服之。

好人提提④,宛然左辟⑤,佩其象揥⑥。维是褊心,是以为刺。

【注释】

①纠纠:缠绕。 ②掺掺(xiān xiān 仙仙):纤巧。 ③要:同"腰"。襋(jí 及):衣领。 ④好人:贵人。提提:傲慢。 ⑤宛然:回转貌。 ⑥揥(tì 替):古首饰,可插头。

【译文】

缠绕编制葛鞋良,穿了可以去踩霜。纤细巧妙女人手,可以缝制新衣裳。先缝腰围再衣领,贵人试穿新衣裳。

贵人态度有傲状,回身就避向左方。发上新插象牙钗,只是褊心没度量,因此作刺成诗章。

诗经

汾沮洳

彼汾沮洳①,言采其莫②。彼其之子,美无度③。美无度,殊异乎公路④。

彼汾一方,言采其桑。彼其之子,美如英。美如英,殊异乎公行⑤。

彼汾一曲,言采其藚⑥。 彼其之子,美如玉。美如玉,殊异乎公族⑦。

【注释】

①汾:水名。源出山西宁武县管涔山,流入黄河。沮洳(jù rù 具褥):低湿地。汾水之低湿地,在汾水入河处。 ②莫(mù 暮):指酸模,根叶花似羊蹄,但叶小味酸为异。采酸模佐食,表魏民崇俭。 ③美无度:指美不可度量。 ④殊异:优异出众。公路:管公家的车子的将军。 ⑤公行(háng 杭):管公家的战车的将军。 ⑥藚(xù 续):泽泻,药用植物。 ⑦公族:管公家的属车的将军。

【译文】

那个汾水的润湿地,我采那个酸模佐食事。他是我自己的人,美好得没有节度可云。美好得没有节度可云,超过管公家车的将军。

那个汾水的一处地方,我采那里的桑。他是我自己的人,美得像花英。美得像花英,超过管公家战车的将军。

那个汾水的弯曲处,我采泽泻好积贮。他是我自己的人,美得像玉一样。美得像玉一样,超过管公家属车的大将。

园 有 桃

园有桃，其实之殽①。心之忧矣，我歌且谣②。不知我者，谓我士也骄。彼人是哉，子曰何其？心之忧矣，其谁知之？其谁知之，盖亦勿思③。

园有棘，其实之食。心之忧矣，聊以行国。不知我者，谓我士也罔极④。彼人是哉，子曰何其？心之忧矣，其谁知之？其谁知之，盖亦勿思。

【注释】

①殽（yáo 姚）：同"肴"。 ②谣：徒歌，不用乐器伴奏的歌。 ③盖（hé 河）：曷，何。 ④罔极：无中正之道。

【译文】

园中有桃，它的桃子可做菜肴。心里忧伤了，我唱歌并且唱谣。不知道我的，说我士子太骄傲。那个人说得对吗，你说怎么样好？心里忧愁了，有什么人知道？有什么人知道，为什么不想到。

园中有枣，枣子可以吃好。心里忧伤了，姑且在国内走各条道。不知道我的，说我士子太偏激。那个人说得对吗，你说怎么样好？心里忧伤了，有什么人知道？有什么人知道，为什么不想到。

陟 岵

陟彼岵兮①，瞻望父兮。父曰："嗟，予子行役，夙夜无已。上慎旃哉②，犹来无止③。"

陟彼屺兮④，瞻望母兮。母曰："嗟！予季行役，夙夜无寐。上慎旃哉，犹来无弃。"

陟彼冈兮，瞻望兄兮。兄曰："嗟！予弟行役，夙夜必偕⑤。上慎旃哉，犹来无死。"

【注释】

①岵（hù 户）：山多草木。 ②上：通"尚"。旃（zhān 毡）：之。 ③犹：可。 ④屺（qǐ 起）：山无草木。 ⑤必偕：指与同行者一起作息，不得自如。

【译文】

登上那座青山啊，看望爸啊。爸说："唉，我儿去服役，早晚不休止。还是谨慎些吧，可以回来不要留滞。"

登上那座光山啊，看望娘啊。娘说："唉！我的老四服役，早晚没有睡觉。还是谨慎些吧，可以回来不要弃掉。"

登上那座山冈啊，看望兄啊。兄说："唉！我弟服役，早晚必定在一起。还是谨慎些吧，可以回来不要去死。"

十亩之间

十亩之间兮，桑者闲闲兮①，行与子逝兮②。
十亩之外兮，桑者泄泄兮③，行与子逝兮。

【注释】

①闲闲：宽闲貌。 ②行：且，将。 ③泄泄（yì yì 意意）：弛缓貌。

【译文】

十亩的中间啊,采桑的悠闲啊,将同你回去啊。

十亩的外啊,采桑的弛缓自在啊,将同你回去啊。

伐 檀

坎坎伐檀兮①,寘之河之干兮②。河水清且涟猗③。不稼不穑④,胡取禾三百廛兮⑤?不狩不猎⑥,胡瞻尔庭有县貆兮⑦?彼君子兮,不素餐兮⑧!

坎坎伐辐兮⑨,寘之河之侧兮。河水清且直兮。不稼不穑,胡取禾三百亿兮⑩?不狩不猎,胡瞻尔庭有县特兮⑪?彼君子兮,不素食兮!

坎坎伐轮兮,寘之河之漘兮⑫。河水清且沦猗⑬。不稼不穑,胡取禾三百囷兮⑭?不狩不猎,胡瞻尔庭有县鹑兮?彼君子兮,不素飧兮⑮!

【注释】

①坎坎:伐木声。 ②干:河岸。 ③涟:风吹水成纹。猗(yī 衣):语助词。 ④稼:种谷。穑:收谷。 ⑤廛(chán 蝉):束。 ⑥狩:冬天打猎。 ⑦尔:是小人,贪得无厌,无功受禄,白吃饭。下文的"彼",是君子,有功才肯受禄,是不白吃饭的。诗人肯定"彼",否定"尔"。县:同"悬",挂。貆(huán 还):幼貉。 ⑧素餐:白吃饭。 ⑨辐(fú 福):车轮中直木。 ⑩亿:束。 ⑪特:三岁的兽。 ⑫漘(chún 纯):河岸。 ⑬沦:小波。 ⑭囷(qūn 逡):束。 ⑮飧(sūn 孙):晚餐。

【译文】

坎坎砍檀树啊,放它在河的岸啊。河水清并且微波连啊。不耕种不收获,怎么取禾三百束啊?不上山去打猎,怎么看你庭内挂貆肉啊?那个君子啊,不白吃饭啊!

坎坎砍树做车辐啊,放在河的边侧啊。河水清并且直啊。不耕种又不收获,怎么取禾三百束啊?不上山去打猎,怎么看你庭有挂的兽肉啊?那个君子啊,不白吃饭啊!

坎坎砍树做车轮啊,放在河的水滨啊。河水清并且起波啊。不耕种又不收获,怎么取禾三百束啊?不上山去打猎,怎么看你庭中挂着鹌鹑肉啊?那个君子啊,不白吃饭啊!

硕 鼠

硕鼠硕鼠[①],无食我黍。三岁贯女[②],莫我肯顾。逝将去女[③],适彼乐土。乐土乐土,爰得我所。

硕鼠硕鼠,无食我麦。三岁贯女,莫我肯德。逝将去女,适彼乐国。乐国乐国,爰得我直[④]。

硕鼠硕鼠,无食我苗。三岁贯女,莫我肯劳。逝将去女,适彼乐郊。乐郊乐郊,谁之永号[⑤]。

【注释】

①硕鼠:土耗子,田鼠。 ②贯:奉侍,养活。 ③逝:同"誓"。 ④直:同"值",价值。 ⑤永号:永远叫苦。

【译文】

土耗子呀土耗子,不要吃我的黄黍。三年养活你,没有肯照顾我。发誓将要离开你,到那乐土。乐土呀乐土,于是得到我的处所。

　　土耗子呀土耗子,不要吃我的麦。三年养活你,没有肯对我感德。发誓将要离开你,到那乐国。乐国呀乐国,于是得到我的价值。

　　土耗子呀土耗子,不要吃我的苗。三年养活你,没有肯对我慰劳。发誓将要离开你,到那乐郊。乐郊呀乐郊,谁会永远把苦叫。

诗经

唐 风

唐,国名,在今山西中部太原一带。周成王封其弟姬叔虞于唐,后来改称晋,唐风就是晋风。

蟋 蟀

蟋蟀在堂,岁聿其莫①。今我不乐,日月其除②。无已大康③,职思其居④。好乐无荒,良士瞿瞿⑤。

蟋蟀在堂,岁聿其逝⑥。今我不乐,日月其迈⑦。无已大康,职思其外。好乐无荒,良士蹶蹶⑧。

蟋蟀在堂,役车其休⑨。今我不乐,日月其慆⑩。无已大康,职思其忧。好乐无荒,良士休休⑪。

【注释】

①聿(yù 域):语助辞。莫:同"暮"。 ②除:过去。 ③大康:同"泰康",过分康乐。 ④职:主要职务。居:所处之事。 ⑤瞿瞿(jù jù 巨巨):收敛。 ⑥逝:过去。 ⑦迈:过去。 ⑧蹶蹶(guì guì 贵贵):敏捷。 ⑨役车:服役的车子。休:止、息。 ⑩慆(tāo 滔):通"滔",过。 ⑪休休:安闲自得。

【译文】

蟋蟀在堂屋里叫,一年快要完了。今天我不快乐,一年日月快过去了。不要过度康乐，想想职分处事不少。爱好快乐不要把事荒掉，善人收敛才算好。

蟋蟀在堂屋里叫，一年快要完了。今天我不快乐，一年日月快过去了。不要过度康乐，想想职分外务不少。爱好快乐不要把事荒掉，善人做事敏捷才好。

蟋蟀在堂屋叫，服役的车子可停息了。今天我不快乐，一年的日月快过去了。不要过度康乐，想想职分处的可忧。爱好快乐不要把事荒掉，善人安闲自得才好。

山有枢

山有枢①，隰有榆。子有衣裳，弗曳弗娄②。子有车马，弗驰弗驱。宛其死矣③，他人是愉。

山有栲④，隰有杻⑤。子有廷内⑥，弗洒弗扫。子有钟鼓，弗鼓弗考⑦。宛其死矣，他人是保⑧。

山有漆，隰有栗。子有酒食，何不日鼓瑟？且以喜乐，且以永日。宛其死矣，他人入室。

【注释】

①枢（shū 书）：树名，即刺榆。 ②曳（yì 义）：拖。娄：古时裳长拖地，需要拖着或提着，娄指提。 ③宛：通"苑"，枯萎。 ④栲（kǎo 考）：树名，即臭椿。 ⑤杻（niǔ 纽）：树名，即菩提树。 ⑥廷：通"庭"，院子。 ⑦考：击。 ⑧保：占有。

【译文】

山上有树叫枢，洼地有树叫榆。你有上衣和下裤，不牵着不提着走。你有车又有马,不让马跑车疾驱。枯萎死了,让别人来快愉。

山上有树叫栲,洼地有树叫杻。你有庭院和内室,不浇水不打扫。你有钟和鼓,不打不敲。枯萎死了,让别人来保。

山上有树叫漆,洼地有树叫栗。你有酒有菜,为什么不每天弹瑟?姑且用来娱乐,姑且用来过日。枯萎死了,让他人入室。

扬之水

扬之水,白石凿凿①。素衣朱襮②,从子于沃③。既见君子,云何不乐。

扬之水,白石皓皓④。素衣朱绣⑤,从子于鹄⑥。既见君子,云何其忧。

扬之水,白石粼粼⑦。我闻有命,不敢以告人。

【注释】

①凿凿:鲜明貌。 ②襮(bó 博):绣黼文的衣领。黼文衣,指绣有斧形文的衣,即锦绣衣,用白布衣罩上,但朱领仍露出。 ③沃:曲沃。 ④皓皓:洁白。 ⑤绣:指领绣,即绣领。 ⑥鹄:曲沃邑名。 ⑦粼粼(lín lín 林林):清澄貌。

【译文】

激扬的河水,白石鲜明。白衣红领,跟你到曲沃。既然看见君子人,说什么不快乐。

激扬的河水,白石洁白。白衣红领,跟你到鹄。既然看见君子人,说什么忧伤不乐。

激扬的河水,白石清澄。我听说有命令,不敢用来告诉人。

椒 聊

椒聊之实①,蕃衍盈升。彼其之子,硕大无朋②。椒聊且,远条且③。

椒聊之实,蕃衍盈匊④。彼其之子,硕大且笃。椒聊且,远条且。

【注释】

①椒聊:花椒多子成串,古人以喻妇人多子。聊指多子成串。②无朋:无比。 ③远条:远长,指香气远而长。 ④匊(jū 居):掬,两手合捧。

【译文】

花椒一串的子,繁多得超过一升。那个人的儿子,魁梧高大得无比竞。像一串串花椒啊,香味远扬啊。

花椒一串的子,繁多得超过一捧。那户人的儿子,魁梧而且笃实隆重。像一串串花椒啊,香气远扬啊。

绸 缪

绸缪束薪①,三星在天②。今夕何夕,见此良人③?子兮子兮,如此良人何?

绸缪束刍④,三星在隅⑤。今夕何夕,见此邂逅⑥?子兮子兮,如此邂逅何?

绸缪束楚,三星在户⑦。今夕何夕,见此粲者⑧?子兮子兮,如此粲者何?

【注释】

①绸缪(chóu móu 仇谋):缠绵。 ②三星:指参星。在天:一指十月。当时以仲春为婚期,十月非婚时。 ③良人:指未婚夫。 ④刍(chú 除):青草。 ⑤三星在隅:一指十一月、十二月,非婚期。 ⑥邂逅:不约而来的爱悦者。 ⑦三星在户:一指一月,亦非婚期。 ⑧粲者:美人。

【译文】

缠绕着捆柴薪,三星在天上明。今夜是何夜,见到这个好人?你啊你啊,像这样好人怎么办啊?

缠绕着捆青草,三星在屋角光皓。今夜是何夜,见这个不约人来得巧?你啊你啊,像这样不约的人怎样办啊。

缠绕着捆荆条,三星在户梢。今夜是何夜,见到这美同胞?你啊你啊,像这样的美人怎样办啊?

杕 杜

有杕之杜①,其叶湑湑②。独行踽踽③。岂无他人,不如我同父④。嗟行之人,胡不比焉⑤?人无兄弟,胡不佽焉⑥?

有杕之杜,其叶菁菁。独行睘睘⑦。岂无他人,不如我同姓⑧。嗟行之人,胡不比焉?人无兄弟,胡不佽焉?

【注释】

①杕（dì 第）：特立貌。杜：赤棠。 ②湑湑（xǔ xǔ 许许）：盛貌。 ③踽踽（jǔ jǔ 举举）：孤独貌。 ④同父：同祖父的族弟。凡是同一父的人，只称兄或弟。称同父的人，指同一祖的族兄或族弟。 ⑤比：辅助。 ⑥佽（cì 刺）：助。 ⑦睘睘（qióng qióng 琼琼）：孤独无依。 ⑧同姓：同父的兄弟叫兄或弟，同祖的昆弟叫同姓。

【译文】

独特生的赤棠，它的叶儿正茂盛。孤零零独自行走。难道没有别人，不像我同族的兄弟亲。叹息独行的人，为什么没有帮助呢？人没有兄弟，怎么能不相济？

独特生的赤棠，它的叶儿正茂盛。孤零零独自行走。难道没有别人，不像我同族的兄弟亲。叹息独行的人，为什么没有帮助呢？人没有兄弟，怎么能不相济？

羔 裘

羔裘豹袪①，自我人居居。岂无他人，维子之故。
羔裘豹褎②，自我人究究③。岂无他人，维子之好。

【注释】

① 袪（qù 区）：袖子。 ②褎（xiù 袖）：同"袖"，指袖口。 ③居居、究究：恶也。

【译文】

羊袍用豹皮做袖子，我们讨厌它。难道没有别人，只是因为对你有故旧啊。

羊袍用豹皮做袖子,我们讨厌它。难道没有别人,只是因为对你有爱好啊。

鸨 羽

肃肃鸨羽①,集于苞栩②。王事靡盬③,不能艺稷黍。父母何怙④。悠悠苍天,曷其有所?

肃肃鸨翼,集于苞棘⑤。王事靡盬,不能艺黍稷。父母何食?悠悠苍天,曷其有极?

肃肃鸨行,集于苞桑。王事靡盬,不能艺稻粱。父母何尝?悠悠苍天,曷其有常?

【注释】

①肃肃:鸨鸟展翅飞行声。鸨(bǎo 保):鸟名。似雁而大,无后趾。 ②苞:丛生。栩(xǔ 许):柞树。 ③盬(gǔ 古):停息。 ④怙(hù 户):依靠。 ⑤棘(jí 及):酸枣树,实较枣小,供药用。

【译文】

沙沙地发响是鸨鸟展翅,停在丛生的栩树。周王的役事没有完,不能种稷黍。父母有什么可依恃。遥远的苍天,怎么能有个依恃?

沙沙地发响是鸨鸟展翅,停在丛生的酸枣树。周王的役事没有完,不能种黍稷。父母靠什么吃?遥远的苍天,怎么能有个完讫?

沙沙地发响是鸨鸟飞行,停在丛生的桑树上。周王的役事没有完,不能种稻粱。父母拿什么来品尝?遥远的苍天,怎么能有个正常?

无 衣

岂曰无衣,七兮。不如子之衣,安且吉兮。
岂曰无衣,六兮。不如子之衣,安且燠兮①。

【注释】

①燠(yù 玉):温暖。

【译文】

难道说我没有衣裳,我的衣裳有七套。不像你的衣裳,安全而且好。

难道说我没有衣裳,我的衣裳有六套。不像你的衣裳,安全而且暖。

有杕之杜

有杕之杜,生于道左。彼君子兮,噬肯适我①。中心好之,曷饮食之?
有杕之杜,生于道周②。彼君子兮,噬肯来游。中心好之,曷饮食之?

【注释】

①噬(shì 式):同"曷",何。 ②周:通作"右"。

【译文】

有独立的赤棠,生在路的左边。那个君子人啊,哪肯到我这边。心中爱好他,何不准备酒饮款待他?

有独立的赤棠,生在路的右边。那个君子人啊,哪肯游逛到面前。心中爱好他,何不准备酒饮招待他?

葛 生

葛生蒙楚,蔹蔓于野①。予美亡此,谁与独处。
葛生蒙棘,蔹蔓于域②。予美亡此,谁与独息。
角枕粲兮③,锦衾烂兮④。予美亡此,谁与独旦。
夏之日,冬之夜⑤,百岁之后,归于其居⑥。
冬之夜,夏之日,百岁之后,归于其室⑦。

【注释】

①蔹(liǎn 脸):白蔹,攀援性草本植物,根可入药。 ②域:指坟地。 ③角枕:牛角枕,敛尸的物品。 ④锦衾:锦缎被子。 ⑤夏之日、冬之夜:夏日长,冬夜长。 ⑥居:坟墓。 ⑦室:指冢坑。

【译文】

葛的茎缠绕荆条,白蔹蔓生在荒郊。我爱的人死在此处,谁可以与他独处。

葛的茎缠绕酸枣树,白蔹蔓生在郊处。我爱的人死在此处,谁与他独安息在此。

牛角枕鲜明啊,锦绣被鲜明啊。我爱的人死在此处,谁与他独到天亮相处。

夏天的日长,冬天的夜长,百年以后,归于他的坟场。
冬天的夜长,夏天的日长,百年以后,归于他的圹场。

采 苓

采苓采苓①,首阳之颠。人之为言②,苟亦无信。舍旃舍旃③,苟亦无然④!人之为言,胡得焉⑤?

采苦采苦,首阳之下。人之为言,苟亦无与⑥。舍旃舍旃,苟亦无然!人之为言,胡得焉?

采葑采葑⑦,首阳之东。人之为言,苟亦无从。舍旃舍旃,苟亦无然!人之为言,胡得焉?

【注释】

①苓(líng 零):甘草。 ②为言:同"伪言",讹言。 ③舍旃(zhān 毡):舍之,放弃它。 ④无然:不以为是。 ⑤胡得:何所得。 ⑥无与:不赞同他。 ⑦葑(fēng 封):芜菁,即芥菜。

【译文】

采苓啊采苓,在首阳山顶。别人的假话,况且也没有可信。放弃它啊放弃它,况且也没真全是假!别人的假话,得到什么啊?

采苦菜啊采苦菜,在首阳山下。别人的假话,况且也没人赞同他。放弃它啊放弃它,况且也没真全是假!别人的假话,得到什么啊?

采芜菁啊采芜菁,在首阳山东。别人的假话,根本没人听从。放弃它啊放弃它,没真全是假!别人的假话,得到什么啊?

诗经

秦 风

秦，本为周的附庸，平王东迁，封秦襄公为诸侯，秦地扩大到今陕西及甘肃东部。

车 邻

有车邻邻①，有马白颠②。未见君子，寺人之令③。阪有漆，隰有栗。既见君子，并坐鼓瑟。"今者不乐，逝者其耋④。"

阪有桑，隰有杨。既见君子，并坐鼓簧。"今者不乐，逝者其亡。"

【注释】

①邻邻：同"辚辚"，车行声。 ②白颠：白顶。 ③寺人：宦官。 ④耋（dié 迭）：八十岁。

【译文】

有车子走时发声辚辚，有马儿白毛白顶。没有看见君子人，只有宦官发命令。山坡上种树有漆，洼地上种树有栗。既然看见君子人，和他并坐弹瑟。"今天不图快乐，过去就变成老疾。"

山坡上种树有桑，洼地里种树有杨。既然看见君子人，和他并坐弹笙簧。"今天不图快乐，过去就转成死亡。"

驷 骥

驷骥孔阜①,六辔在手。公之媚子②,从公于狩。奉时辰牡③,辰牡孔硕。公曰左之,舍拔则获④。

游于北园,四马既闲⑤。𬨎车鸾镳⑥,载猃歇骄⑦。

【注释】

①驷骥:四马黑如铁。骥(tiě 铁),赤黑色的马。阜:肥大。 ②媚子:宠爱的人。 ③奉时:趋奉是,虞人趋奉是,即为公爷赶兽。辰牡:牝鹿和牡鹿。辰通"麎",指牝鹿。 ④舍拔:去箭末,即射箭。 ⑤闲:通"娴",熟练。 ⑥𬨎(yóu 犹)车:轻车。鸾:鸾铃。镳(biāo 标):马衔外铁。 ⑦猃(xiǎn 险):长嘴猎狗。歇骄:短嘴猎狗。

【译文】

四马铁黑雄赳赳,六根缰绳握在手。公爷宠爱的人,跟在公爷打猎后。驱赶鹿儿有牝牡,牡鹿硕壮到处有。公爷说是车向左,一箭正好中牲口。

游猎游到北园遍,四马驾车既熟练。轻车鸾铃马衔镳,二种猎狗车里见。

小 戎

小戎伐收①,五楘梁辀②。游环胁驱③,阴靷鋈续④。文茵畅毂⑤,驾我骐馵⑥。言念君子,温其如玉。在其板屋,乱我心曲。

四牡孔阜,六辔在手。骐骝是中⑦,䯄骊是骖⑧。龙盾之合⑨。鋈以觼軜⑩。言念君子，温其在邑。方何为期，胡然我念之？

俴驷孔群⑪，厹矛鋈镦⑫。蒙伐有苑⑬，虎韔镂膺⑭。交韔二弓⑮，竹闭绲縢⑯。言念君子，载寝载兴。厌厌良人⑰，秩秩德音⑱。

【注释】

①小戎：小的兵车。俴（jiàn 件）：浅。收：收缩。俴收，指小车厢。　②五楘（mù 暮）：五束历录，用五束来连络。梁辀（zhōu 舟）：弯曲的车辕如船状。即用五束皮带系在车辕上。　③游环：活动的环。胁驱：驾马具。一车有四马，外两马称骖，中两马称服。用游环于服马背上，再用皮带连车上，使骖马不入内。　④阴靷（yǐn 隐）：系骖马的革带，不明显。鋈（wù 务）：白铜环。续：接续。在革带上用白铜环相续。　⑤文茵：虎皮垫。畅毂（gǔ 谷）：长毂。毂，车轮中的圆木，中有圆孔，可以插轴。　⑥骐：青黑色的马。馵（zhù 注）：后左足白的马。　⑦骝（liú 留）：赤身黑鬣的马。　⑧騧（guā 瓜）：黄马黑嘴的马。骊：黑色的马。　⑨龙盾：画龙的盾牌。　⑩觼軜（jué nà 决纳）：有舌环穿过骖马的皮带，使内辔固定。軜：骖内辔。　⑪俴驷：四马不披甲。孔群：指马群很和谐。　⑫厹（qiú 求）矛：三棱锋刃的矛。鋈镦（wù duì 务兑）：以白铜镀矛柄底的金属套。　⑬蒙：通"庬"，杂乱绘画。伐：盾牌。苑：文彩。　⑭虎韔（chàng 唱）：以虎皮做的弓囊。镂膺：刻纹。　⑮交韔（chàng 唱）：交错的藏弓袋。　⑯闭：弓檠。绲（gǔn 滚）：绳。縢（téng 藤）：缠束。　⑰厌厌：安静。　⑱秩秩：智慧。

【译文】

小的兵车和小的车厢，五皮革贯铜环绕住车毂。活动的环控制骖马入服，暗的革带贯铜环使骖马接续。老虎皮垫用来舒畅车毂，驾着各色马的家畜。我想念那君子人，温和得真如美玉。他住在板木屋，扰乱我的心曲。

四匹雄马很壮实，六根缰绳拿在手。中间都是杂色马，黄黑骖马向前走。画龙盾牌可配合，铜环扣住内缰钮。我想念那君子人，温和在邑可为友。将在何时作归期，为何我又想他久？

四马不甲很合群，三隅矛杆装铜䥻。盾牌画着有文彩，虎皮弓囊镀了金。弓囊交错放二弓，绳索捆住竹制檠。我想念那君子人，睡睡起起不安宁。那个好人又安静，又有智慧又有德行。

蒹 葭

蒹葭苍苍①，白露为霜。所谓伊人，在水一方。溯洄从之②，道阻且长。溯游从之③，宛在水中央。

蒹葭凄凄④，白露未晞⑤。所谓伊人，在水之湄⑥。溯洄从之，道阻且跻⑦。溯游从之，宛在水中坻⑧。

蒹葭采采⑨，白露未已。所谓伊人，在水之涘⑩。溯洄从之，道阻且右⑪。溯游从之，宛在水中沚⑫。

【注释】

①蒹葭（jiān jiā 兼家）：初生的芦苇。苍苍：青苍。 ②溯（sù 素）洄：逆流而上。 ③溯游：顺流而下。 ④凄凄：同"萋萋"，茂盛貌。 ⑤晞（xī 希）：干。 ⑥湄（méi 眉）：水草相交地。 ⑦跻（jī 几）：登。 ⑧坻（chí 迟）：小水中的小高地。 ⑨采采：茂盛貌。 ⑩涘

(sì 四)：水边。　⑪右：右边，绕弯处。　⑫沚（zhǐ 止）：水中沙洲。

【译文】

初生的芦苇色青苍，夜来白露凝成霜。所说的那个人，在水的那一方。逆流而上去寻他，道路受阻而且长。顺着水流去寻他，仿佛在水的中央。

初生的芦苇很茂盛，路上白露还没干。所说的那个人，在水的草滩。逆流而上去寻他，道路受阻而且攀登难。顺着水流去寻他，仿佛在水中的沙滩。

初生的芦苇很茂盛，路上的白露没有停止。所说的那个人，在水的小渚。逆流而上去寻他，道路受阻而且要转沚。顺着水流去寻他，仿佛在水的小沚。

终　南

终南何有？有条有梅①。君子至止，锦衣狐裘。颜如渥丹，其君也哉！

终南何有？有纪有堂②。君子至止，黻衣绣裳③。佩玉将将，寿考不忘。

【注释】

①条：山楸树。　②纪：通"杞"，杞树。堂：通"棠"，指赤棠树。　③黻（fú 弗）：绣上黑与青相间的礼服。

【译文】

终南山有什么？有山楸树有红梅。君子到这里可住，穿狐袍和锦衣前来。脸色红得像渥丹,他是尊贵的首魁!

终南山有什么?有杞树有赤棠。君子到这里可住,穿着礼服和绣裳。身上佩玉响当当,祝你长寿永不忘。

黄 鸟

交交黄鸟①,止于棘。谁从穆公②?子车奄息③。维此奄息,百夫之特④。临其穴,惴惴其慄⑤。彼苍者天,歼我良人⑥!如可赎兮,人百其身⑦。

交交黄鸟,止于桑。谁从穆公?子车仲行。维此仲行,百夫之防⑧。临其穴,惴惴其慄。彼苍者天,歼我良人!如可赎矣,人百其身。

交交黄鸟,止于楚⑨。谁从穆公?子车鍼虎。维此鍼虎,百夫之御。临其穴,惴惴其慄。彼苍者天,歼我良人!如可赎矣,人百其身。

【注释】

①交交:飞而往来貌。 ②从:从死,即殉葬。 ③子车奄息:子车,氏名。奄息,下面的仲行、鍼虎,皆人名。 ④特:杰出。 ⑤惴惴(zhuì zhuì 缀缀):恐惧。慄(lì 栗):战慄。 ⑥歼(jiān 尖):灭亡。 ⑦人百其身:一人百死也为之。 ⑧防:抵当。 ⑨楚:荆树条。

【译文】

飞去飞来是黄鸟,停在酸枣树杪。啥人陪葬秦穆公?子车氏名奄息了。只有这个奄息,百人杰出才特妙。临到他的墓穴,使人战慄哀悼。那个苍天啊,灭亡我的好人!如果可以赎啊,人愿百死他的身。

飞去飞来是黄鸟,停在枣树杪。啥人陪葬秦穆公?子车氏名仲行了。只有这个仲行,可当百人才特妙。临到他的墓穴,使人战慄哀悼。那个苍天啊,灭亡我的好人!如果可以赎啊,人愿百死他的身。

飞去飞来是黄鸟,停在荆树条。啥人陪葬秦穆公?子车氏名铖虎了。只有这个铖虎,可敌百人才特妙。临到他的墓穴,使人战慄哀悼。那个苍天啊,灭亡我的好人!如果可以赎啊,人愿百死他的身。

晨 风

鴥彼晨风①,郁彼北林②。未见君子,忧心钦钦③。如何如何,忘我实多。

山有苞栎④,隰有六駮⑤。未见君子,忧心靡乐。如何如何,忘我实多。

山有苞棣⑥,隰有树檖⑦。未见君子,忧心如醉。如何如何,忘我实多。

【注释】

①鴥(yù 育):疾飞貌。晨风:鸟名,似鹞。 ②郁:茂盛貌。北林:北面的森林。 ③钦钦:忧愁。 ④栎(lì 力):柞树,落叶乔木,花黄褐色。 ⑤六駮(bó 博):树名,梓榆树,树皮青白像駮马。六指多。 ⑥棣(dì 地):郁李。 ⑦檖(suì 岁):山梨。

【译文】

疾飞那个晨风鸟,茂盛的北林可藏了。没有看见君子人,心里忧愁不算少。为什么啊为什么,把我忘掉不得了。

山上有丛生的柞树,洼地上有树叫六驳。没有看见君子人,心里忧愁不快乐。为什么啊为什么,把我忘掉恩情薄。

山上有丛生的郁李,洼地上有树叫山梨。没有看见君子人,心里忧愁像喝醉。为什么啊为什么,把我忘掉把我弃。

无 衣

岂曰无衣,与子同袍①。王于兴师②,修我戈矛,与子同仇。

岂曰无衣,与子同泽③。王于兴师,修我矛戟,与子偕作。

岂曰无衣,与子同裳。王于兴师,修我甲兵,与子偕行。

【注释】

①袍:长袍,指装有旧丝绵的长袍。 ②王:指周王。 ③泽:亲肤的内衣。

【译文】

难道说没有长袍,我同你同穿长袍。周王发动军队,修理我的戈和矛,与你同对一个仇。

难道说没有内衣,我同你同穿内衣。周王发动军队,修理我的矛和戟,同你一起有所作。

难道说没有下裳,我同你同穿下裳。周王发动军队,修理我的盔甲和刃兵,和你一起前行。

渭 阳

我送舅氏,曰至渭阳①。何以赠之?路车乘黄。
我送舅氏,悠悠我思②。何以赠之?琼瑰玉佩③。

【注释】

①渭阳:渭水北面。 ②悠悠我思:念母也。 ③琼瑰(guī 龟):美玉。

【译文】

我送舅舅,送到渭阳。拿什么来送他?大车子和驾车马儿黄。

我送舅舅,长长地想念我娘。拿什么来送他?美玉作佩来献扬。

权 舆

於,我乎①?夏屋渠渠②。今也每食无余。於嗟乎!不承权舆③。
於,我乎?每食四簋④。今也每食不饱。於嗟乎!不承权舆。

【注释】

①於:叹词。 ②夏屋:大食器。渠渠:盛。 ③权舆:开始,当初。 ④簋(guǐ 鬼):古食器。

【译文】

唉,我吗?大碗菜盛得满满的。现在每顿吃光。唉呀!不能继续当初吃得好。

唉,我吗?每顿四大盆。现在每顿吃不饱。唉呀!不能继续当初吃得好。

诗经

陈 风

陈，国名，今河南开封县以东，安徽亳县以北，皆其地，后为楚所灭。

宛 丘

子之汤兮①，宛丘之上兮②。洵有情兮，而无望兮③。
坎其击鼓④，宛丘之下。无冬无夏，值其鹭羽⑤。
坎其击缶⑥，宛丘之道。无冬无夏，值其鹭翿⑦。

【注释】

①子：指跳舞的巫女。汤：通"荡"，放荡。 ②宛丘：四方高、中央低的土山。 ③望：声望。 ④坎：击鼓声。 ⑤值：持。 ⑥缶（fǒu 否）：小口大腹的瓦器。 ⑦翿（dào 道）：一种舞具，聚鸟羽于柄头而成。

【译文】

你的放荡啊，在宛丘的上啊。确实是多情啊，却没有声望啊。

冬冬地把鼓敲响，在宛丘的丘下。没有冬也没有夏，拿着鹭鸶的羽毛啊。

当当地敲瓦盆，在宛丘的路上。没有冬来没有夏，鹭鸶羽毛拿手上。

东门之枌

东门之枌①,宛丘之栩②。子仲之子,婆娑其下③。
穀旦于差④,南方之原。不绩其麻,市也婆娑。
穀旦于逝,越以鬷迈⑤。视尔如荍⑥,贻我握椒⑦。

【注释】

①枌(fén 坟):白榆树。 ②栩(xǔ 许):柞树。 ③婆娑:舞蹈。 ④穀旦:好日子。穀,善,好。差:选择。 ⑤越以:于以。语助词。鬷(zōng 宗):总。总会合。 ⑥荍(qiáo 桥):锦葵。草本植物,夏开紫或白花。 ⑦椒:花椒,赠椒表结好。

【译文】

东门的白榆树,宛丘的柞树。子仲的姑娘,在树下起舞。
选择那好日子,在南方的平原。不纺织她的麻,却舞蹈在市垣。
好日子快过去,会合男女好共行。看你像荆葵那样美,送我花椒心欢迎。

衡 门

衡门之下①,可以栖迟②。泌之洋洋③,可以乐饥④。
岂其食鱼,必河之鲂⑤?岂其取妻,必齐之姜⑥?
岂其食鱼,必河之鲤?岂其取妻,必宋之子⑥?

【注释】

①衡门:横木为门。 ②栖迟:安居。 ③泌(bì 必):泉水名。

洋洋：水流貌。 ④乐饥：乐而忘饥。 ⑤鲂：亦名鳊鱼，鳞细，肉肥，鱼之美者。 ⑥齐姜、宋子：齐女姓姜，宋女姓子，指贵族姑娘。

【译文】

横木作门的下面，可以作为安居。泌泉水的荡漾，可以快乐忘掉腹饥。

难道吃鱼，一定要黄河里的鲂？难道娶妻，一定要娶齐国的姜姓？

难道吃鱼，一定要黄河的鲤？难道娶妻，一定要娶宋国的子姓？

东门之池

东门之池，可以沤麻①。彼美淑姬，可与晤歌②。
东门之池，可以沤纻③。彼美淑姬，可与晤语。
东门之池，可以沤菅④。彼美淑姬，可与晤言。

【注释】

①沤（òu 怄）：长期浸泡。 ②晤歌：在唱。 ③纻（zhù 注）：苎麻，麻的一种。 ④菅（jiān 肩）：菅草，叶可做绳。

【译文】

东门的池塘，可以长期浸泡麻。她是美丽善良的姬家姑娘，可以和她相对唱啊。

东门的池塘，可以长期浸泡纻麻。她是美丽善良的姬家姑娘，可以和她相对讲啊。

东门的池塘，可以长期浸泡菅草。她是美丽善良的姬家姑娘，可以和她相对说啊。

东门之杨

东门之杨，其叶牂牂①。昏以为期，明星煌煌②。
东门之杨，其叶肺肺③。昏以为期，明星晢晢④。

【注释】

①牂牂（zāng zāng 脏脏）：风吹树叶声。 ②明星：启明星。 ③肺肺（pèi pèi 配配）：同"牂牂"。 ④晢晢（zhé zhé 哲哲）：明亮。

【译文】

东门的杨树，它的叶子发出沙沙响。昏暗作为相约的时期，启明星却闪闪发亮。

东门的杨树，它的叶子沙沙发响。昏暗作为相约的时期，启明星却明明发亮。

墓 门

墓门有棘①，斧以斯之②。夫也不良，国人知之。 知而不已，谁昔然矣③。
墓门有梅，有鸮萃止④。 夫也不良，歌以讯止⑤。讯予不顾，颠倒思予。

【注释】

①墓门：墓道之门。 ②斯：析，砍。 ③谁昔：畴昔。 ④鸮（xiāo 消）：猫头鹰。萃（cuì 翠）：集。 ⑤讯：亦作"谇"。谇，谏，劝。

【译文】

墓道门有酸枣树,用斧头来砍它。那人是不善,国人知道他。知道他还不改,从前就是这样坏。

墓道门有酸枣树,有猫头鹰停栖着。那人是不善,作歌劝谏他。劝谏不理我,颠倒后才想念我。

防有鹊巢

防有鹊巢①,邛有旨苕②。谁侜予美③?心焉忉忉④。
中唐有甓⑤,邛有旨鷊⑥。谁侜予美?心焉惕惕⑦。

【注释】

①防:堤岸。 ②邛(qióng 穷):山丘。苕(tiáo 条):水草。 ③侜(zhōu 舟):欺骗。 ④忉忉(dāo dāo 刀刀):苦恼。 ⑤唐:朝堂前大路。甓(pì 僻):砖。 ⑥鷊(yì 抑):绶草。 ⑦惕惕:忧惧。

【译文】

堤岸上怎么有鹊巢,山丘上怎么有水草。谁欺骗我的爱人?心里很苦恼。

路上怎么用瓦铺道,山丘上怎么有水草。谁欺骗我的爱人?心里忧惧苦恼。

月 出

月出皎兮①,佼人僚兮②。舒窈纠兮③,劳心悄兮④。
月出皓兮,佼人懰兮⑤。舒忧受兮⑥,劳心慅兮⑦。
月出照兮,佼人燎兮⑧。舒夭绍兮⑨,劳心惨兮⑩。

【注释】

①皎（jiǎo 绞）：美好。　②僚（liǎo 了）：好貌。　③窈纠（yǎo jiǎo 咬佼）：行步舒缓。　④悄：忧。　⑤懰（liǔ 柳）：好貌。⑥忧（yǒu 有）受：舒迟貌。　⑦慅（cǎo 草）：忧愁。　⑧燎：明。⑨夭绍：柔美。　⑩惨：惨当作"懆（cǎo 草）"，忧愁。

【译文】

月儿出来亮啊，美人多美啊。缓缓地步行啊，劳苦得我心忧啊。

月儿出来亮啊，美人多好啊。慢慢地行走啊，劳苦得我心忧啊。

月儿出来亮啊，美人多鲜明啊。慢慢地走动啊，劳苦得我心忧啊。

株 林

胡为乎株林①？从夏南②。匪适株林？从夏南。
驾我乘马③，说于株野。乘我乘驹，朝食于株④。

【注释】

①株林：夏姬的住处。　②夏南：夏姬之子夏征舒，字夏南。表面上说看夏南，实际是看夏姬。　③我：指陈灵公。　④朝食：吃早饭。古人常以饥、饱喻男女情欲之事。

【译文】

为什么到株林？跟夏南。不是到株林？跟夏南。

驾起我骑马,停在株林。骑上我的好马,早上到株林行淫。

泽 陂

彼泽之陂①,有蒲与荷。有美一人,伤如之何?寤寐无为②,涕泗滂沱③。

彼泽之陂,有蒲与蕳④。有美一人,硕大且卷⑤。寤寐无为,中心悁悁⑥。

彼泽之陂,有蒲菡萏⑦。有美一人,硕大且俨⑧。寤寐无为,辗转伏枕。

【注释】

①陂(bēi 杯):堤岸。 ②寤寐:睡醒睡着。 ③涕泗:眼泪鼻涕。 ④蕳(jiān 肩):兰草,通莲。 ⑤卷(quàn 劝):通"鬈",头发卷。 ⑥悁悁:忧郁貌。 ⑦菡萏(hàn dàn 汗旦):荷花。 ⑧俨:双下巴。

【译文】

那个池塘的水涯,有蒲草与荷花。有美丽的一个人儿,忧伤得怎么对待她?睡醒睡着无所谓,眼泪鼻涕纷纷落下。

那个池塘的水涯,有蒲草与莲花。有美丽的一个人儿,高大而且卷头发。睡醒睡着无所谓,心中忧郁地想着她。

那个池塘的水涯,有蒲草和荷花。有美丽的一个人儿,高大并且双下巴。睡醒睡着无所谓,辗转伏枕在想她。

桧 风

桧,国名,在今河南密县东北,后为郑所灭。

羔 裘

羔裘逍遥,狐裘以朝。岂不尔思?劳心忉忉。
羔裘翱翔,狐裘在堂。岂不尔思?我心忧伤。
羔裘如膏,日出有曜①。岂不尔思?中心是悼。

【注释】

①如膏:像膏泽。在太阳照耀下,才如膏的,是倒装句。

【译文】

穿着羔裘显得逍遥,穿着狐裘用来上朝。难道不想您吗?想得心里忧劳。

穿着羔裘可以遨游,穿着狐裘在朝堂。难道不想念您吗?想念得我心忧伤。

穿着羔裘像脂膏,太阳出来有光照。难道不想念您吗?想得心中在哀悼。

素 冠

庶见素冠兮①,棘人栾栾兮②,劳心怛怛兮③。

诗经

庶见素衣兮，我心伤悲兮，聊与子同归兮。
庶见素韠兮④，我心蕴结兮，聊与子如一兮。

【注释】

①庶：幸。 ②棘：瘠。栾栾（luán luán 鸾鸾）：瘦瘠貌。 ③抟抟（tuán tuán 团团）：忧思。 ④韠（bì 毕）：蔽膝。用皮革做成。

【译文】

幸能看见戴白帽子啊，人黑又瘦瘠啊，心里悲痛啊。
幸能看见穿白衣啊，我心里悲伤啊，姑且同您一同归去啊。
幸能看见穿白蔽膝啊，我的心里郁闷啊，姑且和您心同一人啊。

隰有苌楚

隰有苌楚①，猗傩其枝②。夭之沃沃③，乐子之无知④。
隰有苌楚，猗傩其华。夭之沃沃，乐子之无家。
隰有苌楚，猗傩其实。夭之沃沃，乐子之无室。

【注释】

①苌（cháng 长）楚：羊桃，猕猴桃。 ②猗傩：美盛貌。 ③夭：少也。沃沃：光实。 ④子：指苌楚。

【译文】

洼地里有羊桃，美盛的是它的嫩枝。又初生又美好，羡你的无知好。

洼地里有羊桃，美盛的开花极妙。又初生又美好，羡你的无家好。

洼地里有羊桃，美盛的结实极妙。又初生又美好，羡你的无室好。

匪 风

匪风发兮，匪车偈兮①。顾瞻周道，中心怛矣②。

匪风飘兮，匪车嘌兮③。顾瞻周道，中心吊兮。

谁能亨鱼④，溉之釜鬵⑤。谁将西归，怀之好音。

【注释】

①偈（jié 结）：疾驰貌。　②怛（dá 达）：悲伤。　③嘌（piāo 飘）：漂摇不定。　④亨：同"烹"。　⑤溉（gài 盖）：洗。鬵（xún 寻）：釜类，即今俗称锅类。

【译文】

不是风吹动啊，不是车子快开啊。回头看看周家的路，心中是忧伤啊。

不是风飘动啊，不是车子摇动啊。回头看看周家的路，心中要凭吊啊。

谁人能够烧鱼，把锅洗干净。谁人要向西进，想托他传一个好音信。

诗经

曹　风

曹，国名，是一个位于齐晋之间的小国，在今山东西南，后为宋所灭。

蜉　蝣

蜉蝣之羽①，衣裳楚楚②。心之忧矣，於我归处。
蜉蝣之翼，采采衣服。心之忧矣，於我归息。
蜉蝣掘阅③，麻衣如雪。心之忧矣，於我归说④。

【注释】

①蜉蝣（fú yóu 浮游）：虫名，也叫渠略，大如指，长三四寸，有翅能飞。夏月阴雨时从地中出，有朝生暮死的，有生六七日的。羽极薄而有光泽。　②楚楚：鲜明貌。　③掘阅：通"掘穴"，即掘地而出。　④说（shuì 税）：通"税"，歇息。

【译文】

蜉蝣的羽毛，像鲜明的衣裳。心里的忧伤，何处是我的归宿。

蜉蝣的翅膀，像漂亮的衣服。心里的忧愁，何处是我的归宿。

蜉蝣掘洞飞出，麻衣像雪白色。心里的忧伤，何处是我的归宿。

候 人

彼候人兮^①，何戈与祋^②。彼其之子，三百赤芾^③。
维鹈在梁^④，不濡其翼。彼其之子，不称其服。
维鹈在梁，不濡其咮^⑤。彼其之子，不遂其媾^⑥。
荟兮蔚兮^⑦，南山朝隮^⑧。婉兮娈兮，季女斯饥。

【注释】

①候人：修路、迎宾的官。 ②何：同"荷"，扛。祋（duì 对）：同"殳"，古兵器。 ③赤芾（fú 扶）：红色的蔽膝，用皮做，为大夫朝服之一部分。 ④鹈（tí 题）：水鸟名。 ⑤咮（zhòu 咒）：鸟嘴。 ⑥不遂其媾：不能成就他的厚禄。媾指厚禄。 ⑦荟蔚（huì wèi 会位）：云雾弥漫貌。 ⑧朝隮（jī 鸡）：彩虹。

【译文】

那个修路迎宾的人啊，还要扛戈与棍。那些他们的人啊，穿红蔽膝有三百人。

鹈鸟在鱼梁，没有打湿它的翅膀。那些他们的人，不配他们的衣裳。

鹈鸟在鱼梁，没有打湿它的嘴。那些他们的人，不能长享他们的奢侈。

云雾弥漫啊，南山早上起彩虹。柔婉啊美好啊，幼小的女儿受饥饿。

诗经

鸤 鸠

鸤鸠在桑①,其子七兮。淑人君子,其仪一兮②。其仪一兮,心如结兮。

鸤鸠在桑,其子在梅。淑人君子,其带伊丝③。其带伊丝,其弁伊骐④。

鸤鸠在桑,其子在棘。淑人君子,其仪不忒。其仪不忒,正是四国⑤。

鸤鸠在桑,其子在榛。淑人君子,正是国人。正是国人,胡不万年?

【注释】

①鸤(shī 尸)鸠:布谷鸟。 ②仪:仪容。 ③伊丝:是丝。 ④弁(biàn 卞):皮帽。伊骐:是马的青黑色。 ⑤正:法则。

【译文】

布谷鸟在桑树,它的儿子有七个啊。善良的君子人,他的仪容是一样啊。他的仪容是一样啊,心像结实的啊。

布谷鸟在桑树,它的儿子在梅树。善良的君子人,他的带子镶边用白丝。他的带子镶边用白丝,他的皮帽镶边用青黑丝。

布谷鸟在桑树,它的儿子在酸枣树。善良的君子人,他的威仪不变色。他的威仪不变色,可以作为各国的法则。

布谷鸟在桑树,它的儿子在榛树。善良的君子人,正好是国人的法则。正好是国人的法则,为什么万年不得?

下 泉

冽彼下泉①,浸彼苞稂②。忾我寤叹③,念彼周京。
冽彼下泉,浸彼苞萧。忾我寤叹,念彼京周。
冽彼下泉,浸彼苞蓍。忾我寤叹,念彼京师。
芃芃黍苗④,阴雨膏之。四国有王⑤,郇伯劳之⑥。

【注释】

①冽(lèi 列):寒冷。 ②稂(láng 郎):童梁,对禾苗有害的草。 ③忾(xì 戏):叹息。 ④芃芃(péng péng 蓬蓬):茂盛。 ⑤四国:四方诸侯之国。有王:有周天子。 ⑥郇(xún 旬)伯:郇国君。

【译文】

那寒冷的下流泉水,浸那丛生的稂草根。我醒时只有长叹息,想念那周朝的京城。

那寒冷的下流泉水,浸那丛生的艾蒿根。我醒时只能长叹息,想念那周朝的京城。

那寒冷的下流泉水,浸那丛生的蓍草根。我醒时只有长叹息,想念那周朝的京城。

黍苗长得茂盛,阴雨来灌溉它。各国有周天子,郇伯来效劳他。

豳 风

豳,古地名,在今陕西,相传为周的始祖公刘所开发。

七 月

七月流火①,九月授衣②。一之日觱发③,二之日栗烈④。无衣无褐⑤,何以卒岁⑥?三之日于耜⑦,四之日举趾⑧。同我妇子⑨,馌彼南亩⑩,田畯至喜⑪。

七月流火,九月授衣。春日载阳⑫,有鸣仓庚。女执懿筐⑬,遵彼微行⑭,爰求柔桑。春日迟迟⑮,采蘩祁祁⑯。女心伤悲,殆及公子同归⑰。

七月流火,八月萑苇⑱。蚕月条桑⑲,取彼斧斨⑳,以伐远扬㉑。猗彼女桑㉒。七月鸣鵙㉓,八月载绩。载玄载黄,我朱孔阳,为公子裳。

四月秀葽㉔,五月鸣蜩㉕。八月其获,十月陨萚。一之日于貉,取彼狐狸,为公子裘。二之日其同㉖,载缵武功㉗。言私其豵㉘,献豜于公㉙。

五月斯螽动股㉚,六月莎鸡振羽㉛。七月在野,八月在宇,九月在户,十月蟋蟀入我床下。穹窒熏鼠㉜,塞向墐户㉝。嗟我妇子,曰为改岁㉞,入此室处。

六月食郁及薁㉟,七月亨葵及菽㊱。八月剥枣㊲,十月获稻。为此春酒㊳,以介眉寿㊴。七月食瓜,八月断壶㊵。九月叔苴㊶,采荼薪樗㊷,食我农夫。

九月筑场圃，十月纳禾稼。黍稷重穋㊸，禾麻菽麦。嗟我农夫，我稼既同，上入执宫功㊹。昼尔于茅，宵尔索绹㊺。亟其乘屋㊻，其始播百谷。

二之日凿冰冲冲，三之日纳于凌阴㊼。四之日其蚤㊽，献羔祭韭。九月肃霜㊾，十月涤场㊿。朋酒斯飨㉛，曰杀羔羊。跻彼公堂，称彼兕觥㉜，万寿无疆！

【注释】

①七月流火：一年从秋季七月开始，火星自西而下，谓之流火。②九月授衣：九月里分发寒衣。 ③一之日：周历正月，夏历十一月。以下二之日、三之日、四之日，可顺序类推。觱（bì 碧）发：风寒。④栗烈：凛烈。寒气。 ⑤褐（hè 鹤）：毛布制的粗衣。 ⑥卒岁：终岁。 ⑦于耜（sì 寺）：修理犁头。 ⑧举趾：举脚而耕。 ⑨妇子：妻子和小孩。 ⑩馌（yè 叶）：送饭到田头。 ⑪田畯（jùn 俊）：田官。 ⑫阳：和暖。 ⑬懿筐：深筐。 ⑭微行：小路。 ⑮迟迟：指春日长。 ⑯蘩：白蒿。 ⑰殆：怕。同归：指去做妾婢。 ⑱萑（huán 环）苇：即芦苇。 ⑲条桑：剪桑枝。 ⑳斨（qiāng 枪）：方孔的斧。㉑远扬：指又长又高的桑枝。 ㉒猗彼女桑：用绳拉着采桑。 ㉓鵙（jú 局）：伯劳鸟。 ㉔秀葽（yāo 腰）：不开花而结实的远志。㉕蜩（tiáo 条）：蝉。 ㉖同：会合。 ㉗缵：继续。武功：武事，指打猎。 ㉘豵（zōng 宗）：小野猪。 ㉙豜（jiān 肩）：大野猪。 ㉚斯螽：一种鸣虫，以股鸣。 ㉛莎鸡：纺织娘，一种虫。㉜穹（qióng 穷）：尽。室（zhì 至）：堵塞。 ㉝向：北窗。墐：用泥涂抹。 ㉞曰：语助词。改岁：除夕。 ㉟郁：郁李。薁（yù 郁）：蘡薁。落叶藤本植物。茎的纤维可以做绳索。 ㊱葵：一种蔬

菜名。　㊲剥：打。　㊳春酒：冬酿春熟的酒。　㊴介：乞求。眉寿：人老眉长，表寿长。　㊵壶：通"瓠"。　㊶叔：拾取。苴（jū 居）：麻子。　㊷荼（tú 涂）：苦菜。樗（chū 初）：木名，臭椿。　㊸重穋（lù 录）：后熟曰重，先熟曰穋。　㊹上：同"尚"。功：事。　㊺绹（táo 陶）：绳。　㊻亟：急。　㊼凌阴：冰室。　㊽蚤：同"早"。　㊾肃霜：下霜。　㊿涤场：涤除场上杂物。　㊀朋酒：两壶酒。　㊁称：举起。

【译文】

　　七月里火星流向下，九月里官家发寒衣。十一月里起寒风，十二月里寒气凛冽。没有长袍和短袄，怎么过年呢？正月里修理农具，二月里举起脚把田犁。同我的妻子女儿，送饭送到田地，田官看了心里喜。

　　七月里火星流向下，九月里官家发寒衣。春天太阳好，黄莺声声啼。姑娘拿深筐，照着小路走，去求柔嫩的桑。春天日子长，采摘白蒿忙。姑娘的心里伤悲，怕和公子一同回归。

　　七月里火星流向下，八月里芦苇长成罢。蚕月里蔪下枝条桑，拿着那斧子，斫掉枝条的远扬。用绳子拉住柔桑。七月里听伯劳鸟叫，八月里纺织麻布料。染上色黑和色黄，我染朱红更鲜丽，为公子做衣裳。

　　四月里远志结子，五月里蝉嘈不止。八月里早稻收获，十月里叶子掉落。十一月上山打貉，取那狐狸皮剥掉，做公子的皮袄。十二月集会共同，继续讲打猎的武功。说私自占有小猪，把三岁大猪献给公。

　　五月里斯螽振动双股，六月里织布娘振动双翅声。七月里在野地，八月里在屋子，九月里在门内，十月里蟋蟀入我床底。塞住漏洞熏老鼠，泥垡上北窗垡住门户。叹说我的妻子和孩子，说是旧年快过去了，进入这间屋里住。

六月吃李和葡萄，七月煮豆和葵苗。八月打枣，十月收稻。做这个春酒，来祝贺长寿。七月吃瓜，八月割断葫芦，九月拣起麻子啰，采苦菜打些柴，养活我们农夫。

九月修筑打谷场，十月把禾稼收藏。早熟晚熟的黍子高粱，禾麻豆麦一起藏。嗟叹我们农夫，我们的庄稼既完工，还进到公爷的宫。白天去割茅草，夜里把绳打好。快些去修屋，到春天忙于种百谷。

十二月凿冰声冲冲忙，正月里把冰往冰室藏。二月里取冰祭祀早，献上韭菜和羔羊。九月里降下霜，十月里清扫打谷场。两壶酒可以上飨，再杀了羔羊，登那公爷堂，举起那兕角觥，说万寿无疆！

鸱鸮

鸱鸮鸱鸮①，既取我子，无毁我室。恩斯勤斯②，鬻子之闵斯③。

迨天之未阴雨，彻彼桑土④，绸缪牖户。今女下民，或敢侮予。

予手拮据⑤，予所捋荼，予所蓄租⑥，予口卒瘏⑦，曰予未有室家。

予羽谯谯⑧，予尾翛翛⑨，予室翘翘⑩，风雨所漂摇，予维音哓哓⑪。

【注释】

①鸱鸮（chī xiāo 痴消）：猫头鹰一类的鸟。　②恩斯勤斯：

斯,语助词。"恩"通"殷",言殷勤于稚子。 ③鬻(yù 育):通"育",养育。闵:病。 ④彻:通"撤",撤去。桑土:即桑杜,为桑根。 ⑤拮(jié 洁)据:辛劳。 ⑥畜租:积聚。 ⑦卒瘏(tú 图):尽瘁。 ⑧谯谯(qiáo qiáo 樵樵):焦敝。 ⑨翛翛(xiāo xiāo 消消):枯焦。 ⑩翘翘(qiáo qiáo 桥桥):危貌,摇晃。 ⑪哓哓(xiāo xiāo 消消):叫声。

【译文】

鸱鸮啊鸱鸮,既经抓取我的小鸟,不要再毁坏我的巢。辛勤地保护小鸟,养育它我已病倒。

等天没有阴雨,撤去那桑根,修理好窗门。现在你们树下的人,还有敢欺侮我的人。

我的手已经疲劳,我还要捋茅草,我还要积蓄枯草,我的嘴已经累坏,我还没有修好我的巢。

我的羽毛已经稀少,我的尾巴已经枯焦,我的巢还在晃摇,风吹雨打显得飘摇,我只有大声喊叫。

东 山

我徂东山①,慆慆不归②。我来自东,零雨其濛。我东曰归,我心西悲。制彼裳衣,勿士行枚③。蜎蜎者蠋④,烝在桑野⑤。敦彼独宿⑥,亦在车下。

我徂东山,慆慆不归。我来自东,零雨其濛。果臝之实⑦,亦施于宇。伊威在室⑧,蟏蛸在户⑨。町疃鹿场⑩,熠燿宵行⑪。不可畏也,伊可怀也⑫。

我徂东山,慆慆不归。我来自东,零雨其濛。鹳鸣于垤⑬,

妇叹于室。洒扫穹室,我征聿至。有敦瓜苦,烝在栗薪。自我不见,于今三年。

我徂东山,慆慆不归。我来自东,零雨其濛。仓庚于飞⑭,熠燿其羽。之子于归,皇驳其马⑮。亲结其缡⑯,九十其仪⑰。其新孔嘉,其旧如之何⑱?

【注释】

①徂(cú殂):往。 ②慆慆(tāo tāo 滔滔):久。 ③勿士行枚:即勿事行枚,勿从事行军衔枚。行军时衔枚,怕发声,今不用衔枚。 ④蜎蜎(yuān yuān 渊渊):蠕动貌。蠋(zhú烛):毛虫。 ⑤烝:乃。 ⑥敦:蜷曲成一团。 ⑦果臝(luǒ裸):植物名,一名瓜蒌,蔓生葫芦科。 ⑧伊威:虫名,一名湿生虫。 ⑨蟏蛸(xiāo shāo消梢):长脚蜘蛛。 ⑩町畽(tǐng tuǎn 挺疃):野外。 ⑪熠(yì意)燿:萤光。宵行:萤火虫。 ⑫伊:是。 ⑬鹳(guàn贯):鸟名,似鹤。垤(dié迭):土堆。 ⑭仓庚:指黄鹂。 ⑮皇驳:马色黄白曰皇,马色赤白曰驳。 ⑯缡(lí离):古妇女的佩巾,嫁时母亲为女结佩巾。 ⑰九十其仪:其仪有九或十,言其仪之多。 ⑱其新孔嘉,其旧如之何:新指新婚。孔嘉,极好。旧指已婚者。

【译文】

我去东山,长久不能回来。我从东方来,小雨迷濛落下来。我从东方回来,我心还向西悲。缝制那新衣裳,不用行军衔枚。蠕动的是毛虫,是在那桑树上。团绕着独宿的兵丁,也在战车下睡。

我去东山,长久不能回来。我从东方来,小雨迷濛落下来。瓜蒌结的子儿,也挂在屋檐边。地虱虫在室内爬,蜘蛛结网挂在门边。野鹿在场上回旋,萤火虫儿亮光妍。这么荒凉不可怕,它是让人更怀念。

我去东山,长久不能回来。我从东方来,小雨迷濛落下来。鹳鸟在蚁堆上叫,妇人在屋里叹了。打扫屋子塞鼠洞,我走路已将到。苦瓜结了一大捧,砍栗做柴始得用。自从我不见这变迁,到了今天已三年。

我去东山,长久不能回来。我从东方来,小雨迷濛落下来。黄鹂到处在飞,闪耀它的毛羽发光。这个姑娘要出嫁,马儿有红又有黄。亲结佩巾推阿母,多种仪式真堂堂。新婚幸福好主张,久别重逢又怎样?

破 斧

既破我斧,又缺我斨①。周公东征,四国是皇②。哀我人斯,亦孔之将③。

既破我斧,又缺我锜④。周公东征,四国是吪⑤。哀我人斯,亦孔之嘉。

既破我斧,又缺我銶⑥。周公东征,四国是遒⑦。哀我人斯,亦孔之休。

【注释】

①斨(qiāng 腔):斧柄方孔者叫斨。 ②四国:管、蔡、商、奄,即管叔、蔡叔、武庚、奄国。奄国在曲阜东。皇:匡正。 ③将:大,美。 ④锜(qí 其):凿类。 ⑤吪(é 俄):教化。 ⑥銶(qiú 求):独头斧。 ⑦遒(qiú 求):安定。

【译文】

既经破坏我的手斧,又弄缺我的方孔斧。周公向东征伐,四国得到安匡。可怜我们这些战士,也得到安康。

既经破坏我的斧子,又弄缺我的凿子。周公向东征伐,四国受到了教化。可怜我们的战士,也得到好评价。

既经破坏我的手斧,又弄缺我的独头斧。周公向东征伐,四国得到安定。可怜我们的士兵,也得到休整。

伐 柯

伐柯如何①,匪斧不克。取妻如何,匪媒不得。

伐柯伐柯,其则不远。我觏之子,笾豆有践②。

【注释】

①柯:斧柄。 ②笾(biān 边):古代祭祀和宴会盛果品的竹器。豆:古代木制盛肉器。践:行列。

【译文】

砍斧柄怎么样,没有斧子不行。娶妻怎么样,没有媒人不行。

砍斧柄啊砍斧柄,它的法则在近旁。我看见这个姑娘,把餐具摆成行。

九 罭

九罭之鱼①,鳟鲂②。我觏之子,衮衣绣裳③。

鸿飞遵渚。公归无所,於女信处④。鸿飞遵陆。公归不复，於女信宿⑤。

是以有衮衣兮⑥，无以我公归兮⑦，无使我心悲兮。

【注释】

①九罭（yù 域）：捕小鱼的细网。 ②鳟（zūn 尊）：赤眼鳟。鲂与鳟，都是大鱼，用捕小鱼网来捕不合式。 ③衮衣：衣上绣着龙的礼服。 ④信：再宿。 ⑤宿：一宿。 ⑥以：已。 ⑦以：与。

【译文】

捕小鱼的细网，捉大鱼的鳟鲂。我看见的这个人，穿着龙袍绣裳。

大雁飞时沿着沙渚。公爷归去没有所处，这里留您住二宿处。大雁飞时沿着大陆。公爷回去后不再回，这里留您住二宿或一宿。

这里有龙袍啊，不要让我公爷归去啊，不要使我心悲啊。

狼 跋

狼跋其胡①，载疐其尾②。公孙硕肤③，赤舄几几④。
狼疐其尾，载跋其胡。公孙硕肤，德音不瑕⑤。

【注释】

①跋（bá 拔）：踩，踏。胡：颔下垂之肉。 ②疐（zhì 至）：踩。 ③硕肤：心广体胖。 ④赤舄（xì 戏）：锡与金合做的鞋头饰物。几几：盛，以状盛服之貌。 ⑤瑕：过。

【译文】

狼向前踩了颔下肉,后退又踩了它尾巴。公孙心宽体又胖,金饰鞋头服很嘉。

狼后退踩它的尾巴,前进踩了它颔下肉。公孙心宽体又胖,他的好声音不含蓄。

卷 四

小 雅

"雅者，正也，正乐之歌也。"（朱熹《诗集传》）雅与风一样，是乐歌之名，又有大小雅之分。二雅大都是贵族士大夫的作品。

鹿鸣之什

"雅、颂无诸国别，故以十篇为一卷，而谓之什，犹军法以十人为什也。"（朱熹《诗集传》）

鹿 鸣

呦呦鹿鸣①，食野之苹②。我有嘉宾，鼓瑟吹笙。吹笙鼓簧③，承筐是将④。人之好我，示我周行⑤。

呦呦鹿鸣，食野之蒿。我有嘉宾，德音孔昭。视民不恌⑥，君子是则是傚。我有旨酒，嘉宾式燕以敖⑦。

呦呦鹿鸣，食野之芩⑧。我有嘉宾，鼓瑟鼓琴。鼓瑟鼓琴，和乐且湛⑨。我有旨酒，以宴乐嘉宾之心⑩。

【注释】

①呦呦（yōu 优）：鹿鸣声，见食相呼。 ②苹：藾蒿，艾蒿。③簧：乐器中用以发声的振动器。 ④承筐是将：承，奉也。将，送也。古代奉筐盛币帛以送宾客。 ⑤周行：大路。 ⑥视：示。恌（tiāo 挑）：轻佻。 ⑦式：语辞。燕：同"宴"。敖：游乐。 ⑧芩

(qín 琴）：蒿类植物。 ⑨湛（dān 耽）：乐之久。 ⑩宴：安。

【译文】

鹿在呦呦地叫，吃野地里的艾蒿。我有好的宾客，弹瑟吹笙簧。吹笙振动簧，送客币帛盛满筐。人们对我很是好，指我大道好主张。

鹿在呦呦地叫，吃野地里的蒿草。我有好的宾客，他的盛名昭昭了。为人榜样不轻佻，君子对好事是仿效。我有好酒，邀客欢宴又逍遥。

鹿在呦呦地叫，吃野地里的芩草。我有好的宾客，弹瑟又弹琴。弹瑟又弹琴，和乐并且尽兴听音。我有好酒，用宴会来欢乐客人的心。

四 牡

四牡骍骍①，周道倭迟②。岂不怀归？王事靡盬③，我心伤悲。

四牡骍骍，啴啴骆马④。岂不怀归？王事靡盬，不遑启处⑤。

翩翩者鵻⑥，载飞载下，集于苞栩⑦。王事靡盬，不遑将父。

翩翩者鵻，载飞载止，集于苞杞。王事靡盬，不遑将母。

驾彼四骆，载骤骎骎⑧。岂不怀归？是用作歌，将母来谂⑨。

诗经

【注释】

①骓骓（fēi fēi 非非）：马行不停貌。 ②倭迟：迂远。 ③靡盬（gǔ 古）：不牢固。 ④啴啴（tān tān 摊摊）：喘气。骆（luò 落）：白毛黑鬣的马。 ⑤启处：安居。 ⑥雉（zhuī 追）：斑鸠。 ⑦苍栩：丛生栎树。 ⑧骎骎（qīn qīn 侵侵）：马速行。 ⑨谂（shěn 审）：念。

【译文】

四匹马在不停地跑，大路又迂回。难道不想回归？周王的事不牢固，我的心里在伤悲。

四匹马在不停地跑，白马跑得光喘气。难道不想回归？周王的事不牢固，没有功夫讲安处。

斑鸠在翩翩飞，飞得高来飞得低，停在丛生栎树里。周王的事不牢固，没有功夫养我父。

斑鸠在翩翩飞，有时飞有时停，停在丛生杞树里。周王的事不牢固，没有功夫养我母。

驾车用那四白马，赶车赶马跑得急。难道不想回归？因此作歌不收敛，用那养母作思念。

皇皇者华

皇皇者华①，于彼原隰②。駪駪征夫③，每怀靡及④。
我马维驹⑤，六辔如濡⑥。载驰载驱，周爰咨诹⑦。
我马维骐⑧，六辔如丝。载驰载驱，周爰咨谋。
我马维骆⑨，六辔沃若。载驰载驱，周爰咨度。
我马维骃⑩，六辔既均。载驰载驱，周爰咨询。

【注释】

①皇皇：同"煌煌"，指光采照耀。 ②原隰（xí 席）：平原洼地。③駪駪（shēn shēn 身身）：众多。征夫：行人。 ④每怀：每次怀念私心。靡及：无及于君命。 ⑤驹：壮马。 ⑥辔：缰绳。 ⑦周：周到。咨：问。诹（zōu 邹）：访事。 ⑧骐（qí 旗）：青黑色的马。 ⑨骆：白毛的马。 ⑩骃（yīn 音）：灰色杂毛的马。

【译文】

光彩照耀的鲜花，在那平原洼地聚集。众多出使的行人，每次怀私停留来不及。

我的马是壮马，六根马缰绳都润湿。又赶马又赶车，周到地访问和谈事。

我的马是青黑色的马，六根马缰绳像丝柔。又赶马又赶车，周到地访问和筹谋。

我的马是白毛的马，六根马缰绳很润泽。又赶马又赶车，周到地访问和谋策。

我的马是杂色的马，六根马缰绳既匀均。又赶马又赶车，周到地访问和咨询。

常　棣

常棣之华①，鄂不韡韡②。凡今之人，莫如兄弟。
死丧之威③，兄弟孔怀。原隰裒矣④，兄弟求矣。
脊令在原⑤，兄弟急难。每有良朋，况也永叹⑥。
兄弟阋于墙⑦，外御其务⑧。每有良朋，烝也无戎⑨。
丧乱既平，既安且宁。虽有兄弟，不如友生⑩。

诗经

傧尔笾豆⑪，饮酒之饫⑫。兄弟既具，和乐且孺⑬。
妻子好合，如鼓瑟琴。兄弟既翕⑭，和乐且湛⑮。
宜尔室家，乐尔妻孥⑯。是究是图，亶其然乎⑰！

【注释】

①常棣：即棠棣，郁李，落叶灌木，高五六尺，春开花五瓣，夏结实为核果。 ②鄂不：同"萼柎"，即萼足。韡韡（wěi wěi 伟伟）：光明貌。 ③威：畏。 ④裒（póu 坏）：聚集。 ⑤脊令：同"鹡鸰"，鸟名。头黑额白，背黑腹白，尾长。是水鸟。今在平原，失其常处，比兄弟有急难。 ⑥况：发语词。 ⑦阋（xì 隙）墙：因恨相争于内。 ⑧务：亦作"侮"。 ⑨烝：通假作"曾"，乃。戎：助。 ⑩友生：友。生，语助词。 ⑪傧（bìn 鬓）：陈设。 ⑫饫（yù 裕）：满足。 ⑬孺：相亲。 ⑭翕（xī 希）：聚合。 ⑮湛（zhàn 栈）：深情。 ⑯孥（nú 奴）：儿女。 ⑰亶（dǎn 胆）：诚然。

【译文】

郁李的花，萼足是光明。凡是如今的人，没有像兄弟相亲。

死丧的可怕，只有兄弟怀念不休。平原或洼地聚葬了，兄弟还是相寻求了。

鹡鸰水鸟在平原上，兄弟救急难。虽有好朋友相慰，只使人长叹。

兄弟在家内相争，对外抗御他们的欺侮。虽有好的朋友，总是没有来相助。

丧乱既经平定，既是平安而且宁静。虽有兄弟，不如朋友相亲。

陈列你设宴的用具,饮酒得到满足。兄弟既经团聚,和好快乐而且永相亲。

妻子既爱好相合,像弹奏琴瑟。兄弟既经聚合,和好快乐而且深情契合。

管好你的家庭,使你妻子儿女快乐呀。研究呀谋划呀,确实是这样的理呀!

伐 木

伐木丁丁①,鸟鸣嘤嘤②。出自幽谷,迁于乔木。嘤其鸣矣,求其友声。相彼鸟矣,犹求友声。矧伊人矣③,不求友生。神之听之④,终和且平。

伐木许许⑤,酾酒有藇⑥。既有肥羜⑦,以速诸父⑧。宁适不来,微我弗顾?於粲洒扫⑨,陈馈八簋⑩。既有肥牡,以速诸舅。宁适不来,微我有咎。

伐木于阪,酾酒有衍⑪。笾豆有践,兄弟无远。民之失德,乾糇以愆⑫。有酒湑我⑬,无酒酤我⑭。坎坎鼓我⑮,蹲蹲舞我⑯。迨我暇矣。饮此湑矣。

【注释】

①丁丁(zhēng zhēng 争争):伐木声。 ②嘤嘤(yīng yīng 莺莺):鸟鸣声。 ③矧(shěn 审):况且,何况。 ④神之听之:审慎听从。神,慎。 ⑤许许(hǔ hǔ 虎虎):众人共力之声。 ⑥酾(shī 师):滤酒。藇(xù 序):美好。 ⑦羜(zhù 助):五个月的小羊。 ⑧速:催请。 ⑨於(wū 乌):感叹词。粲:鲜洁貌。 ⑩馈(kuì 愧):赠送。簋(guǐ 鬼):古盛食物用具,圆口,两耳。 ⑪衍:美

好。 ⑫餱（hóu 侯）：干粮。愆：过失。 ⑬湑（xǔ 许）：滤过的酒。
⑭酤：买酒。 ⑮坎坎：鼓声。 ⑯蹲蹲（cún cún 存存）：舞貌。

【译文】

砍那树木丁丁声，鸟儿叫着嘤嘤鸣。鸟从深谷飞出来，迁到高树争光明。嘤嘤地鸣了，发出求友的叫声。看看那个小鸟呀，还发出求友的叫声。何况还是人呢，怎能不求友生。审慎吧听从吧，终于是和好而且安平。

众人砍树许许声，滤糟的酒更清澄。既有肥美的五月羔，用来快请伯叔情。难道有事不能来，非我不顾心不诚。清洁庭院忙打扫，陈设肴馔和八羹。既有肥羊和清樽，快邀伯叔心极诚。难道有事不能来，非我有错心不诚。

砍树在斜坡上，滤糟的酒更清澄。碗盘排列皆成行，兄弟相会莫疏远。人们失去德音情，干粮待客不真诚。有酒我把它滤清，无酒我买献殷勤。我们击鼓坎坎声，我们跳舞更相亲。等到我们有空了，饮这清酒显情亲。

天 保

天保定尔①，亦孔之固。俾尔单厚②，何福不除③？俾尔多益，以莫不庶④。

天保定尔，俾尔戬穀⑤。罄无不宜⑥，受天百禄。降尔遐福，维日不足。

天保定尔，以莫不兴。如山如阜，如冈如陵，如川之方至，以莫不增。

吉蠲为饎⑦，是用孝享⑧。禴祠烝尝⑨，于公先王⑩。君曰卜尔⑪。万寿无疆。

神之吊矣⑫。诒尔多福。民之质矣，日用饮食。群黎百姓，遍为尔德。

如月之恒⑬，如日之升。如南山之寿，不骞不崩⑭。如松柏之茂，无不尔或承。

【注释】

①保：安也。 ②单厚：尽厚。 ③不除：不予。除、余古通用，余作"予"。 ④庶：富。 ⑤戬（jiǎn 剪）：福。榖：善。 ⑥罄（qìng 庆）：尽。 ⑦蠲（juān 捐）：通"涓"，清洁。馆（chì 斥）：酒食。 ⑧孝享：献祭。 ⑨禴（yuè 跃）：夏祭。祠：春祭。尝：秋祭。烝：冬祭。 ⑩于公先王：于先公先王。 ⑪君：指先公先王。 ⑫吊：至。 ⑬恒（gèng 更）：弦，指月上弦。 ⑭骞（qiān 谦）：亏损。崩：毁坏。

【译文】

上天为了安定你，也把稳固赐给你。使你尽厚待百姓，哪种福气不给你？使你多得好处，没有不富庶呢。

上天为了安定你，使你得到福禄。尽你所得没不宜，受上天的百禄。降给你的远福，惟恐日子不满足。

上天为了安定你，可用的没有不旺兴。像山像阜那样，像山冈像山陵，像百川的流水，因此没有不加增。

吉日清洁作酒食，用来祭献给祖上。春夏秋冬都祭祀，祭祀先公并先王。先公先王说祝你，祝你万寿是无疆。

神的到来了，赐给你多种幸福。人民的质朴呀，日用饮食也不错。群众黎民和百官，普遍感化你的道德。

诗经

好比天上上弦月,好比太阳正高升。好比南山那样寿,不会亏蚀不会崩。好比松柏的茂盛,没有不可你继承。

采 薇

采薇采薇①,薇亦作止②。曰归曰归,岁亦莫止。靡室靡家,狁之故③。不遑启居,狁之故。

采薇采薇,薇亦柔止④。曰归曰归,心亦忧止。忧心烈烈⑤,载饥载渴。我戍未定,靡使归聘⑥。

采薇采薇,薇亦刚止⑦。曰归曰归,岁亦阳止⑧。王事靡盬,不遑启处。忧心孔疚,我行不来。

彼尔维何⑨?维常之华。彼路斯何⑩?君子之车。戎车既驾,四牡业业。岂敢定居?一月三捷。

驾彼四牡,四牡骙骙⑪。君子所依,小人所腓⑫。四牡翼翼⑬,象弭鱼服⑭。岂不日戒?狁孔棘⑮。

昔我往矣,杨柳依依⑯。今我来思,雨雪霏霏。行道迟迟,载渴载饥。我心伤悲,莫知我哀。

【注释】

①薇:野豌豆。 ②作:初生。止:语助词。 ③狁(xiǎn yǔn 险允):古民族名,春秋时为戎狄,秦汉时为匈奴,隋唐时为突厥。 ④柔:嫩。 ⑤烈烈:忧貌。 ⑥聘:问候。 ⑦刚:坚硬。 ⑧阳:阴历十月。 ⑨尔:通"薾",花盛。 ⑩路:大车。 ⑪骙骙(kuí kuí 葵葵):马强壮。 ⑫腓(féi 肥):掩护。 ⑬翼翼:娴熟。 ⑭弭(mǐ 米):弓末弯曲处。鱼服:鱼皮作箭袋。 ⑮棘:急。 ⑯依依:犹"殷殷"。

【译文】

采薇菜呀采薇菜,薇菜刚刚在生长。说归去呀说归去,一年快要过了账。没有妻房没有家,狎狁的缘故要算账。没有功夫讲安居,狎狁的缘故只要讲。

采薇菜呀采薇菜,薇菜变得嫩又柔。说归去呀说归去,不能归去心发愁。心里忧愁像火烧,又饥又渴怎么了。我的驻防没有定,不能使人归问聘。

采薇菜呀采薇菜,薇菜变硬不好采。说归去呀说归去,年到十月不等待。王事没有稳固啊,没有时间可安息。心里忧愁很病痛,我想走了不等待。

那个花是什么? 是棠棣的花。那个大车是谁坐? 是将军的车。兵车既经驾好了,四匹雄马很壮观。怎敢说安定居处? 一个月里三胜战。

驾车用那四雄马,四匹雄马很强壮。战车是将军的依靠,士兵的隐蔽。四匹雄马驾车很熟习,带上象弭鱼皮袋。岂不每天作戒备?狎狁的事很是急。

从前我去参军了,杨柳殷殷情不了。现在我归来了,雨雪纷纷下不了。慢慢走路吧,又渴又饥怎么了。我的心里是悲哀,没有人知道我的悲哀。

出 车

我出我车,于彼牧矣。自天子所,谓我来兮。召彼仆夫,谓之载矣。王事多难,维其棘矣。

我出我车,于彼郊矣。设此旐矣①,建彼旄矣。彼旟旐斯②,胡不旆旆③?忧心悄悄,仆夫况瘁④。

王命南仲⑤,往城于方。出车彭彭,旂旐央央⑥。天子命我，城彼朔方。赫赫南仲⑦，狁于襄⑧。

昔我往矣，黍稷方华。今我来思，雨雪载涂。王事多难，不遑启居。岂不怀归？畏此简书⑨。

喓喓草虫，趯趯阜螽⑩。未见君子，忧心忡忡。既见君子，我心则降。赫赫南仲，薄伐西戎。

春日迟迟，卉木萋萋。仓庚喈喈，采蘩祁祁⑪。执讯获丑⑫，薄言还归。赫赫南仲，狁于夷。

【注释】

①旐(zhào 兆)：古代画龟蛇的旗。 ②旟(yú 于)：古代画隼鸟的旗。 ③旆旆(pèi pèi 配配)：古代旗末有旒下垂。 ④况：通"怳"。 ⑤南仲：宣王时人，为将筑城于朔方，以御北敌。 ⑥央央：鲜明貌。 ⑦赫赫：盛。 ⑧襄：除。 ⑨简书：写在竹简上的军书。 ⑩趯趯(tì tì 惕惕)：跳跃貌。 ⑪祁祁：舒迟。 ⑫执讯：捉敌讯问。获丑：杀敌割左耳。

【译文】

我出了我的车，在那放牧的地方。从天子处，命我来到这地方。召集那些车夫，叫他们快装光。周王的事多外患，事情急迫着忙。

我出了我的车，在那郊区了。装饰这面旗子了，竖立那面旗子了。那各种旗子，为什么不让旒下垂？我暗中担忧，想那车夫劳瘁。

周王命令南仲，去筑城北方。出发的兵车浩盛，旗子飘动有光。天子命令我，筑城在那朔方。威严的大将南仲，除去狁固国防。

从前我去了，黍稷正开花。现在我来了，满路雨雪花花。周王的事多外患，没功夫安居。难道不想回去，怕这种紧急兵书。

草虫嘤嘤地叫，阜螽追赶地跳。没有看见君子人，心里忧愁忡忡地跳。既经看见那君子人，我的心平静不动摇。威严的南仲，去讨伐那西戎。

春天日子慢慢过，花木生长繁盛时。黄莺正在喈喈叫，人们从容采蒿芝。捉敌审讯或割耳，凯旋班师正得时。威严大将称南仲，狁狁得到平定时。

杕 杜

有杕之杜，有睆其实①。王事靡盬，继嗣我日②。日月阳止，女心伤止，征夫遑止③。

有杕之杜，其叶萋萋。王事靡盬，我心伤悲。卉木萋止，女心悲止，征夫归止。

陟彼北山，言采其杞④。王事靡盬，忧我父母。檀车幝幝⑤，四马痯痯⑥，征夫不远。

匪载匪来，忧心孔疚。期逝不至，而多为恤⑦。卜筮偕止⑧，会言近止，征夫迩止⑨。

【注释】

①睆（huǎn 缓）：光泽。　②嗣：继续。　③遑：空暇。　④杞：枸杞。　⑤檀车：檀木做的役车。幝幝（chǎn chǎn 产产）：破敝貌。　⑥痯痯（guǎn guǎn 管管）：疲乏貌。　⑦恤（xǔ 许）：忧。　⑧偕：通"嘉"。　⑨迩（ěr 尔）：近。

【译文】

　　特生的赤棠,光泽是它的果实。王爷的事没止息,继续延留我月日。又延留到十月,妇人的心里忧愁,征人没功夫得休。

　　特生的赤棠,它的叶儿茂盛。王爷的事没止息,我的心里伤悲。花木终是茂盛,妇人的心里伤悲,征人怎能回归。

　　登上那座北山,采摘那里的枸杞。王爷的事没止息,忧我父母没人理。役车已经敝坏,四匹马儿已疲软,征人已经走不远。

　　车不见载人不见来,忧心成病想不开。约期已过人不至,多为忧愁伤怀。又卜又筮都说好,合说他来期近了,征人回家近了。

南　陔（佚）

白华之什

白 华（佚）
华 黍（佚）

鱼 丽

鱼丽于罶①，鲿鲨②。君子有酒，旨且多。
鱼丽于罶，鲂鳢③。君子有酒，多且旨。
鱼丽于罶，鰋鲤④。君子有酒，旨且有。
物其多矣，维其嘉矣。
物其旨矣，维其偕矣⑤。
物其有矣，维其时矣⑥。

【注释】

①丽（lí 离）：通"罹"，陷入。罶（liǔ 柳）：竹篓，用竹编制，鱼进入竹篓即不能出。篓有大小，小篓只能捉小鱼，大篓可以捉大鱼，这里当指大篓。　②鲿（cháng 尝）：黄颊鱼，较大。鲨（shā 沙）：吹沙鱼，较小。　③鲂（fáng 房）：鳊鱼，银灰色，腹部隆起。身阔鳞细。鳢（lǐ 礼）：也叫黑鱼。　④鰋（yǎn 偃）：也叫鲇鱼。　⑤偕：通"嘉"。　⑥时：适时。

【译文】

鱼儿陷入竹篓,鳡鱼和鲨鱼都有。君子有酒,鱼味美且多酒。
鱼儿陷入竹篓,鲂鱼鳢鱼都有。君子有酒,鱼味美且多酒。
鱼儿陷入竹篓,鳏鱼鲤鱼都有。君子有酒,鱼味美且多酒。
食物真是多呀,只有它是好呀。
食物真是美呀,只有它是好呀。
食物真是丰富呀,只有它是适合时令呀。

由 庚(佚)

南有嘉鱼

南有嘉鱼①,烝然罩罩②。君子有酒,嘉宾式燕以乐。
南有嘉鱼,烝然汕汕③。君子有酒,嘉宾式燕以衎④。
南有樛木⑤,甘瓠累之⑥。君子有酒,嘉宾式燕绥之。
翩翩者鵻⑦,烝然来思。君子有酒,嘉宾式燕又思⑧。

【注释】

①南:南方。嘉鱼:美好的鱼。 ②罩罩:指用多罩来捉鱼,不限于一罩。 ③汕汕(shàn shàn 善善):用众抄网捕鱼。汕即抄网,汕汕即不止一汕。 ④衎(kàn 看):乐。 ⑤樛(jiū 纠)木:向下弯曲的树。 ⑥瓠:葫芦。 ⑦鵻(zhuī 追):斑鸠。 ⑧又:通"右",劝酒。

【译文】

南方有美好的鱼,用众渔具捉鱼。君子有美酒,好宾客快乐地欢宴饮酒。

南方有美好的鱼,用众网捕捉鱼。君子有美酒,好宾客舒畅地欢宴饮酒。

南方有向下弯曲的树,甜葫芦缠绕这树。君子有美酒,好宾客安然地欢宴饮酒。

斑鸠翩翩地飞来,众多地飞过来。君子有美酒,好宾客参加宴会又劝酒。

崇 丘(佚)

南山有台

南山有台①,北山有莱②。乐只君子,邦家之基。乐只君子,万寿无期。

南山有桑,北山有杨。乐只君子,邦家之光。乐只君子,万寿无疆。

南山有杞③,北山有李。乐只君子,民之父母。乐只君子,德音不已。

南山有栲④,北山有杻⑤。乐只君子,遐不眉寿。乐只君子,德音是茂。

南山有枸⑥,北山有楰⑦。乐只君子,遐不黄耇⑧?乐只君子,保艾尔后⑨。

【注释】

①台:莎草,可作蓑衣。 ②莱:藜,亦称灰菜,嫩叶可食。 ③杞(qǐ 起):木名,一说枸杞,一说杞柳。 ④栲(kǎo 考):山樗,像漆树。 ⑤杻(niǔ 纽):檍木,可作弓材。 ⑥枸(jǔ 举):

枳枸。树高大，子大如指，味甘美，亦名木蜜。　⑦梄（yú 于）：虎梓，槚楸。　⑧黄耇（gǒu 苟）：少年发黑，老变白，白久变黄，为老寿。　⑨保艾：安长。

【译文】

南山有莎草，北山有黎草。快乐的君子人，国家基础的宝。快乐的君子人，万寿无时可考。

南山有桑，北山有杨。快乐的君子人，是为国家增光。快乐的君子人，万寿无疆。

南山有枸杞，北山有李。快乐的君子人，民的父母亲。快乐的君子人，道德的声誉不停。

南山有山樗树，北山有檍树。快乐的君子人，怎么不会长寿。快乐的君子人，道德的声誉是盛茂。

南山有梄树，北山有楸树。快乐的君子人，怎么不成黄发老人？快乐的君子人，安定地长养您的后代人。

由　仪（佚）

蓼　萧

蓼彼萧斯①，零露湑兮②。既见君子，我心写兮③。燕笑语兮，是以有誉处兮④。

蓼彼萧斯，零露瀼瀼⑤。既见君子，为龙为光⑥。其德不爽，寿考不忘。

蓼彼萧斯，零露泥泥⑦。既见君子，孔燕岂弟⑧。宜兄宜弟，令德寿岂⑨。

蓼彼萧斯,零露浓浓。既见君子,鞗革冲冲⑩。和鸾雝雝⑪,万福攸同⑫。

【注释】

①蓼(lù 录):长大貌。萧:白蒿。 ②零:落下。湑(xǔ 许):湑指滤过的酒,有清澄意。 ③写:舒泄。 ④誉:通"豫",乐。 ⑤瀼瀼(ráng ráng 攘攘):盛貌。 ⑥龙:光宠。 ⑦泥泥:濡湿。 ⑧岂弟:同"恺悌",和易近人。 ⑨岂:同"恺",乐。 ⑩鞗(tiáo 条)革:马缰绳。冲冲:垂饰貌。 ⑪和鸾:车上的铃铛。 ⑫攸:所。同:聚集。

【译文】

长大的白蒿啊,降下的露珠清啊。既经看见君子人,我的心里舒畅啊。在宴会上笑着说啊,因此有快乐啊。

长大的白蒿啊,降下的露水满穰穰。既经看见君子人,又受宠又增光。他的德行既不差,愿他长寿永安康。

长大的白蒿啊,落下的露水濡穰。既经看见君子人,又欢宴又和畅。作为兄弟很相宜,好的德行乐寿长。

长大的白蒿啊,落下的露水浓浓。既经看见君子人,马缰绳停下从容。鸾铃声锵锵和衷,降下的万福会同。

湛 露

湛湛露斯①,匪阳不晞②。厌厌夜饮③,不醉无归。
湛湛露斯,在彼丰草。厌厌夜饮,在宗载考④。
湛湛露斯,在彼杞棘。显允君子,莫不令德。

其桐其椅⑤，其实离离⑥。岂弟君子，莫不令仪。

【注释】

①湛湛（zhàn zhàn 占占）：露重貌。　②晞（xī 希）：干。③厌厌：安然。　④宗：同族。考：成。指宴饮之礼。　⑤椅（yī 医）：类桐树。　⑥离离：下垂貌。

【译文】

浓重的露水啊，不是太阳晒不干。安闲的夜间饮酒，不醉不归看。

浓重的露水啊，落在丰草上。安闲的夜间饮酒，在同族中的宴礼上。

浓重的露水啊，落在枸杞酸枣上。光明诚恳的君子人，没有不是好德上。

那桐树和椅树，它的结实是下垂。平易的君子人，没有不是好威仪。

彤弓之什

彤 弓

彤弓弨兮①,受言藏之②。我有嘉宾,中心贶之③。钟鼓既设,一朝飨之④。

彤弓弨兮,受言载之⑤。我有嘉宾,中心喜之。钟鼓既设,一朝右之⑥。

彤弓弨兮,受言櫜之⑦。我有嘉宾,中心好之。钟鼓既设,一朝酬之⑧。

【注释】

①彤弓:朱红的弓。周代天子有赐弓礼。弨(chāo 超):放松。②言:语助词。 ③贶(kuàng 况):爱戴。 ④飨(xiǎng 响):用酒食款待人。 ⑤载:装载。 ⑥右:通"侑",劝酒。 ⑦櫜(gāo 高):隐藏。 ⑧酬:劝酒。

【译文】

朱弓弦放松啊,接受赏赐藏起它。我有好宾客,心中喜爱他。钟鼓既经设置,一朝设宴款待他。

朱弓弦放松啊,接受赏赐载藏它。我有好宾客,心中喜爱他。钟鼓既经设置,一朝摆酒款待他。

朱弓弦放松啊,接受赏赐藏好它。我有好宾客,心中爱好他。钟鼓既经设置,一朝用酒食款待他。

菁菁者莪

菁菁者莪①,在彼中阿②。既见君子,乐且有仪。
菁菁者莪,在彼中沚③。既见君子,我心则喜。
菁菁者莪,在彼中陵④。既见君子,锡我百朋⑤。
泛泛杨舟,载沉载浮⑥。既见君子,我心则休⑦。

【注释】

①菁菁(jīng jīng 精精):盛貌。莪(é 俄):莪蒿。多年生草本植物,生在水边。 ②阿:大丘陵。 ③沚:水中小洲。 ④陵:土山。 ⑤朋:古货币,五贝为一朋。 ⑥载:则。 ⑦休:喜。

【译文】

茂盛的莪蒿,在那大山中。既经看见君子人,有威仪且在快乐中。

茂盛的莪蒿,在那小洲中。既经看见君子人,我的高兴在心中。

茂盛的莪蒿,在那土山中。既经看见君子人,他赐给我在百朋中。

杨木船儿水中游,或是下去或是上浮。既经看见君子人,我是欢喜在心头。

六 月

六月栖栖①，戎车既饬②。四牡骙骙③，载是常服④。狁狁孔炽⑤，我是用急⑥。王于出征，以匡王国。

比物四骊⑦，闲之维则。维此六月，既成我服⑧。我服既成，于三十里⑨。王于出征，以佐天子。

四牡修广⑩，其大有颙⑪。薄伐狁狁，以奏肤公⑫。有严有翼⑬，共武之服⑭。共武之服，以定王国。

狁狁匪茹⑮，整居焦获，侵镐及方，至于泾阳⑯。织文鸟章⑰，白旆央央⑱。元戎十乘⑲，以先启行。

戎车既安，如轾如轩⑳。四牡既佶㉑，既佶且闲。薄伐狁狁，至于大原。文武吉甫，万邦为宪。

吉甫燕喜，既多受祉㉒。来归自镐，我行永久。饮御诸友㉓，炰鳖脍鲤㉔。侯谁在矣㉕，张仲孝友㉖。

【注释】

①栖栖：通"栖栖"，遑遑不安貌。 ②饬：整顿。 ③骙骙（kuí kuí 葵葵）：马强壮貌。 ④常服：画日月的旗。服：指旗。 ⑤炽：盛。 ⑥急：紧急。 ⑦比物：指力气均齐。骊：黑马。 ⑧服：军服。 ⑨于三十里：军行三十里。 ⑩修：长。广：大。 ⑪颙（yóng 喁）：大。 ⑫奏：为。肤公：大功。 ⑬严：威严。翼：恭敬。 ⑭服：事。 ⑮匪茹：不自量。 ⑯焦获、镐、方、泾阳：皆周之地名。 ⑰织：通"帜"，指旗。 ⑱白旆：帛做的旗。 ⑲元戎：大兵车。 ⑳如轾（zhì 至）：车子前低后高。如轩（xuān 宣）：车子前高后低。指车子安稳前进。 ㉑佶（jí 吉）：壮健貌。 ㉒祉（zhǐ 止）：福。 ㉓御：进。 ㉔炰（páo 袍）：烹煮。脍（kuài

569

快）：细切。　㉕侯：语助，惟。　㉖张仲：吉甫之友。

【译文】

六月里惶惶不安，兵车整顿上前方。四匹雄马都强壮，插的日月旗风光。玁狁兵力很盛旺，我因此很急忙。周王命令我出征，来使王国得安匡。

均齐力气四黑马，熟习战斗法度良。只有在这六月里，既经成就我军装。我的军装既成就，日行卅里兵力强。周王命令我出征，来辅天子固国防。

四匹雄马大而长，头大显得更勇壮。讨伐那个玁狁，用来建立那个大功。武有威严文敬恭，用武对敌方共同。共同用武对敌方，用来安定王国防。

玁狁可真不自量，整占焦获我地方，侵入镐地又及方，一直进入到泾阳。旗上画着隼鸟章，帛做旗子极鲜亮。大的兵车我十辆，先行开拔到战场。

大的兵车既安全，忽低忽高冲向前。四匹雄马既强壮，既是强壮又熟娴。讨伐玁狁到边疆，到了太原直向前。文武兼备尹吉甫，万邦取法人所羡。

吉甫设宴表欢喜，既多受福把功酬。他从镐地班师回，我们行军时间久。设宴饮食待诸友，烹煮切鲤样样有。谁人在座列席了，原来张仲是孝友。

采　芑

薄言采芑①，于彼新田②，于此菑亩③。方叔莅止④，其车三千⑤，师干之试⑥。方叔率止，乘其四骐⑦，四骐翼翼⑧。路车有奭⑨，簟茀鱼服⑩，钩膺鞗革⑪。

薄言采芑，于彼新田，于此中乡⑫。方叔莅止，其车三千，旂旐央央。方叔率止，约軧错衡⑬，八鸾玱玱⑭。服其命服，朱芾斯皇，有玱葱珩⑮。

鴥彼飞隼⑯，其飞戾天⑰，亦集爰止。方叔莅止，其车三千，师干之试。方叔率止，钲人伐鼓⑱，陈师鞠旅⑲。显允方叔⑳，伐鼓渊渊㉑，振旅阗阗㉒。

蠢尔蛮荆，大邦为仇。方叔元老，克壮其猷㉓。方叔率止，执讯获丑。戎车啴啴，啴啴焞焞㉔，如霆如雷㉕。显允方叔，征伐玁狁，蛮荆来威。

【注释】

①芑（qǐ 起）：苦菜。 ②新田：开垦两年的田。 ③菑（zī 资）：开垦一年的田。 ④方叔：周宣王时大将。 ⑤其车三千：一说三千辆兵车，是夸张军威，非实数。 ⑥师干之试：师，士卒。干，捍敌。试，试用。士兵有扞敌之用。 ⑦骐：青黑色的马。 ⑧翼翼：整饬有次序。 ⑨奭（shì 式）：赤貌。 ⑩簟茀（diàn fú 电拂）：簟，竹席，用竹席蔽车窗叫簟茀。鱼服：用鲛鱼皮作箭袋。 ⑪钩膺：用钩子连锁皮带绕住马的胸腹部。鞗（tiáo 条）革：马缰绳所用的皮革。 ⑫中乡：指新田中。 ⑬约軧（qí 其）：用皮带约束车毂上。错衡：再连车上横木。 ⑭八鸾：八个铃。马口旁有两铃，四匹马有八铃。 ⑮玱（qiāng 枪）：玉声。葱珩：青色佩玉。 ⑯鴥（yù 育）：飞捷貌。 ⑰戾：至。 ⑱钲：一种乐器，击钲使士兵进退的。 ⑲陈师：整齐队伍。鞠旅：告诫士众。鞠，告。 ⑳允：语助词。 ㉑渊渊：鼓声。 ㉒振旅：休整军队。阗阗（tián tián 田田）：击鼓声。 ㉓猷：谋。 ㉔啴啴（tān tān 摊摊）：众多。焞焞（tūn tūn 吞吞）：盛貌。 ㉕霆：打雷。

【译文】

说是采苦菜啊，在那二年耕的田，在这一年耕的田。方叔亲自到来，他的兵车有三千，士兵都有捍卫的作用。方叔领他们来前，他坐车用四匹青黑马，四匹青黑马顺序相连。大车有红色的，竹席蔽窗鱼皮做箭袋，钩车缰绳套马胸腹相连。

说是采苦菜啊，在那二年耕的田，在这一年耕的田。方叔亲自来到，他的兵车有三千，画龙画龟蛇的旗子光鲜。方叔率领士兵来前，用皮缠车毂跟横木相连，八个鸾铃锵锵响连。穿上他的军装，红的蔽膝是辉煌，有青玉作佩声煌煌。

飞得快的有隼鸟，它的高飞飞到天，飞下停留在树颠。方叔亲自来到，他的兵车有三千，士兵捍卫齐向前。方叔率领着士兵，击钲人击鼓进军，整顿军队告诫整编。声名赫赫的方叔啊，击鼓声音渊渊，整顿军队声阗阗。

愚蠢的你们蛮荆，和大国作仇。方叔是元老，能够展现他的智谋。方叔率领部队到来，捉敌讯问割耳除丑。兵车众多前来，众多啊盛大啊，好像天上在打雷。声名赫赫的方叔，讨伐猃狁显震威，蛮荆跟着来服威。

车 攻

我车既攻①，我马既同②。四牡庞庞③，驾言徂东④。
田车既好，四牡孔阜⑤。东有甫草⑥，驾言行狩。
之子于苗⑦，选徒嚣嚣⑧。建旐设旄，搏兽于敖⑨。
驾彼四牡，四牡奕奕。赤芾金舄，会同有绎⑩。
决拾既佽⑪，弓矢既调，射夫既同⑫，助我举柴⑬。
四黄既驾，两骖不猗。不失其驰⑭，舍矢如破⑮。

萧萧马鸣，悠悠旆旌。徒御不惊⑯，大庖不盈⑰。
之子于征，有闻无声。允矣君子⑱，展也大成⑲。

【注释】

①攻：坚固。 ②同：一样。 ③庞庞（lóng 隆）：壮大。 ④徂东：往东，往洛阳。 ⑤阜：壮大。 ⑥甫草：甫田之草。郑有甫田。 ⑦苗：夏猎。 ⑧选：通"算"。嚣嚣（áo áo 熬熬）：喧哗。 ⑨敖：郑国地。 ⑩会同：诸侯朝见天子。绎：连续不断。 ⑪决拾既佽：决，钩弦具。拾，护臂具。佽（cì 次），调动好。 ⑫同：协同。 ⑬柴（zì 字）：积兽。 ⑭不失其驰：御者驾车得法。 ⑮舍矢如破：发箭皆中。 ⑯徒御：兵士和驾车人。不惊：不喧哗。 ⑰大庖：大厨子。不盈：不使饭菜过多。 ⑱允：信。 ⑲展：确实。

【译文】

我的车子修整既牢固，我的马儿行动既相同。四匹雄马真充实，驾着车子跑向东。

打猎车子既备好，四匹雄马很服帖。东有甫田好野草，驾车可以去冬猎。

这个人在夏猎时，选择徒众闹讻嚣。竖起龙旗龟蛇旗，捉住野兽在郑敖。

驾着那四匹雄马，四匹雄马既习熟。红皮蔽膝金头鞋，朝见天子相陆续。

扳指护袖既安好，张弓射箭又调正。射箭的人既心同，帮我积兽举得正。

四匹黄马即驾车，两匹骖马不偏差。驾车的人不错失，一箭中的不出差。

马儿萧萧地叫,旗帜悠悠地飘。士兵驾车不喧哗,大厨子烧菜不多饶。

这个人去打猎,有名望无声音。确实是君子人,确是有大的功成。

吉 日

吉日维戊①,既伯既祷②。田车既好,四牡孔阜。升彼大阜,从其群丑③。

吉日庚午④,既差我马⑤。兽之所同⑥,麀鹿麌麌⑦。漆沮之从⑧,天子之所。

瞻彼中原⑨,其祁孔有⑩。儦儦俟俟⑪,或群或友⑫。悉率左右,以燕天子。

既张我弓,既挟我矢。发彼小豝⑬,殪此大兕⑭。以御宾客,且以酌醴⑮。

【注释】

①戊:指初五日,为刚日,即十日中一、三、五、七、九为单日,即甲、丙、戊、庚、壬,余为双日。 ②既伯既祷:伯,马祖神。祷,向神祷告。 ③从:追逐。群丑:成群野兽。 ④庚午:指初七日。 ⑤差:选择。 ⑥同:犹聚。 ⑦麀(yōu 优)鹿:母鹿。麌麌(yǔ yǔ 雨雨):麀群聚貌。 ⑧漆沮:漆水、沮水流域。 ⑨中原:原中。 ⑩祁(qí 其):指大兽。 ⑪儦儦(biāo biāo 标标):奔跑貌。俟俟(sì sì 四四):行走貌。 ⑫群:兽三为群。友:兽二为友。 ⑬豝(bā 巴):野猪。 ⑭殪(yì 意):射死。兕(sì 似):野牛。 ⑮醴(lǐ 礼):甜酒。

【译文】

吉祥的日子是初五,既祭马祖神还祷告。打猎车子既备好,四匹雄马很强壮。登上大坡真是好,追赶群兽不算少。

吉祥日子是初七,既选我马在猎中。野兽聚集水泽中,母鹿成群好相从。漆沮流域可追从,天子打猎处所同。

看望那个平原中,多有大兽类不同。有的奔跑有的走,或三或两是相从。尽率左右来打猎,以请天子欢宴中。

既拉开我的弓,既挟起我箭头。射中那小野猪,射死这大野牛。用来款待我宾客,并且用来佐甜酒。

鸿 雁

鸿雁于飞,肃肃其羽①。之子于征,劬劳于野②。爰及矜人③,哀此鳏寡④。

鸿雁于飞,集于中泽。之子于垣,百堵皆作⑤。虽则劬劳,其究安宅⑥。

鸿雁于飞,哀鸣嗷嗷。维此哲人⑦,谓我劬劳。维彼愚人,谓我宣骄⑧。

【注释】

①肃肃:羽声。 ②劬(qú 渠)劳:辛苦劳累。 ③爰:语助词。矜人:可怜人。 ④鳏(guān 官):老而无妻者。寡:老而无夫者。 ⑤堵:墙壁。一丈为板,五板为堵。 ⑥究:终究。宅:居。 ⑦哲人:聪明人。 ⑧宣骄:逞强。

【译文】

鸿雁在飞,翅膀发出肃肃响。这个人服役,在野地里劳苦难状。于是连到可怜人,哀伤这些鳏寡苦状。

鸿雁在飞,停在沼泽中。这个人在筑墙,几百丈高墙极高崇。虽极辛劳,终究安民居宅中。

鸿雁在飞,嗷嗷地哀叫。只有这聪明人,说我辛劳。只有那愚蠢人,说我宣扬骄傲。

庭 燎

夜如何其?夜未央①。庭燎之光②。君子至止③,鸾声将将。
夜如何其?夜未艾④。庭燎晣晣⑤。君子至止,鸾声哕哕⑥。
夜如何其?夜乡晨。庭燎有辉。君子至止,言观其旂。

【注释】

①夜未央:夜未尽。 ②庭燎:庭中火炬,庭中大烛。 ③君子:指诸侯。 ④艾:止,尽。 ⑤晣晣(zhé zhé 哲哲):光明。 ⑥哕哕(huì huì 会会):铃声。

【译文】

夜怎样了?夜没有亮。庭院里大烛的光。君子人到来了,鸾铃锵锵地响。

夜怎样了?夜没有亮。庭院里大烛的一点亮。君子人到来了,銮铃暗暗地响。

夜怎样了?夜将亮。庭院里大烛有光。君子人到来了,看见他的旗在飘扬。

沔 水

沔彼流水^①，朝宗于海^②。鴥彼飞隼，载飞载止。嗟我兄弟，邦人诸友^③，莫肯念乱^④，谁无父母。

沔彼流水，其流汤汤。鴥彼飞隼，载飞载扬。念彼不迹^⑤，载起载行。心之忧矣，不可弭忘^⑥。

鴥彼飞隼，率彼中陵。民之讹言，宁莫之惩。我友敬矣^⑦，谗言其兴。

【注释】

①沔（miǎn 免）：水流满貌。　②朝宗：以河水入海，比诸侯朝见天子。　③兄弟：比同姓诸侯。邦人：比异姓臣。　④念乱：止乱。　⑤不迹：不规则的事，不道德的事。　⑥弭（mǐ 米）：止，息。　⑦敬：通"警"，警惕。

【译文】

满满的流水，流向大海像朝见帝王。疾飞的那隼鸟，有时飞有时停藏。感叹我的兄弟，国人诸侯友方，不肯止乱复礼，谁没有父母可启。

满满的流水，它的流声洋洋。疾飞的那隼鸟，有时飞有时高扬。想那不规则的人，有时起来有时行。我的心是忧了，不可以停止轻忘。

疾飞的那隼鸟，飞向那土山中。人们的谣言，怎么可以不惩凶。我的朋友警惕了，谗言怎能兴从。

577

鹤 鸣

鹤鸣于九皋①,声闻于野。鱼潜在渊,或在于渚。乐彼之园,爰有树檀,其下维萚②。它山之石,可以为错③。

鹤鸣于九皋,声闻于天。鱼在于渚,或潜在渊。乐彼之园,爰有树檀,其下维榖④。它山之石,可以攻玉。

【注释】

①九皋(gāo 高):九折泽,泽中水溢出称一折,九折指极远处。 ②萚(tuò 唾):树脱落的皮。 ③错:可琢玉的石。 ④榖:即楮树,皮可制纸。

【译文】

鹤在极远处叫,声音传到野处。鱼儿潜伏在深渊,有时在绕水的小渚。喜欢那个园子,在园里种有檀树,它的下面有落下萚。别的山里的石,可以做磨刀石。

鹤在极远处叫,声音传到天际处。鱼儿在绕水的小渚,有时潜伏在深渊。喜欢那个园子,在园里种有檀树,它的下面有榖树。别的山里的石,可以磨玉使它白。

卷 五

小 雅

祈父之什

祈 父

祈父①,予王之爪牙②。胡转予于恤③,靡所止居。
祈父,予王之爪士④。胡转予于恤,靡所底止⑤。
祈父,亶不聪⑥。胡转予于恤,有母之尸饔⑦。

【注释】

①祈父:即圻父,官名,是职掌边处兵甲的司马。 ②爪牙:指将军。 ③转:移,陷。恤(xù 序):忧。 ④爪士:虎臣。 ⑤底:至。 ⑥亶(dǎn 胆):诚。 ⑦尸:主。饔(yōng 庸):熟食。

【译文】

司马,我是王的爪牙。为什么陷我到忧患呀,没有安居呀。
司马,我是王的爪牙。为什么陷我到忧患呀,没有安居呀。
司马,确实是不聪呀。为什么陷我到忧患呀,有母谁主熟食呀。

白 驹

皎皎白驹①,食我场苗。絷之维之②,以永今朝。所谓伊人,于焉逍遥③。

皎皎白驹,食我场藿。絷之维之,以永今夕。所谓伊人,于焉嘉客。

皎皎白驹,贲然来思④。尔公尔侯,逸豫无期⑤。慎尔优游,勉尔遁思⑥。

皎皎白驹,在彼空谷⑦。生刍一束,其人如玉。毋金玉尔音⑧,而有遐心⑨。

【注释】

①皎皎:洁白,光明,指马毛说。 ②絷(zhí 执):绊。维:系住。 ③焉:此,这儿。 ④贲(bì 闭)然:光彩貌。 ⑤逸豫:安乐。 ⑥勉尔遁思:望他勿遁。勉,抑止。遁,隐遁。 ⑦空谷:无人的山谷。 ⑧音:音信。 ⑨遐:远去。

【译文】

洁白有光的白马,吃我场里的豆苗。绊住它来系住它,来留住他过今朝。所说的那个人,在这儿可以逍遥。

洁白有光的白马,吃我场里的豆茎。绊住它来系住它,留住他过今夜这时辰。所说的那个人,在这儿是好客人。

洁白有光的白马,有光采地到来。封您公爷或侯爷,安乐过活没期限。谨慎您的游乐,望您不要隐遁不来。

洁白有光的白马,跑在没有人的山谷。有嫩青草一束,那个人像白玉。别爱惜您像金玉的声音,对我有疏远的心。

黄 鸟

黄鸟黄鸟,无集于榖①,无啄我粟。此邦之人,不我肯榖②。言旋言归,复我邦族③。

黄鸟黄鸟,无集于桑,无啄我粱。此邦之人,不可与明④。言旋言归,复我诸兄。

黄鸟黄鸟,无集于栩⑤,无啄我黍。此邦之人,不可与处。言旋言归,复我诸父。

【注释】

①榖(gǔ谷):树名,即楮树,皮可制纸。 ②榖(gǔ谷):善。 ③复:回运: ④明(méng盟):通"盟"。 ⑤栩(xǔ许):柞树。《唐风·鸨羽》:"集于苞栩。"

【译文】

黄鸟呀黄鸟,不要集中在榖树,不要吃我的粟。这个侯国的人,不肯好好地待我活。说要转身回去,回到我国的宗族。

黄鸟呀黄鸟,不要集中在柔桑,不要吃我的高粱。这个侯国的人,不可以同他结盟。说要转身回去,回去找我众兄。

黄鸟呀黄鸟,不要集中在苞栩,不要啄我的黍。这个侯国的人,不可以和他们相处。说要转身回去,回去找我众伯父叔父。

我行其野

我行其野,蔽芾其樗①。昏姻之故,言就尔居。尔不我畜②,复我邦家。

我行其野,言采其蓫③。昏姻之故,言就尔宿。尔不我畜,言归思复。

我行其野,言采其葍④。不思旧姻,求尔新特⑤。成不以富⑥,亦祇以异。

【注释】

①蔽芾(fèi 费):幼小貌。樗(chū 初):臭椿,叶有臭味。 ②畜:养。 ③蓫(zhú 逐):草名,一称羊蹄。 ④葍(fú 福):多年生蔓草,一名小旋花,地下茎可食。 ⑤特:匹配。 ⑥成:通"诚"。

【译文】

我在野地里走,看到臭椿的幼芽。因为婚姻的缘故,我到你住处不差。你不肯养育我,我回到我的邦家。

我在野地里走,采羊蹄草充腹。因为婚姻的缘故,我就来你处住宿。你不肯养育我,我回去想归复。

我在野地里走,采那种小旋花。你不念那旧婚姻,求那新的匹偶嘉。虽实不因为贪富,也只因你异心吧。

斯 干

秩秩斯干①,幽幽南山②。如竹苞矣③,如松茂矣。兄及弟矣,式相好矣,无相犹矣④。

似续妣祖⑤,筑室百堵,西南其户。爰居爰处,爰笑爰语。

约之阁阁⑥,椓之橐橐⑦。风雨攸除,鸟鼠攸去,君子攸芋⑧。

如跂斯翼⑨，如矢斯棘⑩，如鸟斯革⑪，如翚斯飞⑫，君子攸跻⑬。

殖殖其庭⑭，有觉其楹⑮。哙哙其正⑯，哕哕其冥⑰，君子攸宁。

下莞上簟⑱，乃安斯寝。乃寝乃兴，乃占我梦。吉梦维何？维熊维罴⑲，维虺维蛇⑳。

大人占之㉑，维熊维罴，男子之祥；维虺维蛇，女子之祥。

乃生男子，载寝之床，载衣之裳，载弄之璋㉒。其泣喤喤，朱芾斯皇㉓，室家君王。

乃生女子，载寝之地，载衣之裼㉔，载弄之瓦㉕。无非无仪㉖，唯酒食是议，无父母诒罹。

【注释】

①秩秩：流行貌。于：溪涧。　②幽幽：深远貌。南山：终南山，在陕西西安市南。　③苞：本。　④犹：通"尤"，过失。　⑤似续：通"嗣续"，继承。　⑥约：束。阁阁：犹历历，言束板之绳历历可数。　⑦椓（zhuó 酌）：夯打。橐橐（tuó tuó 驼驼）：用杵击土声。　⑧攸：语助。芋：通"宇"，居。　⑨跂（qì 气）：企，颠起脚后跟站着。翼：如鸟张翼。　⑩棘（jí 吉）：急也，矢行缓则枉，急则直，急有直义。此章用四个比喻来比建筑物的各种形态，线条的整齐挺耸，以及装饰的华彩。　⑪革：变也，鸟飞则变静止状态。　⑫翚（huī 辉）：野鸡毛羽五彩称翚。　⑬跻（jī 基）：登，升上。　⑭殖殖：平正。　⑮觉：高大。楹：通"楹"，柱子。　⑯哙哙（kuài kuài 快快）：宽明貌。正：昼也。　⑰哕哕（huì huì 会会）：光明貌。冥：

夜。　⑱莞（guān 关）：蒲席。　⑲罴（pí 皮）：熊的一种，比熊更猛。　⑳虺（huǐ 毁）：小蛇。　㉑大人：即太卜，占梦官。　㉒璋：玉器。　㉓朱芾（fèi 费）：蔽膝，古代天子、诸侯的一种服饰，用以蔽膝的。㉔裼（tì 惕）：婴儿的包被。　㉕瓦：古代纺线的纺锤。　㉖仪：善。

【译文】

　　流动的溪涧，幽深的终南山。像竹子的丛生了，像松树的茂盛了。兄和弟，互相友好了，没有相指责了。

　　继承先妣和先祖，建筑宫室墙百堵，门户朝着西南向，于是用这里作居处，于是笑于是语。

　　捆束墙版声阁阁，敲打泥土声托托。风雨免除不为虐，鸟鼠赶去不作恶，君子以此住新作。

　　像企望那样站稳，像发箭那样笔直，像鸟飞那样变革，像野鸡那样展翅，君子人登堂进入。

　　平正的前庭，有高大柱子直陈。白天显得明亮，夜里显得光明，君子住了安宁。

　　下面蒲席上竹席，是可以安寝最嘉。是寝了是起来，是吉卜我的梦啊。吉梦是什么？是熊是罴，是小蛇和大蛇。

　　请太卜占梦，是熊是罴，是生男儿的吉祥；是小蛇是大蛇，是生女儿的吉祥。

　　是生男儿，睡在大床，穿上衣裳，玩弄玉璋。他的哭泣喤喤，穿上蔽膝辉煌，成立家庭为君王。

　　是生女儿，睡在大地，穿上抱衣，玩弄纺线锤。没有是没有非，只有酒食可商议，不要使父母遭非议。

无 羊

谁谓尔无羊？三百维群。谁谓尔无牛？九十其犉①。尔羊来思，其角濈濈②。尔牛来思，其耳湿湿③。

或降于阿，或饮于池。或寝或讹④，尔牧来思，何蓑何笠⑤，或负其餱。三十维物⑥，尔牲则具。

尔牧来思，以薪以蒸⑦，以雌以雄。尔羊来思，矜矜兢兢⑧，不骞不崩⑨。麾之以肱，毕来既升⑩。

牧人乃梦，众维鱼矣⑪，旐维旟矣⑫。大人占之，众维鱼矣，实维丰年。旐维旟矣，室家溱溱⑬。

【注释】

①犉（rún）：牛七尺为犉。 ②濈濈（jí jí 辑辑）：聚集貌。 ③湿湿（qì qì 泣泣）：牛反刍时摇动耳朵。 ④讹（é 哦）：行动。 ⑤何：通"荷"，披戴。 ⑥物：色。 ⑦蒸：粗曰薪，细曰蒸。 ⑧矜矜、兢兢：紧张貌。 ⑨骞、崩：亏损，群疾。 ⑩升：登入，入牢。 ⑪众：通"螽"，蝗虫。 ⑫旐、旟：画龟蛇旗为旐，画隼鸟旗为旟。见《诗·鄘风·干旄》。 ⑬溱溱（zhēn zhēn 真真）：众多。

【译文】

谁说你没有羊群？三百头羊成一群。谁说你没有牛？七尺黄牛九十头。你的羊群来了，它的角集合成群好。你的牛来了，反刍时候把耳摇。

有的牛羊下坡岗，有的喝水在池旁。有的睡觉有的游逛，你的牧人来了，披着蓑衣戴着笠，有时背着那干粮。牛羊毛色三十种，作为牲口都备得。

你的牧人来了,带来粗柴和细草,带来雌兽和雄鸟。你的羊来了,都是强壮个个好,没有亏损没病了。用臂来指挥它,全都进入圈儿好。

牧人于是做好梦,蝗虫变做鱼儿了,龟蛇旗变做隼鸟旗了。太卜因此占卜它,蝗虫变成鱼儿了,这是丰年征兆好。龟蛇旗变做隼鸟旗了,子孙众多室家好。

节 南 山

节彼南山①,维石岩岩②。赫赫师尹③,民具尔瞻④。忧心如惔⑤,不敢戏谈。国既卒斩⑥,何用不监⑦!

节彼南山,有实其猗⑧。赫赫师尹,不平谓何?天方荐瘥⑨,丧乱弘多。民言无嘉,憯莫惩嗟⑩!

尹氏大师,维周之氐⑪,秉国之均⑫,四方是维⑬,天子是毗⑭,俾民不迷。不吊昊天⑮,不宜空我师⑯。

弗躬弗亲,庶民弗信。弗问弗仕⑰,勿罔君子。式夷式已⑱,无小人殆,琐琐姻亚⑲,则无膴仕⑳。

昊天不傭㉑,降此鞠讻㉒。昊天不惠,降此大戾㉓。君子如届㉔,俾民心阕㉕。君子如夷㉖,恶怒是违。

不吊昊天,乱靡有定。式月斯生,俾民不宁。忧心如酲㉗,谁秉国成?不自为政,卒劳百姓。

驾彼四牡,四牡项领㉘。我瞻四方,蹙蹙靡所骋㉙!

方茂尔恶,相尔矛矣!既夷既怿㉚,如相酬矣㉛。

昊天不平,我王不宁。不惩其心,覆怨其正。

家父作诵㉜,以究王讻。式讹尔心㉝,以畜万邦㉞。

【注释】

①节：高峻貌。　②岩岩：积石貌。　③师尹：太师尹氏。太师，周三公之一，掌兵权。尹氏，周大臣尹吉甫的后代。　④具：俱。　⑤惔（tán 谈）：火烧。　⑥卒：尽。斩：灭绝。　⑦监：监察。　⑧有实其猗：实指广大。猗指山坡。山坡广大。　⑨荐：重。瘥（cuó 矬）：疫病。　⑩憯：同"惨"，语助词，犹曾。惩：止。嗟：语末助词。　⑪氐：柢，根柢。　⑫秉钧：掌握大权。　⑬维：维系。　⑭毗（pí 疲）：辅助。　⑮吊：善。　⑯空：空乏。　⑰仕：察事。"仕"通"事"。　⑱式夷式已：受伤或停职。夷，伤。已，完结。　⑲琐琐：小貌。姻亚：婿之父曰姻，两婿相谓曰亚。　⑳膴（wǔ 舞）仕：厚加任用，即高位厚禄。　㉑俾：均。　㉒鞫讻：极凶。　㉓戾：灾祸。　㉔届：极，止。　㉕阕（què 却）：止息。　㉖夷：伤。　㉗醒（chéng 成）：病于酒。　㉘项领：头颈粗大. 不能驾车，喻马不能用，比大臣不能用。　㉙蹙蹙（cù cù 促促）：局促不舒展。　㉚怿：喜悦。　㉛酬：应酬，言反复无常。　㉜作诵：通"作讽"，作诗讽谏。　㉝讹（é 俄）：化。　㉞畜：养，休养，安定。

【译文】

那高峻的终南山，只有大石堆积成山峦。威风凛凛的尹太师，人民都在向您看。心中忧愁像火烧，不敢戏笑作谈端。国家既经尽灭绝，为什么不起来察看！

那高峻的终南山，有广大的山坡。威风凛凛的尹太师，做事不平说什么？天正要降严重的瘟疫，死丧混乱大而多。人民没有好话说，曾经没有惩戒乎！

尹氏您是太师，是周朝的根柢，掌握国家的政权，四方靠您来纲维,天子是依靠您,使人民不受迷。不善的上天,不该困乏我们大众受饥。

对事不亲自过问,人民对您不相信。您不问不察事,不要欺骗君子问讯。或被伤害或停职,不要受小人斥摈。小小的亲眷,不要高官厚禄相允。

上天不公匀,降下这个极凶灾。上天不恩惠,降下这个大灾难。君子如果到来过问,使人民心里不为难。君子如果受伤残,恶怒您是违背亲规。

不善的上天,乱没有安定。乱子月月在发生,使得人民不安宁。忧心像酒醉,谁掌握国政?不自己管好国政,终于劳苦百姓。

四匹雄马驾着车,四匹雄马粗项领。我看那四方天下,局促得没法驰骋。

正在增加您的罪恶,观察您的矛对谁啊!既然又和平又快乐,像相酬对啊。

上天不公平,我王不安宁。您不去惩戒您的心,还怨劝您改正的人。

家父作了这篇讽,用来追究王的凶。快快改变您的心,用来安定万邦中。

正 月

正月繁霜①,我心忧伤。民之讹言,亦孔之将②。念我独兮,忧心京京③。哀我小心,癙忧以痒④。

父母生我,胡俾我瘉⑤?不自我先,不自我后。好言自口,莠言自口⑥。忧心愈愈⑦,是以有侮。

忧心惸惸⑧,念我无禄。民之无辜,并其臣仆⑨。哀我人斯,于何从禄?瞻乌爰止⑩,于谁之屋?

瞻彼中林,侯薪侯蒸⑪。民今方殆,视天梦梦⑫。既克有定⑬,靡人弗胜⑭。有皇上帝⑮,伊谁云憎⑯?

谓山盖卑?为冈为陵,民之讹言,宁莫之惩。召彼故老,讯之占梦。具曰予圣,谁知乌之雌雄?

谓天盖高⑰?不敢不局⑱。谓地盖厚?不敢不蹐⑲。维号斯言,有伦有脊⑳。哀今之人,胡为虺蜴㉑?

瞻彼阪田㉒,有菀其特㉓。天之扤我㉔,如不我克,彼求我则㉕,如不我得,执我仇仇㉖,亦不我力㉗。

心之忧矣,如或结之。今兹之正㉘,胡然厉矣?燎之方扬,宁或灭之。赫赫宗周㉙,褒姒灭之㉚!

终其永怀,又窘阴雨。其车既载,乃弃尔辅㉛。载输尔载㉜,将伯助予㉝。

无弃尔辅,员于尔辐㉞。屡顾尔仆,不输尔载。终逾绝险,曾是不意㉟。

鱼在于沼,亦匪克乐。潜虽伏矣,亦孔之炤㊱。忧心惨惨㊲,念国之为虐。

彼有旨酒,又有嘉肴。洽比其邻㊳,昏姻孔云㊴。念我独兮,忧心慇慇㊵。

佌佌彼有屋㊶,蔌蔌方有穀㊷。民今之无禄,天夭是椓㊸。哿矣富人㊹,哀此惸独!

【注释】

①正月:夏历四月。繁:多。 ②将:大。 ③京京:忧愁不止。 ④瘋(shǔ 鼠)忧:极忧。痒(yǎng 氧):病。 ⑤癙(yù

诗经

育）：病，转为痛苦。 ⑥莠：恶。 ⑦愈愈：忧惧貌。 ⑧惸惸（qióng qióng 琼琼）：忧念貌。 ⑨并：使。臣仆：奴仆。 ⑩瞻乌爰止：相传乌落在谁家，即谁家富。 ⑪侯薪侯蒸：维薪维蒸，维集薪处维集草，维集贤处维集小人。 ⑫梦梦：昏愦。 ⑬定：定乱。 ⑭弗胜：不胜过王为乱。 ⑮皇上帝：指君王。 ⑯伊：是。憎：恨。 ⑰盖：同"盍"。 ⑱局：同"跼"。 ⑲蹐：小步累足。 ⑳伦：道也。脊：同"迹"。 ㉑胡为虺蜴：言人畏惧官吏何以如虺蜴。 ㉒阪田：山坡上的田。 ㉓菀（wǎn 碗）：茂盛貌。特：特出的苗。 ㉔扤（wù 误）：动摇。 ㉕则：语助词。 ㉖仇仇：傲慢貌。 ㉗不我力：即不我用。 ㉘正：指执政者。 ㉙宗周：指西周。 ㉚褒姒：褒国之女，周幽王后。 ㉛辅：车箱版。 ㉜输：堕也。 ㉝伯：长者。 ㉞员：益也。 ㉟曾是不意：乃不以是为意。 ㊱炤：一作"昭"，明也。 ㊲惨惨：忧郁貌。 ㊳洽：和协。邻：亲近的人。 ㊴云：周旋。 ㊵慇慇：同"殷殷"，指悲痛。 ㊶佌佌（cǐ cǐ 此此）：低微。 ㊷蔌蔌（sù sù 素素）：鄙陋。穀：俸禄。 ㊸夭：摧残。椓：以斧劈柴，喻打击。 ㊹哿（gě 舸）：表称许。

【译文】

四月里下了许多霜，使我的心里很忧伤。民间的谣言，也是很猖狂。念我孤独啊，心里惊恐忧难忘。悲哀我的小心，极忧得发病那样。

父母生养我，为什么使我受痛苦？不在我以前，不在我以后。好话出自口，恶话出自口。心里越来越忧愁，越是有人来欺侮。

心里非常忧愁，想我没有福禄。人们本来没有罪，牵连到他的奴仆。悲哀我这个人啊，从什么地方得到福禄？看到乌鸦所停处，在谁家的房屋？

看看那树林里，只可樵柴和割草。人们如今正苦难，看天昏昏也不晓。既然能够使乱定，没有人不能取胜。高高在上的君王，是谁敢对他憎恨？

说山为何说它低？可它都是大冈陵，民间的谣言，难道没法加以戒惩。召集那些旧的老人，问他占卜梦兆。都说自己圣明，谁知道乌鸦的雌雄？

说天何以这样高？却不敢不弯腰。说地何以这样厚？却不敢不小心走路。说这样呼号的话，有道理有根据。悲哀现在的人，为什么把上者看做虮蜴？

看那坡上田，有茂盛的苗。天要来动摇我，如果不能制胜我，他便求我，惟恐求不到我，求到我又傲慢我，也不用我。

心里忧愁啊，像有什么结扎它。今天这样政治，为什么这样暴虐？火烧得正旺，难道有人灭它。威严的西周，褒姒来灭亡它！

既经永久伤怀，又碰上天的阴霾。车既把东西装载，抛弃了你的车箱板。堕下你的运载，呼叫大哥帮运材。

不要抛弃你的车箱板，加固你的车子辐。屡次顾看你的奴仆，不要使你的运载有失落。终于越过危险地，可是你却不以为意。

鱼在池沼，不能快乐。潜水虽然伏了，但仍清楚见到了。忧心惨惨，想国家的政事浑浊。

他有美酒，又有好的菜肴。和好了他的邻居，跟亲眷非常好。念我孤独啊，心里忧愁怎么了。

小小的人他有屋，鄙陋的人他有禄。人们今天没有福禄，天摧残他是虐。好过的是富人，哀怜我这孤独！

十月之交

十月之交①，朔日辛卯②，日有食之，亦孔之丑③。彼月而微，此日而微④。今此下民，亦孔之哀。

日月告凶⑤，不用其行⑥。四国无政，不用其良。彼月而食，则维其常，此日而食，于何不臧。

烨烨震电⑦，不宁不令，百川沸腾，山冢崒崩⑧；高岸为谷，深谷为陵。哀今之人，胡憯莫惩⑨？

皇父卿士，番维司徒，家伯维宰，仲允膳夫，棸子内史，蹶维趣马，楀维师氏⑩。艳妻煽方处⑪。

抑此皇父，岂曰不时？胡为我作，不即我谋？彻我墙屋，田卒汙莱⑫。曰予不戕，礼则然矣。

皇父孔圣⑬，作都于向。择三有事⑭，亶侯多藏。不憖遗一老⑮，俾守我王。择有车马，以居徂向。

黾勉从事，不敢告劳。无罪无辜，谗口嚣嚣。下民之孽⑯，匪降自天。噂沓背憎⑰，职竞由人⑱。

悠悠我里⑲，亦孔之痗⑳。四方有羡㉑，我独居忧。民莫不逸，我独不敢休。天命不彻㉒，我不敢效我友自逸。

【注释】

①十月：当时称谓纯阴之月，阴盛阳衰，所以发生日蚀。经今人研究，是周幽王六年十月朔日，即公元前776年9月6日的日蚀，是世界上最早的有明确记录的日蚀。交：交替。　②朔日辛卯：初一辛卯日。当时用天干地支记日期，故称这天为辛卯。朔指初一。　③丑：恶。当时认为日蚀是不好的，所以称丑。　④微：月无光，指月蚀。日无光，指日蚀。　⑤告凶：告天下凶兆。当时人迷信日蚀是天告凶。　⑥行：

道。 ⑦烨烨（yè yè 叶叶）：声光之盛。震电：如打雷闪电。 ⑧冢：山顶。崒（zú 足）：碎。 ⑨憯（cǎn 惨）：乃。 ⑩皇父、家伯、仲允：人名，皆称字。番、聚（zōu 邹）、蹶（guì 贵）、楀（jǔ 举）：皆氏。师氏：掌司朝得失之事。 ⑪艳：美色。煽：炽。方：正时。 ⑫汙：水不通。莱：草丛生。 ⑬圣：聪明。 ⑭择三：选择人任三公。 ⑮憖（yìn 印）：愿。 ⑯孽：灾难。 ⑰噂（zǔn 樽）沓：议论纷杂。 ⑱职：主。竞：强。 ⑲悠悠：忧思。里：病。 ⑳痗（mèi 妹）：病。 ㉑羡：宽裕。 ㉒天命不彻：天命不合正道。

【译文】

十月开头，初一是辛卯，又是次日蚀，也是很不好。那月光不亮，这天太阳也不亮。现在这儿老百姓，也很哀痛怎么了。

日蚀月蚀告凶象，不用走在轨道上。四方国家无善政，不用他们的贤良。那个月儿现月蚀，则是走路还从常。这天出现了日蚀，有什么事情是不良。

光采照耀像雷电，政事不善不安宁。有像百川要沸腾，有像山顶石碎崩；高岸降下变深谷，深谷上升变山陵。悲哀现在的人民，什么惨事不戒惩？

国家大臣是皇父，番氏做了司徒。家伯做了冢宰，仲允做了膳夫。聚子做了内史，蹶氏做了养马夫，楀氏做了师氏，与美艳的皇后煽惑在一处。

叹息这皇父，难道肯说自己不是？为什么让我服劳役，不和我谈事？拆毁我的墙屋，田里水不流草不治。反说我没伤害你，礼治便是如此。

皇父以为很明圣，在向邑筑了都城。有事用人选三卿，专权敛财多宝珍。不愿遗留一元老，使他守卫我王作大臣。选择富有车马人,用来迁居到向城。

我勉力做事,不敢说辛劳。没有罪没有辜,谗人的嘴却说说。百姓受了灾祸,不是天上降一遭。议论纷杂背后憎,专力争逐由人搞。

忧思在我心里,过于忧愁转成疾。四方的人有富裕,我独处忧不敢息。人们没有不安逸,我独不敢自休息。天命不遵道理行,我不敢效我友自安逸。

雨无正

浩浩昊天,不骏其德①。降丧饥馑②,斩伐四国。旻天疾威③,弗虑弗图。舍彼有罪,既伏其辜④。若此无罪,沦胥以铺⑤。

周宗既灭,靡所止戾⑥。正大夫离居⑦,莫知我勚⑧。三事大夫⑨,莫肯夙夜。邦君诸侯,莫肯朝夕。庶曰式臧⑩,覆出为恶。

如何昊天,辟言不信⑪?如彼行迈,则靡所臻⑫。凡百君子,各敬尔身。胡不相畏?不畏于天!

戎成不退⑬,饥成不遂。曾我暬御⑮,憯憯日瘁⑯。凡百君子,莫肯用讯。听言则答⑰,谮言则退⑱。

哀哉不能言!匪舌是出⑲,维躬是瘁。哿矣能言⑳,巧言如流,俾躬处休。

维曰于仕㉑,孔棘且殆㉒。云不可使,得罪于天子。亦云可使,怨及朋友。

谓尔迁于王都,曰予未有室家。鼠思泣血㉓,无言不疾㉔!昔尔出居,谁从作尔室?

【注释】

①骏：长。 ②饥馑：谷不熟曰饥，菜不熟曰馑。 ③疾威：暴虐。 ④伏其辜：隐其罪。 ⑤沦胥以铺：无罪的人皆因牵连而无辜受害。沦，陷。胥，相。铺，遍。 ⑥戾：至。 ⑦正大夫：大夫中的正，指大官。 ⑧勩（yì 义）：劳。 ⑨三事：三公。 ⑩庶：庶几，近乎。 ⑪辟言：法度之言。 ⑫臻（zhēn 贞）：至。 ⑬戎成不退：即战争不息。 ⑭遂：安也。 ⑮暬（xiè 泄）御：侍御，王亲近之臣。 ⑯憯憯（cǎn cǎn 惨惨）：忧貌。瘁（cuì 翠）：病。 ⑰听言：顺从的话。 ⑱谮（zèn）言：谏诤的话。 ⑲出：通"绌"，绌劣。 ⑳哿（kě 可）：嘉许。 ㉑于：往。 ㉒棘：急。殆：危。 ㉓鼠：同"癙（shǔ 鼠）"，忧思。 ㉔疾：通"嫉"，嫉恨。

【译文】

大大的上天，不能长赐恩德。降下这饥荒，残害我四方的邦国。上天暴虐，不考虑不谋图。舍弃那有罪，尽隐藏他的罪过。像这些无罪，都沦没牵连把罪坐。

周朝的宗亲既已灭绝，没有地方住定当。正大夫离开所居住，没有人知道我辛苦备尝。三公大夫，莫肯早夜为国忙。各国诸侯，莫肯早夜为国忙。王做事近乎有改善，但又出来作恶那能忘。

怎样的上天，法度的话不相信？像那走远路，就没有知道止境。凡是众多的君子，各自戒慎你的身。为什么不互相畏惧？不怕天的雷震！

战争不停，饥荒不退。曾经是我这小侍御，忧愁得日以憔瘁。凡是众位君子，没有用心箴规。中听的就答对，谏诤的就斥退。

595

悲哀我不能说话！不是舌头拙于应对，只是身子怕憔悴。可是能够说的，巧言像水流，使自身处于安乐休。

只说可以出仕，国事很急难任事。如说坏事不可使，得罪于天子。如说坏事可以使，怨到朋友怎么使。

叫你迁到王的首都，说我那里还没有家室。忧思到哭泣出血，没有我的话不嫉。从前你迁出居处时，谁肯作好你家室？

小旻之什

小旻①

旻天疾威，敷于下土②。谋犹回遹③，何日斯沮④？谋臧不从，不臧覆用。我视谋犹，亦孔之邛⑤！

潝潝訿訿⑥，亦孔之哀。谋之其臧，则具是违⑦；谋之不臧，则具是依。我视谋犹，伊于胡底⑧！

我龟既厌，不我告犹⑨。谋夫孔多，是用不集⑩。发言盈庭，谁敢执其咎？如匪行迈谋⑪，是用不得于道。

哀哉为犹，匪先民是程⑫，匪大犹是经⑬；维迩言是听，维迩言是争！如彼筑室于道谋，是用不溃于成⑭。

国虽靡止⑮，或圣或否⑯。民虽靡膴⑰，或哲或谋⑱，或肃或艾⑲。如彼泉流，无沦胥以败。

不敢暴虎⑳，不敢冯河㉑。人知其一㉒，莫知其他。战战兢兢，如临深渊，如履薄冰。

【注释】

①小旻（mín 民）：小天。旻指天，因诗称天不向人民施恩德，故称小天。　②敷：布施。　③犹：通"猷"：指谋策。回遹（yù 域）：邪僻。　④沮（jǔ 举）：阻止。　⑤邛（qióng 穷）：病。　⑥潝潝（xì xì 细细）：对上不满。訿訿（zǐ zǐ 紫紫）：同"訾訾"，对上诋毁。

⑦具:通"俱"。 ⑧于:往。底:止。 ⑨犹:道。 ⑩集:成就。 ⑪匪行迈谋:即不进而谋。 ⑫程:法。 ⑬经:行。 ⑭溃:遂,达到。 ⑮靡止:狭小无所居。 ⑯否:相对于"圣"者,当指不智者。 ⑰肝(hū 呼):大,多。 ⑱谋:聪。 ⑲肃:恭谨严肃。艾(yì 义):治,治事。 ⑳暴虎:徒手搏虎。 ㉑冯(píng 凭)河:涉水过河。 ㉒其一:指暴虎、冯河这一类危险。

【译文】

上天大发威风,暴虐遍布下面土地中。谋划邪僻,那一天才不用?谋划善的不从,不善的反而用。我看这些谋划,也是弊病多又重!

人们不满又诋毁,也很可悲哀伤恸。谋划是善的,便都是违反不用;谋划不善的,便都是依从。我看这些谋划,到什么时候才不用。

我的龟甲既已厌倦,不告诉我什么是吉凶。谋臣太多,因此不能成功。发言的充满朝廷,谁敢承担那个凶?像远行不进问路人,因此谋事不能成功。

可哀的是谋划,不以先人的为标准,不以大谋划为定论;只有浅近的话听,只有浅近的话争!像那造屋问路人,因此谋事不能完成。

国虽狭小无居处,有圣人和不智人。人虽说没太多,有谨慎人有聪敏人。像那泉水的流快,不要都沦没失败。

不敢徒手搏虎,不敢徒步过河。人们知道这危险,不知还有其他危险。战战兢兢要小心,像临近深渊难过,像踏上薄冰求过。

小 宛①

宛彼鸣鸠，翰飞戾天②。我心忧伤，念昔先人。明发不寐③，有怀二人④。

人之齐圣⑤，饮酒温克⑥。彼昏不知，壹醉日富⑦。各敬尔仪，天命不又。

中原有菽，庶民采之。螟蛉有子⑧，蜾蠃负之⑨。教诲尔子，式穀似之⑩。

题彼脊令，载飞载鸣。我日斯迈，(而)尔月斯征。夙兴夜寐，无忝尔所生⑪。

交交桑扈⑫，率场啄粟。哀我填寡⑬，宜岸宜狱⑭，握粟出卜，自何能穀？

温温恭人，如集于木。惴惴小心，如临于谷。战战兢兢，如履薄冰。

【注释】

①小宛：小而短尾，宛通"屈"，指鸠短尾。这诗指民有识见短的，以鸠相比，故称小而短尾。鸠：一说斑鸠，指短尾鸠。 ②翰飞：高飞。戾：至。 ③明发：天亮。 ④二人：指父母。 ⑤齐圣：正直聪明。 ⑥温克：蕴藉自持。 ⑦壹醉日富：一喝醉，自以为日富。 ⑧螟蛉：螟蛾的幼虫。 ⑨蜾蠃（guǒ luǒ 果裸）：细腰蜂。细腰蜂捉螟蛾的幼虫作为它自己幼虫的食品。古人不察，错认为细腰蜂领养螟蛉为己子。 ⑩式穀似之：用善似它。古人误认细腰蜂用善使螟蛉像它。 ⑪忝：辱没。尔所生：你所生，指父母。 ⑫桑扈：鸟名，一名青雀，相传食肉。今无肉可食，惟啄粟而已。 ⑬填寡：填通"殄"，穷苦而寡财。 ⑭岸：通"犴"，牢房。

【译文】

小而秃尾的鸠鸟叫,高飞想上到天。我的心里忧愁伤痛,想念先人从前。从夜到天亮没有睡着,想念父母二人都贤。

人的正直和聪明,饮酒蕴藉能克制。那昏庸的人不知道,一醉便夸有财资。各人敬慎你威仪,天命一去没来时。

原野里有野生的豆,百姓都可去采它。螟蛾有儿子,细腰蜂背起它。教诲那个儿子,用善教它像它。

看那鹡鸰鸟,一边飞一边鸣。我每天在前进,你是每月在前行。早起夜睡,不要辱没你父母亲。

青雀交交地叫没吃肉,顺着农场吃我粟。哀伤我穷苦寡财,应该入牢应该入狱。拿着小米去问卜,自己何从能得吉卦?

温和恭谨的人,好像鸟栖息在树木。我是惴惴小心,像临到那山谷。我是战战兢兢,好像踏上那冰又薄。

小 弁①

弁彼鸒斯,归飞提提②。民莫不榖,我独于罹。何辜于天?我罪伊何?心之忧矣,云如之何?

踧踧周道③,鞫为茂草④。我心忧伤,惄焉如捣⑤。假寐永叹⑥,维忧用老。心之忧矣,疢如疾首⑦。

维桑与梓,必恭敬止⑧。靡瞻匪父,靡依匪母。不属于毛,不罹于里⑨。天之生我,我辰安在?

菀彼柳斯⑩,鸣蜩嘒嘒⑪。有漼者渊⑫,萑苇淠淠⑬。譬彼舟流,不知所届⑭。心之忧矣,不遑假寐。

鹿斯之奔,维足伎伎⑮。雉之朝雊⑯,尚求其雌。譬彼坏木,疾用无枝。心之忧矣,宁莫之知。

600

相彼投兔⑰，尚或先之。行有死人，尚或墐之⑱。君子秉心，维其忍之⑲。心之忧矣，涕既陨之。

君子信谗，如或酬之。君子不惠，不舒究之。伐木掎矣⑳，析薪扡矣㉑。舍彼有罪，予之佗矣㉒。

莫高匪山，莫浚匪泉。君子无易由言，耳属于垣。无逝我梁，无发我笱！我躬不阅，遑恤我后！

【注释】

①小弁（pán 盘）：小乐。这首诗的开头讲鹬（yù 誉），即乌鸦。又说乌鸦群飞，但它的为乐是小的，所以称小弁。斯：语助词。　②提提：群飞。　③踧踧（dí dí 敌敌）：指平坦。　④鞠（jū 鞠）：尽。　⑤怒（nì 溺）：思。搗（dǎo 捣）：捣碎。　⑥假寐：不脱衣裳睡。　⑦疢（chèn 趁）：热病。　⑧维桑与梓，必恭敬止：桑树与梓树，是父母所栽种，所以一定要恭敬。　⑨不属于毛，不罹于里：毛在外属阳，指父。里在内属阴，指母。　⑩菀（yù 郁）：茂盛。　⑪蜩（tiáo 条）：蝉。嘒嘒（huì huì 惠惠）：蝉鸣声。　⑫漼（cuǐ 璀）：深。　⑬淠淠（pèi pèi 配配）：茂盛。　⑭届：至。　⑮伎伎（qí qí 其其）：宽舒。　⑯雊（gòu 够）：野鸡叫。　⑰投：掩，关闭。　⑱墐（jìn 晋）：通"殣"，埋葬。　⑲忍：残忍。　⑳掎（jǐ 几）：先挖树根，再用粗绳把树扳倒。　㉑扡（chǐ 齿）：纹理。　㉒佗（tuó 驼）：加。

【译文】

快乐的乌鸦，成群地飞回来呀。人们生活没有不好，我独自陷在网罗。我对天犯了什么罪呀？我的罪是什么？心里无限忧愁呀，叫我到底怎么办呀？

平坦的大路，全是茂盛的草。我的心里忧伤，想起来像心在捣。穿衣裳睡只长叹，只有忧使人老。心里无限忧愁呀，烦热头痛怎了。

故乡的桑树和梓树，一定要恭敬它。没有瞻仰不是父，没有依靠不是母。我既不属于父，我也不属于母。上天生育我，我的时运在何处？

茂密那柳枝啊，蝉儿在鸣叫不休。深沉的渊泉边，芦苇长得密而稠。好比船儿顺水流，不知到何处才休。心里无限忧愁呀，和衣躺着只缘愁。

鹿儿狂跑呀，只是四脚像飞时。野鸡清晨叫呀，还是找个雌。好像那被浸坏的树，因病不能长枝。心里无限忧愁呀，难道没有人知。

观察那捕兔网捉兔，尚且有人放了它。路上有死人，尚且有人埋葬他。君子居着何心，这狠心怎忍受它。心里无限忧愁呀，涕泪不断落下它。

君子听信谗言，像有人呈酒酬答他。君子不讲恩惠，不是从容研究它。斫树用绳揹倒它，劈薪顺理分开它。舍弃那有罪人，却把罪状加给我啊。

没有高的不是山，没有深的不是渊。君子不要轻易出言，人有耳朵靠近墙垣。不要弄断我的鱼梁。不要弄动我的鱼篓！我的身子不自由，不考虑我的身后！

巧　言

悠悠昊天①，曰父母且②。无罪无辜，乱如此怃③。昊天已威，予慎无罪④。昊天泰怃，予慎无辜。

乱之初生，僭始既涵⑤。乱之又生，君子信谗。君子如怒，乱庶遄沮⑥；君子如祉⑦，乱庶遄已。

君子屡盟，乱是用长。君子信盗，乱是用暴。盗言孔甘，乱是用餤⑧。匪其止共，维王之邛⑨。

奕奕寝庙⑩，君子作之。秩秩大猷，圣人莫之⑪。他人有心，予忖度之。跃跃毚兔⑫，遇犬获之。

荏染柔木⑬，君子树之。往来行言⑭，心焉数之。蛇蛇硕言⑮，出自口矣。巧言如簧，颜之厚矣。

彼何人斯？居河之麋⑯。无拳无勇，职为乱阶⑰。既微且尰⑱，尔勇伊何？为犹将多，尔居徒几何？

【注释】

①悠悠：指长远。 ②且：语助词。 ③怃（hū 呼）：大。 ④慎：诚。 ⑤僭（jiàn 荐）：谗言。涵：包容。 ⑥遄沮（chuán jū 船居）：很快制止。 ⑦祉：福，指贤人。 ⑧餤（tán 谈）：进。 ⑨匪其止共，维王之邛：止，职。共：恭。职恭，尽责。邛（qióng 穷），病。 ⑩奕奕：大貌。 ⑪莫：谋。 ⑫毚（chán 蝉）兔：狡兔。 ⑬荏（rěn 忍）染：柔弱。 ⑭行言：流言。 ⑮蛇蛇（yí yí 夷夷）：轻率。 ⑯麋：水边。 ⑰职：主。 ⑱微：足病。尰：通"肿"，指足肿。

【注释】

遥远的上天，说像父和母。没有罪孽受罚，乱这样大。上天已经发威，我谨慎地没有犯罪。上天降祸太广大，我谨慎地没有犯错误。

暴乱开始发生，谗言开始既经容许。暴乱再发生，君子相信谗言相与。君子如果发怒，暴乱近乎快阻止；君子如果用贤人，暴乱近乎快停止。

君子屡次和暴乱结盟，暴乱因此增添。君子相信盗窃，暴乱因此更坚。盗窃的话很甜，暴乱因此更前。盗窃谗佞不职恭，只是为王造罪愆。

大的宗庙，君子造它。明智的大计划，圣人谋划它。他人有什么心，我能猜测它。活跃的狡兔，碰上狗捉住它。

柔软的树，君子种它。来往的流言，心中有数对付它。浮夸的大话，从嘴里说出了。巧妙的话像奏笙簧，脸皮太厚了。

他是什么人呀？住在河的边堤。没有拳力没有勇气，专门成为乱的阶梯。腿有溃疡脚且肿，你的勇气是什么？施行诡计真太多，你的徒侣有几多？

何 人 斯

彼何人斯？其心孔艰①。胡逝我梁②，不入我门？伊谁云从？维暴之云。

二人从行，谁为此祸？胡逝我梁，不入唁我？始者不如今，云不我可③。

彼何人斯？胡逝我陈④？我闻其声，不见其身。不愧于人，不畏于天。

彼何人斯？其为飘风⑤。胡不自北？胡不自南？胡逝我梁？只搅我心。

尔之安行⑥，亦不遑舍；尔之亟行⑦，遑脂尔车⑧。壹者之来⑨，云何其盱⑩？

尔还而入，我心易也⑪；还而不入，否难知也。壹者之来，俾我祇也⑫。

伯氏吹埙⑬,仲氏吹篪⑭。及尔如贯⑮,谅不我知。出此三物⑯,以诅尔斯⑰。

为鬼为蜮⑱,则不可得。有靦面目⑲,视人罔极⑳。作此好歌,以极反侧㉑。

【注释】

①艰:险也,指心险而难测,心狠。 ②胡逝我梁:指为什么过我的鱼梁。 ③不我可:即不可我,不同意我。 ④陈:堂前的路。 ⑤飘风:暴风。 ⑥安行:缓行。 ⑦亟行:急行。 ⑧脂:通"支",即支车使不行。 ⑨壹者:犹云乃者。 ⑩盱(xū 虚):张目。 ⑪易:改变,指转愁为喜。 ⑫祇:通"疧",病也。 ⑬埙(xūn 勋):古代用陶土制的乐器,吹奏用。 ⑭篪(chí 池):古代竹制乐器,吹奏用。 ⑮贯:用绳串物。 ⑯三物:指犬、豕、鸡。 ⑰诅(zǔ 祖):誓词。 ⑱蜮(yù 域):古代以为短狐一类害人的动物。 ⑲靦(tiǎn 舔):狡猾貌。 ⑳视:通"示"。罔极:不可靠。 ㉑反侧:反覆无常,指不正直。

【译文】

那人是什么人啊?他的心很阴沉。为什么走过我鱼梁,不进入我家大门?是听从什么人的话?只听从暴公的言论。

二人跟着走路,啥人造出这个祸?为什么走过我鱼梁,不进来安慰我?开始时不像如今,说不赞成我。

那人是什么人啊?为什么走过我堂路滨?我听到他的声音,不看见他的人身。他既对人没有惭愧,也不怕天神。

那人是什么人啊?他是暴风入侵。为什么不从北边来?为什么不从南入侵？为什么只走我鱼梁？只搅乱我的心。

你的缓缓走，不休息也成；你的快快走，没功夫使你车子停。上次你的到来，说什么我把眼睁？

你回来时就进门，我心变得高兴；你回来不进门，使我难知情。上次你的到来，使我气得病不轻。

你如阿哥吹埙，我如阿弟吹篪。我和你像一绳串，你竟对我不深知。摆出豕犬鸡，对神发个誓。

你如作鬼作蜮，那对我就不可见得。你有狡猾的面目，让人终究靠不得。我作这首好歌，用来探究你的不正直。

巷 伯

萋兮斐兮①，成是贝锦②。彼谮人者，亦已大甚！
哆兮侈兮③，成是南箕④。彼谮人者，谁适与谋？
缉缉翩翩⑤，谋欲谮人。慎尔言也，谓尔不信。
捷捷幡幡⑥，谋欲谮言。岂不尔受，既其女迁。
骄人好好，劳人草草⑦。苍天苍天，视彼骄人，矜此劳人！
彼谮人者，谁适与谋？取彼谮人，投畀豺虎⑧；豺虎不食，投畀有北⑨；有北不受，投畀有昊。
杨园之道，猗于亩丘⑩。寺人孟子，作为此诗。凡百君子，敬而听之⑪。

【注释】

①萋斐（qī fěi 妻匪）：文采错杂貌。　②贝锦：像贝壳的织锦。　③哆（chǐ 齿）：大。　④南箕：即二十八宿中的箕宿，四星连成梯形，像簸箕。古人认为南箕星主口舌，故比谗人。　⑤缉缉：

口舌声。翩翩：本指鸟的飞翔，这里比人的往来。 ⑥捷捷：指口舌声。幡幡（fān fān 翻翻）：指往来。 ⑦草草：劳心。 ⑧畀（bì 毕）：给。 ⑨有北：极北寒冷处。 ⑩猗（yǐ 倚）：加。 ⑪敬：通"警"，警惕，警戒。

【译文】

文彩错杂啊，成功这贝壳样的织锦。那个进谗言的人，也已经太过分！

夸大啊夸大啊，成功这南箕的星宿。那个进谗言的人，谁好同他联谋？

往来窃窃私语声，谋用谗言来害人。劝你说话要谨慎，说你的话不可信。

往来窃窃私语声，谋用谗言来害人。岂能不接受你的话？既而迁怒到你的身。

骄人得意很高兴，劳人辛苦常艰辛。苍天啊苍天，瞧瞧那骄横的人，哀怜那辛劳的人！

那个进谗言的人，谁好同他联谋？把那个进谗言的人，投给豺虎；豺虎不吃，投给有北去受苦；有北不受，投给上天去受侮。

到杨园去的路，先从亩丘过。我是寺人孟子，作这首诗。凡是众君子，警戒地来听这首诗。

谷 风

习习谷风①，维风及雨。将恐将惧②，维予与女。将安将乐，女转弃予。

习习谷风，维风及颓③。将恐将惧，寘予于怀。将安将乐，弃予如遗。

习习谷风，维山崔嵬④。无草不死，无木不萎。忘我大德，思我小怨。

【注释】

①习习：指微风和煦。谷风：山谷中风，东风。 ②将：且。 ③颓（tuí 颓）：龙卷风。 ④崔嵬（wéi 维）：山巅。

【译文】

和暖的东风吹着，只有风和雨。且恐且惧的时候，只有我与你。且安且乐的时候，你转而把我抛弃。

和暖的东风吹着，只有暖风和狂风在一起。且恐且惧的时候，抱我在你怀里。且安且乐的时候，抛弃我像丢东西。

和暖的东风吹着，只有狂风吹上山顶。在狂风中没有草不死，没有树不枯陨。忘记我的大恩德，想我的小怨恨。

蓼 莪

蓼蓼者莪①，匪莪伊蒿。哀哀父母，生我劬劳。

蓼蓼者莪，匪莪伊蔚②。哀哀父母，生我劳瘁。

缾之罄矣，维罍之耻③。鲜民之生，不如死之久矣！无父何怙④？无母何恃？出则衔恤，入则靡至。

父兮生我，母兮鞠我。拊我畜我，长我育我，顾我复我，出入腹我。欲报之德，昊天罔极⑤！

南山烈烈⑥，飘风发发⑦。民莫不穀⑧，我独何害！

南山律律⑨，飘风弗弗⑩。民莫不穀，我独不卒⑪！

【注释】

①蓼蓼（lù lù 路路）：长大貌。莪（é 俄）：一名萝，三月中茎可生食，又可蒸煮而食，香美。至秋老为蒿，则不可食。　②蔚（wèi 卫）：牡蒿，花如胡麻花，紫赤。实像角，无子，故称牡蒿。　③缾罄罍耻：缾同"瓶"，瓶小罍大，罍中物分装瓶中，瓶空无物即固罍空所致，故罍以为耻。喻己小如瓶，瓶空不得养父母。瓶空由于罍空，比上之人征役不息，不能养父母。　④怙（hù 户）：依靠。　⑤昊天罔极：言父母之恩如天，广大无边，不知所以为报也。　⑥烈烈：艰阻貌，难于攀登。　⑦发发：疾貌。　⑧榖：善，指养。　⑨律律：同"烈烈"。　⑩弗弗：犹"发发"。　⑪卒：终，指终养父母。

【译文】

长大的莪菜，那不是莪是蒿。悲哀的父母，生育我辛劳。

长大的莪菜，那不是莪是蔚。悲哀的父母，生育我太劳瘁。

盛酒的小瓶空了，是盛酒大罍的耻了。少德无靠的人活着，不如死去的久了。没有父亲何所依？没有母亲何所靠？出门含着忧愁，入门像没有到。

父亲啊生我，母亲啊养我。抚爱我来培育我，拉大我来教育我，照顾我来照顾我，出进抱我。要报他们的恩德，像上天那样广大怎么报得！

终南山攀登难，狂风吹得利害。人没有不养父母，我独为什么受这害！

终南山攀登难，狂风吹得利害。人没有不养父母，我独为什么终养难。

诗经

大 东

有饛簋飧①,有捄棘匕②。周道如砥③,其直如矢。君子所履,小人所视。睠言顾之④,潸焉出涕⑤。

小东大东⑥,杼柚其空⑦。纠纠葛屦,可以履霜。佻佻公子⑧,行彼周行。既往既来,使我心疚。

有冽氿泉⑨,无浸获薪。契契寤叹⑩,哀我惮人⑪。薪是获薪,尚可载也。哀我惮人,亦可息也。

东人之子,职劳不来。西人之子⑫,粲粲衣服。舟人之子⑬,熊罴是裘。私人之子⑭,百僚是试。

或以其酒,不以其浆⑮。鞙鞙佩璲⑯,不以其长。维天有汉⑰,监亦有光。跂彼织女⑱,终日七襄⑲。

虽则七襄,不成报章⑳。睆彼牵牛㉑,不以服箱㉒。东有启明,西有长庚。有捄天毕㉓,载施之行。

维南有箕,不可以簸扬。维北有斗㉔,不可以挹酒浆。维南有箕,载翕其舌㉕。维北有斗,西柄之揭。

【注释】

①饛(méng 蒙):满簋貌。簋(guǐ 鬼):古代盛食物器,圆口,青铜或陶制。 ②捄(qiú 求):长貌。匕(bǐ 比):勺,匙类。 ③砥(dǐ 底):磨刀石。 ④睠:同"眷"。 ⑤潸(shān 衫):泪流貌。 ⑥小东大东:东方大小侯国。 ⑦杼:织布机上持纬线的。柚:受经线的。 ⑧佻佻:轻薄的。 ⑨氿(guǐ 鬼)泉:侧出的泉。 ⑩契契:忧苦貌。 ⑪惮(dàn 但):劳。 ⑫西人:西周来人。 ⑬舟人:有舟的人,指西人中的富人。 ⑭私人之子:指家庭奴隶。 ⑮浆:薄酒。 ⑯鞙鞙(juān juān 捐捐):通"琄琄",玉

貌。瑳（suì 遂）：玉佩。长：余，剩余。 ⑰汉：银河。 ⑱跂：通"歧"，分歧。织女三星，故称歧。 ⑲七襄：七次移动位置。 ⑳报章：指织布。 ㉑睆（huǎn 缓）：明星貌。 ㉒服：牛负。箱：车箱。 ㉓毕：星名，共八星，似网。 ㉔斗：北斗星。 ㉕翕（xì 细）：引。

【译文】

　　装满古器是晚餐，再有长柄进食匙。大路好像磨石平，它的笔直像箭矢。君子可在路上走，小民只能用眼看。眷恋地看着它，涕泣交流为着它。

　　东方侯国有大小，用杼柚织布都成空。仔细织成的葛布鞋，可以踏霜还成功。轻佻的公子，走那大路是从容。既是前去又回来，使我看了心发痛。

　　有寒冷的侧出泉，不要浸所获柴薪。忧苦地叹息，悲哀我们辛苦人，砍伐获得的柴薪，还可载运回来。悲哀我们辛苦人，也该休息安身。

　　东方侯国的子弟，职务劳苦无人理。西方人的子弟，衣服鲜明是华丽。富人的子弟，熊皮做裘暖身体。小人的子弟，他们也来试做吏。

　　有人醉于美酒，有人不得浆汤。有人身上挂的是宝玉，有人不得碎玉长。天上有银河，看上去也有光。分歧的看那织女星，整天搬迁了七场。虽则搬迁了七场，不成织锦的纹章。看那牵牛星，不能用来背车箱。东方有启明星，长庚星亮在西方。有弯曲的天毕星，排成行列没用场。

　　南方有箕星，不可以用来簸米糠。北方有北斗星，不可用来舀酒浆。南方有箕星，它的舌头能吸北方。北方有北斗星，它的柄儿举向西方。

四 月

四月维夏，六月徂暑①。先祖匪人，胡宁忍予？
秋日凄凄，百卉俱腓②。乱离瘼矣③，爰其适归。
冬日烈烈，飘风发发。民莫不穀，我独何害？
山有嘉卉，侯栗侯梅。废为残贼④，莫知其尤。
相彼泉水，载清载浊。我日构祸，曷云能穀？
滔滔江汉，南国之纪⑤。尽瘁以仕，宁莫我有⑥？
匪鹑匪鸢⑦，翰飞戾天。匪鳣匪鲔，潜逃于渊。
山有蕨薇，隰有杞桋⑧。君子作歌，维以告哀。

【注释】

①徂：往。　②腓（féi 肥）：枯萎。　③瘼（mò 莫）：病。
④废：大。　⑤纪：作为众川的纲纪。　⑥有：通"友"，相亲。
⑦鹑：指雕。　⑧桋（yí 夷）：树名。

【译文】

四月是夏天，六月到暑天。先祖不是他人，为何宁可忍我受熬煎？

秋天凄凉，百草都枯萎。乱离苦了，在何处适宜可以回归。

冬天凛冽，北风不歇。人们没有不好过，我独自为何受逼？

山上有好的草木，有栗树直和梅树稠。有谁做残害树的贼，不知道谁是树的仇。

观察那泉水，有时清有时浊。我是天天遭祸，怎么说能有好生活？

滔滔的长江汉水，南国水流的纲纪。尽瘁去做官，难道对我没点情谊?

不是老雕不是鸢,高飞可以飞上天。不是鳣鱼不是鲔鱼,潜逃可以到深渊。

山里有蕨薇菜,洼地有杞桋材。君子做这首歌,只是用来诉悲哀。

诗经

北山之什

北 山

陟彼北山，言采其杞①。偕偕士子②，朝夕从事。王事靡盬，忧我父母。

溥天之下③，莫非王土。率土之滨④，莫非王臣。大夫不均，我从事独贤⑤。

四牡彭彭⑥，王事傍傍⑦。嘉我未老⑧，鲜我方将⑨。旅力方刚⑩，经营四方。

或燕燕居息⑪，或尽瘁事国，或息偃在床⑫，或不已于行。

或不知叫号，或惨惨劬劳⑬；或栖迟偃仰⑭，或王事鞅掌⑮。

或湛乐饮酒⑯，或惨惨畏咎；或出入风议⑰，或靡事不为。

【注释】

①言：我。　②偕偕：强壮貌。　③溥：大。　④率土之滨：循着土地的水涯，即海内的国土，即四海之内，即中国。　⑤贤：贤劳，艰苦。　⑥彭彭：不得息。　⑦傍傍：不得止。　⑧嘉：夸奖。　⑨鲜：珍视，重视。将：强壮。　⑩旅力：体力。　⑪燕燕：安息。　⑫偃：仰卧。　⑬惨惨：忧愁。　⑭栖迟：游息。　⑮鞅掌：指公事忙

碌。　⑯湛（dān 丹）乐：过度欢乐。　⑰风议：放言，讽谕。

【译文】

登上那北山，我采那枸杞。壮健的士子，早晚做事。王事没尽头，忧我没供养的父母。

广大的天下，没有不是王的疆土。沿着土地到海滨，没有不是王的臣。大夫派劳逸不均匀，我做的事独自艰辛。

四匹雄马不安宁，王事紧急不得停。赞我年未老，夸我强壮正是好。我的体力正刚强，可以经管走四方。有人安逸地居住休息，有人为国事用尽全力。有人休息躺着在床，有人不停地干他行当。

有人不知道征召，有人忧郁地辛劳；有人为游息而仰躺，有人为王事着忙。

有人狂欢饮酒，有人愁苦引咎；有人出进放言，有人事事都作。

无将大车

无将大车①，衹自尘兮。无思百忧，衹自疧兮②。
无将大车，维尘冥冥。无思百忧，不出于颎③。
无将大车，维尘雝兮④。无思百忧，衹自重兮⑤。

【注释】

①无将大车：将，率领，指推。大车本用牛拉，改用人推，力微车重，无济于事。　②疧（qí 其）：忧病。　③颎（jiǒng 炯）：同"炯"，火光明亮。　④雝：同"壅"，蔽。　⑤重：加重。

【译文】

不要推大车,只是自己吃灰尘。不要想各种忧愁,只是自己病上身。

不要推大车,只是尘土暗暗。不要想各种忧愁,不出于光明是憾。

不要推大车,只是尘土遮蔽。不要想各种忧愁,只是自己加重此弊。

小 明

明明上天,照临下土。我征徂西,至于艽野①。二月初吉②,载离寒暑。心之忧矣,其毒大苦。念彼共人③,涕零如雨。岂不怀归?畏此罪罟④。

昔我往矣,日月方除⑤。曷云其还,岁聿云莫?念我独兮,我事孔庶⑥。心之忧矣,惮我不暇⑦。念彼共人,睠睠怀顾。岂不怀归,畏此谴怒。

昔我往矣,日月方奥⑧。曷云其还,政事愈蹙?岁聿云莫,采萧获菽。心之忧矣,自诒伊戚⑨。念彼共人,兴言出宿⑩。岂不怀归?畏此反覆⑪。

嗟尔君子,无恒安处,靖共尔位⑫,正直是与。神之听之⑬,式穀以女(汝)。

嗟尔君子,无恒安息。靖共尔位,好是正直。神之听之,介尔景福⑭。

【注释】

①艽(qiú 求)野:荒远之野。 ②初吉:初次来的吉日,指阴

历初一、二、三月亮初生时称为吉日。　③共人：恭谨的人，指同僚。④罪罟（gǔ 古）：罪网。　⑤除：除旧生新。　⑥庶：众多。　⑦惮：劳。　⑧奥：通"燠"，和暖。　⑨戚：忧。　⑩兴：起来。　⑪反覆：反反覆覆，乱加罪名。　⑫靖：安定。　⑬神之听之：见《小雅·伐木》注释。　⑭介：给与。景：大。

【译文】

　　明明的上天，光芒照着下土。我出征到西方，到荒远的野处。二月开始的吉日，经历了寒和暑。心里的忧愁啊，它的毒害太苦。想那恭谨的人，涕泪落下像雨。难道不想回来？怕这罪像网罟。

　　从前我出征时，日月正在布新除故。怎么说那回来，一年又到岁暮。念我孤独啊，我事很多难数。心的忧愁啊，怕我没空难顾。想那恭谨的人，眷眷多情来回顾。难道不想回来，怕这里责备发怒。

　　从前我出征时，日月正在暖气恢复。怎么说那回来，政事越来越迫麇？一年又到岁暮，采蒿草又得豆熟。心里的忧愁啊，自己造成忧独。想那恭谨的人，起身出外去住宿。难道不想回去，怕这里反反覆覆。

　　叹息你君子啊，不要长期安处。安定地恭谨你的位置，和正直的人相处。审慎吧听从吧，用善道来赐你安处。叹息你君子啊，不要长期安居休息。安定地恭谨你的位置，爱好亲近人的正直。审慎吧听从吧，赐给你大的幸福。

鼓　钟

　　鼓钟将将①，淮水汤汤。忧心且伤。淑人君子，怀允不忘②。

鼓钟喈喈③，淮水湝湝④。忧心且悲。淑人君子，其德不回⑤。

鼓钟伐鼛⑥，淮有三洲。忧心且妯⑦。淑人君子，其德不犹⑧。

鼓钟钦钦，鼓瑟鼓琴。笙磬同音。以《雅》以《南》⑨，以籥不僭⑩。

【注释】

①将将：同"锵锵"，钟声。 ②允：诚实。 ③喈喈（jiē jiē 皆皆）：钟声。 ④湝湝（jiē jiē 皆皆）：水流声。 ⑤回：邪僻。 ⑥鼛（gāo 高）：大鼓。 ⑦妯（chōu 抽）：哀悼。 ⑧犹：奸邪。 ⑨以：为。《雅》：《诗经》中有《雅》。《南》：《诗经》中有《周南》、《召南》。 ⑩籥（yuè 跃）：古乐器，似笛，吹以节舞。僭（jiàn 荐）：乱。

【译文】

敲钟的声音锵锵，淮水的声音泱泱。忧心又痛伤，善人君子人，怀念确实不能忘。

敲钟的声音皆皆，淮水的声音皆皆。忧心又悲咤。善人君子人，他的道德不枉邪。

敲钟又敲大鼓，声响遍及淮地三洲。心中忧伤又发愁。善人君子人，他的道德一点诈没有。

敲钟声音钦钦，弹瑟又弹琴。吹笙击磬发同音。奏二《雅》和二《南》音，吹籥节舞不乱阵。

楚 茨

楚楚者茨①，言抽其棘②。自昔何为？我蓺黍稷。我黍与与③，我稷翼翼④。我仓既盈，我庾维亿⑤。以为酒食，以享以祀，以妥以侑⑥，以介景福。

济济跄跄⑦，絜尔牛羊⑧，以往烝尝⑨。或剥或亨⑩，或肆或将⑪。祝祭于祊⑫，祀事孔明⑬。先祖是皇，神保是飨⑭。孝孙有庆，报以介福⑮，万寿无疆！

执爨踖踖⑯，为俎孔硕⑰，或燔或炙，君妇莫莫⑱。为豆孔庶，为宾为客，献酬交错。礼仪卒度，笑语卒获。神保是格⑲，报以介福，万寿攸酢⑳！

我孔熯矣㉑，式礼莫愆。工祝致告㉒，徂赉孝孙㉓。苾芬孝祀㉔，神嗜饮食。卜尔百福，如几如式㉕。既齐既稷㉖，既匡既敕㉗。永锡尔极㉘，时万时亿！

礼仪既备，钟鼓既戒㉙，孝孙徂位，工祝致告。"神具醉止"，皇尸载起。鼓钟送尸，神保聿归。诸宰君妇，废彻不迟㉚。诸父兄弟，备言燕私。

乐具入奏，以绥后禄。尔肴既将㉛，莫怨具庆。既醉既饱，小大稽首。神嗜饮食，使君寿考。孔惠孔时，维其尽之。子子孙孙，勿替引之㉜！

【注释】

①楚楚：丛生貌。茨：蒺藜。 ②抽：除。棘：植物的刺。 ③与与：茂盛貌。 ④翼翼：繁盛貌。 ⑤庾（yǔ 羽）：露天积谷物处。 ⑥侑（yòu 幼）：劝饮食。 ⑦济济：众多。跄跄（qiāng qiāng 腔腔）：走路有节拍。 ⑧絜：同"洁"。 ⑨烝：冬祭。尝：秋祭。 ⑩亨：同"烹"。

⑪肆：陈设。将：捧持。　⑫祊（bēng 崩）：宗庙门内设祭处。　⑬明：指祭礼洁净。　⑭神保：祭时用人作尸的美称。　⑮报：报祭，国祭。　⑯爨（cuàn 窜）：烧饭。踖踖（jí jí 及及）：敏捷。　⑰俎（zǔ 阻）：古祭器。　⑱莫莫：安静。　⑲格：至。　⑳酢（zuò 祚）：回敬酒。　㉑煁（nǎn 赧）：敬惧。　㉒工祝：主祭司仪的人。　㉓赉（lài 赖）：赏赐。　㉔苾（bì 必）芬：芬芳。　㉕几：期。式：法。　㉖稷：急。通"亟"。　㉗匡：端正。敕：严正。　㉘极：穷极。　㉙戒：戒备。　㉚彻：通"撤"，除。　㉛将：美好。　㉜引：引长。

【译文】

　　植物丛生是蒺藜，那时除刺靠用犁。自古以来做什么？我自种下黍和稷。我的黍子很茂盛，我的稷子很茂密。我的仓库既装满，我的露仓数有亿。用来做酒和吃食，用来供神和祭祀，用来安坐饮酒足嗜，用来助我得大福祉。

　　众人奔走有节度，祭神洁净你牛羊，用作秋祭及冬祭。有的剥皮有煮汤，有的陈设有的供场。司仪先祭庙门旁，祭祀的事很洁净。先祖神道最堂皇，作尸的人得安享。孝孙得会有赐赏，报祭用来赐大福，赐的是万寿无疆！

　　庖人烧火很恭谨，作为器具用大好，有的烧烤有的炒，主妇安静态度好。食器陈列得很多，作宾作客真不少，献酒酬酒相交错。礼节合法极周到，笑着说话都恰好。作尸的人是来了，报祭用来赐大福，用万寿来做答报。

　　我是很恭敬了，用礼没有过错好。司仪向神来报告，神往赐福孝孙好。馨香祭祀用得到，神爱酒食吃得了。赐你百种幸福好，福来有期又有程。既是整齐又快好，既是正规又坚妙。永远赐你福气好，是万是亿都得到！

礼仪既经完备，钟鼓既经备好。孝孙既已到位，司仪向神祷告。"神都吃醉了"，做尸的人起来了。打鼓敲钟送尸了，做尸的人回去了。诸个宰夫和主妇，撤掉祭神酒席不迟了。诸父兄弟另设席，完备地饮宴私自好。

乐器具备入奏好，用来安享祭后肴。你的肴既已摆好，没有怨言全说好。既喝醉又吃饱，小子大人叩头报道。神爱好饮酒吃肉，使你能够得寿考。很顺礼很及时，你尽礼又尽孝。你的子子孙孙，不要改变长存好。

信 南 山

信彼南山①，维禹甸之②。畇畇原隰③，曾孙田之。我疆我理④，南东其亩。

上天同云，雨雪雰雰。益之以霢霂⑤。既优既渥⑥，既霑既足，生我百谷。

疆埸翼翼⑦，黍稷彧彧⑧。曾孙之穑，以为酒食。畀我尸宾，寿考万年！

中田有庐⑨，疆埸有瓜。是剥是菹⑩，献之皇祖。曾孙寿考，受天之祐。

祭以清酒，从以骍牡⑪，享于祖考。执其鸾刀⑫，以启其毛，取其血膋⑬。

是烝是享，苾苾芬芬⑭。祀事孔明⑮，先祖是皇。报以介福，万寿无疆！

【注释】

①信：通"申"，长貌。　②甸（diàn 佃）：治理。　③畇

畇（yún yún 云云）：平整。 ④疆理：分界治理。 ⑤霢霂（mài mù 脉沐）：小雨。 ⑥优：雨水足。渥：沾润。 ⑦埸（yì 亦）：田畔。翼翼：整饬。 ⑧彧彧（yù yù 玉玉）：茂盛。 ⑨庐：通"芦"，萝卜。 ⑩菹（zū 租）：腌菜。 ⑪骍（xīn 辛）：赤色。 ⑫鸾刀：有鸾铃的刀。 ⑬膋（liáo 辽）：脂肪。 ⑭苾苾（bì bì 必必）：芳香。 ⑮明：犹"洁"。

【译文】

　　申展那终南山，只有禹来治理它。平整那高原和洼地，曾孙曾经种过它。我划疆界和治理，田亩从南从东我治它。

　　上天有阴云，下雪又纷纷。加上又小雨。既是水足又润渥，既经霑湿又满足，可以生长我百谷。

　　田地疆界很整饬，黍稷种得很密植。曾孙把它来收获，用作我们的酒食。给我作尸和宾客，神赐寿考万年值。

　　田中种得有萝卜，田边种得有杂瓜。是剥萝卜是醃瓜，献给皇祖不为差。曾孙因此得长寿，受天赐福得称嘉。

　　祭祀用的是清酒，跟着一头红牡牛，拿去献给先祖考。拿着他的鸾刀头，用来开脱它皮毛，取出它的血和油。

　　冬祭请神来受享，芬芬芳芳是馨香。祭祀的事很洁净，先祖受祭得安享。报祭用来赐大福，赐给万寿称无疆！

甫　田

　　倬彼甫田①，岁取十千。我取其陈，食我农人，自古有年②。今适南亩，或耘或耔③，黍稷薿薿④。攸介攸止⑤，烝我髦士⑥。

以我齐明⑦,与我牺羊⑧,以社以方⑨。我田既臧,农夫之庆。琴瑟击鼓,以御田祖⑩,以祈甘雨,以介我稷黍,以穀我士女⑪。

曾孙来止,以其妇子,馌彼南亩⑫,田畯至喜⑬。攘其左右⑭,尝其旨否。禾易长亩⑮,终善且有。曾孙不怒,农夫克敏⑯。

曾孙之稼,如茨如梁⑰。曾孙之庾,如坻如京⑱。乃求千斯仓,乃求万斯箱。黍稷稻粱,农夫之庆。报以介福,万寿无疆。

【注释】

①倬(zhuō 卓):大。甫田:大田。 ②有年:丰年。 ③耘:锄草。耔(zǐ 子):培土。 ④薿薿(nǐ nǐ 你你):茂盛。 ⑤攸介攸止:攸,语助词。介,长之。止,停止,指结实。 ⑥烝:进。髦(máo 毛)士:英俊的男人。 ⑦齐(zī 咨)明:在古器中所盛食品皆洁净。明指洁净。齐通"齍(zī 咨)",盛谷物的祭器。 ⑧牺:牺牲用牛。 ⑨社:土地神。方:四方神。 ⑩御(yà 亚):迎。田祖:田神。 ⑪穀:养。 ⑫馌(yè 叶):送饭给耕者。 ⑬喜:通"饎",吃酒食。 ⑭攘:通"让"。 ⑮易:禾盛貌。 ⑯敏:敏捷。 ⑰茨:积。 ⑱坻(chí 池):水中高地。京:高丘。

【译文】

广大的那大田,每年收粮取十千。我取其中陈旧粮,养活农夫不可怜,从古以来尽丰年。今到南亩去种田,或是除草或培土,黍稷茂盛结实坚。青苗长大结实止,献我俊士称崇贤。

诗经

用我器物讲洁净，祭神用我牛和羊，祭祀社神和四方。我田既是收获昌。农夫庆贺面有光，琴瑟击鼓声高扬，用来迎接那田祖，用求甘雨来帮忙，用来长大我稷黍，用来养好我男女。

曾孙亲自来到，同他的妻和子，送酒饭到南亩，田官到了用酒饭。让开他的左右，尝尝味道好否。稻禾容易长田亩，终于长好年成有。曾孙看了不发怒，农夫能快种田亩。

曾孙所有的庄稼，多如屋盖高如梁。曾孙的露天仓，多如沙堆高如冈。于是求千个仓，于是求万个箱。有黍稷有稻粱，农夫庆贺面有光。报祭用来赐大福，赐给他万寿无疆。

大 田

大田多稼，既种既戒①，既备乃事。以我覃耜②，俶载南亩③，播厥百谷，既庭且硕④，曾孙是若⑤。

既方既皁⑥，既坚既好，不稂不莠⑦。去其螟螣⑧，及其蟊贼⑨。无害我田稚⑩！田祖有神，秉畀炎火⑪。

有渰萋萋⑫，兴雨祁祁⑬。雨我公田，遂及我私。彼有不获稚，此有不敛穧⑭。彼有遗秉⑮，此有滞穗⑯，伊寡妇之利！

曾孙来止，以其妇子，馌彼南亩，田畯至喜。来方禋祀，以其骍黑⑰。与其黍稷，以享以祀，以介景福。

【注释】

①种：选种。戒：准备，包括修农具，事耦耕。　②覃（yǎn 眼）：锋利。　③俶载：开始从事。　④庭：直。　⑤若：顺。　⑥方：谷穗空壳。皁（zào 造）：谷结实未坚。　⑦稂：空谷。　⑧螟（míng 冥）：蛀稻心的害虫。螣（tè 特）：食苗叶的害虫。　⑨蟊（máo 毛）：

食稻根的害虫。贼：食稻茎的害虫。 ⑩稚（zhì 至）：幼禾。 ⑪秉畀：执与。 ⑫渰（yǎn 掩）：云起。萋萋：云行貌。 ⑬祁祁：众多貌。 ⑭穧（jì 计）：已割而未收的农作物。 ⑮秉：谷把。 ⑯滞穗：遗弃的谷穗。 ⑰骍黑：赤色牛、黑色豕。

【译文】

　　大田里边多庄稼，既选种子又备戒，既完备了这些事。用我锋利的耜器，开始南亩种了田，播种各种谷子事，既挺直又肥大，曾孙看了是顺事。

　　稻既抽穗又结实，结实既坚硬又好，没有空壳与害草。除去螟虫和螣虫，蟊虫贼虫也除掉。不要害我的幼苗！田祖有神通，拿了害虫给我烧。

　　有云流动众多，兴起下雨田有利。雨落我的公家田，遂即到我私田里。有没收嫩谷在那里，有没收谷类在这里。有遗漏禾把在那里，有漏落禾穗在这里，这都是寡妇得的利！

　　曾孙到来了，同他的妻和子，送酒饭到南亩田里，田官来到用饮食。曾孙来祭四方神，用他的牛和豕，与他的稷和黍，用来献神行祭祀，求神赐给大福祉。

瞻彼洛矣

　　瞻彼洛矣①，维水泱泱②。君子至止，福禄如茨③。韎韐有奭④，以作六师。

　　瞻彼洛矣，维水泱泱。君子至止，鞞琫有珌⑤。君子万年，保其家室。

　　瞻彼洛矣，维水泱泱。君子至止，福禄既同。君子万年，保其家邦。

625

【注释】

①洛:洛水。 ②泱泱:水深广貌。 ③茨:屋盖,指广而大。④韎韐(mèi gé 妹格):蔽膝,用熟皮制,遮住膝部,用茜草染绛色。奭(shì 士):赤色。 ⑤鞞琫(bǐ běng 比绷):刀鞘上的饰物。珌(bì 必):刀鞘下的饰物。

【译文】

看那洛水呀,只有水声洋洋。君子到了这里,福禄多比屋盖强。披着蔽膝红灿灿,总领六军练兵忙。

看那洛水呀,只有水声洋洋。君子到了这里,刀鞘上下饰物都有光。君子长寿活万年,永保家室有荣光。

看那洛水呀,只有水声洋洋。君子到了这里,禄禄聚拢合一样。君子长寿活万年,保护家邦永无恙。

裳裳者华

裳裳者华①,其叶湑兮②。我觏之子,我心写兮③。我心写兮,是以有誉处兮。

裳裳者华,芸其黄矣④。我觏之子,维其有章矣⑤。维其有章矣,是以有庆矣。

裳裳者华,或黄或白。我觏之子,乘其四骆。乘其四骆,六辔沃若。

左之左之⑥,君子宜之。右之右之,君子有之⑦。维其有之,是以似之⑧。

【注释】

①裳裳：犹堂堂。　②湑（xǔ 许）：茂盛。　③写：通"泻"，泻去。　④芸：黄盛。　⑤章：文章，指文采、礼乐。　⑥左之、右之：或左或右，指左右辅弼，无不相宜。　⑦有：有此宜。　⑧似：通"嗣"。

【译文】

堂堂的鲜花，它的叶儿茂盛啊。我看见这个人，我心忧愁泻尽啊。我心忧愁泻尽啊，因此有安乐可处啊。

堂堂的鲜花，它的花儿黄啊。我看见这个人，只是他有文章了。只是他有文章了，因此该有庆贺了。

堂堂的鲜花，有的黄有的白。我看见这个人，驾着四匹黑鬃白毛的马。驾着四匹黑鬃白毛的马，六根辔绳很柔滑。

左就左，君子适宜它。右就右，君子适宜它。只是因为适宜它，因此继承祖业可靠他。

卷 六

小 雅

桑扈之什

桑 扈

交交桑扈①,有莺其羽②。君子乐胥③,受天之祜。
交交桑扈,有莺其领④。君子乐胥,万邦之屏。
之屏之翰⑤,百辟为宪⑥。不戢不难⑦,受福不那⑧。
兕觥其觩⑨,旨酒思柔⑩。彼交匪敖⑪,万福来求。

【注释】

①交交:鸟叫声。桑扈:鸟名,亦叫小桑鹰。 ②莺:指文彩。 ③乐胥:指乐兮。胥,语助词。 ④领:头颈。 ⑤翰:指屏障。 ⑥辟:君主。 ⑦不戢不难:不,语助词。戢指和,难指敬。 ⑧那:多。 ⑨觩(qíu 求):角上曲。 ⑩思:语助词。 ⑪彼交匪敖:当作"匪交匪敖",交通"儌",侮慢。

【译文】

交交是桑扈鸟叫,有文采的是羽毛。君子是快乐啊,接受上天的福好。

交交是桑扈鸟叫,有文彩是它颈毛。君子是快乐啊,是万国的屏障了。

作屏障作藩翰，诸侯把它作为法。又和平又恭敬，受天降福岂不多啊。

牛角杯呀曲角口，美酒味道真和柔。不侮慢不骄傲，万种福气自来求。

鸳　鸯

鸳鸯于飞，毕之罗之①。君子万年，福禄宜之。

鸳鸯在梁②，戢其左翼。君子万年，宜其遐福。乘马在厩，摧之秣之③。君子万年，福禄艾之④。

乘马在厩，秣之摧之。君子万年，福禄绥之。

【注释】

①毕：小网，用小网来捕。罗：大网，用大网来捕。　②梁：鱼梁，拦鱼的水坝。　③摧（cuò 错）：铡草。秣（mò 末）：以草喂马。④艾（ài 爱）：养护。

【译文】

鸳鸯在飞，用小网大网来捉它。君子活万年，福禄适宜他。

鸳鸯在鱼梁上，收敛它的左翅膀。君子活万年，适宜他永远的福望。骑的马在马棚里，铡草来喂它。君子活万年，用福禄来养他。

骑的马在马棚里，用铡草来喂它。君子活万年，用福禄来安抚他。

诗经

颊 弁

　　有颊者弁①，实维伊何②？尔酒既旨，尔肴既嘉。岂伊异人，兄弟匪他。茑与女萝③，施于松柏④。未见君子，忧心奕奕。既见君子，庶几说怿。

　　有颊者弁，实维何期⑤？尔酒既旨，尔肴既时。岂伊异人，兄弟具来。茑与女萝，施于松上。未见君子，忧心怲怲⑥。既见君子，庶几有臧。

　　有颊者弁，实维在首。尔酒既旨，尔肴既阜⑦。岂伊异人，兄弟甥舅。如彼雨雪，先集维霰⑧。死丧无日，无几相见⑨。乐酒今夕，君子维宴。

【注释】

　　①颊（kuǐ 傀）：戴皮帽倾向前。弁（biàn 便）：皮帽。 ②实：当作"寔"，这。伊何：为何。 ③茑（niǎo 鸟）、女萝：两种寄生植物，比兄弟亲戚相依附。 ④施（yì 异）：蔓延。 ⑤期：语助词。 ⑥怲怲（bǐng bǐng 丙丙）：很忧。 ⑦阜：丰富。 ⑧霰（xiàn 线）：雪珠。 ⑨无几：没有多少。

【译文】

　　戴着前倾的皮帽，这是为什么？你的酒既是美好，你的菜肴又是好。岂是接待外姓人，兄弟不是他人了。桑寄生和菟丝子，攀着松柏相连络。没有看见君子人，忧心时时发作。既然看见君子人，心情近乎有喜乐。

　　戴上前倾的皮帽，实在是为什么？你的酒既是美好，你的菜肴既是新作。岂是接待外姓人，兄弟全来非是外族。桑寄生和菟丝子，攀在松上做连络。没有看见君子人，忧心时时发作。既然看见君子人，心情近乎有快乐。

戴上前倾的皮帽，实在是因为在头。你的酒既是美好，你的菜肴又丰厚。岂是接待外姓人，是兄弟和甥舅。像那天上落雪，先聚集雪珠岂能后。死去丧亡没日期，我们相见不久。快乐饮酒在今夕，君子只在宴会情投。

车 辖

间关车之辖兮①，思娈季女逝兮②。匪饥匪渴，德音来括③。虽无好友④，式燕且喜⑤。

依彼平林⑥，有集维鷮⑦。辰彼硕女，令德来教。式燕且誉，好尔无射⑧。

虽无旨酒，式饮庶几。虽无嘉肴，式食庶几。虽无德与女，式歌且舞。

陟彼高冈，析其柞薪。析其柞薪⑨，其叶湑兮⑩。鲜我觏尔⑪，我心写兮。

高山仰止，景行行止⑫。四牡騑騑⑬，六辔如琴。觏尔新昏，以慰我心。

【注释】

①间关：车轴铁头的转动声。辖（xiá 辖）：车轴铁头。 ②娈（luán 峦）：美好。季女：少女。逝：去，指出嫁。 ③德音：美誉。括：会合。 ④友：指女方。 ⑤式：语助词。 ⑥依：通"殷"，茂盛。平林：平地的树林。 ⑦鷮（jiāo 骄）：雉。 ⑧射（yì 亦）：厌烦。 ⑨柞（zuò 作）：麻栎。 ⑩湑（xǔ 许）：盛。 ⑪鲜：善。觏

（gòu 够）：见。　⑫仰止：仰望。止：语助词。景行：大路。　⑬骈骈（fēi fēi 非非）：马行不止貌。

【译文】

车的铁轴头发声啊，这美好少女要出嫁啊。不再饿不再渴，有德音来会合。虽则没有好的朋友，在宴会上且喜乐相合。

茂盛的那平地树林，集中的有雉群。适时而嫁的那大姑娘，用好德行来教誉。且开宴且赞誉，喜爱你没有厌弃。

我虽然没有美酒，你饮一点也算数。我虽没有好菜肴，你吃一点也算数。我虽没有美德给你，你还唱歌并且跳舞。

登那高的山冈，斫它麻栎作柴薪。斫它麻栎作柴薪，它的叶儿很茂盛。我欢喜能看见你啊，我心里的愁苦泻尽啊。

高山仰望就停止，大路前行行又止。四匹雄马不停进，使那六根缰绳像弹琴。看见你的新婚，用来安慰我的心。

青　蝇

营营青蝇①，止于樊②。岂弟君子③，无信谗言。
营营青蝇，止于棘④。谗人罔极⑤，交乱四国。
营营青蝇，止于榛。谗人罔极，构我二人。

【注释】

①营营：往来貌。　②樊：篱笆。　③岂弟：同"恺悌"，和乐平易。　④棘：荆棘。　⑤罔极：不中正。

【译文】

飞来飞去的苍蝇,停在篱笆上。和乐平易的君子人,不要听信谗言乱放。

飞来飞去的苍蝇,停在荆棘上。谗人没有中正话,只把四方国家说冤枉。

飞来飞去的苍蝇,停在榛树上。谗人没有中正话,挑拨你我二人相乱攘。

宾之初筵

宾之初筵,左右秩秩①。笾豆有楚②,肴核维旅③。酒既和旨,饮酒孔偕④。钟鼓既设,举酬逸逸⑤。大侯既抗⑥,弓矢斯张。射夫既同,献尔发功。发彼有的,以祈尔爵。

籥舞笙鼓⑦,乐既和奏。烝衎烈祖⑧,以洽百礼⑨。百礼既至,有壬有林⑩。锡尔纯嘏⑪,子孙其湛⑫。其湛曰乐,各奏尔能⑬。宾载手仇⑭,室人入又⑮。酌彼康爵⑯,以奏尔时⑰。

宾之初筵,温温其恭。其未醉止,威仪反反⑱。曰既醉止,威仪幡幡⑲。舍其坐迁⑳,屡舞僊僊㉑。其未醉止,威仪抑抑㉒。曰既醉止,威仪怭怭㉓。是曰既醉,不知其秩。

宾既醉止,载号载呶㉔。乱我笾豆,屡舞僛僛㉕。是曰既醉,不知其邮㉖。侧弁之俄㉗,屡舞傞傞㉘。既醉而出,并受其福。醉而不出,是谓伐德㉙。饮酒孔嘉,维其令仪。

凡此饮酒,或醉或否。既立之监,或佐之史。彼醉不臧,不醉反耻。式勿从谓㉚,无俾大怠。匪言勿言,匪由勿语。由醉之言,俾出童羖㉛。三爵不识,矧敢多又㉜。

诗经

【注释】

①秩秩：肃敬。 ②楚：成列。 ③肴：肉食。核：果品。旅：陈设。 ④偕：通"嘉"。 ⑤酢：同"酬"，主人劝酒。逸逸：往来有次序。 ⑥大侯：箭靶。抗：举起。 ⑦籥（yuè 月）：古乐器，竹制，称舞籥，比笛长而六孔，吹籥以节舞。 ⑧烝（zhēng 蒸）：进。衎（kàn 看）：乐。烈祖：有功的先祖。 ⑨洽：合。 ⑩壬：状礼大。林：状礼多。 ⑪纯嘏（gǔ 古）：大福。 ⑫湛（dān 丹）：喜悦。 ⑬奏：献。能：技能。 ⑭手仇：对手，仇指相对。 ⑮室人：指主人。 ⑯康爵：空杯。 ⑰尔时：你这时所尊者。 ⑱反反：慎重。 ⑲幡幡（fān fān 翻翻）：旗帜翻动。 ⑳坐迁：迁动当坐之礼。 ㉑僊僊（xiān xiān 仙仙）：轻举貌。 ㉒抑：慎密，指庄重。 ㉓怭怭（bì bì 必必）：不庄重，轻佻。 ㉔呶（náo 挠）：叫喊。 ㉕僛僛（qī qī 欺欺）：不自正。 ㉖邮：通"尤"，过错。 ㉗侧：倾侧。 ㉘傞傞（suō suō 蓑蓑）：醉舞不止。 ㉙伐德：败坏道德。 ㉚勿从谓：不要从为之。 ㉛童羖（gǔ 古）：没有生角的黑色公羊，指酒后妄言。 ㉜又：通"侑"，劝酒。

【译文】

宾客初到就筵席，左右严肃有礼节。笾豆摆设有秩序，肉食果品都陈列。酒既醇和又美好，饮酒合礼无不悦。钟鼓奏乐既陈设，举杯敬客有序列。箭靶既然已举起，张弓射箭心头热。射箭的人既然齐，献你发功效果切。发箭射靶能中的，来求你杯酒不绝。

用籥节舞笙鼓奏，音乐既和奏调新。进献有功的先祖，用来配礼皆得申。众礼既然到了庭，又盛大又隆重。神赐给你大福气，子子孙孙喜无伦。他们喜悦称快乐，各献你能把酒斟。宾客比箭找对手，主人献酒又相亲。酌那空杯的客人，来敬你这位能人。

宾客的初到酒筵，态度温和又恭虔。他没有吃醉时，他的仪容自相连。说是既醉了，他的仪容不相连。放弃坐礼有改变，屡次舞蹈像成仙。他没有吃醉时，仪容自相连。既经吃醉了，仪容不相连。说既经醉了，不知礼仪应相连。

宾客既经吃醉了，有的号叫有的嚷。弄乱我放的笾豆，屡次跳舞像发狂。说是既经醉了，不知失礼真荒唐。侧着皮帽的时候，屡次跳舞又发狂。既醉出门回家睡，宾主都受福分强。既醉不肯出门去，这叫败德不可忘。饮酒本是很好事，只要好的礼节不相妨。

凡是饮这酒，有的喝醉有的否。既经确立了酒监，再设酒史为他友。那吃醉的不知不善，不醉的反而负咎。不要从醉者作为，不要使他见大丑。不该说的不要说，不该从的不要受。从醉汉的话，使你拿出童羊又。三杯吃了不认识，怎敢再多劝饮酒。

鱼 藻

鱼在在藻，有颁其首①。王在在镐②，岂乐饮酒③。
鱼在在藻，有莘其尾④。王在在镐，饮酒乐岂。
鱼在在藻，依于其蒲⑤。王在在镐，有那其居⑥。

【注释】

①颁（fén 坟）：大头。 ②镐：镐京。 ③岂（同"恺"）乐：欢乐。 ④莘（shēn 身）：长。 ⑤蒲：多年生水草。 ⑥那：安闲。

【译文】

鱼儿游在水藻中，摆动它的大头。武王住在镐京里，欢乐地饮酒。

鱼儿游在水藻中,有长的尾巴。武王住在镐京里,饮着酒又欢乐。

鱼儿游在水藻中,依靠在它的蒲草。武王住在镐京,有他安闲居处了。

采 菽

采菽采菽①,筐之筥之②。君子来朝,何锡予之?虽无予之,路车乘马③。又何予之?玄衮及黼④。

觱沸槛泉⑤,言采其芹。君子来朝,言观其旂。其旂淠淠⑥,鸾声嘒嘒⑦。载骖载驷,君子所届。

赤芾在股⑧,邪幅在下⑨。彼交匪纾⑩,天子所予。乐只君子,天子命之。乐只君子,福禄申之⑪。

维柞之枝,其叶蓬蓬。乐只君子,殿天子之邦⑫。乐只君子,万福攸同⑬。平平左右⑭,亦是率从。

汎汎杨舟,绋纚维之⑮。乐只君子,天子葵之⑯。乐只君子,福禄膍之⑰。优哉游哉,亦是戾矣⑱。

【注释】

①菽(shū 叔):豆。 ②筥(jǔ 举):圆竹筐。 ③路车。 ④玄衮(gǔn 滚):浅黑色画卷龙袍。黼(fǔ 甫):绣在裳上斧形用黑白色。 ⑤觱(bì 必):沸。槛泉:正出泉水。 ⑥淠淠(pèi pèi 佩佩):飘动。 ⑦嘒嘒(huì huì 彗彗):有节奏。 ⑧芾(fú 芙):通"韨",古代官服上的蔽膝。 ⑨邪幅:像绑腿。 ⑩纾:缓,怠慢。 ⑪申:重。 ⑫殿:镇定。 ⑬攸:所。同:聚。 ⑭平平:闲雅。 ⑮绋(fú 弗):大索。纚(lí 厘):拴。 ⑯葵:

通"揆",量才使用。 ⑰脾(pí 皮):厚赐。 ⑱戾:至,至极。

【译文】

采大豆呀采大豆,用筐用筥来盛它。诸侯远路来朝见,什么东西赐给他?虽然没有赐给他,送他车子和驾马。又有什么赐给他?龙衣绣裳赐给他。

沸腾正流泉水边,我去采摘那香芹。诸侯远路来朝见,我去看他车和旌。他的旌旗在飘动,车上鸾铃节奏匀。驾车三马或四马,诸侯已经是亲临。

红色蔽膝披在股,绑腿裹在膝盖下。他的交情不急慢,车马天子赐给他。音乐是使诸侯乐,天子策命赏赐他。音乐是使诸侯乐,再用福禄重赏他。

只有柞木的枝条,它的叶儿丰庞。音乐是使诸侯乐,他能镇定天子的侯邦。音乐是使诸侯乐,万福齐聚拢。左右闲雅的人,也是相率顺从。

杨木船在河里泛,用大绳来拴住它。音乐是使诸侯乐,天子度量赏赐他。音乐是使诸侯乐,福禄加重他。优游自在呀!也美好至极轮到他。

角 弓

骍骍角弓①,翩其反矣②。兄弟昏姻,无胥远矣③。
尔之远矣,民胥然矣④。尔之教矣,民胥效矣。
此令兄弟⑤,绰绰有裕⑥。不令兄弟,交相为瘉⑦。
民之无良,相怨一方。受爵不让,至于己斯亡。
老马反为驹⑧,不顾其后。如食宜饫⑨,如酌孔取。

毋教猱升木⑩，如涂涂附⑪。君子有徽猷⑫，小人与属⑬。
雨雪瀌瀌⑭，见晛曰消⑮。莫肯下遗，式居娄骄⑯。
雨雪浮浮⑰，见晛曰流。如蛮如髦⑱，我是用忧。

【注释】

①骍骍（xīn xīn 辛辛）：弓调理貌。角弓：以牛角饰的弓。 ②翩其：自然地。反矣：弹弓弦，弓弦自然回弹了。 ③胥：相。 ④胥：皆。 ⑤令：善。 ⑥绰绰：宽裕。 ⑦瘉（yù 育）：病。 ⑧老马反为驹：老马反而视为壮马。 ⑨饫（yù 裕）：饱。 ⑩猱（náo 挠）：猿类。 ⑪涂：同"塗"。如涂涂附，在污泥上面涂一层污泥。 ⑫徽：美。猷：道。 ⑬与属：附属。 ⑭瀌瀌（biāo biāo 标标）：雪盛。 ⑮晛（xiàn 现）：日气。 ⑯式居娄骄：陈奂《传疏》："小人不肯卑下加礼于人，唯数数骄慢自用。"式，用。居，通"倨"，傲慢。娄，收敛。 ⑰浮浮：雪盛。 ⑱髦：西南少数民族名。

【译文】

调理好牛角饰的弓，去弦自然反弹了。兄弟是亲骨肉，不要互相疏远了。

你疏远兄弟了，百姓都是这样了。你是这样教导了，百姓互相效法了。

这样善良的兄弟，彼此宽容得有裕。不善良的兄弟，互相作恶害自己。

百姓的不善良，互相怨恨那一方，受到爵位不相让，直到自己的死亡。

老马反而当作为壮马，不顾自己后来老。好像吃饭应吃饱，好像饮酒酌量好。

不要教猴子爬树,不要像用泥来涂附。君子有美德,小人要来依附。

下雪纷纷,看见日光就消。不肯谦下,用自律收敛骄傲。

下雪纷纷,看见日光变水流。像南蛮像髦族,我因此而心忧。

菀 柳

有菀者柳①,不尚息焉②。上帝甚蹈③,无自暱焉④。俾予靖之⑤,后予极焉⑥。

有菀者柳,不尚愒焉⑦。上帝甚蹈,无自瘵焉⑧。俾予靖之,后予迈焉⑨。

有鸟高飞,亦傅于天⑩。彼人之心,于何其臻?曷予靖之?居以凶矜⑪。

【注释】

①菀(yù 欲):树茂盛。 ②尚:庶几,希望。 ③上帝:指君王。蹈:变动。 ④暱(nì 溺):亲近。 ⑤靖:安定。 ⑥极:诛杀。 ⑦愒(qì 气):休息。 ⑧瘵(zhài 债):接近。 ⑨迈:行,放逐。 ⑩傅:至。 ⑪居:语助词。凶矜:凶危。

【译文】

茂盛的柳树,岂不希望在它下休息。上帝很会变化,不要自己向他亲热。用我去安定他,后来对我用刑罚。

茂盛的柳树,岂不希望在它下休息。上帝很会变化,不要自已去亲接。用我去安定他,后来对我放逐不息。

　　有鸟高飞,直到高天。那人的心,在什么地方相连?为何用我安定他?他必置我于凶险。

都人士之什

都人士

彼都人士，狐裘黄黄。其容不改，出言有章。行归于周①，万民所望。

彼都人士，台笠缁撮②。彼君子女，绸直如发③。我不见兮，我心不说。

彼都人士，充耳琇实④。彼君子女，谓之尹吉⑤。我不见兮，我心菀结⑥。

彼都人士，垂带而厉⑦。彼君子女，卷发如虿⑧。我不见兮，言从之迈。

匪伊垂之，带则有余。匪伊卷之，发则有旟⑨。我不见兮，云何盱矣⑩！

【注释】

①周：忠信。　②台：草名，可以作笠。缁撮：缁布冠。　③绸：细密。　④琇（xiù 秀）：美石。　⑤尹吉：尹氏吉氏，两个大姓氏。　⑥菀结：郁结。　⑦厉：带之垂者。　⑧虿（chài 瘥）：蝎子类有毒的虫。　⑨旟（yú 余）：扬上。　⑩盱（xū 吁）：盼望。

【译文】

那个都市的士人，黄黄的狐皮袍穿上。他的容貌不改变，说的话有文章。行为归结到忠信，成为万民所瞻仰。

那个都市的士人，戴着草笠或缁布冠。那个贵族的女儿，细密直直头发不乱。我不看见她啊，我的心里不喜欢。

那个都市的士人，用宝石作充耳饰。那个贵族的女儿，称作尹氏和吉氏。我不看见她啊，我心里郁结不止。

那个都市的士人，带子垂下飘左右。那个贵族的女儿，发像蝎尾翘在首。我不看见她啊，我想跟她一起走。

不是他把带垂下，带是有多余啊。不是她有意把发卷起，发有的是上扬啊。我看不见她啊，说什么盼望啊。

采 绿

终朝采绿①，不盈一匊②。予发曲局③，薄言归沐。
终朝采蓝④，不盈一襜⑤。五日为期，六日不詹⑥。
之子于狩，言韔其弓⑦。之子于钓，言纶之绳。
其钓维何？维鲂及鱮⑧。维鲂及鱮，薄言观者⑨。

【注释】

①绿：王刍，花深绿，古时作绿色用。 ②匊（jū 掬）：同"掬"，两手合捧。 ③局：卷。 ④蓝：草名，汁可染蓝色。 ⑤襜（chān 搀）：围裙。 ⑥詹：到。 ⑦韔（chàng 唱）：弓袋。 ⑧鱮（xù 叙）：大头鲢。 ⑨观：多。

【译文】

整个早晨采绿草，采的不满两手掬。我的头发曲而卷，我要回去把头沐。

整个早晨采蓝草,采的不满一围裙。约定五天为一期,六天不回怎么云。

这个人去打猎,我用弓袋藏他弓。这个人去钓鱼,我用钓绳供他用。

他钓的是什么鱼?有鲂鱼和鲢鱼。有鲂鱼和鲢鱼,我看他钓得真多鱼。

黍 苗

芃芃黍苗①,阴雨膏之。悠悠南行②,召伯劳之。
我任我辇③,我车我牛④。我行既集⑤,盖云归哉⑥!
我徒我御⑦,我师我旅。我行既集,盖云归处!
肃肃谢功⑧,召伯营之。烈烈征师⑨,召伯成之。
原隰既平,泉流既清。召伯有成,王心则宁。

【注释】

①芃芃(péng péng 彭彭):长大貌。 ②悠悠:远行。 ③任:担任。辇:拉车。 ④车:手扶车。牛:牵牛。 ⑤集:成。 ⑥盖:通"盍",何不。 ⑦徒:步行。御:驾驶。 ⑧谢:指谢邑,在河南省。肃肃:严正。 ⑨烈烈:威武。

【译文】

长大的黍苗,阴雨润泽它。远远地向南走,召伯慰劳他。

我任管车又拉车,我扶牛车我牵牛。我的南走既经成功,何不说归去休!

我步行我驾驶,我属师我属旅。我南走既经完成,何不说归去安处!

严正的谢邑工程,召伯经营它。威武前进的军队,召伯成就它。

原野洼地既治平,泉流既经澄清。召伯有了成功,周王心里就安宁。

隰 桑

隰桑有阿①,其叶有难②。既见君子,其乐如何?
隰桑有阿,其叶有沃③。既见君子,云何不乐?
隰桑有阿,其叶有幽④。既见君子,德音孔胶⑤。
心乎爱矣,遐不谓矣⑥?中心藏之,何日忘之?

【注释】

①阿:美貌。 ②难(nuó 挪):盛貌。 ③沃:柔。 ④幽:黑。 ⑤胶:固定。 ⑥遐不:何不。

【译文】

洼地桑树长得好,它的叶儿茂盛了。既然看见君子人,她的快乐怎么了?

洼地桑树长得好,它的叶儿柔软了。既然看见君子人,说什么不快乐了?

洼地桑树长得好,它的叶儿色深妙。既然看见君子人,情思确实很牢靠。

心里真是爱了,怎么不说了?内心深处藏着他,什么时候忘记掉他?

白 华

白华菅兮①,白茅束兮。之子之远,俾我独兮。
英英白云②,露彼菅茅③。天步艰难④,之子不犹⑤。
滮池北流⑥,浸彼稻田。啸歌伤怀,念彼硕人。
樵彼桑薪,卬烘于煁⑦。维彼硕人,实劳我心。
鼓钟于宫⑧,声闻于外。念子懆懆⑨,视我迈迈⑩。
有鹙在梁⑪,有鹤在林。维彼硕人,实劳我心。
鸳鸯在梁,戢其左翼。之子无良,二三其德。
有扁斯石⑫,履之卑兮。之子之远,俾我疧兮⑬。

【注释】

①白华:白花。菅(jiān 肩):茅草,茎可作绳织履。白花认为菅草,一说比幽王把申后看作坏女人。 ②英英:云起貌。 ③露彼菅茅:露滋润菅草。 ④天步:天行,一说比幽王行动。 ⑤犹:可。 ⑥滮(biāo 标)池:在陕西长安县西。 ⑦卬:同"昂",指我。煁(shén 神):灶火。 ⑧宫:古代房子的通称,秦后始为帝王专用。 ⑨懆懆(cǎo cǎo 草草):忧愁不安。 ⑩迈迈:不悦。 ⑪鹙(qiū 秋):水鸟名,似鹤,头颈上无毛。 ⑫扁:卑下。 ⑬疧(qí 齐):病。

【译文】

白花认为菅草啊,用白茅草来捆它。这个人疏远我,使我孤独啊。

朵朵的白云,下露水润泽那菅草。天神走路艰难,这个人不可我了。

滮池水向北流,浸润那稻田。长啸唱歌伤胸怀,想那大人总相连。

砍那桑枝做柴薪,我烧柴在那灶。只有那个大人,确实使我心劳。

在宫内敲钟,声音听见在宫外。想念你使我忧愁,你看我讨厌心烦。

有鹫鸟在鱼梁,有白鹤在树林。只有那个大人,确实忧劳我的心。

鸳鸯在鱼梁,收敛它的左翅膀。这个人真无良心,三心两意不一样。

有块扁的石头,踏上去低下啊。这个人疏远我,使我生病啊。

绵 蛮

绵蛮黄鸟①,止于丘阿②。道之云远,我劳如何?饮之食之,教之诲之。命彼后车③,谓之载之。

绵蛮黄鸟,止于丘隅。岂敢惮行④,畏不能趋⑤。饮之食之,教之诲之。命彼后车,谓之载之。

绵蛮黄鸟,止于丘侧。岂敢惮行,畏不能极⑥。饮之食之,教之诲之。 命彼后车,谓之载之。

【注释】

①绵蛮:小鸟貌。 ②阿:山坳。 ③后车:正车后面的副车。 ④惮:怕。 ⑤趋:快走。 ⑥极:至。

【译文】

小小的黄鸟,停在山坳。路是很远,我是怎样疲劳?命他饮酒，命他吃饭，教导他还告诫他。命他趁副车，让用车载他。

小小的黄鸟，停在山腰。难道怕走路，怕不能快跑。命他饮酒，命他吃饭，教导他还告诫他。命他趁副车，让用车载他。

小小的黄鸟，停在丘边了。难道怕走路，怕不能到。命他饮酒，命他吃饭，教导他还告诫他。命他趁副车，让用车载他。

瓠 叶

幡幡瓠叶①，采之亨之②。君子有酒，酌言尝之。
有兔斯首③，炮之燔之④。君子有酒，酌言献之。
有兔斯首，燔之炙之⑤。君子有酒，酌言酢之⑥。
有兔斯首，燔之炮之。 君子有酒，酌言酬之。

【注释】

①幡幡（fān fān 翻翻）：翻动。瓠：葫芦。 ②亨：同"烹"，煮。 ③斯首：白头。 ④炮（páo 庖）：烧，将兔裹泥在火上烧。燔（fán 凡）：烧。 ⑤炙：将肉在火上烤。 ⑥酢（zuò 坐）：回敬酒。

【译文】

飘动的葫芦叶，采它来煮它。君子人有酒，酌酒品尝它。

有小兔头是白的，用泥涂了烧它煮它。君子人有酒，酌酒与客敬献它。

有小兔子头是白的，用泥涂了烧它烤它。君子人有酒，宾客酌酒回敬他。

有小兔头是白的，用泥涂了烧它烤它。君子人有酒，酌酒再劝宾客品尝它。

渐渐之石

渐渐之石①，维其高矣。山川悠远，维其劳矣②。武人东征，不皇朝矣③。

渐渐之石，维其卒矣④。山川悠远，曷其没矣⑤。武人东征，不皇出矣⑥。

有豕白蹢⑦，烝涉波矣⑧。月离于毕⑨，俾滂沱矣⑩。武人东征，不皇他矣。

【注释】

①渐渐：通"巉巉（chán chán 谗谗）"，山石高峻。 ②劳：通"辽"，指广阔。 ③不皇：不暇。不皇朝，犹无暇日。 ④卒：通"崒（zú 族）"，高峻危险。 ⑤曷：何。没：尽。 ⑥出：脱险。 ⑦蹢（dí 敌）：蹄。 ⑧烝：多。 ⑨离：通"丽"，接近。毕：毕星。月接近毕星，有雨。 ⑩滂沱：大雨貌。

【译文】

高峻的山石，真是那样的高了。山河长远，真是那样的广阔了。武人出兵向东征。无闲暇的日子了。

高峻的山石，真是那样的高险了。山河长远，何处是它的尽头了。武人向东出征，无暇出离险地了。

有豕白蹄，众豕都渡过水了。月接近毕星，大雨落下了。武人向东出征，无暇顾及其他了。

苕之华

苕之华①，芸其黄矣②。心之忧矣，维其伤矣。

苕之华，其叶青青。知我如此，不如无生！
牂羊坟首③，三星在罶④。人可以食，鲜可以饱！

【注释】

①苕（tiáo 条）：凌霄花，藤本，蔓生，花将落则黄。 ②芸黄：指花将落色黄，黄指蔫黄。 ③牂（zāng 脏）羊：母羊。坟：大。母羊瘦则头大。 ④罶（liǔ 柳）：竹篓，鱼可以进不可以出。

【译文】

凌霄花，花落时黄了。心中忧愁了，是伤透心了。
凌霄花，它的叶儿青青茂盛。知我活得像这样，不如不要生！
母羊大头，三颗星照在鱼篓。人可得饭吃，少有人可吃饱相求！

何草不黄

何草不黄？何日不行？何人不将①？经营四方。
何草不玄②？何人不矜③？哀我征夫，独为匪民！
匪兕匪虎④，率彼旷野⑤。哀我征夫，朝夕不暇。
有芃者狐⑥，率彼幽草⑦。有栈之车⑧，行彼周道。

【注释】

①将：行。 ②玄：黑色。 ③矜：通"鳏"，老而无妻的人。 ④兕（sì 似）：野牛。 ⑤率：循，沿着。 ⑥芃（péng 蓬）：毛蓬松。 ⑦幽：深暗。 ⑧栈车：役车。

【译文】

哪种草不枯黄？哪一天人不行？哪个人不出行？去经营那四方。

哪种草不死不黑？哪个人不独身？悲哀我的士兵，独独不算人！

不是野牛不是老虎，沿着旷野日夜奔走。悲哀我的战士，早晚不得休。

尾毛蓬松的狐狸，沿着旷野深藏在草里。有役事的车子，跑在那大道里。

【说明】

许渊冲之《小雅》英译篇目排列所据为《毛诗正义》，分为七个部分，不列《南陔》等六篇佚诗。兹录其目如下：

鹿鸣之什

鹿鸣 四牡 皇皇者华 常棣 伐木 天保 采薇 出车 杕杜 鱼丽

南有嘉鱼之什

南有嘉鱼 南山有台 蓼萧 湛露 彤弓 菁菁者莪 六月 采芑 车攻 吉日

鸿雁之什

鸿雁 庭燎 沔水 鹤鸣 祈父 白驹 黄鸟 我行其野 斯干 无羊

节南山之什

节南山 正月 十月之交 雨无正 小旻 小宛 小弁 巧言 何人斯 巷伯

谷风之什

谷风 蓼莪 大东 四月 北山 无将大车 小明 鼓钟 楚茨 信南山

甫田之什

甫田 大田 瞻彼洛矣 裳裳者华 桑扈 鸳鸯 頍弁 车舝 青蝇 宾之初筵

鱼藻之什

鱼藻 采菽 角弓 菀柳 都人士 采绿 黍苗 隰桑 白华 绵蛮 瓠叶 渐渐之石 苕之华 何草不黄

卷七

大 雅

文王之什

文 王

文王在上①，於昭于天②。周虽旧邦，其命维新。有周不显③，帝命不时④。文王陟降⑤，在帝左右⑥。

亹亹文王⑦，令闻不已⑧。陈锡哉周⑨，侯文王孙子⑩。文王孙子，本支百世⑪。凡周之士，不显亦世⑫。

世之不显，厥犹翼翼⑬。思皇多士⑭，生此王国。王国克生，维周之桢⑮。济济多士⑯，文王以宁。

穆穆文王⑰，於缉熙敬止⑱。假哉天命⑲，有商孙子。商之孙子，其丽不亿⑳。上帝既命，侯于周服㉑。

侯服于周，天命靡常。殷士肤敏㉒，祼将于京㉓。厥作祼将，常服黼冔㉔。王之荩臣㉕，无念尔祖㉖。

无念尔祖，聿修厥德。永言配命，自求多福。殷之未丧师㉗，克配上帝。宜鉴于殷，骏命不易㉘。

命之不易，无遏尔躬㉙。宣昭义问，有虞殷自天。上天之载㉚，无声无臭。仪刑文王㉛，万邦作孚㉜。

【注释】

①文王在上：周文王既死，他的神在民上。 ②於（wū 乌）：赞叹。昭：明著。 ③有周：周朝。不显：显，光明。 ④不时：时，是。 ⑤陟降：升降。 ⑥帝：上帝。 ⑦亹亹（wěi wěi 伟伟）：勉力。 ⑧令闻：好的声闻。 ⑨陈锡：重赐，厚赐。 ⑩侯：于。 ⑪本支百世：本宗，即文王子孙。支，支子，即文王庶出子孙，均传百代。 ⑫不显亦世：显世，光显于世。 ⑬厥犹翼翼：其谋恭敬。 ⑭皇：美。 ⑮桢：支柱。 ⑯济济：众多貌。 ⑰穆穆：美好。 ⑱於：叹美。辑熙：光明。敬：诚敬。止：语助词。 ⑲假：大。 ⑳其丽不亿：其数亿。 ㉑侯于周服：维服从周。 ㉒殷士肤敏：殷臣美好敏疾。 ㉓祼（guàn 贯）：用酒祭祖。将：行。 ㉔黼（fǔ 甫）：绣白黑色斧形的礼服。冔（xǔ 许）：礼帽。称殷臣穿戴殷的礼服礼帽，说明文王以德不以强。 ㉕荩（jìn 尽）臣：忠臣。 ㉖无念：念。 ㉗丧师：丧失众人心。师：众。 ㉘骏命不易：保大命不容易。 ㉙遏：止。 ㉚载：事。 ㉛刑：法。 ㉜孚：相信。

【译文】

文王的神在上，光明显现在天上。周虽然是旧邦，承受天命是新上。周朝是光明显耀，上帝任命适时新上。文王神的升降，在上帝左右两旁。

勤勉的文王，好的声望不止。厚赐啊周朝，只有文王孙孙子子。文王的孙孙子子，本宗支子相传百世。凡是周朝的士子，光明也能照世。

照世的光明，他的谋划谨慎。赞美众多士子，在这个王国里诞生。王国里能够诞生，都是周朝的干桢。靠众多的臣子，使文王得到安宁。

美好的文王,啊,光明诚敬为是。伟大啊天命,商朝的孙孙子子。商朝的孙孙子子,它的数目上亿计。上帝既然命令,只服从周朝做臣子。

殷人臣服于周朝,天命无常没一定。殷朝的士人美好敏疾,在周京用酒祭祖相称。他们用酒祭祖时,经常穿殷朝礼服相应。作周王的忠臣,想念你祖先相称。

想念你的祖先,修明你的德行。永久配合天命,自己求多福分。殷的未失掉众心,能够配合上帝天命。应该以殷为鉴戒,不容易保持大命。

不容易保持大命,不要断送大命在你身。宣扬昭示好的声誉,殷的喜悲从天命。上天的事,没有味儿也没有声。效法文王,万邦才会对你信任。

大 明

明明在下①,赫赫在上。天难忱斯②,不易维王。天位殷适③,使不挟四方④。

挚仲氏任⑤,自彼殷商,来嫁于周,曰嫔于京⑥。乃及王季⑦,维德之行。大任有身⑧,生此文王。

维此文王,小心翼翼。昭事上帝,聿怀多福。厥德不回,以受方国⑨。

天监在下,有命既集⑩。文王初载,天作之合。在洽之阳⑪,在渭之涘⑫。

文王嘉止⑬,大邦有子。大邦有子,伣天之妹⑭。文定厥祥⑮,亲迎于渭。造舟为梁⑯,不显其光。

有命自天,命此文王,于周于京⑰。缵女维莘⑱,长子维行⑲,笃生武王⑳。保右命尔,燮伐大商㉑。

殷商之旅㉒,其会如林㉓。矢于牧野㉔,维于侯兴。上帝临女,无贰尔心。

牧野洋洋㉕,檀车煌煌㉖。驷騵彭彭㉗,维师尚父㉘,时维鹰扬。凉彼武王㉙,肆伐大商㉚,会朝清明㉛。

【注释】

①明明在下:明显的恩德施给下面人民。 ②忱(chén 沉):信。③适:通"嫡",嫡子。 ④挟:达到。 ⑤挚仲氏任:挚国的中女姓任,叫太任。 ⑥嫔(pín 贫):为妇。 ⑦王季:太任的丈夫。 ⑧有身:有孕。 ⑨方国:四方诸侯之国。 ⑩集:就。 ⑪洽(hé 合):水名,源出陕西郃阳县北。阳:水北。 ⑫渭:水名,渭水亦经此入河。涘(sì 四):水边。 ⑬嘉:嘉礼,订婚礼。 ⑭俔(qiàn 欠):好比。 ⑮文定:订婚礼。祥:吉。 ⑯梁:浮桥。 ⑰于周于京:改号为周,易邑为京。 ⑱缵(zuǎn 纂):继娶。莘:国名。娶莘国女,即太姒。 ⑲长子:指周文王长子伯邑考,先死。行:德行。 ⑳笃:语助词。 ㉑燮(xiè 谢):和协。 ㉒旅:众。 ㉓会:通"旝",旗。 ㉔矢:陈列。 ㉕洋洋:广大。 ㉖煌煌:明显。 ㉗騵(yuán 元):赤毛白腹的马。 ㉘师尚父:太师吕望。 ㉙凉:假为亮,辅佐。 ㉚肆:疾。 ㉛会:合。

【译文】

明显的恩德在下面,烜赫的神灵在天上。天意很难相信,不易做的是治天下王。天位本属殷嫡子,使命不能达四方。

挚国中女名太任，从那个商朝挚城，来嫁到那周家，说做新妇到周京。是认王季做丈夫，只有道德才施行。太任嫁后有了孕，生下文王这个人。

只有这个文王，既是小心又谨慎。勤勉地奉事上帝，获取众多的福分。他对道德不违背，而受四方侯国的信任。

上天监视在下面，天命既然成就他。文王即位的初年，天作配合成了家。在那洽水的北面，在那渭水的水涯。

文王嘉礼已经详，大邦有个好姑娘。大邦有个好姑娘，好比天帝妹子样。定婚卜卦都吉祥，亲迎就在渭水旁。造船作为浮桥样，显耀亲迎的辉光。

有那天命从天降，天命这个周文王，定国为周城为京，继娶女儿国号莘，长子亡故讲德行，生个武王好继承。上天命令保佑他，和协诸国伐殷商。

殷商的众很是强，旗子插得像林样。陈兵牧野是我军，只有周侯可以兴。上帝亲自来照临，你们不要有二心。

牧野这里很宽广，檀木作车很辉煌。四匹骍马很威武，太师吕望称尚父，这时就像鹰飞扬。辅佐武王战疆场，疾驰前去伐大商，会合朝见天下亮。

绵

绵绵瓜瓞①，民之初生②，自土沮漆③。古公亶父④，陶复陶穴⑤，未有室家。

古公亶父，来朝走马，率西水浒，至于岐下。爰及姜女⑥，聿来胥宇⑦。

周原膴膴⑧，堇荼如饴⑨。爰始爰谋⑩，爰契我龟⑪。曰止曰时⑫，筑室于兹。

迺慰迺止⑬，迺左迺右，迺疆迺理，迺宣迺亩⑭。自西徂东⑮，周爰执事。

乃召司空，乃召司徒⑯，俾立室家。其绳则直，缩版以载⑰，作庙翼翼。

捄之陾陾⑱，度之薨薨⑲，筑之登登⑳，削屡冯冯㉑。百堵皆兴㉒，鼛鼓弗胜㉓。

迺立皋门，皋门有伉㉔。迺立应门，应门将将㉕。迺立冢土㉖，戎丑攸行㉗。

肆不殄厥愠㉘，亦不陨厥问㉙。柞棫拔矣，行道兑矣㉚，混夷駾矣㉛，维其喙矣㉜。

虞芮质厥成㉝，文王蹶厥生㉞。予曰有疏附，予曰有先后，予曰有奔奏㉟，予曰有御侮。

【注释】

①绵绵：长而不断绝。瓜瓞（dié 迭）：大瓜叫瓜，小瓜叫瓞。从小瓜长到大瓜，它的蔓长而不断绝。 ②民：周人。 ③土：通"杜"，水名。沮、漆：皆水名。杜水，在陕西麟游县杜山下，南流折东入武水。漆水在陕西邠县西，西南流与沮水相会，注于渭水。 ④古公亶父：古代的公，名亶父，是周代太王名。 ⑤陶复陶穴：挖土为室，旁穿为复，直穿为穴。旁穿指在地上挖洞，直穿指在地下挖洞。陶指挖洞。 ⑥爰及：于是与。 ⑦胥宇：察看居处。 ⑧妩妩（wǔ wǔ 午午）：美好。 ⑨堇（jǐn 仅）：堇葵。荼（tú 图）：苦菜。饴（yí 姨）：用淀粉制成的糖。 ⑩始：始谋。 ⑪契龟：求龟壳裂纹，古人用龟壳卜吉凶，用火烧龟壳求裂纹。 ⑫时：居住。 ⑬迺慰迺止：迺，同"乃"。慰，慰劳。止，定居。 ⑭左右：分左分右。疆理：分疆界和治理。宣亩：导沟洫

诗经

和治田亩。 ⑮自西徂东：从西往东，指分阡陌道路。 ⑯司空：管土地的官。司徒：管徒役的官。 ⑰缩版：用绳捆木板，为两层，中实土为墙。载：指版上去。 ⑱捄（jiū 鸠）：用器盛土。陾陾（réng réng 仍仍）：众多。 ⑲度：通"墢"，填土。薨薨（hōng hōng 烘烘）：指人众多。 ⑳登登：指用力声。㉑削屡（lóu 楼）：削去墙上隆高的泥土。屡，同"偻"，土墙隆起处。冯冯（píng píng 平平）：削土声。 ㉒堵（dǔ 睹）：墙，五版为堵。兴：起。 ㉓鼛（gāo 高）：大鼓。 ㉔皋门：王的郭门。伉（kàng 抗）：高貌。 ㉕应门：王宫的正门。将将：严正。 ㉖冢土：大社神坛。有大事，必先祭大社神。 ㉗戎丑：戎狄丑类。行：去，遁去。 ㉘肆：遂。殄（tiǎn 舔）：断绝。愠（yùn 运）：怨愤。 ㉙陨：废弃。问：聘问。 ㉚兑：通行。 ㉛混夷：西戎名。駾（tuì 退）：逃窜。 ㉜喙（huì 惠）：困。 ㉝虞芮：相传二国争田。质厥成：成其和平。二国到周求正，看见周人相让，以致自动相让，趋于和平。 ㉞蹶（guì 贵）：感动。生：通"性"，善良的本性。 ㉟疏附：疏者亲附上者。先后：分清先后。奔奏：同"奔走"。

【译文】

长长不断的小瓜大瓜，周人最初的生涯，从杜水、沮水到漆水。古公亶父就留下，挖地上洞到地下洞，他还没有居室的家。

古公亶父不停下，从早上骑马走着，顺着西面的水边，直到岐山山脚下。于是跟了姜姓女，来相居处做观察。

岐周原野是肥美，苦菜也是像糖类。于是始谋又再谋，于是龟卜定祥瑞。停在这里作居处，筑室在此真是美。

于是慰劳定居正，分出左右定彼此，划定疆界便治理，疏通田亩好整治。从西到东有田地，周遍事情有管理。

是召司空来管地,是召司徒来管人,使立室家是他们。丈量绳子直又正,用绳捆版得上升,筑庙墙版严又整。

用筐运土人纷纷,填土版内人群群,筑土为墙声登登,削平墙土声平平。百堵高墙都起来,大鼓声音不能胜。

于是建立起郭门,郭门建立高相应。于是建立起正门,正门建立真严整。于是建立大社坛,西戎丑类望风行。

遂不灭掉他怨愤,也不废掉他聘问。柞树棫树都拔了,道路通畅了,混夷逃遁了,喘息困顿了。

虞芮求正得和平,文王感动他善性。我说使疏的亲附,我说分先后有良臣,我说讲奔走有功臣,我说讲抗敌有武臣。

棫 朴

芃芃棫朴①,薪之槱之②。济济辟王③,左右趣之。
济济辟王,左右奉璋④。奉璋峨峨⑤,髦士攸宜。
淠彼泾舟⑥,烝徒楫之⑦。周王于迈⑧,六师及之。
倬彼云汉⑨,为章于天。周王寿考,遐不作人⑩。
追琢其章⑪,金玉其相⑫。勉勉我王,纲纪四方⑬。

【注释】

①芃芃(péng péng 蓬蓬):树木茂盛。棫(yù 育):柞树。朴:丛生。 ②槱(yóu 犹):积。 ③辟:君。 ④璋:古祭祀用的酒器,用玉制。 ⑤峨峨:庄严。 ⑥淠(pì 譬):舟行。泾:水名,源出甘肃,东南流入陕西,注于渭水,有泾清渭浊之称。 ⑦烝徒:众人。楫:用楫划船。 ⑧于迈:往行。 ⑨倬(zhuō 卓):大。云汉:天河。 ⑩遐不:何不。 ⑪追:雕。章:文章,文采。 ⑫相:本质。 ⑬纲纪:张网为纲,理网为纪。

【译文】

柞树丛生多茂盛,砍它做柴积起来。肃然起敬周文王,左右奔去积柴来。

肃然起敬周文王,左右助祭捧玉璋。捧璋群臣威仪盛,俊美贤士宜称强。

譬如那只泾水船,众人拿楫划着它。文王兴师去征伐,六军及时跟着他。

广阔的那天河,作为文彩在上天。周文王长寿,何不作培养人才年。

雕琢他的文章,金玉是它的质量。我勤勉的周文王,忙于整顿四方。

旱 麓

瞻彼旱麓①,榛楛济济②。岂弟君子③,干禄岂弟④。
瑟彼玉瓒⑤,黄流在中。岂弟君子,福禄攸降。
鸢飞戾天,鱼跃于渊。岂弟君子,遐不作人⑥?
清酒既载,骍牡既备⑦,以享以祀,以介景福。
瑟彼柞棫⑧,民所燎矣。岂弟君子,神所劳矣⑨。
莫莫葛藟⑩,施于条枚⑪。岂弟君子,求福不回⑫。

【注释】

①旱:山名。旱山在陕西南郑县西南。麓:山脚。 ②榛(zhēn 真):树名,乔木。实为坚果,果仁可吃,可榨油。楛(hù 户):树名,似荆而赤。济济:众多。 ③岂弟:同"恺悌",快乐平易。 ④干:求。 ⑤瑟:鲜洁。玉瓒(zàn 赞):古代以玉为柄的酒勺,可以斟酒祭神。 ⑥遐不:何不。 ⑦骍牡:红色公牛。 ⑧瑟:众密。柞

（zuò 作）、棫（yù 玉）：均树木名。　⑨劳：劳来，保佑。　⑩莫莫：茂盛。葛藟（lěi 磊）：野葛。　⑪施（yì 异）：蔓延。　⑫回：违背正道。

【译文】

遥望那旱山脚，榛树楛树真多哩。快乐平易的君子，求禄得禄真乐易。

鲜洁的玉杓，黄酒流在杓中。快乐平易的君子，福禄来得丰隆。

鸢鸟高飞到上天，鱼儿跳跃在深渊。快乐平易的君子，怎能不作培养人？

清酒既经陈设了，纯色的牺牲既经备了，用来献神用来祭，用来求得大福气。

茂密的柞棫枝，人民祭天所烧了。快乐平易的君子，神所保佑了。

茂盛的野葛，蔓延到树干枝条上。快乐平易的君子，求福不用在邪法上。

思 齐

思齐大任①，文王之母。思媚周姜②，京室之妇。大姒嗣徽音③，则百斯男④。

惠于宗公⑤，神罔时怨，神罔时恫⑥。刑于寡妻⑦，至于兄弟，以御于家邦⑧。

雝雝在宫，肃肃在庙⑨。不显亦临，无射亦保⑩。

肆戎疾不殄⑪，烈假不瑕⑫。不闻亦式，不谏亦入⑬。

肆成人有德，小子有造。古之人无斁⑭，誉髦斯士⑮。

【注释】

①思：语助词。齐（zhāi 斋）：肃敬。大任：太任，王季的妃。 ②媚：爱慕。周姜：周太王妻。 ③大姒：太姒，文王妻。嗣：继承。徽：美。 ④百斯男：文王妻太姒生十男，文王众妾合太姒宜生百子。 ⑤惠于宗公：顺于先公。 ⑥时恫（tōng 通）：是痛。 ⑦刑：通"型"，法。寡妻：嫡妻。 ⑧御：治。 ⑨雝雝（yōng yōng 庸庸）：和气。肃肃：恭敬。 ⑩不显亦临，无射亦保：不显的人也观察，无射才的人也保用，重在贤，不在显与射。 ⑪肆戎疾不殄：故大病不灭。大病自灭，故不灭。 ⑫烈假不瑕：烈，光。假，大。瑕，过。 ⑬不闻亦式，不谏亦入：即闻式谏入。不，语助词。 ⑭无斁（yì 亦）：无厌。 ⑮髦（máo 毛）：俊。

【译文】

肃敬的太任，是文王的母亲。这敬爱的周姜，她是主妇在周京。太姒继承了德音，她生了很多男人。

文王顺从先公，先公神没有怨痛，先公神没有悲痛。立法先施于谪妻，连及到兄弟，再用到治理国中。

和气的人在王宫，恭敬的人在宗庙。不显赫的人也让他照耀，无射才的人也加爱保。

因此大病不灭，光大不过头不息。听见好话就采纳，听见谏劝也采纳。

成年人有德业，年轻人有造就事业。古人对教育人不厌，赞誉有俊才的事业。

皇 矣

皇矣上帝，临下有赫。监视四方，求民之莫①。维此二国②，其政不获。维彼四国③，爰究爰度。上帝耆之④，憎其式廓⑤。乃眷西顾，此维与宅。

作之屏之⑥，其菑其翳⑦。修之平之，其灌其栵⑧。启之辟之，其柽其椐⑨。攘之剔之⑩，其檿其柘⑪。帝迁明德，串夷载路⑫。天立厥配，受命既固。

帝省其山⑬，柞棫斯拔，松柏斯兑⑭。帝作邦作对⑮，自太伯、王季。维此王季，因心则友。则友其兄，则笃其庆⑯，载锡之光。受禄无丧，奄有四方⑰。

维此王季，帝度其心，貊其德音⑱。其德克明，克明克类⑲，克长克君。王此大邦，克顺克比⑳。比于文王，其德靡悔。既受帝祉，施于孙子。

帝谓文王："无然畔援㉑，无然歆羡，诞先登于岸㉒。"密人不恭，敢距大邦，侵阮徂共。王赫斯怒，爰整其旅，以按徂旅㉓，以笃于周祜，以对于天下㉔。

依其在京，侵自阮疆。陟我高冈："无矢我陵㉕，我陵我阿，无饮我泉，我泉我池。"度其鲜原，居岐之阳，在渭之将㉖。万邦之方㉗，下民之王。

帝谓文王："予怀明德，不大声以色㉘，不长夏以革㉙。不识不知，顺帝之则。"帝谓文王："询尔仇方㉚，同尔兄弟。以尔钩援㉛，与尔临冲㉜，以伐崇墉。"

临冲闲闲㉝，崇墉言言㉞，执讯连连，攸馘安安㉟。是类是祃㊱，是致是附㊲，四方以无侮。临冲茀茀㊳，崇墉仡仡㊴，是伐是肆㊵，是绝是忽㊶，四方以无拂㊷。

【注释】

①莫：安定。　②二国：指夏和殷。古人常以夏商兴衰为戒。③四国：四方的侯国。　④耆（qí 其）：恶。　⑤憎：恨。廓：大。　⑥作：通"斫"，砍。　⑦菑（zì 自）：树立着枯死。翳（yì 亦）：树倒地枯死。　⑧灌：丛生。栵（lì 例）：再生枝条。　⑨柽（chēng 称）：三春柳。椐（jū 居）：灵寿树。　⑩攘（rǎng 让）：排除。　⑪檿（yǎn 掩）：山桑。柘（zhè 这）：树名，野桑。　⑫串夷：即混夷，西戎的一种。路：贫瘠。　⑬省：察看。　⑭兑：易伸直。　⑮作对：作配，即为君。　⑯笃其庆：厚其亲。　⑰奄有：广有。　⑱貊（mò 陌）：静。　⑲克类：能分善恶。　⑳克比：能顺比。　㉑畔援：跋扈。　㉒诞：语助词。登于岸：升岸。　㉓按：止。徂旅：往莒。旅当作莒。　㉔对：遂。　㉕矢：陈列。　㉖将：侧。　㉗方：效法。　㉘声以色：声与色。　㉙夏以革：夏楚与鞭革。夏楚，木棍；鞭革，皮鞭，都是刑具。　㉚仇方：与国。指邻国。　㉛钩援：攻城工具。　㉜临冲：两种战车，上临下，冲击。　㉝闲闲：整齐貌。　㉞言言：高大貌。　㉟攸馘（guó 国）：从敌首级上割左耳。安安：从容貌。　㊱类：出征前祭神。祃（mà 骂）：至所征地祭神。　㊲致：送还。附：抚慰。　㊳茀茀（fú fú 福福）：强盛貌。　㊴仡仡（yì yì 义义）：高耸貌。　㊵肆：杀。　㊶忽：灭。　㊷拂：违抗。

【注释】

伟大啊上帝，亲自观察下面严明。监视四方形势，寻求人民的安定。夏和殷二国，它们的政治不行。四方侯国谁可受天命，于是研究量评。上帝恨殷纣他们，恨他们的廓争。于是眷念向西看顾，只此可与它经营。

除掉它和摒弃它,立死和枯死的树。修剪它和平整它,丛生和再生的树。开发它和开辟它,是河柳和灵寿树。除掉它和剔掉它,是山桑和柘树。上帝迁就明白德行人,混夷贫瘠而自狴。上天立了太王配偶,他接受天命既得巩固。

上帝察看岐山,柞树棫树都拔光,松树柏树往上长。上帝立国又立君,从太伯到王季。只有这个王季,因他心里有友爱。友爱他兄长,厚待他亲人,赐给他们荣光。接受福禄没有丧失,广博地拥有四方。

只有这个王季,上帝度量他的心,静修他道德行为。他的美德是非明,能分是非分善恶,能做族长能做君,做这个大国的国王,能顺势能顺民情。影响一直到文王,他在道德上没有悔恨。既然受了上帝赐福,就要传给他的子孙。

上帝对文王说:"不要跋扈,不要羡慕贪婪,先登上高岸罢。"密国人不恭顺,敢拒绝大国教化,侵犯阮进到共啦。文王赫然发怒,于是整顿他的军队,用来阻止敌往莒,用来加厚周家的福分,用来安民心于天下。

依靠他在周京的力量,息兵归自阮国边疆。登上我的高冈:"不要陈兵在我山陵,我的山陵我的山冈,不要饮我的泉水,我的泉水我的池塘。"量度那广阔的平原,在岐山的南方,在渭水的侧旁。作为万邦所效法,是天下人民的王。

上帝对文王说:"我眷念你显明的美德,不用声威和怒色,不用罚打和鞭革。好像不知不识,顺从上帝的法则。"上帝对文王说:"事要征询你邻国,协同好你的兄弟国。用你钩梯等物,同你的临车冲车,用攻崇城来破贼。"

临车冲车整齐好,崇国城墙高高耸,捉住俘虏连连问,杀敌割耳也从容。祭祀神灵求福佑,送还民物抚民众,四方不敢来欺

诗经

攻。临车冲车称强雄,崇国城墙高高耸,是攻破是杀戮,是斩绝是消灭,四方没有违抗都服从。

灵 台

经始灵台①,经之营之②,庶民攻之③,不日成之。经始勿亟④,庶民子来。

王在灵囿,麀鹿攸伏⑤;麀鹿濯濯⑥,白鸟翯翯⑦。王在灵沼,於牣鱼跃⑧。

虡业维枞⑨,贲鼓维镛⑩。於论鼓钟⑪,於乐辟雍⑫。

於论鼓钟,於乐辟雍。鼍鼓逢逢⑬,矇瞍奏公⑭。

【注释】

①灵台:台名,在陕西西安市西北。下章灵囿、灵沼同。 ②经营:规划。 ③攻:制作。 ④亟:同"急"。 ⑤麀(yōu 优):雌鹿。 ⑥濯濯(zhuó zhuó 浊浊):娱游。 ⑦翯翯(hè hè 贺贺):肥泽。 ⑧牣(rèn 认):满。 ⑨虡业维枞:挂钟磬的直柱横梁上的木板,上刻着牙形。虡(jù 巨):直柱。业:木板。枞(cōng 匆):牙形。 ⑩贲鼓:大鼓。镛:大钟。 ⑪论:通"抡",敲击。 ⑫辟(bì 壁)雍:水环丘如璧曰辟雍。古代大学,大射行礼处,在水环绕处。 ⑬鼍(tuó 驼)鼓:鳄鱼皮的鼓。 ⑭矇瞍(méng sǒu 蒙叟):瞎子,古以瞎子作音乐师。公:通"功"。

【译文】

开始设计造灵台,设计它规划它,人们都来建筑它,不到几天造成它。开始设计并不急,人们像儿子般来完成它。

文王在灵囿,母鹿很贴伏;母鹿优游,白鸟肥泽自降落。文王在灵沼,赞美满池鱼在跳。

木柱横板上崇牙耸,挂上大鼓与大钟。赞美敲击鼓钟,赞美同乐在辟雍。

赞美敲击鼓钟,赞美同乐在辟雍。鼍鼓声音蓬蓬,音乐师奏乐祝成功。

下 武

下武维周①,世有哲王。三后在天②,王配于京③。
王配于京,世德作求④。永言配命⑤,成王之孚⑥。
成王之孚,下土之式。永言孝思⑦,孝思维则。
媚兹一人,应侯顺德⑧。 永言孝思, 昭哉嗣服⑨。
昭兹来许⑩,绳其祖武⑪。于万斯年,受天之祜。
受天之祜,四方来贺。于万斯年,不遐有佐⑫。

【注释】

①下武:后继。维周:只有周家。后人能继先祖的,只有周家。②三后:指太王、王季、文王。 ③王配于京:武王配行其道于周京。配,配天,秉承天命。 ④作求:作述,作配。 ⑤永言配命:永远配合天命。 ⑥孚:信。 ⑦孝思:孝心。一说"孝"指美德总称。 ⑧应侯顺德:当乃顺从祖德。 ⑨嗣服:继承祖业。 ⑩来许:后进。 ⑪祖武:祖迹,祖业。 ⑫不遐:胡不。

【译文】

后人继承的只有周家,世世有明圣的国君。三王已经在天上,武王作配在周京。

武王作配在周京,当世道德作配允。永远秉承着天命,成为周王得信任。

成为周王得信任,天下人民的法式。永远继承着孝思,继承孝思是法则。

爱慕武王这一人,当是顺从祖先德。永远留下了孝思,诏示后人要继承。

诏示那后进,继承祖先的德行。在一万多年分,享受天赐的福分。

享受天赐的福分,四方前来祝贺。在一万多年分,怎能没有辅佐。

文王有声

文王有声,遹骏有声①,遹求厥宁,遹观厥成②。文王烝哉③!
文王受命,有此武功;既伐于崇,作邑于丰。文王烝哉!
筑城伊淢④,作丰伊匹⑤。匪棘其欲⑥,遹追来孝。王后烝哉!
王公伊濯⑦,维丰之垣。四方攸同,王后维翰⑧。王后烝哉!
丰水东注,维禹之绩。四方攸同,皇王维辟⑨。皇王烝哉!
镐京辟雍,自西自东,自南自北,无思不服。皇王烝哉!
考卜维王,宅是镐京。维龟正之,武王成之。武王烝哉!
丰水有芑,武王岂不仕!诒厥孙谋⑩,以燕翼子⑪。武王烝哉!

【注释】

①遹(yù 愈):语助词。骏(jùn 俊):大。　②观:示人。厥:

其。　③烝：君道。　④伊：语助词。淢（xù 序）：护城河。　⑤匹：配对。　⑥棘：同"急"。　⑦公：通"功"。濯（zhuó 浊）：大。⑧翰：骨干。　⑨辟：君。　⑩诒：传。孙谋：顺天下之谋。　⑪燕翼：安乐警戒。

【译文】

文王有声誉，有大的声誉，谋求人民安宁，展现功业完成。文王的君道得完成啊！

文王接受天命，才有这样的武功；既经讨伐崇国，建立都邑在丰。文王的君道得畅通啊！

筑城要挖护城河，建立丰邑要配牢。不是急求满他欲，只是追念先代的孝。文王的君道能得道啊！

文王的功劳大，有丰邑的城墙。四方同归向，称文王作骨干宣扬。文王的君道强啊！

丰水向东流去，是禹的功劳。四方同归向，文王行得是君道。文王的君道劳啊！

镐京里建立辟雍，从西到东，从南到北，没有哪国不服从。文王的君道雄啊！

考查占卜只推王，定居在镐京。龟卜能决断它，武王能建成它，武王的君道成就它啊！

丰水边上有芑草，武王岂有不建业啊！传授给子孙的谋划，用来安定警戒儿子，武王的君道真是好啊！

生民之什

生 民

厥初生民，时维姜嫄①，生民如何？克禋克祀②，以弗无子③。履帝武敏歆④，攸介攸止⑤，载震载夙⑥，载生载育，时维后稷。

诞弥厥月⑦，先生如达⑧。不坼不副⑨，无菑无害⑩。以赫厥灵⑪，上帝不宁⑫。不康禋祀，居然生子。

诞寘之隘巷⑬，牛羊腓字之⑭。诞寘之平林，会伐平林。诞寘之寒冰，鸟复翼之。鸟乃去矣，后稷呱矣。实覃实訏⑮，厥声载路⑯。

诞实匍匐⑰，克岐克嶷⑱，以就口食。蓺之荏菽⑲，荏菽旆旆⑳，禾役穟穟㉑，麻麦幪幪㉒，瓜瓞唪唪㉓。

诞后稷之穑，有相之道。茀厥丰草㉔，种之黄茂。实方实苞㉕，实种实褎㉖，实发实秀㉗，实坚实好，实颖实栗㉘。即有邰家室㉙。

诞降嘉种，维秬维秠㉚，维穈维芑㉛。恒之秬秠㉜，是获是亩；恒之穈芑，是任是负㉝。以归肇祀。

诞我祀如何？或舂或揄㉞，或簸或蹂㉟；释之叟叟㊱，烝之浮浮㊲；载谋载惟，取萧祭脂，取羝以軷㊳；载燔载烈，以兴嗣岁㊴。

卬盛于豆⑩，于豆于登㊶。其香始升，上帝居歆㊷。胡臭亶时㊸。后稷肇祀，庶无罪悔，以迄于今。

【注释】

①姜嫄（yuán 原）：姜姓部落的女酋长。 ②禋（yīn 因）：祭天的典礼。 ③以弗无子：用来除去无子。弗，指除灾去邪。 ④履帝武敏歆：践踏上帝脚迹忻然。履，踏。帝武，上帝脚步。敏歆，很快忻然。 ⑤攸介攸止：腹大得孕。介，大。止，得到。这是踏脚印会得孕，是神话，实际是姜嫄同人野合而得孕。 ⑥载震载夙：指胎动。震，指震动。夙也指动。 ⑦诞弥厥月：生育满足它月份。弥，满。月，月份。 ⑧达：羊胎。 ⑨不坼不副：不，语助词。坼，指胞衣分裂；副，指胎盘分离。 ⑩菑：同"灾"。 ⑪赫：显耀。 ⑫上帝不宁：姜嫄恐"履帝武"孕受罚，故有"帝不宁"之忧，而居然生后稷，故以不祥而弃之。 ⑬寘：置，放在。 ⑭腓（féi 肥）：庇护。字：慈爱。 ⑮覃（tán 谈）：长。訏（xū 须）：大。 ⑯载路：满路。 ⑰匍匐（pú fú 婆伏）：爬行。 ⑱岐：知意。嶷（yí 宜）：识。 ⑲蓺：同"艺"。荏（rěn 忍）：大。 ⑳旆旆（pèi pèi 沛沛）：长大。㉑禾役：禾之行列。穟穟（suì suì 遂遂）：美好。 ㉒幪幪（měng měng 猛猛）：茂盛。 ㉓唪唪（běng běng 绷绷）：甚多貌。 ㉔茀（fú 伏）：除去。 ㉕实：语助词。方：发芽。苞：含苞。 ㉖褎（yòu 右）：长。 ㉗发：发展。秀：扬花。 ㉘颖：垂头。栗：结实。 ㉙邰（tái 台）：姜嫄的国名，在陕西武功县西南。 ㉚秬（jù 巨）：黑黍。秠（pī 披）：麦子。 ㉛穈（mén 门）：赤苗，红米。芑（qǐ 起）：白苗，白米。 ㉜恒：遍种。 ㉝任：犹抱。 ㉞揄（yóu 由）：舀取。 ㉟蹂：通"揉"，搓米。 ㊱释：淘米。叟叟：淘米声。 ㊲浮浮：蒸米热气。

㊳羝（dī 低）：公羊。 。 **较**（bá 拔）：祭路神。　㊴以兴嗣岁：用来兴起新年，祝新年丰收。　㊵卬：通"昂"，我。　㊶豆：木制盛熟物器。登：瓦制的器。　㊷居：语助词。歆：饗。　㊸胡臭：大芳香。亶时：诚善。

【译文】

开始生育周人，是由姜嫄女子，生育周人是怎样？能祭天能祭祀，怎能没有儿子。踏上帝脚印很欢欣，肚子大了怀孕了，胎儿震动又震动，生下了好培植，这就是后稷。

生时满足月份，头生顺利像羊胎。胎衣破裂胎盘分离，无灾无害。上帝显示神威灵，上帝还是不安宁。不安还是来祭祀，居然生下了儿子。

把他放在窄巷里，牛羊包庇爱护它。把他放在树林里，碰上砍林救了他。把他放在寒冰上，鸟儿展翅暖着他。鸟儿飞去了，后稷呱呱哭了。哭声又长又是大，他的声音满路了。

他已经会爬行了，能够有知又有识，能够就去找口食。他种那大豆，大豆长得好。禾穗排列好，麻麦长得好，小瓜大瓜多又好。

后稷种庄稼，有助长的门道。除去茂盛的草，种的植物黄又好。发荣又含苞，粗壮又长好，发茎又扬花，坚挺结实好，垂头又结实。封到邰地立家妙。

好的种子天降下，是黑黍是麦子，是赤米是白米。遍种黑黍和麦子，是收获是用亩计；遍种赤米和白米，是抱还是背起。用来回去开始祭。

我的祭祀怎么样？或是舂米或舀米，或是簸糠或搓米；淘起米来声叟叟，蒸起米来气浮浮；出主意来出计谋，取蒿和油来祭神,取公羊来祭路神;就烧熟来再用烤,且来求得明年好。

我把食物装木豆,装了木豆装瓦登。它的香气开始升,上帝降临来受歆。香味大好又好闻。后稷开始来祭祀,几乎没有罪和悔,自从那时直到今。

行 苇

敦彼行苇①,牛羊弗践履。方苞方体②,维叶泥泥③。戚戚兄弟④,莫远具尔⑤。或肆之筵⑥,或授之几⑦。

肆筵设席,授几有缉御⑧。或献或酢,洗爵奠斝⑨。醓醢以荐⑩,或燔或炙。嘉殽脾臄⑪,或歌或咢⑫。

敦弓既坚⑬,四鍭既钧⑭,舍矢既均⑮,序宾以贤。敦弓既句,既挟四鍭。四鍭如树,序宾以不侮。

曾孙维主,酒醴维醹⑯,酌以大斗,以祈黄耇。黄耇台背⑰,以引以翼⑱。寿考维祺,以介景福。

【注释】

①敦(tuán 团):聚集。行(háng 杭)苇:路边的芦苇。 ②苞:含苞。体:成形。 ③泥泥:茂盛。 ④戚戚:亲善。 ⑤尔:同"迩",近。 ⑥筵(yán 延):竹席,作为坐具。 ⑦几:似矮桌。坐时可凭倚。 ⑧缉御:续侍。 ⑨奠斝(jiǎ 甲):献酒器,即敬酒。 ⑩醓(tǎn 坦):多汁肉酱。醢(hǎi 海):肉酱。 ⑪脾(pí 琵):牛胃。臄(jué 觉):牛舌。 ⑫咢(è 厄):只击鼓,不唱歌。 ⑬敦(diāo 雕):画弓。 ⑭鍭(hóu 侯):箭。钧:同"均"。 ⑮均:均射中。 ⑯醹(rú 儒):酒质醇厚。 ⑰黄耇(gǒu 苟):长寿老人。台背:同"鲐背",指老人背有黑纹如鲐鱼背也。 ⑱以引以翼:对老人在前牵引在旁扶持。

【译文】

聚生路边的芦苇,牛羊不要乱踩紊。它正含苞正成形,它的叶儿正茂盛。相亲的兄弟,不要疏远要亲近。或摆好了筵席,或给与几表尊敬。

陈列筵席请客坐,授与几子有侍候。有人献酒有回敬,洗杯献杯实敬酒。肉酱肉汁用来献,或烧或烤正火候。好菜牛胃兼牛舌,有唱有咢来助欢。

雕弓既是很坚劲,四箭既是极钧衡,发箭既是均中的,序列都是好客人。雕弓既是都引满,既挟四箭中的均。四箭中的如树立,不去侮慢好客人。

周王真是好主人,甜酒真是味道醇,酌用大杯来敬客,来求寿考祝客人。寿考都像鲐鱼背,有行有扶有人敬。祝他寿考是祥瑞,用求大福受人敬。

既 醉

既醉以酒,既饱以德。君子万年,介尔景福。
既醉以酒,尔肴既将①。君子万年,介尔昭明。
昭明有融②,高朗令终。令终有俶③,公尸嘉告④。
其告维何?笾豆静嘉。朋友攸摄⑤,摄以威仪。
威仪孔时,君子有孝子。孝子不匮,永锡尔类⑥。
其类维何?室家之壶⑦。君子万年,永锡祚胤⑧。
其胤维何?天被尔禄。君子万年,景命有仆⑨。
其仆维何?釐尔女士⑩。釐尔女士,从以孙子⑪。

【注释】

①将:精美。　②有融:又明。　③俶(chù 触):始。　④公

尸：代公作尸的人。　⑤摄：辅佐，指助祭。　⑥类：法程。　⑦壸（kǔn 捆）：古时宫中巷，引申为广。　⑧祚（zuò 做）：福。胤（yìn 印）：后代。　⑨仆：附。《笺》："天之大命又附着于女。"女：汝，你。　⑩釐尔女士：予汝女子有士行。釐（lí 离）：给予。　⑪从以孙子：相从以好孙子。

【译文】

既已饮用了醉酒，既已饱受了恩德。君子人活一万年，上天赐你大福泽。

既已饮用了醉酒，你的菜肴美而精。君子人活一万年，天赐给你是光明。

光明又盛又久长，高明用善求始终。善终有个好开始，代公的人好作颂。

他的作颂是什么？笾豆洁美又得宜。群臣宾客来辅助，辅助讲究是威仪。

威仪用得很适时，君子又都是孝子。孝子永远不穷乏，天赐给他大法子。

他的法子是什么？治家推广到治国。君子活到一万年，永赐子孙多福泽。

天赐子孙是什么？天给你的是禄福。君子活到一万年，天赐大命有着附。

天附大命是什么？赐你生女像士子。赐你生女像士子，从而给你好孙子。

凫　鹥

凫鹥在泾①，公尸来燕来宁。尔酒既清，尔肴既馨。公尸燕饮，福禄来成②。

凫鹥在沙③，公尸来燕来宜，尔酒既多，尔肴既嘉。公尸燕饮，福禄来为④。

凫鹥在渚，公尸来燕来处。尔酒既湑，尔肴既脯⑤。公尸燕饮，福禄来下。

凫鹥在潨⑥，公尸来燕来宗⑦。既燕于宗⑧，福禄攸降。公尸燕饮，福禄来崇⑨。

凫鹥在亹⑩，公尸来止熏熏。旨酒欣欣⑪，燔炙芬芬。公尸燕饮，无有后艰。

【注释】

①凫（fú 扶）：野鸭。鹥（yī 医）：鸥鸟。泾（jīng 京）：水名。 ②成：成就，指以福禄成全之。 ③沙：沙滩。 ④为：助。 ⑤脯（fǔ 府）：干肉。 ⑥潨（zhōng 中）：水涯。 ⑦宗：尊敬。 ⑧于宗：在宗庙。 ⑨崇：申，重，增加。 ⑩亹（mén 门）：峡中两岸对峙如门处。 ⑪"来止熏熏"与"旨酒欣欣"，俞樾《古书疑义举例》认为当作"来止欣欣"，"旨酒熏熏"。"熏"同"醺"，指酒味。

【译文】

野鸭鸥鸟聚泾水，代公人宴来安宁。你的美酒既澄清，你的菜肴既香馨。代公的人来宴饮，天赐福禄成就你。

野鸭鸥鸟在沙滩，代公人宴会相宜。你的美酒既然多，你的菜肴又新奇。代公的人来宴饮，天赐福禄相助你。

野鸭鸥鸟在水渚，代公人宴来安处。你酒既滤得澄清，你的菜肴干肉煮。代公的人来宴饮，天把福禄降你处。

野鸭鸥鸟在水涯,代公人宴会极好。既经宴会在宗庙,天把福禄降下来。代公的人来宴饮,福禄重重来得好。

野鸭鸥鸟在峡门,代公人来到欣欣。好酒香气可以闻,烧的烤的味芬芬。代公的人来宴饮,没有后难可以云。

假 乐

假乐君子①,显显令德。宜民宜人,受禄于天。保右命之②,自天申之。

干禄百福③,子孙千亿。穆穆皇皇,宜君宜王,不愆不忘④,率由旧章。

威仪抑抑⑤,德音秩秩⑥。无怨无恶,率由群匹⑦。受福无疆,四方之纲。

之纲之纪,燕及朋友。百辟卿士⑧,媚于天子。不解于位,民之攸墍⑨。

【注释】

①假:同"嘉",美好。君子:指成王。 ②右:同"佑",佑助。 ③干:求。 ④愆(qiān 千):过失。 ⑤抑抑:美好。 ⑥秩秩:有秩序。 ⑦群匹:群臣。 ⑧百辟(bì 必):百君,指诸侯。卿士:指诸侯的大臣。 ⑨墍(jì 既):安息。

【译文】

美好的成王,明显德行有善良。适宜安民和用人,受到天赐福禄长。天命保佑他,天神告诫他。

求得福禄有多样,子孙多到千亿强。做人美好又堂皇,宜做国君又做王,没有过错没遗忘,一切都照旧规章。

所有仪容都美好,所有德音都守常。没有怨恨没有恶,都从群臣好主张。接受福禄多无限,作为四方的纪纲。

作为四方的纪纲,欢宴朋友真是好。诸侯卿士都说好,面对天子都亲好。不懈怠他的职位,人民安心都守道。

公 刘

笃公刘①,匪居匪康,迺场迺疆②,迺积迺仓③;迺裹餱粮④,于橐于囊⑤,思辑用光⑥。弓矢斯张,干戈戚扬⑦,爰方启行⑧。

笃公刘,于胥斯原⑨。既庶既繁,既顺迺宣⑩,而无永叹。陟则在巘⑪,复降在原。何以舟之⑫?维玉及瑶,鞞琫容刀⑬。

笃公刘,逝彼百泉,瞻彼溥原;迺陟南冈,乃觏于京。京师之野,于时处处,于时庐旅⑭,于时言言,于时语语。

笃公刘,于京斯依,跄跄济济⑮,俾筵俾几,既登乃依⑯。乃造其曹⑰,执豕于牢,酌之用匏⑱。食之饮之,君之宗之。

笃公刘,既溥既长,既景迺冈⑲,相其阴阳⑳,观其流泉,其军三单㉑;庶其隰原,彻田为粮㉒,度其夕阳㉓,豳居允荒。

笃公刘,于豳斯馆。涉渭为乱㉔,取厉取锻㉕。止基乃理㉖,爰众爰有㉗。夹其皇涧㉘,遡其过涧㉙。止旅迺密㉚,芮鞫之即㉛。

【注释】

①笃(dǔ 赌)：忠厚。 ②迺：同"乃"。场(yì 亦)：田界。疆：边界。 ③积：露积。 ④餱(hóu 侯)粮：干粮。 ⑤橐(tuó 托)：小袋。 ⑥辑：和睦。 ⑦戚扬：斧钺。戚，小斧；扬，大斧。 ⑧爰：语助词。方：始。 ⑨胥：相，察看。 ⑩宣：宣畅，通畅。 ⑪巘(yǎn 演)：小山。 ⑫舟：带。 ⑬鞞琫(bǐng běng 丙绷)：刀鞘上的饰物。容刀：佩刀。 ⑭庐旅：房舍。 ⑮跄跄：步趋有节。济济：庄严。 ⑯既登：指登席。乃依：指依几。几，坐时凭倚的矮桌。 ⑰造：通"祰"，指告祭。曹：通"禣"，指祭豕神。 ⑱匏(páo 袍)：葫芦。 ⑲景：同"影"。冈：山冈。 ⑳阴阳：山北山南。㉑三单：轮流当兵。㉒彻：开发。 ㉓夕阳：山的西边。 ㉔乱：横渡。 ㉕厉：通"砺"，磨刀石。锻：石。 ㉖止：居。乃理：理田野。 ㉗众：指人口增多。有：指物丰。 ㉘皇：涧名。 ㉙过：涧名。 ㉚旅：众。密：安。 ㉛芮(ruì 锐)：水涯。鞠(jū 居)：水曲。

【译文】

诚厚的公刘，不敢安居图安康，于是划田界划地界，于是露囤是装仓；于是裹了干粮，放进小袋和大囊，人民和睦国有光芒。对敌弓箭就开张，还用干戈和斧扬，于是方才开始出行。

诚厚的公刘，于是察看这田原。既是人多又繁荣，既顺民情人心宽，没有人怨发长叹。登上小山望田原，往下又走在平原。用什么来佩带呢？用美玉和琼瑶，还有刀鞘饰物和佩刀。

诚厚的公刘，看逝去那百泉流，望那广阔的平原；登山上南面山丘，于是看见那京丘。那是京师的野地头，于是处处可居，于是可以建新居，于是话他当说那个话，于是语他当讲那个语。

诗经

　　诚厚的公刘，在京地依居后，趋走有节的众多臣，使设筵席使几留，有登筵席有依几留。于是祭猪神把神求，捉猪在猪牢，酌酒用葫芦瓢。给他们吃和饮，做国君、族长尊敬他。

　　诚厚的公刘，土地既广又是长，既是测影在山冈，观察它的阴和阳，观察流泉定方向，轮流当兵来驻防；洼地平原好测量，治理田亩好种粮，测量西山的夕阳，豳地居住确是广。

　　诚厚的公刘，在豳地作公馆。横渡渭河把工施，取砺石又取细锻。立定基址治田亩，人口众多物富有。夹着皇涧是住处，逆遡过涧是田亩。众人居住是密集，水边河曲住处有。

泂　酌

　　泂酌彼行潦^①，挹彼注兹^②，可以餴饎^③。岂弟君子，民之父母。

　　泂酌彼行潦，挹彼注兹，可以濯罍^④。岂弟君子，民之攸归。

　　泂酌彼行潦，挹彼注兹，可以濯溉^⑤。岂弟君子，民之攸塈^⑥。

【注释】

　　①泂（jiǒng窘）：远。行潦（lǎo老）：路上积水。　②挹：舀。注：倒下。　③餴（fēn分）：蒸饭。饎（chì翅）：酒食。　④罍（lěi雷）：古瓦器名，可以盛酒。　⑤濯（zhuó浊）：洗涤。溉（gài盖）：通"概"，漆尊，酒器。　⑥塈（xì戏）：休息。

【译文】

远远舀那路积水，舀水倒在这里后，可以蒸饭可热酒，平易的君子人，是人民的父母。

远远舀那路积水，舀水倒在这里后，可以洗净瓦杯向客酬。平易的君子人，人民归顺的好友。

远远舀那路积水，舀水倒在这里后，可以洗净漆杯向客酬。平易的君子人，可使人民休息久。

卷 阿

有卷者阿①，飘风自南。岂弟君子，来游来歌，以矢其音②。

伴奂尔游矣③，优游尔休矣。岂弟君子，俾尔弥尔性④，似先公酋矣⑤。

尔土宇昄章⑥，亦孔之厚矣。岂弟君子，俾尔弥尔性，百神尔主矣。

尔受命长矣，茀禄尔康矣⑦。岂弟君子，俾尔弥尔性，纯嘏尔常矣⑧。

有冯有翼⑨，有孝有德。以引以翼。岂弟君子，四方为则。

颙颙卬卬⑩，如圭如璋，令闻令望。岂弟君子，四方为纲。

凤凰于飞，翙翙其羽⑪，亦集爰止。蔼蔼王多吉士⑫，维君子使，媚于天子。

凤凰于飞，翙翙其羽，亦傅于天。蔼蔼王多吉人，维君子命，媚于庶人。

凤凰鸣矣，于彼高岗。梧桐生矣，于彼朝阳。萋萋萋萋⑬，雝雝喈喈。

君子之车，既庶且多。君子之马，既闲且驰。矢诗不多⑭，维以遂歌。

【注释】

①卷（quán 权）：曲。阿：大土山。　②矢：陈述。　③伴奂：优游闲暇。　④俾尔弥尔性：使你终其寿命。弥，终。性，寿命。　⑤似先公酋：继承祖宗功业长久。"似"通"嗣"。酋，久。　⑥土宇：土地屋宅，代指领土封地。昄（bǎn 板）章：犹版图。　⑦茀（fú 福）：小福。康：安康。　⑧纯嘏（gǔ 古）：大福。纯，大。　⑨冯（píng 凭）：依托。翼：庇护。　⑩颙颙（yóng yóng 喁喁）：仰慕。卬卬（áng áng 昂昂）：繁盛。　⑪翙翙（huì huì 汇汇）：众多。　⑫蔼蔼（ǎi ǎi 矮矮）：众多而有容仪。　⑬萋萋（běng běng 绷绷）：茂盛。　⑭矢诗不多：献诗多。矢，献。不，语助词。

【译文】

有卷曲的大土山，疾风从南方吹来。快乐平易的君子，游玩来又唱歌来，陈述他的德音来。

优游闲暇你游了，逍遥自得你休息了。快乐平易的君子，使你终养你性命，继承先公大业久了。

你的领土版图，也是得天独厚了。快乐平易的君子，使你终养你性命，百神做你的主了。

你受天命长久了，福禄使你安康了。快乐平易的君子，使你终养你性命，天赐大福是经常了。

有依靠有辅助，有孝行有美德。导引辅助在亲侧。快乐平易的君子，四方用你做法则。

人民仰望志高昂，有像玉圭像玉璋，有美名和好声望。快乐平易的君子，四方用你做纪纲。

凤凰在飞，众多鸟儿展两翅，聚集树上才息止。王朝有众多善士，只听君子驱使，他们敬爱天子。

凤凰在飞，众多鸟儿展两翅，高飞飞到了上天。王朝有众多善士，只听君子命令，亲爱众人和善士。

凤凰叫了，在那高岗。梧桐生长了，在那朝阳照的地方。梧桐长得茂盛，凤凰叫得和顺。

君子的车，既是众来又是多。君子的马，训练有素善奔波。我献诗多，只是用它成为歌。

民 劳

民亦劳止，汔可小康①。惠此中国②，以绥四方。无纵诡随③，以谨无良。式遏寇虐④，憯不畏明⑤。柔远能迩⑥，以定我王。

民亦劳止，汔可小休。惠此中国，以为民逑⑦。无纵诡随，以谨惛怓⑧。式遏寇虐，无俾民忧。无弃尔劳，以为王休。

民亦劳止，汔可小息。惠此京师，以绥四国。无纵诡随，以谨罔极。式遏寇虐，无俾作慝⑨。敬慎威仪，以近有德。

民亦劳止，汔可小愒⑩。惠此中国，俾民忧泄⑪。无纵诡随，以谨丑厉⑫。式遏寇虐，无俾正败⑬。戎虽小子⑭，而式弘大。

民亦劳止，汔可小安。惠此中国，国无有残。无纵诡随，以谨缱绻⑮。式遏寇虐，无俾正反。王欲玉女⑯，是用大谏⑰。

【注释】

①汔（qì 气）：求。 ②中国：指京师。 ③谲随：谲诈谩欺之人。 ④式遏：用以制止。 ⑤憯（cǎn 惨）：乃。明：高明。 ⑥柔远：怀柔远方人。能迩：能从近处人。 ⑦逑：聚。 ⑧憎怓（hūn náo 昏挠）：喧哗。 ⑨慝（tè 特）：罪恶。 ⑩愒（qì 迄）：休息。 ⑪泄（xiè 屑）：通"渫"，除去。 ⑫丑厉：众恶。 ⑬无俾正败：无使正道败坏。 ⑭戎：你。 ⑮缱绻（qiǎn quǎn 浅犬）：紧紧缠绕。比喻小人固结其君。 ⑯玉女：玉汝，成就你。 ⑰大谏：力谏。

【译文】

人民也劳苦够了，求得可以稍稍安康。惠爱这些京师人，用来安定四方。不要放纵谲诈的人，用来谨防不善良。用来遏止暴虐抢掠，不要怕高明人强梁。怀柔远人能及近，用来安定我周王。

人民也劳苦够了，求得可以稍休处。惠爱这些京师人，用作人民的相聚。不要放纵谲诈的人，用来谨防喧吵咒诅。用来遏止暴虐抢掠，无使人民多忧虑。不要抛弃你的功劳，用来作为王的美誉。

人民也劳苦够了，求得可以稍稍休息。惠爱这些京师人，用来安定四方侯国。不要放纵谲诈的人，用来谨防没有准则。用来遏止暴虐和掠夺，无使有人作恶。敬慎在人民的仪容，用来接近美德。

人民也劳苦够了，求得可以小休一会。惠爱这些京师人，使人民忧愁疏散。不要放纵谲诈的人,用来谨防众恶为害。用来遏制暴虐和掠夺。不要使正道失败。你虽是年轻人,可是作用广大。

人民也劳苦够了,求得可以稍稍安闲。惠爱这些京师人,国内没有残患。不要纵容谲诈的人,用来谨防奉迎成患。用来遏制暴虐掠夺,不要使政治变幻。王啊!我想成就你,特此用力劝谏。

板

上帝板板①,下民卒瘅②。出话不然③,为犹不远④。靡圣管管⑤,不实于亶⑥。犹之未远,是用大谏。

天之方难,无然宪宪⑦。天之方蹶⑧,无然泄泄⑨。辞之辑矣⑩,民之洽矣。辞之怿矣⑪,民之莫矣⑫。

我虽异事⑬,及尔同僚。我即尔谋,听我嚣嚣⑭。我言维服⑮,勿以为笑。先民有言,询于刍荛⑯。

天之方虐,无然谑谑⑰。老夫灌灌⑱,小子蹻蹻⑲。匪我言耄,尔用忧谑⑳。多将熇熇㉑,不可救药。

天之方懠㉒,无为夸毗㉓。威仪卒迷㉔,善人载尸㉕。民之方殿屎㉖,则莫我敢葵㉗。丧乱蔑资㉘,曾莫惠我师㉙。

天之牖民㉚,如埙如篪㉛,如璋如圭㉜,如取如携㉝。携无曰益㉞,牖民孔易。民之多辟㉟,无自立辟㊱。

价人维藩㊲,大师维垣㊳。大邦维屏,大宗维翰㊴。怀德维宁,宗子维城。无俾城坏,无独斯畏㊵。

敬天之怒,无敢戏豫。敬天之渝㊶,无敢驰驱㊷。昊天曰明,及尔出王㊸。昊天曰旦㊹,及尔游衍。

诗经

【注释】

①板板：反常。 ②瘅(dān 丹)：病。 ③出话不然：发出好话，不以为对。 ④犹：指谋划。 ⑤靡圣管管：眼中没有圣人，无所依靠。管管，指无所依靠。 ⑥亶(dǎn 胆)：诚。《笺》："不能用实于诚信之言，言行相违。" ⑦宪宪：犹欣欣。 ⑧蹶(guì 贵)：动。 ⑨泄泄：多言。 ⑩辞：指政教。辑：指和睦。 ⑪怿(yì 译)：通"斁"，败坏。 ⑫莫：通"瘼"，病。 ⑬异事：职务有异。 ⑭嚣嚣(áo áo 敖敖)：通"敖敖"，不听善言。 ⑮服：事。 ⑯刍荛(ráo 饶)：割草打柴的人。 ⑰谑谑(xuè xuè 血血)：戏笑。 ⑱灌灌：诚恳。 ⑲蹻蹻(jué jué 决决)：骄傲。 ⑳忧：当作"优"，调戏。 ㉑熇熇(hè hè 贺贺)：火盛。 ㉒怿(qí 齐)：怒。 ㉓夸毗(pí 皮)：柔顺貌，指屈己卑身。 ㉔卒迷：尽迷乱。 ㉕载尸：如尸，不语。 ㉖殿屎(xī 希)：呻吟。 ㉗葵：通"揆"，猜度。 ㉘蔑资：无财。 ㉙师：众民。 ㉚牖：通"诱"，诱导。 ㉛如埙如篪：埙(xūn 勋)，土制乐器，有六孔，吹奏用。篪(chí 池)，竹制器，像笛，有八孔。两乐器吹奏可相和。 ㉜如璋如圭：半圭叫璋，合璋为圭，指相配合。 ㉝如取如携：取携极易。 ㉞益：通"隘"，塞。 ㉟多辟：多邪行为。 ㊱立辟：立法。 ㊲价(jiè 介)人：披甲人，武人。 ㊳大师：太师，三公之一。维垣：作为城墙。 ㊴大宗：大的宗族。 ㊵畏：通"威"，指威严。 ㊶渝：变。 ㊷驰驱：指放纵。 ㊸王：往。 ㊹旦：明。

【译文】

上帝行为反常，下面人民尽遭难。说的好话不算数，做的谋划没远算。没有圣人只有乱，没有诚信不忠善。作的谋划没远算，因此用了大谏劝。

上天正要降灾难，不要高兴弄戏玩。上天正要降动乱，不要多话来论断。如果政教协和了，人民就安定了。如果政教败坏了，人民就受苦了。

我们虽然管不同的事，我和你是同僚。我就同你商量，听我说话你骄傲。我的说话是实事，不要认为开玩笑。古人曾经有句话，有事问到割草和老樵。

上天正在暴虐，不要这样来戏谑。老夫谆谆和你讲，小子骄傲是轻薄。不是我话是老昏，是你用了多戏谑。多把气盛对待人，真是不可以救药。

上天正在发怒，不要卑身顺着干。人的威仪尽迷乱，善人好比死尸般。人民正在苦呻吟，对我猜疑都不敢。人民经乱财资空，怎不施恩于民众。

上天的引导人民，像埙和篪的和洽，像圭和璋的合璧，像取和携的合一。不要说携有阻塞，引导人民很容易。人多邪狭，不要自己多立法。

武人是国的藩篱，太师是国的城墙。大邦是国的屏障，大宗是国的栋梁，怀有美德使国安宁，大宗的儿子是国的城。不要使城坏，不要害怕孤独众人。

敬畏上天的发怒，不敢当儿戏。敬畏上天的变化，不敢放纵自己奔马。上天那么明朗，连你可以出去游荡。上天那么光明，连你可以游逛外出。

荡之什

荡

荡荡上帝①,下民之辟②。疾威上帝③,其命多辟④。天生烝民,其命匪谌⑤。靡不有初,鲜克有终。

文王曰咨,咨女殷商。曾是强御⑥,曾是掊克⑦,曾是在位,曾是在服⑧。天降滔德⑨,女兴是力⑩。

文王曰咨,咨女殷商。而秉义类⑪,强御多怼⑫,流言以对⑬,寇攘式内⑭。侯作侯祝⑮,靡届靡究⑯。

文王曰咨,咨女殷商。女炰烋于中国⑰,敛怨以为德。不明尔德,时无背无侧⑱。尔德不明,以无陪无卿。

文王曰咨,咨女殷商。天不湎尔以酒⑲,不义从式⑳。既愆尔止㉑,靡明靡晦。式号式呼,俾昼作夜。

文王曰咨,咨女殷商。如蜩如螗㉒,如沸如羹。小大近丧,人尚乎由行。内奰于中国㉓,覃及鬼方㉔。

文王曰咨,咨女殷商。匪上帝不时,殷不用旧。虽无老成人,尚有典刑。曾是莫听,大命以倾。

文王曰咨,咨女殷商。人亦有言,颠沛之揭㉕,枝叶未有害,本实先拨㉖。殷鉴不远,在夏后之世。

【注释】

①荡荡：指法度败坏。 ②辟（bì 壁）：君王。 ③疾威：暴戾。 ④辟（pì 僻）：邪僻。 ⑤谌（chén 臣）：诚。 ⑥曾：乃。强御：强暴。 ⑦掊（póu 抔）克：聚敛。 ⑧在服：在职。 ⑨滔德：慢德，不好的行为。 ⑩女兴是力：汝兴起是用力。 ⑪而秉义类：尔执持强族。义类，指强族。 ⑫怼（duì 队）：怨。 ⑬对：遂，成就。 ⑭攘（rǎng 嚷）：夺取。 ⑮侯作侯祝：侯，是。作，诅。祝，咒。 ⑯靡届靡究：无穷无尽。 ⑰炰烋（páo xiāo 袍肖）：即咆哮，怒吼。 ⑱无背无侧：不知反叛不知反侧。背，背逆。侧，倾仄，邪僻。 ⑲湎（miǎn 免）：沉迷。 ⑳不义从式：不宜纵试。 ㉑尔止：你行止。 ㉒蜩（tiáo 条）：蝉。蟷（táng 唐）：蝉的一种。 ㉓奰（bì 必）：怒。 ㉔覃：延。鬼方：远方。 ㉕颠沛之揭：颠倒拔起的根露。揭，指见根。 ㉖拨：败坏。

【译文】

法度败坏的上帝，像下面人民的暴君。暴戾的上帝，他的命令多邪淫。上天生下众民，他的命令不真诚。不是没有好开头，却很少能够有所成。

文王说：唉，唉叹你们殷商。曾是强横，曾是聚敛，曾是在位称王，曾是各在职事。上天降下不好的行藏，你们是出力帮忙。

文王说：唉，唉叹你们殷商。你们执持强族，强横多得怨恨，流言可以成就，强抢强取得猖狂。于是怨谤于是诅咒，没穷没尽没收场。

文王说：唉，唉叹你们殷商。你们在国中咆哮，招集怨恨以为德。不明是你们的德，不知反叛不知反侧。你们对德是不明，因此无陪臣无卿相。

文王说:唉,唉叹你们殷商。天不沉醉你们用酒,不宜放纵你们发狂。既经行止失当,无论晴明或阴凉。你们大号又大呼,把那白天作夜场。

文王说:唉,唉叹你们殷商。像蝉那样噪,像沸的羹汤。小事大事都近丧亡,人们还在学样。国中怨着那怨恨,沿及到远方。

文王说:唉,唉叹你们殷商。不是上帝不善良,是殷商不用旧规章。虽然没有老成人,但还是有典刑。怎么就是不去听,国家的大命只好倾。

文王说:唉,唉叹你们殷商。人有这样的话,颠倒的树根露出土壤,枝叶没有害,本根先受伤。殷商的鉴不远,就在夏王的世上。

抑

抑抑威仪①,维德之隅②。人亦有言,靡哲不愚。庶人之愚,亦职维疾。哲人之愚,亦维斯戾③。

无竞维人④,四方其训之。有觉德行⑤,四国顺之。讦谟定命⑥,远犹辰告⑦。敬慎威仪,维民之则。

其在于今,兴迷乱于政⑧;颠覆厥德,荒湛于酒。女虽湛乐,弗念厥绍⑨。罔敷求先王⑩,克共明刑。

肆皇天弗尚⑪,如彼泉流,无沦胥以亡。夙兴夜寐,洒扫廷内⑫,维民之章。修尔车马,弓矢戎兵,用戒戎作⑬,用逷蛮方⑭。

质尔人民⑮,谨尔侯度,用戒不虞。慎尔出话,敬尔威仪,无不柔嘉⑯。白圭之玷,尚可磨也;斯言之玷,不可为也。

无易由言，无曰苟矣⑰。莫扪朕舌，言不可逝矣⑱。无言不雠⑲，无德不报。惠于朋友，庶民小子。子孙绳绳⑳，万民靡不承。

视尔友君子，辑柔尔颜㉑，不遐有愆。相在尔室，尚不愧于屋漏㉒。无曰不显，莫予云觏，神之格思㉓，不可度思，矧可射思㉔！

辟尔为德㉕，俾臧俾嘉。淑慎尔止，不愆于仪。不僭不贼，鲜不为则。投我以桃，报之以李。彼童而角㉖，实虹小子㉗。

荏染柔木㉘，言缗之丝㉙。温温恭人，维德之基。其维哲人，告之话言，顺德之行。其维愚人，覆谓我僭㉚，民各有心。

於呼小子，未知臧否。匪手携之，言示之事。匪面命之，言提其耳。借曰未知㉛，亦既抱子。民之靡盈，谁夙知而莫成㉜？

昊天孔昭，我生靡乐。视尔梦梦㉝，我心惨惨㉞。诲尔谆谆，听我藐藐㉟。匪用为教，覆用为虐㊱。借曰未知，亦聿既耄㊲。

於乎小子，告尔旧止。听用我谋，庶无大悔。天方艰难，曰丧厥国。取譬不远，昊天不忒㊳。回遹其德㊴，俾民大棘㊵。

【注释】

①抑抑：静密。　②隅：屋角，比方正。　③戾（lì 吏）：罪。　④无竞维人：无强于得贤人。无竞，竞也。　⑤觉：指正直。　⑥訏（xū）谟：大谋。　⑦辰：时。告：宣告。　⑧兴：语辞。　⑨绍：继承。指继承先人传统。　⑩傅：铺。　⑪肆：于是。尚：祐。　⑫廷内：

朝堂内。 ⑬戎作：伐戎事。 ⑭逷（tì 替）：治理。 ⑮质：诚。 ⑯柔嘉：安善。 ⑰苟：苟且。 ⑱逝：往。 ⑲雠（chóu 仇）：应验。 ⑳绳绳（mǐn mǐn 敏敏）：戒慎。 ㉑辑柔：和安。 ㉒屋漏：居之西北隅，即暗处，为藏神之处，代指神。 ㉓格：至。 ㉔矧（shěn 沈）：况。射：厌。 ㉕辟：法。 ㉖童：童羊。 ㉗虹（hóng 宏）：同"讧"，指溃乱。 ㉘荏染：柔弱。 ㉙缗（mín 民）：安上弦。 ㉚僭（jiàn 建）：不信。 ㉛借：假如。 ㉜莫：同"暮"。 ㉝梦梦：昏乱。 ㉞惨惨：悲伤。 ㉟藐藐：忽略貌。 ㊱覆：反。 ㊲耄（mào 冒）：老。 ㊳忒（tè 特）：差。 ㊴遹（yù 育）：邪僻。 ㊵棘：通"急"，危难。

【译文】

缜密威严的仪容，只是表示品德的方正。人有这样的话，没有哲人不愚蠢。众人的愚蠢，也是本身造成的毛病。哲人的愚蠢，也是只怕罪刑。

要想争强靠贤人，四方国家有教训。有了真正的德行，四方国家都归顺。大谋决定好发令，远的谋划报国人。敬慎威严的仪容，这是人民的模型。

事情到当今，迷乱在国政；颠倒了德行，沉湎在于酒。你喜欢纵情嗜酒，不顾祖业的继承。不广求先王的遗训，怎能执掌用明刑。

于是遭皇天厌弃，像那泉水流一样，不要沉沦都败亡。早早起来深夜睡，洒扫室内地方，这是人民的规章。修好你的马车，弓箭兵器各样，用来戒备西戎打仗，用来治理蛮方。

告诫你的人民，谨慎你诸侯的法度，用来防备突发的事件。谨慎你发出的话语，慎重你威严的行举，没有安善不赞许。白圭上的污点，还可以磨去；这话的缺点，不可除去。

不要轻易发言，不要说苟且了。没人扪住我舌头，话不可追回了。无话没有回应，无德行没有报答。施恩惠给朋友，以及庶民年轻人。子孙相戒慎，万民没有不相顺。

对你结交的君子人，容颜柔和又有神，没有一点小过错。看你在室有精神，还不愧在暗处。不要说暗室不显明，不要说不能看见我，神的亲临，不可猜测，何况可以厌倦神！

修明你的美德，做善做美。好好谨慎你容止，不错失于威仪。没过失不害人，很少不为当法则。投给我用桃子，报答他用李子。那童羊装上角，实际上败坏了你小子。

柔软的木料，安上丝线可发音。温和恭敬的人，有美德可任。他是哲人，告诉他好话，顺着美德去行。他是愚人，反说我不可信，人各自有心。

唉，小子，还不知道坏和好。不但亲手提携你，话里示你事相告。不但当面命令你，说话提你耳朵相教。假使说你不知道，也已经把儿子抱。人若没有自满，谁说早知晚成好？

上天很明白，我的生活没有快乐。看你懵懂，我心作痛。教你谆谆，听我藐藐。不是作教，反当戏谑。假使说你无知，也难说既老。

唉，小子，告你旧的章程。听用我的谋划，近乎没有大悔恨。天正在降灾难，要亡掉你的国和京。打比方不远，上天岂能不明。你邪僻你德行，使人民危急难行。

桑　柔

菀彼桑柔①，其下侯旬②，捋采其刘③。瘼此下民④，不殄心忧⑤。仓兄填兮⑥，倬彼昊天⑦，宁不我矜？

四牡骙骙⑧,旟旐有翩。乱生不夷,靡国不泯⑨。民靡有黎⑩,具祸以烬⑪。於乎有哀,国步斯频⑫。

国步蔑资⑬,天不我将⑭。靡所止疑⑮,云徂何往?君子实维⑯,秉心无竞⑰。谁生厉阶,至今为梗⑱?

忧心慇慇⑲,念我土宇。我生不辰,逢天僤怒⑳。自西徂东,靡所定处。多我觏痻㉑,孔棘我圉㉒。

为谋为毖㉓,乱况斯削。告尔忧恤,诲尔序爵。谁能执热,逝不以濯?其何能淑,载胥及溺。

如彼遡风,亦孔之僾㉔。民有肃心㉕,荓云不逮㉖。好是稼穑,力民代食㉗。稼穑维宝,代食维好。

天降丧乱,灭我立王。降此蟊贼㉘,稼穑卒痒。哀恫中国,具赘卒荒㉙。靡有旅力,以念穹苍㉚。

维此惠君,民人所瞻。秉心宣犹㉛,考慎其相。维彼不顺,自独俾臧。自有肺肠,俾民卒狂。

瞻彼中林,甡甡其鹿㉜。朋友已谮㉝,不胥以穀㉞。人亦有言,进退维谷。

维此圣人,瞻言百里。维彼愚人,复狂以喜。匪言不能,胡斯畏忌㉟。

维此良人,弗求弗迪㊱。维彼忍心,是顾是复。民之贪乱㊲,宁为荼毒㊳?

大风有隧㊴,有空大谷。维此良人,作为式穀。维彼不顺,征以中垢。

大风有隧,贪人败类㊵。听言则对,诵言如醉。匪用其良,复俾我悖㊶。

嗟尔朋友,予岂不知而作㊷。如彼飞虫㊸,时亦弋获。既之阴女㊹,反予来赫㊺。

民之罔极,职凉善背㊻。为民不利,如云不克。民之回遹,职竞用力。

民之未戾㊼,职盗为寇㊽。凉曰不可㊾,复背善詈㊿。虽曰匪予,既作尔歌。

【注释】

①菀(wǎn 碗):茂盛。 ②旬:树荫蔽遮均匀。 ③刘:剥落而稀,叶子稀少。 ④瘼(mò 莫):病。 ⑤殄(tiǎn 舔):断绝。 ⑥仓兄填兮:《笺》:"丧亡之道滋久长。"仓,丧;兄,滋;填,久。桑树叶采完了,等于丧亡。 ⑦倬(zhuō 捉):明察。 ⑧骙骙(kuí kuí 葵葵):不息。 ⑨泯(mǐn 敏):乱。 ⑩民靡有黎:黎民没有。黎,黑首。 ⑪具:通"俱"。烬:灰烬。 ⑫国步斯频:国运危急。频,急。 ⑬蔑资:无资财。 ⑭将:助。 ⑮疑:定。 ⑯实维:是作。 ⑰秉心无竞:执心好争。无,语辞。 ⑱梗(gěng 耿):指害人。 ⑲慇慇(yīn yīn 因因):忧伤。 ⑳僤(dàn 旦)怒:重怒。 ㉑瘨(mín 民):病。 ㉒圉(yǔ 宇):边疆。 ㉓毖:慎重。 ㉔僾(ài 爱):窒息。 ㉕肃:进取。 ㉖茀云不逮:前进的使不及门。茀(pīng 乒),使。 ㉗好是稼穑,力民代食:爱好居家吝啬的人,令人民力作代食。稼穑,通"家啬",指家居吝啬聚敛。 ㉘蟊贼:虫食苗根曰蟊,食节曰贼。 ㉙具赘卒荒:具备像赘疣的人,则田荒。 ㉚念:感动。 ㉛宣犹:遍谋。 ㉜牲牲(shēn shēn 申申):众多。 ㉝谮(zèn):诬陷,中伤。 ㉞穀:善。 ㉟胡斯畏忌:何此畏惧。 ㊱求:贪求。迪:钻营。 ㊲贪乱:贪欲作乱。 ㊳荼毒:毒害。 ㊴隧:状迅疾。 ㊵败类:败坏宗族。 ㊶复俾我悖:反使我悖逆。复:反。 ㊷而:

你。 ㊸飞虫：飞鸟。 ㊹阴：同"荫"，庇护。 ㊺反予来赫：反而迁怒于我。 ㊻职凉善背：主信小人，善于背正道。凉：信，通"谅"。㊼戻：安定。 ㊽职盗为寇：主作盗，为寇害。 ㊾凉：语助。 ㊿善：大。詈（lì 利）：骂。

【译文】

　　茂盛的桑树叶子嫩，它的下面绿荫匀，采了叶子没绿荫。晒苦树下的人民，人民不断心忧愁。类似丧亡来已久啊，广大明察的上天，难道不哀怜我人民？

　　四匹雄马不停跑，鸟旗龟旗车上飘。祸乱产生不平静，没有一国不纷扰。国的中间没黎民，都遭灾祸成灰烬。叹息之中有悲哀，国运危急心不平。

　　国运穷困没资财，天不助我实难办。没有居处终疑难，说走不知何处去？君子实干也是难，存心没有好争竞。谁人生出这祸根，直到今天还作梗。

　　忧心隐隐还痛苦，常常想念我国土。我生不逢好时辰，碰上上天发重怒。自从西方到东方，没有一所定居处。我是遭逢很多苦，十分紧急我疆土。

　　为国出谋要谨慎，乱情可能得减削。告你怎样忧国家，教你怎样封官爵。谁遇到了苦热，能不在水洗濯？可这怎能做得好，只能相互水中溺。

　　像面向那个暴风，也很像气喘哮。人民本有进取心，却使他们做不到。喜好聚敛又吝啬，使民出力代替吃。聚敛吝啬算是宝，代替吃食算做好。

　　上天降下丧乱，灭掉我拥立的王。降下这些吃苗虫，田里庄稼都吃光。哀痛国中的人民，都像赘疣田都荒。没有众力怎宣扬，用来感动穹苍。

只有这样好仁君，人民认同好瞻仰。执心遍求好谋划，考虑谨用他的相。只有那个不顺君，用人独行以为良。独自有那肺与肠，使那人民都发狂。

看那个树林中，许多野鹿步从容。朋友已经不相信，不相友好记心中。人也有过这样说，进退维谷走不通。

只有这样的圣人，眼睛远看有百里。只有那些愚蠢人，又像发狂又自喜。不是有话不能说，话说一下怕猜忌。

只有这个是好人，不去贪求不钻营。只有那个忍心人，是顾望来是反复。人民作乱有原因，谁愿为此受荼毒？

大风吹得很迅猛，有从空洞大山谷。只有这个善良人，所作善事无过错。只有那个不顺眼，做事不正又混浊。

大风吹得很迅猛，贪人败坏那宗族。听到顺话便对答，听到谏言像醉客。不是用人好的话，反而使我遭逆悖。

叹息你的朋友，我岂不知你所作。像那飞鸟，有时也被捉。既然我在庇护你，反而对我来威赫。

人民的不中正，主要相信善背人。这样做事民不利，还说恐怕不能胜。人民的邪僻，主要你崇尚暴力争。

人民生活不安定，主要朝廷有盗行。说你不可这样做，又是背后大骂人。虽说不是来骂我，还是作歌求你正。

云 汉

倬彼云汉①，昭回于天②。王曰於呼，何辜今之人？天降丧乱，饥馑荐臻③。靡神不举，靡爱斯牲。圭璧既卒④，宁莫我听？

旱既大甚，蕴隆虫虫⑤。不殄禋祀，自郊徂宫⑥。上下奠瘗⑦，靡神不宗。后稷不克⑧，上帝不临。耗斁下土⑨，宁丁我躬？

旱既大甚，则不可推。兢兢业业⑩，如霆如雷。周余黎民，靡有孑遗⑪。昊天上帝，则不我遗⑫。胡不相畏，先祖于摧⑬？

旱既大甚，则不可沮。赫赫炎炎⑭，云我无所⑮。大命近止⑯，靡瞻靡顾。群公先正⑰，则不我助。父母先祖，胡宁忍予？

旱既大甚，涤涤山川⑱。旱魃为虐，如惔如焚。我心惮暑，忧心如熏。群公先正，则不我闻。昊天上帝，宁俾我遯⑲？

旱既太甚，黾勉畏去⑳。胡宁瘨我以旱㉑，憯不知其故㉒。祈年孔夙，方社不莫。昊天上帝，则不我虞。敬恭明神，宜无悔怒。

旱既大甚，散无友纪㉓。鞫哉庶正㉔，疚哉冢宰㉕，趣马师氏㉖，膳夫左右。靡人不周㉗，无不能止。瞻卬昊天，云如何里？

瞻卬昊天，有嘒其星㉘。大夫君子，昭假无赢㉙。大命近止，无弃尔成。何求为我，以戾庶正。瞻卬昊天，曷惠其宁？

【注释】

①倬（zhuō 桌）：大。云汉：天河。　②昭：光。回：运转。　③荐臻（zhēn 贞）：接连来。　④卒：尽。　⑤蕴隆虫虫：暑雷而热。蕴，指暑。隆，指雷。虫虫，指热。　⑥宫：指宗庙。　⑦奠：祭天。礼神之物，置之于地。瘗：祭地。礼神之物，埋之于土。　⑧克：能。　⑨斁（dù

妒）：败坏。　⑩兢兢：恐。业业：危。　⑪孑遗：遗留。　⑫遗：赠物。　⑬于摧：将毁。　⑭赫赫：旱。炎炎：热。　⑮云：遮蔽。　⑯大命：国命。　⑰群公：指先世诸侯。先正：指先世卿士。　⑱涤涤：除尽。　⑲遯：通"困"。　⑳黾（mǐn 敏）勉：勉力。去：除去。　㉑瘨（diān 颠）：病害。　㉒憯（cǎn 惨）：曾，竟。　㉓友：通"有"。纪：纲纪。　㉔鞫哉庶正：鞫（jū 居），穷困。庶正，众官之长。相当于后世宰相。　㉕冢宰：众长之长。相当于后世宰相。　㉖趣马师氏：管马的做教育官。　㉗周：周济。　㉘嘒（huì 彗）：微光。　㉙昭假无赢：祭祀无差。

【译文】

那个广大的天河，光芒在天上转运。王说：唉，今天的人有何罪？上天降下这丧乱，饥荒相接都发生。没有神道不祭祀，没有吝惜那牺牲。玉圭玉璧已用完，难道我诉不听闻？

旱得既然太厉害，暑天打雷热得很。没有断绝那祭祀，从祭天到宫祭神。祭上祭下或埋压，没有神道无不敬。祖宗后稷不能救，昊天上帝不亲临。破坏天下的土地，难道正当我的身？

旱得既然太厉害，灾情就是不可推。害怕危险没有用，好像霹霹像打雷。周朝余下的百姓，好像没有留下来。昊天上帝降大旱，也不对我来问慰。为什么不怕旱灾，祖宗的神不怕毁？

旱得既然太厉害，就是不可以阻拦。旱气迫人热气来，使我无处逃这灾。大命接近停止了，没有看前看后来。诸侯卿士众位神，不能助我除灾情。父母先祖的神灵，怎么忍心我受灾情？

旱得既然太厉害，山川干涸无水神。旱鬼对人作虐待，到处像烧又像焚。我的心里怕暑热，心里忧愁像火熏。诸侯卿士众位神，对我祷告不恤问。昊天上帝降灾情，难道使我长受困。

旱得既然太厉害,怕旱勉强除痛苦。为什么用旱来害我,还不知道它缘故。求年成好祭祀办得早,祭四方祭社神不迟暮。昊天上帝降旱灾,就不把我来忖度。我恭敬神明,应该没有触犯众神怒。

旱得既然太厉害,散乱无纪使人愁。穷困小人成庶正,怀着疚心冢宰愁,管马的做教育官,膳夫做王的左右。没有一人不用赒,没有不能而停止不救。仰头看看那上天,说什么呢使我忧?

仰头看看那上天,有光闪闪它的星。大夫和君子们,祭祀无不用真诚。大命接近停止了,不要放弃你功勋。何必为我有要求,用来安定众官心。仰头看看那上天,何时安惠民安宁?

崧 高

崧高维岳①,骏极于天②。维岳降神,生甫及申③。维申及甫,维周之翰,四国于蕃④,四方于宣⑤。

亹亹申伯⑥,王缵之事,于邑于谢,南国是式⑦。王命召伯:"定申伯之宅。登是南邦⑧,世执其功。"

王命申伯:"式是南邦。因是谢人,以作尔庸⑨。"王命召伯:"彻申伯土田。"王命傅御⑩:"迁其私人。"

申伯之功⑪,召伯是营。有俶其城⑫,寝庙既成,既成藐藐⑬。王锡申伯,四牡蹻蹻⑭,钩膺濯濯⑮。

王遣申伯,路车乘马。"我图尔居,莫如南土。锡尔介圭⑯,以作尔宝。往辽王舅⑰,南土是保。"

申伯信迈⑱,王饯于郿。申伯还南,谢于诚归⑲。王命召伯,彻申伯土疆。以峙其粻⑳,式遄其行㉑。

申伯番番㉒,既入于谢,徒御啴啴㉓。周邦咸喜,戎有良翰㉔。不显申伯，王之元舅，文武是宪㉕。

申伯之德，柔惠且直。揉此万邦㉖，闻于四国。吉甫作诵，其诗孔硕，其风肆好㉗，以赠申伯㉘。

【注释】

①崧（sōng 松）：山高。岳：指四岳，东岳泰山，西岳华山，南岳衡山，北岳恒山。那个中岳嵩山是后起的，所以先说四岳。②骏（jùn 俊）：通"峻"。③生甫及申：甫侯和申伯，皆周宣王时大臣。一说甫即仲山甫，一说甫即甫侯，即穆王时作《吕刑》之甫侯之子孙。今即释为甫侯。④四国：四方诸侯国。于蕃：为藩篱。⑤于宣：为垣，做墙。宣，指墙。⑥亹亹（wěi wěi 委委）：勤勉。⑦南国：南方国家。式：法，取法。⑧登：成为。⑨庸：通"墉"，城墙。⑩傅御：家臣之长。⑪功：指建筑谢城的功业。⑫俶（chù 绌）：修缮。⑬藐藐（miáo miáo 秒秒）：美好。⑭蹻蹻（jué jué 决决）：强壮。⑮濯濯（zhuó zhuó 浊浊）：光明。⑯介：通"玠"，大圭。⑰迋（jì 记）：犹了。⑱信：再宿。迈：走。⑲谢于诚归：诚心要回到谢邑去。⑳峙（zhì 至）：储备。粻（zhāng 章）：粮食。㉑遄（chuán 传）：速。㉒番番：勇武。㉓徒御：徒步乘车两种人。啴啴（tān tān 摊摊）：和乐。㉔戎：你们。㉕宪：法则。㉖揉（róu 柔）：使服从。㉗风：清风。肆好：极好。㉘赠：增。

【译文】

山极高的是名山，高到极点高到天。只有名山降生神，降生甫侯和申伯相连。只有申伯及甫侯，使周朝的屏障保全，四方侯国的藩篱，四方侯国的城垣。

勤勉的申伯:王使申伯办他事,使他建邑在谢地,南方侯国作统治。王命令召伯:"决定申伯住宅事。成为南方的侯国,执掌他功传后世。"

王命令申伯:"作为南方侯国的法程。依靠谢邑的人,建好你的城。"王命令召伯:"申伯田地你治成"。王命令申伯家臣,"迁申伯的家人"。

申伯的功业,召伯来经营。修缮他的城,寝宫宗庙既建成,建成官庙很壮美。王赐申伯有功臣,四匹雄马很雄壮,金钩胸缨都光明。

王派申伯回国,赐他大车乘马好。"我算计你的住处,没有像南方好。赐你大玉圭,用作你的宝。去吧王的舅,南方土地是安保。"

申伯过宿回国去,王饯申伯在郿地。申伯回到南方去,诚心回到谢邑去。王又命令给召伯,治理申伯的疆地。用来备好你的粮,加快申伯回国去。

申伯威武回了国,既到谢邑就进入。徒步坐车都欣欣,全国臣民都喜悦。你们今天有好君,光荣显耀的申伯,王的大娘舅,文德武功是法则。

申伯的美德,柔和惠爱并正直。用来安顺那万国,声誉闻达四方侯国。吉甫作了这篇颂,他的诗意有特色,他的风格非常好,用来增美贤申伯。

烝 民

天生烝民①,有物有则②。民之秉彝③,好是懿德。天监有周,昭假于下④。保兹天子,生仲山甫⑤。

仲山甫之德,柔嘉维则。令仪令色,小心翼翼。古训是式,威仪是力。天子是若⑥,明命使赋⑦。

王命仲山甫,式是百辟。缵戎祖考,王躬是保。出纳王命,王之喉舌。赋政于外,四方爰发⑧。

肃肃王命⑨,仲山甫将之⑩。邦国若否⑪,仲山甫明之。既明且哲,以保其身。夙夜匪懈,以事一人。

人亦有言,柔则茹之⑫,刚则吐之。维仲山甫,柔亦不茹,刚亦不吐。不侮矜寡,不畏强御。

人亦有言,德輶如毛⑬,民鲜克举之。我仪图之⑭,维仲山甫举之,爱莫助之⑮。衮职有缺⑯,维仲山甫补之。

仲山甫出祖⑰,四牡业业⑱,征夫捷捷⑲,每怀靡及⑳。四牡彭彭㉑,八鸾锵锵。王命仲山甫,城彼东方。

四牡骙骙㉒,八鸾喈喈㉓。仲山甫徂齐,式遄其归㉔。吉甫作诵,穆如清风。仲山甫永怀,以慰其心。

【注释】

①烝(zhēng 蒸):众。 ②物:事物,行事。则:法则。 ③彝(yí 移):常规,常道。 ④昭假:明致,精神明显地到达神。 ⑤仲山甫:周的诸侯之一,封于樊,今河南济源县西南阳城。 ⑥若:顺从。 ⑦明命使赋:王的明命使他传布。赋,传布。 ⑧发:行。 ⑨肃肃:庄严。 ⑩将:奉行。 ⑪若否:善恶。 ⑫茹:吃。 ⑬輶(yóu 由):轻。 ⑭仪图:度量谋画。仪:度。 ⑮爱:爱惜。 ⑯衮:天子的龙衣。衮职:指天子职。 ⑰祖:路祭。 ⑱业业:指高大。 ⑲捷捷(qiè qiè 切切):指喜乐。 ⑳每怀靡及:每人怀其私,无及于事。 ㉑彭彭:蹄声。 ㉒骙骙(kuí kuí 葵葵):强壮。 ㉓喈喈(jié jié 杰杰):车铃声。 ㉔遄(chuán 船):速。

【译文】

上天生了众民,有事物就有法则。人民执持常规,爱好的是美德。上天察视周朝,明显地到达下面侯国。保佑这个天子,生仲山甫这英哲。

仲山甫的美德,柔和美好是准则。好仪容加好脸色,小心谨慎真难得。古来教训是法式,威望仪表他用力。天子这就选择他,政令使他布侯国。

周王命令仲山甫,作为诸侯的法式。继承祖先的事业,保佑王身的业绩。接受传达王命令,作为周王的喉舌。传布政令在朝外,四方诸侯于是发。

尊严周王的命令,仲山甫执行它。朝廷上的善恶,仲山甫辨明它。既辨明又聪哲,用来保全他身子。早晚不懈怠难得,用来侍奉一人责。

人有这样的话,柔软的吃掉它,刚强的吐出它。只有仲山甫,柔软的也不吃它,刚强的也不吐它。不欺侮孤寡的人,不害怕强横的人。

人有这样的话,道德虽轻像根毛,人少能够举起它。我曾度量它,只有仲山甫举起它,可惜没人帮助他。天子的职务有缺点,只有仲山甫补救他。

仲山甫出去祭路神,四匹雄马壮又强,跟随的人喜洋洋,每有怀私顾不上。四匹雄马声彭彭,八个鸾铃响当当。周王命令仲山甫,筑城在那个东方。

四匹雄马真强壮,八个鸾铃响当当。仲山甫到齐国去,催他速回能发光。吉甫作了这篇颂,柔和如像清风扬。永远怀念仲山甫,用来安慰他衷肠。

韩 奕

奕奕梁山①,维禹甸之②。有倬其道③,韩侯受命。王亲命之:"缵戎祖考④,无废朕命!夙夜匪解,虔共尔位!朕命不易。榦不庭方⑤,以佐戎辟⑥。"

四牡奕奕,孔修且张⑦。韩侯入觐,以其介圭,入觐于王。王锡韩侯,淑旂绥章⑧,簟茀错衡。玄衮赤舄,钩膺镂钖⑨,鞹鞃浅幭⑩,鞗革金厄⑪。

韩侯出祖,出宿于屠。显父饯之,清酒百壶。其肴维何?炰鳖鲜鱼。其蔌维何?维笋及蒲。其赠维何?乘马路车。笾豆有且⑫,侯氏燕胥⑬。

韩侯取妻,汾王之甥⑭,蹶父之子⑮。韩侯迎止,于蹶之里。百两彭彭,八鸾锵锵,不显其光。诸娣从之,祈祈如云。韩侯顾之⑯,烂其盈门。

蹶父孔武,靡国不到,为韩姞相攸,莫如韩乐。孔乐韩土,川泽訏訏,鲂鱮甫甫⑰,麀鹿噳噳⑱,有熊有罴,有猫有虎⑲。庆既令居,韩姞燕誉⑳。

溥彼韩城,燕师所完。以先祖受命,因时百蛮。王锡韩侯,其追其貊㉑,奄受北国,因以其伯。实墉实壑㉒,实亩实籍㉓。献其貔皮㉔,赤豹黄罴㉕。

【注释】

①奕奕(yì yì 亦亦):高大。梁山:在陕西韩城县西北。 ②甸:治理。 ③倬(zhuō 卓):宽大。道:路。 ④缵(zuǎn 纂):继承。戎:你。 ⑤榦(gàn 干):匡正。不庭方:不朝见朝廷之国。方,指国。 ⑥戎辟:你君。 ⑦修张:长大。 ⑧淑旂:美丽的画,交龙的旗。绥

章：安全挂起。 ⑨钖（yáng 阳）：马头上饰物。 ⑩鞹鞃（kuò hòng 扩宏）：用皮裹的车中供人凭的皮包横木。浅幭（miè 蔑）：用浅毛皮裹的车上覆盖物。 ⑪鞗（tiáo 条）革：皮的马缰绳。金厄：金属环，缠辔头。 ⑫笾（biān 边）：盛果脯的竹器。豆：木制食器，高足。且（jū 居）：多。 ⑬侯氏：诸侯。燕胥：皆宴。胥，皆。 ⑭汾王：周厉王逃到山西汾水附近，人们称他为汾王。 ⑮蹶（jué 决）父：周朝的卿大夫。 ⑯顾：当时嫁娶的礼。 ⑰甫甫：大。 ⑱噳噳（yǔ yǔ 雨雨）：众多。 ⑲猫：指山猫。 ⑳燕誉：安乐。 ㉑追：西戎。貊（mò 末）：北狄。 ㉒壑：深沟。 ㉓籍：税。 ㉔貔（pí 皮）：白狐。 ㉕黑（pí 皮）：棕熊。

【译文】

高大的梁山，禹来治理它。宽广的路，韩侯接受王命用它。周王亲自命令他："继承你的先祖好，不要把我命令废掉。早晚不要懈怠，虔诚恭敬你职位好！我的命令不改变，纠正不朝国的路遥，用来辅佐你君的正道。"

四匹雄马气昂昂，马身很长又强壮。韩侯进京来朝见，用他大圭来献上，进京朝拜见周王。王赐韩侯有多样，善旂妥帖显文章，车帘文彩交错光。黑袍红鞋都堂皇，金钩胸饰兼辔饰，皮裹车板虎皮张，皮缰金木饰金黄。

韩侯出门作路祭，路远出宿在屠地。显父设席来饯他，清酒百壶在席里。他的菜肴是什么？烹鳖鲜鱼都在里。他的蔬菜是什么？有笋和嫩蒲在里。他的赠送是什么？乘马大车都在里。食器笾豆花样多，诸侯参加都在里。

韩侯娶妻要行礼，妻是汾王的甥女，又是蹶父的女子。韩侯自作迎亲礼，迎亲自到蹶父里。百辆彩车声彭彭，八个鸾铃声锵锵，大显荣耀的光芒。诸位娣女跟从她，多得像云能飞扬。韩侯看了心欢喜，光彩满门喜气扬。

蹶父为人很勇武，没有侯国不曾去。为女儿韩姞相女婿，没有像韩土快乐可与。最快乐是韩地可据，那河川可羡慕，鲂鱼鲔鱼大而著，麋鹿众多在林下，有熊有黑都可据，有猫有虎胜别处。既以为善好居处，韩姞安居有好誉。

广大的那韩城，燕国人所经营。因为祖先曾受命，统有百蛮的能人。周王赐地给韩侯，那是西戎北狄人。统有北方诸侯国，以他为霸而称伯。增城墙深城池，清田亩征户籍。献他的白狐皮，再献赤豹和黄黑。

江 汉

江汉浮浮①，武夫滔滔②。匪安匪游，淮夷来求③。既出我车，既设我旟。匪安匪舒④，淮夷来铺⑤。

江汉汤汤⑥，武夫洸洸⑦。经营四方，告成于王。四方既平，王国庶定⑧。时靡有争⑨，王心载宁。

江汉之浒，王命召虎："式辟四方，彻我疆土⑩。匪疚匪棘⑪，王国来极⑫。"于疆于理，至于南海。王命召虎："来旬来宣⑬。文武受命，召公维翰⑭。无曰予小子，召公是似⑮。肇敏戎公⑯，用锡尔祉。"

"釐尔圭瓒⑰，秬鬯一卣⑱。告于文人，锡山土田。于周受命，自召祖命。"虎拜稽首⑲，"天子万年！"

虎拜稽首，"对扬王休⑳，作召公考㉑，天子万寿！"明明天子㉒，令闻不已。矢其文德㉓，洽此四国㉔。

【注释】

①浮浮：强盛貌。　②滔滔：水广大。当作"江汉滔滔，武夫浮浮"。③求：征伐。　④舒：缓慢。　⑤铺：通"抚"，安抚。　⑥汤汤（shāng shāng 商商）：水势广。　⑦洸洸（guāng guāng 光光）：威武。　⑧庶：幸。　⑨时：是。　⑩彻：开发。　⑪疚：病。棘：急。　⑫极：准则。　⑬来旬来宣：来，语助词。旬，巡视。宣，宣抚。　⑭召公：召虎的先祖，指助武王灭商的召公奭，谥康公。维翰：是桢干。　⑮似：通"嗣"，继承。　⑯肇敏：勉力。戎公：汝功，你的功业。　⑰釐：赐。圭瓒（zàn 赞）：玉柄酒勺。　⑱秬鬯（jù chàng 具畅）：黑黍酒。卣（yǒu 友）：古酒器。　⑲稽（jī 鸡）首：叩头礼。　⑳对扬：颂扬。王休：王的美德。　㉑作召公考：作召穆公辞，这辞刻在庙器上。　㉒明明：勤勉。　㉓矢：施行。　㉔洽：协和。

【译文】

　　长江汉水滚滚流，武人气势雄赳赳。不是求安不是出游，而是把淮夷来挽救。既然发出我的车，既把鸟旗挡车头。不是求安不是求舒服，淮夷来归好怀柔。

　　长江汉水流洋洋，武人威风凛凛强。平定四方叛变国，报告成功给宣王。四方叛变既平定，王国安定国势张。这就没有战争事，宣王心里就安康。

　　长江汉水的水边，宣王命令召伯虎："用法开辟四方国，发展我朝的疆土。不是有病不求急，王国从来用法辅。"治好国疆治田地，一直到达南海土。宣王命令召伯虎："要巡视要安抚。文王武王受天命，召康公是国的柱。不要自说我是小子，召康公事业要继嗣。勉力建立功业成，就把福泽赐给你。"

　　"赐你圭柄好玉勺，黑黍香酒一杯焉。祭告文德人，赐你山川和土田。你在周朝受王命,封同召祖受命焉。"召虎下拜来叩头,"天子寿命有万年!"

召虎拜谢来叩头,"颂扬周王有美德,制作召公考上辞,天子万寿多福泽!"勤奋不已好天子,美好声望不能息。施行他的美好德,协和这个四方国。

常 武

赫赫明明①,王命卿士,南仲大祖②,大师皇父③。"整我六师,以修我戎,既敬既戒④,惠此南国!"

王谓尹氏⑤:"命程伯休父⑥,左右陈行。戒我师旅,率彼淮浦⑦,省此徐土⑧。"不留不处⑨,三事就绪⑩。

赫赫业业⑪,有严天子。王舒保作⑫,匪绍匪游⑬。徐方绎骚⑭,震惊徐方。如雷如霆,徐方震惊。

王奋厥武,如震如怒。进厥虎臣,阚如虓虎⑮。铺敦淮濆⑯,仍执丑虏⑰。截彼淮浦⑱,王师之所。

王旅啴啴⑲,如飞如翰⑳,如江如汉,如山之苞㉑,如川之流,绵绵翼翼㉒。不测不克,濯征徐国㉓。

王犹允塞㉔。徐方既来㉕,徐方既同,天子之功。四方既平,徐方来庭㉖。徐方不回㉗,徐方还归。

【注释】

①赫赫:威严貌。明明:明智貌。 ②南仲大祖:在太祖庙里立南仲为卿,表示这是太祖的意思。 ③大师皇父:命令皇父做太师。 ④既敬既戒:既是警惕,又是戒备。敬同"警"。 ⑤尹氏:指尹吉甫。 ⑥命程伯休父:命令程伯,字休父,任大司马。 ⑦淮浦:淮水

水边。 ⑧省：察看。徐土：徐国国土。 ⑨不留不处：不，语助词。留同"刘"，杀，即杀其君。处：吊，即吊其民。 ⑩三事：指立三个卿。 ⑪业业：指军队前进。 ⑫王舒保作：王行军舒缓安全。即军队不舒缓，王舒缓。 ⑬匪绍：不是舒缓，指军队不舒缓。游：遨游，游逛。 ⑭绎（yì 亦）骚：乱动，乱扰。 ⑮阚（hǎn 罕）：虎怒。虓（xiāo 逍）：虎叫。 ⑯铺敦：大陈列。濆（fén 坟）：大堤。 ⑰仍：就。 ⑱截：截断。 ⑲啴啴（tān tān 坍坍）：盛大。 ⑳翰（hàn 汉）：高飞鸟。 ㉑苞：根本。 ㉒緜緜：绵绵，连续不断。翼翼：壮盛。 ㉓濯（zhuó 浊）：大。 ㉔王犹允塞：王谋信实。 ㉕来：归顺。 ㉖来庭：来朝见。 ㉗不回：不违反。

【译文】

声威烜赫又明智，宣王命令封卿士，托名太祖封南仲，命令皇父做太师。"整顿我国的六军，用来训练我兵士，既已警惕又戒备，加爱这个南国是！"

宣王告诉尹吉甫："命封程伯大司马，左右排列好战阵。勤戒我们的队伍，率领他们到淮浦，视察这个徐国土。" 诛其君来吊其民，三卿建立就安抚。

军威烜赫向前进，威严天子不急行。宣王舒缓保安是，军不舒缓不游行。徐国内部正扰乱，徐国君臣都震惊。像打霹雳像打雷，徐国君臣都震惊。

宣王奋起他威武，有像打雷像发怒。进用虎臣领大军，咆哮有像那猛虎。大设阵势淮水边，就捉那些众俘虏。截断敌方在淮浦，送俘直到王师所。

王师盛大有威力，好像鸷鸟飞得疾，好像长江像汉水，像山本根能确立，像河水流永不灭，继续接连不断绝。不可测量不可胜，大兵讨徐一定入。

宣王谋划确信诚。徐国既经来称臣，徐国既经来会同，这是天子立了功。四方既然已太平，徐国既然来朝廷。徐国不敢违王命，王说回朝不必停。

瞻卬

瞻卬昊天①，则我不惠。孔填不宁②，降此大厉③。邦靡有定，士民其瘵。蟊贼蟊疾，靡有夷届④。罪罟不收⑤，靡有夷瘳⑥。

人有土田，女反有之。人有民人，女复夺之。此宜无罪，女反收之。彼宜有罪，女复说之⑦。

哲夫成城，哲妇倾城。懿厥哲妇⑧，为枭为鸱。妇有长舌，维厉之阶。乱匪降自天，生自妇人！匪教匪诲，时维妇寺⑨。

鞫人忮忒⑩，谮始竟背。岂曰不极，伊胡为慝？如贾三倍，君子是识。妇无公事，休其蚕织。

天何以刺？何神不富⑪？舍尔介狄⑫，维予胥忌。不吊不祥⑬，威仪不类⑭。人之云亡，邦国殄瘁！

天之降罔⑮，维其优矣。人之云亡，心之忧矣。天之降罔，维其几矣⑯。人之云亡，心之悲矣。

觱沸槛泉⑰，维其深矣。心之忧矣，宁自今矣！不自我先，不自我后。藐藐昊天，无不克巩。无忝皇祖，式救尔后。

【注释】

①瞻卬：同"瞻仰"。 ②填（chén 尘）：通"陈"，久。 ③厉：

恶。 ④夷：语助词。 ⑤收：逮捕。 ⑥瘳（chōu 抽）：病愈。 ⑦说：通"脱"，脱罪。 ⑧懿：通"噫"，叹词。 ⑨寺：寺人，阉人。 ⑩鞫（jū 鞠）人：奸人。忮忒（zhì tè 治特）：害人。 ⑪富：福。 ⑫介狄：元凶。 ⑬吊：善。 ⑭类：善。 ⑮罔：通"网"。 ⑯几：危。 ⑰觱（bì 必）沸：涌出。槛（jiàn 建）泉：喷涌而出的泉水。

【译文】

抬头望着那上天，对我就是不施恩。很久不能来安宁，降下这个是大恶。国家没有能安定，士民都是害了病。禾苗受到害虫病，没有到头没有尽。罪人入网网不收，病人没有见病瘳。

人家有田地，你却反去占有它。人家有家奴，你却又是去夺他。这人应该没有罪，你却反去逮捕他。那人应该有罪，你却再去解脱他。

智慧的男子能建筑城墙，智慧的妇人却能毁城墙。唉，那个智慧的妇人，是枭是鸱都一样。妇人有长舌，是败坏的祸殃。乱不是从天上降，生在妇人的身上！没人教她做坏事，她和阉人是一样。

奸人巧弄害人术，谗言开始终背逆。难道说是不极坏，她为什么作恶迹？好像经商利三倍，君子对此有见识。妇人没有做女功，放弃她们的蚕织。

上天为何来责问？神道为何不施恩？放纵你的大坏人，只是对我相怨恨。你是不善又不祥，威仪不修怎样论。好人都说已散去，国家失人更贫困！

上天降下那罗网，只是它那宽大了。好人都说已散去，心里真是忧伤了。上天降下那罗网，只是那样危险了。好人都说已散去，心里很是悲伤了。

沸腾上涌的槛泉,是那样的深了。心里有忧伤了,难道从今天生了!不先从我生,不后从我生。广大的上天,没有不能固自身。不要有辱你祖宗,要救你后代子孙。

召 旻

旻天疾威①,天笃降丧。瘨我饥馑②,民卒流亡。我居圉卒荒③!

天降罪罟,蟊贼内讧。昏椓靡共④,溃溃回遹⑤;实靖夷我邦⑥。

皋皋訿訿⑦,曾不知其玷。兢兢业业,孔填不宁。我位孔贬。

如彼岁旱,草不溃茂⑧,如彼栖苴⑨。我相此邦,无不溃止。

维昔之富不如时,维今之疚不如兹。彼疏斯粺⑩,胡不自替?职兄斯引⑪!

池之竭矣,不云自频⑫。泉之竭矣,不云自中⑬。溥斯害矣,职兄斯弘。不灾我躬!

昔先王受命,有如召公,日辟国百里。今也日蹙国百里。於乎哀哉!维今之人,不尚有旧⑭!

【注释】

①旻(mín 民)天:上天。 ②瘨(diān 颠):灾害。 ③居圉(yǔ 禹):居御,住处。 ④椓(zhuó 酌):宫刑的人,指阉人。《郑笺》:"昏、椓皆奄人也。椓,椓毁阴者也。"共:同"供",供职。 ⑤溃溃:乱。回遹:邪僻。 ⑥靖夷:平定。 ⑦皋皋:顽固。訿訿(zǐ zǐ子子）：懒惰。 ⑧溃：遂。 ⑨苴（chá 茶）：水中草。 ⑩疏：糙米。稗（bài 败）：细米。昔贤者禄薄食粗，今反之。 ⑪职兄斯引：主况斯退。职：主。兄：况。引：长，延长。指奸佞小人长居高位。⑫自频：由于海滨。 ⑬自中：来自中央。 ⑭旧：旧的事功。

【译文】

上天急着使威风，天降灾荒使人丧。病我粮荒又菜荒，人民到处都流亡。我的住处尽荒凉！

上天降下有罪网，贼人内争自相伤。昏阉完全不供职，胡乱邪僻多冤枉；实在毁灭我家邦。

态度顽固又懒惰，不知他们都点污。虽然小心自惊恐，很久不安怎能过。我的职位贬低过。

像那年荒有旱象，百草不能茂盛长，像那水中浮的草。我是观察这个邦，没有不是溃烂亡。

昔富不像今日贫，今贫又加今日病。那些吃粗粮今反细，何不自己来告退？主职况是引长计！

池水枯竭了，不说水从滨外来。泉水枯竭了，不说水从泉中来。灾害已经普遍了，主职况是扩大哉。灾害怎不向我来！

从前先王受天命，贤臣有的像召公，每天开拓国土有百里。如今日减百里中。呜呼哀哉！只有今天的人中，不崇尚有旧的事功！

卷 八

颂

颂是配有音乐又有舞蹈的诗,颂的特点就是有舞蹈。《左传》襄公二十九年,称吴公子季札聘问鲁国,请观周朝赐给鲁国的音乐。他看到颂,加以赞美。总的说来,颂的音乐是和平的,有节度的,不过分的。《毛诗序》说:"颂者,美盛德之形容,以其成功,告于神明者也。"要用音乐来表演盛德,季札的话或可供想象。朱熹《诗集传》:"盖颂与容,古字通用,故《序》以此言之。"

颂分周颂、鲁颂、商颂三部分。周颂是西周初期的作品,产生于西周首都镐京。鲁颂产生于春秋时代,产生于鲁国国都(今山东曲阜)。商颂即宋颂,产生于春秋时代宋国国都(今河南商丘)。

周颂

清庙之什

清 庙

於穆清庙①,肃雍显相②。济济多士,秉文之德,对越在天③。骏奔走在庙④,不显不承⑤,无射于人斯⑥!

【注释】

①於:叹词。穆:美好。清庙:祭文王的庙。 ②肃雍:严敬和好。显相:指有明德光显的公卿诸侯助祭。 ③对越:对扬。 ④骏:

快。　⑤不显不承：不，语助词。显，光耀。承，继承。　⑥射（yì 亦）：同"斁"，厌。

【译文】

啊，美好的清庙，严敬雍和光显的助祭好。众多仪容美好的朝臣，秉承文王的美德，颂扬他在天英灵好。快些奔走在宗庙，光荣地继承，对人没什么烦恼！

维天之命

维天之命，於穆不已。於乎不显①，文王之德之纯！假以溢我②，我其收之③。骏惠我文王，曾孙笃之④。

【注释】

①显：指光明。　②假以溢我：借文王之美德来增我。　③收：受。　④曾孙：自称。笃：厚行。

【译文】

只有上天的命令，啊！美好不停。啊！这是光明啊，文王的德美而纯！借来丰富我，我来接受它。快谢厚爱我的文王，孙辈切实厚待他。

维 清

维清缉熙①，文王之典。肇禋②，迄用有成③，维周之祯④。

【注释】

①缉熙:光明。 ②肇禋(yīn 音):开始祭祀。指文王征伐前的祭天。 ③迄:至。有成:有天下。 ④祯:吉祥。

【译文】

只有清明才光明,文王的典章是清明。开始祭祀,直到有功业成,这是周家的祥祯。

烈 文

烈文辟公①,锡兹祉福,惠我无疆,子孙保之。无封靡于尔邦②,维王其崇之③。念兹戎功④,继序其皇之⑤。无竞维人,四方其训之。不显维德,百辟其刑之。於乎前王不忘!

【注释】

①烈:指功。文:指德。辟(bì 必)公:君公。文王起初不称王,为诸侯之一。 ②封靡:大累,指大罪,封通"丰"。靡为羁縻。 ③维:乃。崇:尊敬。 ④戎功:大功。 ⑤皇:美好,光大。

【译文】

有功烈文德的君公,赐给这个福泽安康。惠爱我们没有止境,子孙永远安保它。不要有大罪对你邦,你们一定要崇敬王。想念他的大功,继承弘扬他的光芒。最强的只有得贤人,来归顺的有四方。光显的只有美德,诸侯都依他作榜样。唉,前王美德不能忘!

诗经

天 作

天作高山①,大王荒之②。彼作矣,文王康之③。彼徂矣④,岐有夷之行⑤,子孙保之。

【注释】

①作:生长。高山:指岐山。 ②荒:大,治理。 ③康:安定。 ④徂(cú 殂):往,到。 ⑤夷之行:平的路。

【译文】

天生万物在岐山,太王治理它。太王经营它,文王安定它。他们到过了,岐山有了平路,子孙安保它。

昊天有成命

昊天有成命①,二后受之②。成王不敢康,夙夜基命宥密③。於缉熙,单厥心④,肆其靖之⑤。

【注释】

①成命:犹明命。 ②二后:指文王、武王。 ③夙夜:日夜。基命:王者始承的天命。宥密:宽宁。宥,通"有",语助词。 ④单:同"亶",信。 ⑤靖:安和。

【译文】

上天有明白的命令,文王、武王接受它。成王不敢求安乐,承受天命日夜信从宽仁安静,唉,光明,专诚他的心,故他得到天下的安定。

我 将

我将我享①,维羊维牛,维天其右之②。仪式刑文王之典③,日靖四方④。伊嘏文王,既右飨之⑤。我其夙夜,畏天之威,于时保之⑥。

【注释】

①我将我享:我大献祭。将,大。享,献祭。 ②右:佑助。之:代国家,下同。 ③仪式刑:则用法。仪,则。式,用。刑,法。 ④靖:求。 ⑤既右飨之:既佑助而祭享之。飨,神来受享。 ⑥时:是。

【译文】

我献大祭,是用羊用牛来祭,只是求上天佑助他。用文王的典章方法,天天求安定四方。伟大的文王,既经受祭上天帮助他。我还是日夜不懈怠,敬畏上天的威严,于是保住他。

时 迈

时迈其邦①,昊天其子之。实右序有周②,薄言震之③,莫不震叠④。怀柔百神,及河乔岳⑤。允王维后,明昭有周,式序在位。载戢干戈,载櫜弓矢⑥。我求懿德,肆于时夏⑦。允王保之⑧。

【注释】

①迈:行,指巡视。 ②右序:保佑帮助。 ③薄:语助词。 ④震叠:震动惧怕。叠,借作"慴",故为惧。 ⑤乔岳:高山。 ⑥櫜(gāo

高）：藏弓箭的袋，指装袋。　⑦肆：遂。夏：华夏。　⑧允：确实。

【译文】

按时巡视诸侯国，上天对周像爱子啊。诚心保佑帮周朝，武王威力震天下，没有一国不害怕。再怀安百神，连及河神岳神。武王不愧是国君，明显地保护周朝，序列在位百官在朝。把干戈聚拢来，把弓箭藏起来。我求有美德，于是布达到中国。确实是武王长保这美德。

执 竞

执竞武王①，无竞维烈②。不显成康③，上帝是皇④，自彼成康，奄有四方，斤斤其明⑤，钟鼓喤喤⑥。磬筦将将⑦，降福穰穰⑧。降福简简⑨，威仪反反⑩。既醉既饱，福禄来反⑪。

【注释】

①执竞：执持自强。执，持。竞，自强。　②竞：自强。烈：功业，指伐纣克商。　③成康：指成王、康王。　④皇：美。　⑤斤斤：明察。　⑥喤喤（huáng huáng 皇皇）：指声大而和。　⑦筦：通"管"，指竹制乐器。将将：指管乐器会集声。　⑧穰穰（ráng ráng）：众多貌。　⑨简简：盛大貌。　⑩反反：慎重。反，假作"昄"。　⑪反：反复。

【译文】

执持自强的是武王，功业无比的是克殷商。显耀的是成王康王，上帝赞美的君王。自从那成王康王，统治侯国的四方，考察英明无错差,钟鼓声相和声皇皇。磬管应和声锵锵,降下福泽多穰穰。降下福泽盛而大,威风容仪重堂皇。既醉饱而无礼违,福禄复来惠赐长。

思 文

思文后稷①,克配彼天。立我烝民②,莫匪尔极③。贻我来牟④,帝命率育。无此疆尔界,陈常于时夏⑤。

【注释】

①思:语助词。文:文德。　②立:假借为粒,谷粒。烝民:众民。烝同"蒸",众也。　③极:至德。　④来牟:来,小麦。牟(móu谋),大麦。　⑤陈常:布政。时:是。夏:华夏。

【译文】

后稷的文德,能够配享那个上天。种粮养活了众民,没有不是与你德相连,天赐给我瑞麦,上帝命令与民种育相连。没有此疆那界分划,布陈农政于华夏。

诗经

臣工之什

臣 工

嗟嗟臣工①！敬尔在公。王釐尔成②，来咨来茹③。嗟嗟保介④！维莫之春，亦又何求⑤？如何新畬⑥？於皇来牟⑦，将受厥明⑧。明昭上帝，迄用康年⑨。命我众人：庤乃钱镈⑩，奄观铚艾⑪。

【注释】

①臣工：臣官，指诸侯的卿士。 ②王釐尔成：王理汝之收成。釐通理，董理。成，指收获。 ③咨：谋。茹：度。 ④保介：保护田界的人。介通"甲"，指武士。 ⑤又：有。 ⑥新畬（yú 于）：新田熟田。耕未三年叫新，过三年叫畬。 ⑦皇：美。 ⑧将受厥明：大受其成。明，成，指收成。 ⑨迄用康年：至今用丰年赐我。 ⑩庤（zhì 至）：储备。钱（jiǎn 检）：农具，似铁铲。镈（bó 博）：锄。 ⑪铚（zhì 至）：小镰刀。艾（yì 刈）：割。

【译文】

唉唉！臣子做侯国官，敬谨你们在公家称能。王董理你们的收成，来询问来度称。唉唉！保护收成的人！在这暮春，还有什么要求？怎么对新田熟田去耕耘？好美啊天赐的麦，大受它的收成。明见的上帝,到现在都使年成丰登。命令我的众人:准备好农具,察看镰刀割麦收成。

噫 嘻

噫嘻成王,既昭假尔①。率时农夫,播厥百谷。骏发尔私②,终三十里。亦服尔耕,十千维耦③。

【注释】

①昭假:招请。假,通"格",至,降临。尔:指所请的神,即成王之灵。 ②骏发:快开发。 ③耦(ǒu 偶):两人各持一耜,并肩耕种。

【译文】

啊啊!成王,既经招请了您。统帅农民百姓,播种那百谷忙耕耘。快开发你们私田,尽在三十里耕耘。竭力从事你们的耕耘,十千个人是耦耕。

振 鹭

振鹭于飞①,于彼西雝②。我客戾止③,亦有斯容④。在彼无恶⑤,在此无斁⑥。庶几夙夜⑦,以永终誉⑧。

【注释】

①振:群飞貌。 ②雝(yōng 庸):水泽。 ③我客:指宋国诸侯微子。戾(lì 吏):到。 ④斯容:这样的容貌,指像白鹭一样的高洁。 ⑤无恶:无人厌恶。 ⑥无斁(yì 亦):无人厌弃。 ⑦夙

夜:从早到夜。 ⑧永:永远。终誉:终久称誉。

【译文】

成群的白鹭在飞,在那西边的水泽里。我的客人到来,也有这样高洁的容仪。在那个国里没人厌恶,在这里没人厌弃。早晚勤勉差不多,永远保持着美誉。

丰 年

丰年多黍多稌①。亦有高廪②,万亿及秭③。为酒为醴,烝畀祖妣④,以洽百礼,降福孔皆⑤。

【注释】

①稌(tú 途):稻。 ②廪(lǐn 凛):仓库。 ③秭(zǐ 子):万万为亿,亿亿为秭。 ④烝:进。畀(bì 币):给与。 ⑤皆:通"嘉"。

【译文】

丰收年多黍多稻。也有仓库很是高,积粮万万及亿亿。做酒做甜酒都好,进献先祖和先妣,用来配合百礼好,降下福禄都是好。

有 瞽

有瞽有瞽①,在周之庭。设业设虡②,崇牙树羽③,应田县鼓④,鞉磬柷圉⑤。既备乃奏,箫管备举⑥。喤喤厥声⑦,肃雍和鸣⑧,先祖是听。我客戾止,永观厥成⑨。

【注释】

①有：语助词。瞽（gǔ 古）：瞎子，古以瞎子为乐师。 ②业：大版。虡（jù 俱）：木架。木架上有大版，可以挂钟鼓。 ③崇牙：设在大版上，像象牙齿，可以挂钟鼓的。树羽：在崇牙上饰的五彩鸟羽。 ④应：小鼓。田：大鼓。县鼓：应田都是悬挂的鼓。 ⑤鞉（táo 陶）：摇鼓。磬：石磬，击之则鸣。柷（zhù 祝）：如漆桶，中有椎柄，令左右击，为开始演奏的信号。圉（yǔ 语）：状如伏虎，敲击以止乐。 ⑥备举：一齐奏乐。 ⑦喤喤（huáng 皇）：宏亮和谐。 ⑧肃雍：舒缓和谐。 ⑨成：乐一终为一成。

【译文】

盲乐师盲乐师，在周朝的朝廷。设立木版和木架，崇牙上面饰羽形，小鼓大鼓都悬挂，鞉磬柷圉都可听。既经备齐就可奏，箫管齐奏无不灵。它的声音喤喤响，舒缓协调声和鸣，先祖神灵下来听。我的客人到来后，长久观到乐奏成。

潜

猗与漆沮①，潜有多鱼②。有鳣有鲔③，鲦鲿鰋鲤④。以享以祀，以介景福⑤。

【注释】

①猗（yī 衣）与：好啊。漆沮（jū 居）：岐山下面的两条河，在今陕西省境内。 ②潜：水中柴堆，供鱼止息，以便捕捉。 ③鳣（zhān 毡）：大鲤鱼。鲔（wěi 诿）：鲟鱼。 ④鲦（tiáo 条）：白条鱼。鲿（cháng 尝）：黄颊鱼。鰋（yǎn 偃）：鲇鱼。 ⑤介：求。景：大。

【译文】

好啊那漆水和沮水,水里柴堆上有多鱼。有大鲤鱼有鲟鱼,有白条鱼、黄颊鱼、鲇鱼、鲤鱼。用来献祖用来祭祀,用来求得大福气。

雍

有来雍雍①,至止肃肃②。相维辟公③,天子穆穆④。於荐广牡⑤,相予肆祀⑥。假哉皇考⑦,绥予孝子⑧。宣哲维人⑨,文武维后。燕及皇天⑩,克昌厥后。绥我眉寿,介以繁祉。既右烈考⑪,亦右文母⑫。

【注释】

①雍雍:和顺貌。 ②肃肃:严肃恭敬貌。 ③相:助祭。辟公:诸侯。 ④穆穆:庄严和气貌。 ⑤於(wū 乌):语助词。荐:进献。广牡:大的雄牛。 ⑥肆祀:陈列祭祀。 ⑦假哉:美哉。 ⑧绥:安定。 ⑨宣哲:明哲,指文王为人明哲睿智。 ⑩燕:安。 ⑪右:保佑。烈考:有功业的先父。 ⑫文母:有文德的先母。

【译文】

这来的人极和顺,到来以后严肃又恭敬。助祭的有诸侯,天子庄严又和顺。啊,进献的大雄牛,助我陈列那祭品。美啊,我的先父,安定我这孝子身。明哲的只有贤人,能文能武只有君。安抚及到上天意,能够昌盛他的后。安定我来赐我寿,用多种福气来保佑。既然保佑有功业的先父,有文德的先母亦保佑。

载 见

载见辟王①，曰求厥章。龙旂阳阳②，和铃央央③，鞗革有鸧④，休有烈光⑤。率见昭考⑥，以孝以享。以介眉寿，永言保之，思皇多祜⑦。烈文辟公⑧，绥以多福，俾缉熙于纯嘏⑨。

【注释】

①载：开始。辟（bì 必）王：君王，指成王。 ②龙旂：龙旗，画龙的旗。阳阳：色彩鲜明。 ③和铃：两种铃，和在车上，铃在旗上。央央：铃声。 ④鞗（tiáo 条）革：马辔头。鸧（qiāng 枪）：马辔头的金饰有光彩。 ⑤休：美。烈光：大光。 ⑥率：相率。昭考：指武王。 ⑦思皇：指成王。 ⑧烈文：有功，业，有文德。辟（bì 必）公：诸侯。 ⑨俾：使。缉熙：光明。纯嘏（gǔ 骨）：大福。

【译文】

开始朝见到君王，礼仪要求合规章。龙旗色彩很鲜明，和铃发声声央央，马辔饰物都有光，美好饰物有大光。相率来祭那武王，用孝思来献祭享。以求长寿的荣光，永远保有周天下，多种福气沾成王。武烈文德的诸侯，天用多福来安定，使有大福作明光。

有 客

有客有客，亦白其马。有萋有且①，敦琢其旅②。有客宿宿③，有客信信④，言授之絷⑤，以絷其马。薄言追之，左右绥之⑥。既有淫威⑦，降福孔夷⑧。

【注释】

①萋:文采交错。且(jū 拘):盛,多。 ②敦(duī 堆)琢:妆饰打扮。 ③宿宿:住二夜。 ④信信:住四夜。 ⑤言:我。縶(zhí 直):拴马索。 ⑥左右:用计。 ⑦淫:大。威:德。 ⑧孔夷:很大。

【译文】

客人来客人来,他用白马驾车乘。有文彩又壮盛,妆饰着他随从人。客人住一宿又一宿,客人住一信又一信,我给他用拴马索,用拴他马不让行。他走了又去追他,左右想法安定他。既然有大的威德,神把很大福降给他。

武

於皇武王①,无竞维烈②。允文文王③,克开厥后。嗣武受之,胜殷遏刘④,耆定尔功⑤。

【注释】

①於(wū 乌):赞叹词。 ②烈:功业。 ③允:确实。 ④刘:残杀。 ⑤耆(zhǐ 旨):致.

【译文】

啊,伟大的武王,没有强过他的功业。确实讲美德的文王,能够开创后人基业。武王继承接受它,战胜殷商遏残杀,致使确定您的功业。

闵予小子之什

闵予小子

闵予小子①,遭家不造②,嬛嬛在疚③。於乎皇考④,永世克孝⑤!念兹皇祖⑥,陟降庭止⑦。维予小子,夙夜敬止。於乎皇王,继序思不忘⑧!

【注释】

①闵(mǐn 敏):可怜。予小子:我小子,成王自称。 ②不造:不幸。 ③嬛嬛(qióng qióng 穷穷):孤独貌。 ④於乎:呜呼。皇考:指武王。 ⑤永世:终于一世。 ⑥皇祖:指祖父。 ⑦陟降:升降,上下。庭:通"廷"。 ⑧继序:继承王业。

【译文】

可怜我小子,遭遇家里的不幸了,孤独的在忧伤中。唉,伟大的王考,永世能够尽孝!想念这位伟大的祖考,神灵升降在朝廷了。我小子一人,早晚恭敬谨慎。唉,伟大的武王,继承大业永思不忘!

访 落

访予落止①,率时昭考②。於乎悠哉③,朕未有艾④!将予就之⑤，继犹判涣⑥。维予小子，未堪家多难。绍庭上下⑦，陟降厥家。休矣皇考，以保明其身⑧！

【注释】

①访：访问。指向群臣谋政。落：开始。止：语助词。　②率：遵循。时：是。昭考：显赫的先父，指武王。　③於乎：呜呼。悠：远。　④朕：成王自称。艾：阅历，指成王年幼无知。　⑤就之：接近他，指就位。　⑥继犹：继续图谋。判涣：分散。　⑦绍：继续。上下：或升上或降下。　⑧保明：保佑。

【译文】

谋政我开始怎样，是遵循显赫的先父执行。唉，太遥远啊，我未有经历进行。我勉强继承王位，继谋恐分散难行。我小子一人，家有多难不堪担任。神灵继续在朝廷升降，升降在我家进行。美啊，伟大的先父，用来保佑我一身！

敬 之

敬之敬之①，天维显思②，命不易哉③！无曰高高在上！陟降厥士④，日监在兹。维予小子，不聪敬止？日就月将⑤，学有缉熙于光明⑥。佛时仔肩⑦，示我显德行。

【注释】

①敬：戒慎。　②天维显：天道善恶明显。思：语助词。　③易：容易。　④士：《说文》："士，事也。"《笺》："天上下其事，谓转日月，施其所行，日月瞻视，近在此也。"　⑤日就：每日成就。月

将：每月奉行。　⑥缉熙：积渐广大。　⑦佛：通"弼（bì 毕）"，辅佐。时：是。仔肩：责任。

【译文】

戒慎啊戒慎啊，天道善恶是显明，秉承天命不易啊！不说高高在上不显明，升上降下巡察，每天监视都在此。我小子一人，敢不聪达不戒慎？日有成就月有奉行，学问靠广大积累到光明。有人辅佐我担当责任，指示我显出德行。

小 毖

予其惩而毖后患①！莫予荓蜂②，自求辛螫③。肇允彼桃虫④，拼飞维鸟⑤。未堪家多难，予又集于蓼⑥。

【注释】

①惩：警戒。毖（bì 必）：谨防。　②荓（píng 萍）蜂：扰动蜂群。　③辛螫（zhē 遮）：辛辣痛。　④肇：开始。允：相信。桃虫：鹪鹩，小鸟。古人认为桃虫能生雕。　⑤拼（fān 翻）飞：翻飞。⑥蓼（liǎo 了）：一种有苦味的草。

【译文】

我是警戒而谨防后患！不要引我扰乱群蜂，自己惹得蜂来辣刺。开始相信是那桃虫，翻飞就是一只鸟儿。不堪忍受我家多难容，我又聚集在蓼草中。

诗经

载 芟

载芟载柞①，其耕泽泽②。千耦其耘③，徂隰徂畛④。侯主侯伯，侯亚侯旅，侯彊侯以⑤。有嗿其馌⑥，思媚其妇，有依其士⑦。有略其耜⑧，俶载南亩⑨。播厥百谷，实函斯活⑩。驿驿其达⑪，有厌其杰⑫。厌厌其苗⑬，绵绵其麃⑭。载获济济⑮，有实其积，万亿及秭⑯。为酒为醴，烝畀祖妣⑰，以洽百礼。有飶其香⑱，邦家之光。有椒其馨⑲，胡考之宁⑳。匪且有且㉑，匪今斯今，振古如兹㉒。

【注释】

①芟（shān 山）：除草。柞（zé 责）：伐树。 ②泽泽：土地分解貌。 ③千耦：一千对两人并耕。耘：除草。 ④徂（cú 殂）：前往。隰（xí 隙）：新开垦的低田。畛（zhěn 枕）：以前开垦的田界。 ⑤侯主：侯国的主，国君。侯伯：国君长子。侯亚：国君次子。侯旅：国君以外的众子弟。侯彊：国君手下强壮的奴隶。侯以：侯与，其他帮忙的人。 ⑥嗿（tǎn 坦）：众吃饭声。馌（yè）：送饭。 ⑦依：爱悦。 ⑧略：锋利。耜（sì 四）：犁头。 ⑨俶（chù 触）载：首先耕好。南亩：向阳的田。 ⑩实：种子。函：充满。活：生机。 ⑪驿驿：接连不断。达：指出土。 ⑫有厌：美好。其杰：它的壮苗。 ⑬厌厌：美好。 ⑭绵绵：细密。麃（biāo 标）：禾苗末梢。 ⑮济济：众多。 ⑯万亿：万万。秭（zǐ 子）：亿亿。指粮多。 ⑰烝（zhēng 蒸）：进献。畀（bì 闭）：给予。 ⑱飶（bì 必）：芬香。 ⑲椒（jiāo 焦）：香气缭绕。馨（xīn 欣）：芳香。 ⑳胡考：老人。 ㉑匪且有且：非此有此。 ㉒振古：从古以来。

【译文】

开始除草除树木,开垦耕地土分崩。一千对耦耕来除草,到新开湿地到旧田埂。国君和他长子,国君次子和他众子都来耕,国中壮人和助耕人。有送饭和吃饭声,讨好送饭的妇女,爱悦耕作的男人。有锋利的犁头,始耕向阳的田塍。种下那些百种谷,种子饱满能够生。接连不断地出土,美好的苗茁壮生。美好的是它禾苗,细密的是它末梢。开始收割的人多,果实堆积露天里,多到万万及亿亿。做成清酒和甜酒,进献先祖和先妣,用来和协成百礼。饭菜缭绕的喷香,这为国家增荣光。酒醴缭绕的香气,这使老人得安康。不料有此竟如此,不料有今竟如今,从古以来都如此。

良 耜

畟畟良耜①,俶载南亩。播厥百谷,实函斯活。或来瞻女,载筐及筥②,其饟伊黍③。其笠伊纠④,其镈斯赵⑤。以薅荼蓼⑥,荼蓼朽止。黍稷茂止,获之挃挃⑦。积之栗栗⑧,其崇如墉⑨,其比如栉⑩。以开百室,百室盈止,妇子宁止。杀时犉牡⑪,有捄其角⑫。以似以续⑬,续古之人⑭。

【注释】

①畟畟(cè cè 册册):耜深耕入地。耜(sì 四):犁头。 ②筐:方形竹器。筥(jǔ 举):圆形竹器。 ③饟(xiǎng 响):送来的饭。黍:黄米饭。 ④纠:纠结,结实。 ⑤镈(bó 博):锄头。赵(tiāo 条):锋利。 ⑥薅(hāo 蒿):除草。荼蓼:陆上或水中的秽草。 ⑦挃挃(zhì zhì 至至):镰刀割禾声。 ⑧栗栗:众多貌。 ⑨墉(yōng

庸）：城墙。　⑩比：排列。栉（zhì 智）：梳篦齿。　⑪时：是。犉（rún）牡：七尺高的大公牛。　⑫捄（qiú 求）：长而弯曲。　⑬似：通"嗣"，继承。　⑭续古之人：继续古人的做法。

【译文】

深耕入土的好犁头，开始耕种向阳田。播种那百类好谷，种子生机满相连。有人前来看望你，载了方筐和圆筥，他的饭是黄小米。他的斗笠真结实，他的犁头真好使。用来除去荼和蓼，荼草蓼草都朽死。小米高粱茂盛长，镰刀收割声吱吱。堆积谷物多又多，它的高像城墙起，排列紧密像梳齿。打开上百储藏库，装满百室好停止，妇子心里才安止。杀那公牛来祭祀，有那弯曲的犄角。延续前人来继续，继续古人讲农事。

丝 衣

丝衣其紑①，载弁俅俅②。自堂徂基③，自羊徂牛。鼐鼎及鼒④，兕觥其觩，旨酒思柔。不吴不敖⑤，胡考之休⑥！

【注释】

①丝衣：丝织祭服。紑（fóu）：鲜洁貌。　②载：通"戴"。弁（biàn 汴）：皮帽。俅俅（qiú qiú 求求）：恭顺貌。　③基：台阶。　④鼐（nài 奈）：大鼎。鼒（zī 资）：小鼎。　⑤吴：喧哗。敖：通"傲"。　⑥胡考：长寿。休：美好。

【译文】

丝制祭服多鲜净，戴了皮帽很恭顺。从堂到阶都查过，从羊到牛查祭牲。大鼎小鼎查祭品,兕角杯弯曲空陈,好酒想起文德好。不喧哗来不骄傲,故能长寿是美好!

酌①

於铄王师②,遵养时晦③。时纯熙矣④,是用大介⑤。我龙受之⑥,蹻蹻王之造⑦。载用有嗣⑧,实维尔公允师⑨。

【注释】

①酌:言武王能酌量取得祖先之道以养民。 ②於(wū 乌):赞美。铄(shuò 朔):美。 ③遵养时晦:即遵时养晦。时,时势。晦,韬晦。 ④纯熙:大光明。 ⑤大介:大甲兵。 ⑥龙:光荣,荣宠。⑦蹻蹻(jiǎo jiǎo 矫矫):勇武貌。造:成就。 ⑧嗣:继承。 ⑨实:是。维:语助词。尔:你,指武王。公:通"功"。允师:确实效法。

【译文】

好啊武王的军队,遵循时势计韬晦。一朝大光明了,于是用大甲兵。我的荣宠受天命,勇武是周王造就成。王用的人有继承,您的功业确可效法成。

桓①

绥万邦,娄丰年②,天命匪解③。桓桓武王,保有厥士,于以四方。克定厥家,於昭于天④,皇以间之⑤。

【注释】

①桓:桓桓,威武貌。 ②娄:通"屡",经常。 ③解:通"懈",懈怠。 ④於(wū 乌):叹词。 ⑤间:代替。

【译文】

安定成万诸侯国,经常得到丰收年,天命对周不懈怠。桓桓的是武王威严,保有他的功业,更四方相连。能够安定他的家,啊,功德明显在上天,用美德来取代纣天下。

赉①

文王既勤止,我应受之。敷时绎思②,我徂维求定③,时周之命④。於绎思⑤!

【注释】

①赉(lài 赖):赏赐。武王赏赐功臣。 ②敷:布。时:是。绎(yì 亦):连续不断。思:语助词。 ③徂(cú 殂):往。 ④时:是。周之命:周朝所接受的天命。 ⑤於(wū 乌):叹词。

【译文】

文王既然勤劳啊,我应当继承他。布陈恩泽不断继承他,我去伐纣只求安定,是上天给周朝的命令。啊,应该不断继承他!

般①

於皇时周②,陟其高山③,嶞山乔岳④。允犹翕河⑤,敷天之下⑥，裒时之对⑦，时周之命⑧。

【注释】

①般：乐。写周成王的快乐，故称《般》。 ②於（wū 乌）：叹词。时：是。 ③陟（zhì 至）：登上。 ④隋（duò 舵）山：小山。 ⑤允：通"沇"，亦名济水。犹：通"洍"，水名。翕：合。河：黄河。允犹二水，合于黄河。 ⑥敷：普。 ⑦裒（póu 抔）：聚集。对：配，指配祭。 ⑧时：是。周之命：周朝的命令。

【译文】

啊，伟大的是周朝，登上四岳的高山，还有小山和高山，允水犹水合于黄河。普天之下，聚集群神来配祭，是周朝接受了天命啊。

诗经

鲁 颂

朱熹《诗集传》:"鲁,少皞之墟,在《禹贡》徐州蒙羽之野,成王以封周公长子伯禽。今袭庆、东平府,沂、密、海等州即其地也。成王以周公有大勋劳于天下,故赐伯禽以天子之礼乐,鲁于是乎有颂,以为庙乐。其后又作诗以美其君,亦谓之颂。"

驷①

驷驷牡马②,在坰之野③。薄言驷者④,有骄有皇⑤,有骊有黄⑥,以车彭彭⑦。思无疆⑧,思马斯臧⑨。

驷驷牡马,在坰之野。薄言驷者,有骓有驲⑩,有骍有骐⑪,以车伾伾⑫。思无期⑬,思马斯才。

驷驷牡马,在坰之野。薄言驷者,有䮄有骆⑭,有骝有雒⑮,以车绎绎⑯。思无斁⑰,思马斯作⑱。

驷驷牡马,在坰之野。薄言驷者,有駰有騢⑲,有驔有鱼⑳,以车祛祛㉑。思无邪,思马斯徂㉒。

【注释】

①驷(jiōng 扃):歌颂鲁侯养马肥壮。 ②牡马:雄马。 ③坰(jiōng 扃):远郊。城外叫郊,郊外叫牧,牧外叫野,野外叫林,林外叫坰。 ④薄、言:皆语助词。 ⑤骄(yù 浴):黑马白股。皇:黄白相杂的马。 ⑥骊:黑马。黄:黄马。 ⑦彭彭:强壮有力貌。 ⑧思无

疆：想念这些马跑没有止境。思，思虑。 ⑨思：语助词。斯臧：这些马实优良。 ⑩骓（zhuī 追）：苍白杂色马。骃（pī 丕）：黄白杂色马。 ⑪骍（xīn 辛）：赤黄色的马。骐：青黑色的马。 ⑫伾伾（pī pī 丕丕）：强壮有力貌。 ⑬思无期：想念这些马跑无穷期。 ⑭驒（tuó 佗）：青黑色马。骆（luò 落）：黑鬃白马。 ⑮骝（liú 留）：赤身黑鬣的马。雒（luò 洛）：黑身白鬣的马。 ⑯绎绎：跑得快。 ⑰思无斁（yì 亦）：想这些马跑无厌倦。 ⑱作：振作。 ⑲骃（yīn 因）：浅黑带白的马。騢（xiá 霞）：赤白色的马。 ⑳驔（diàn 店）：脚胫有长毛的马。鱼：二目外长白毛的马。 ㉑祛祛（qū qū 区区）：强健貌。 ㉒徂：善跑。

【译文】

　　肥壮的雄马，在极远的荒野。肥壮的马是那些，有黑白马和黄白马，有黑马和黄马，用车来驾都是强壮马，想它们跑得没止境，这些马是很好的马。

　　肥壮的雄马，在极远的荒野。肥壮的马是那些，有苍白马和黄白马，有赤黄马和青黑马，用车来驾都是强壮马，想它们跑得没穷期，这些马是有才的马。

　　肥壮的雄马，在极远的荒野。肥壮的马是那些，有青黑马和黑白马，有赤黑马和黑白马，用车来驾都是强壮马。想它们跑得没厌倦，这些马是能够振作的马。

　　肥壮的雄马，在极远的荒野。肥壮的马是那些，有黑白马和赤白马，有脚胫长毛和眼边长毛的马，用车来驾都是强壮马。专诚无邪念，这些马是会跑的好马。

有 駜

有駜有駜①,駜彼乘黄②。夙夜在公③,在公明明④。振振鷺⑤,鷺于下。鼓咽咽⑥,醉言舞。于胥乐兮⑦!

有駜有駜,駜彼乘牡。夙夜在公,在公饮酒。振振鷺,鷺于飞。鼓咽咽,醉言归。于胥乐兮!

有駜有駜,駜彼乘駽⑧。夙夜在公,在公载燕。自今以始,岁其有。君子有穀⑨,诒孙子。于胥乐兮!

【注释】

①駜(bì 必):马强壮貌。这首诗称为《有駜》,是用诗句的开头两字做题目。 ②乘黄:四匹黄马。乘,指四匹。 ③夙夜:从早到夜。 ④明明:通"勉勉",勤勉。 ⑤振振:群飞貌。鷺:白鹭鸟,以比洁白之士。 ⑥鼓咽咽:鼓声有节奏。 ⑦胥乐:皆乐。 ⑧駽(xuān 宣):青黑色马。 ⑨穀:善。

【译文】

肥壮马肥壮马,他驾四匹肥壮黄马。从早到晚在公家,勤勉在公家。群飞白鹭鸟,白鹭飞向下。鼓声有节奏,醉醺醺地起舞。都快乐啊!

肥壮马肥壮马,他驾车四匹肥壮雄马。从早到晚在公家,饮酒在公家。群飞白鹭鸟,白鹭振飞下。鼓声有节奏,醉醺醺地归去。都快乐啊!

肥壮马肥壮马,他驾四匹肥壮青骊马。从早到晚在公家,宴会在公家。从现在开始,年年有丰收啊。君子僖公有善政,留给孙子。都快乐啊!

泮 水①

思乐泮水,薄采其芹②。鲁侯戾止③,言观其旂④。其旂茷茷⑤,鸾声哕哕⑥。无小无大,从公于迈。

思乐泮水,薄采其藻。鲁侯戾止,其马蹻蹻⑦。其马蹻蹻,其音昭昭⑧。载色载笑,匪怒伊教⑨。

思乐泮水,薄采其茆⑩。鲁侯戾止,在泮饮酒⑪。既饮旨酒,永锡难老⑫。顺彼长道,屈此群丑⑬。

穆穆鲁侯⑭,敬明其德⑮。敬慎威仪,维民之则⑯。允文允武⑰,昭假烈祖⑱。靡有不孝⑲,自求伊祜。

明明鲁侯,克明其德。既作泮宫,淮夷攸服。矫矫虎臣⑳,在泮献馘㉑。淑问如皋陶㉒,在泮献囚。

济济多士㉓,克广德心。桓桓于征㉔,狄彼东南㉕。烝烝皇皇㉖,不吴不扬㉗。不告于讻㉘,在泮献功。

角弓其觩㉙,束矢其搜㉚。戎车孔博,徒御无斁。既克淮夷,孔淑不逆。式固尔犹,淮夷卒获。

翩彼飞鸮㉛,集于泮林。食我桑黮㉜,怀我好音㉝。憬彼淮夷㉞,来献其琛㉟。元龟象齿,大赂南金㊱。

【注释】

①泮(pàn 判)水:泮宫前的半月形水池。泮宫是诸侯国的学官,这首诗名为《泮水》,即从第一句话中取两字为诗题。 ②薄:赶快。芹:水芹菜。 ③鲁侯:指鲁僖公。戾:到来。 ④言:我。 ⑤茷茷(pèi pèi 沛沛):飘扬貌。 ⑥哕哕(huì huì 慧慧):铃和声。 ⑦蹻蹻(jiǎo jiǎo 矫矫):雄壮貌。 ⑧昭昭:嘹亮貌。 ⑨伊教,维教,只是教导。 ⑩茆(mǎo 卯):莼菜,蓴菜。 ⑪在泮:在泮宫。

⑫难老：长寿。　⑬群丑：对敌人的蔑称，指淮夷。　⑭穆穆：庄重和善貌。　⑮敬明：恭敬修明。　⑯则：法则。　⑰允：确实。　⑱昭假：明至。假通"格"，至也。烈祖：有功业的祖先。　⑲孝：同"效"。　⑳矫矫：壮健貌。　㉑献馘（guó 国）：不服者杀而献其左耳。　㉒皋陶：舜的法官，善于断狱。　㉓济济：众多。　㉔桓桓：威武貌。　㉕狄：扫荡。　㉖烝烝：生气勃勃。皇皇：声势大。　㉗不吴：不喧哗。　㉘讻（xióng 凶）：争辩。㉙觩（qiú 求）：弓弯曲弦松，换弦急的。　㉚束矢：众矢。搜：飕飕发箭声。　㉛鸮（xiāo 销）：猫头鹰。　㉜桑黮：同"桑葚"，桑树果实。㉝怀：馈。　㉞憬（jǐng 景）：悔悟。　㉟琛（chēn 抻）：珍宝。　㊱南金：南方产的黄金。

【译文】

　　快乐啊泮水，在水中采那芹菜忙。鲁侯来到了，我看他的旂上有文章。他的旗在飘扬，鸾铃丁当响。官不论大小，跟从僖公前行。

　　快乐啊泮水，在水中采那水藻。鲁侯来到了，他的马勇骁。他的马勇骁，他的声音明嘹。脸色和善还带笑，不会发怒唯指教。

　　快乐啊泮水，在水中采那蓴菜好。鲁侯来到了，在泮宫饮酒了。既饮了好酒，永久赐给他难老。顺着他走远征路，制服这些群丑了。

　　庄重和善的鲁侯，恭敬修明他的道德。敬慎他威严的仪容，作为人民的法则。确实有文才有武略，有功先祖感召到。家法没个不效法，日求天赐他福好。

　　勤勉的鲁侯，能够修明他的道德。既然造好了泮宫，淮夷服从来就职。勇武如虎的大臣，在泮宫献馘。善于断问像皋陶，泮宫审囚献给国。

众多贤良的士子，能推仁德的心胸。威武军队去出征，扫荡淮夷南到东。生气勃勃又威风，不喧哗不宣扬，不诉讼不争功。只在泮宫献武功。

角弓弦松改弦急，众箭成束声搜搜。兵车大又大，步行坐车无倦容。既然战胜淮夷敌，化为善良不背叛。因为固守你计谋，淮夷终究得服从。

翩翩飞的那鸮鸟，停在泮水的树林。吃我的桑葚，送给我善德音。觉悟的那淮夷，来赠他的宝珍。大龟和象牙，厚献的是南金。

闵 宫

闵宫有侐①，实实枚枚②。赫赫姜嫄③，其德不回④。上帝是依⑤，无灾无害，弥月不迟⑥。是生后稷，降之百福。黍稷重穋⑦，稙穉菽麦⑧。奄有下国⑨，俾民稼穑⑩。有稷有黍，有稻有秬⑪。奄有下土，缵禹之绪⑫。

后稷之孙⑬，实维大王⑭，居岐之阳⑮，实始翦商⑯。至于文武⑰，缵大王之绪，致天之届⑱，于牧之野⑲。无贰无虞，上帝临女！敦商之旅⑳，克咸厥功。王曰叔父㉑，建尔元子㉒，俾侯于鲁。大启尔宇，为周室辅。

乃命鲁公，俾侯于东。锡之山川，土田附庸㉓。周公之孙，庄公之子㉔，龙旂承祀，六辔耳耳㉕。春秋匪解，享祀不忒㉖。皇皇后帝！皇祖后稷！享以骍牺㉗，是飨是宜，降福既多。周公皇祖，亦其福女！

秋而载尝㉘，夏而楅衡㉙，白牡骍刚㉚。牺尊将将㉛，毛炰胾羹㉜。笾豆大房㉝，万舞洋洋㉞，孝孙有庆，俾尔炽而昌，俾尔寿而臧！保彼东方，鲁邦是常。不亏不崩，不震不腾。三寿作朋㉟，如冈如陵。

公车千乘，朱英绿縢㊱，二矛重弓㊲。公徒三万，贝胄朱綅㊳，烝徒增增㊴。戎狄是膺，荆舒是惩，则莫我敢承。俾尔昌而炽，俾尔寿而富！黄发台背㊵，寿胥与试。俾尔昌而大，俾尔耆而艾㊶！万有千岁，眉寿无有害。

泰山岩岩㊷，鲁邦所詹。奄有龟蒙㊸，遂荒大东，至于海邦，淮夷来同㊹。莫不率从，鲁侯之功。

保有凫绎㊺，遂荒徐宅㊻，至于海邦，淮夷蛮貊㊼，及彼南夷，莫不率从。莫敢不诺，鲁侯是若。

天赐公纯嘏，眉寿保鲁。居常与许㊽，复周公之宇。鲁侯燕喜，令妻寿母，宜大夫庶士。邦国是有，既多受祉，黄发儿齿㊾。

徂徕之松㊿，新甫之柏[51]，是断是度，是寻是尺。松桷有舄[52]，路寝孔硕[53]。新庙奕奕[54]，奚斯所作[55]；孔曼且硕[56]，万民是若[57]。

【注释】

①閟（bì 闭）宫：神秘的宫殿，指祭祀后稷母亲姜嫄的庙，这诗也以诗首两字为题。侐（xù 序）：清静。 ②实实：广大。枚枚：雕饰细密。 ③赫赫：威严。 ④回：邪僻。 ⑤依：依靠。 ⑥弥月：满月，指满足十月。 ⑦重：先种后熟的。穋（lù 路）：后种先熟的。 ⑧稙（zhí 直）：先种的庄稼。穉（zhì 置）：后种的庄稼。菽（shū

叔）：大豆。 ⑨奄有：全有。下国：天下的国家。 ⑩俾（bǐ 鄙）：使。 ⑪秬（jù 巨）：黑谷子。 ⑫缵（zuǎn 纂）：继承。绪：事业。⑬孙：后代。 ⑭大王：太王，指古公亶父。 ⑮岐：岐山。阳：南面。 ⑯翦商：消灭商朝。 ⑰文武：文王、武王。 ⑱致：执行。届：通“殛”，罚。 ⑲牧：牧野，今河南淇县西南。 ⑳敦：通“凋”，凋残。旅：军队。 ㉑王：周成王。叔父：指周公旦。 ㉒元子：长子。㉓附庸：附属国家。 ㉔庄公：鲁庄公。 ㉕耳耳：柔和貌。 ㉖不忒（tè 特）：没有差错。 ㉗骍（xīn 辛）牺：赤色牛作牺牲。 ㉘载尝：始祭，指秋祭。尝，秋祭名。 ㉙楅（bì 壁）衡：指修牛栏。 ㉚骍刚：红色公牛。 ㉛牺尊：牛角杯。将将：杯撞击声。 ㉜毛炰（páo 袍）：连毛烧熟的肉。胾（zì 字）：切块的肉。 ㉝大房：大杯。 ㉞万舞：一种舞名。洋洋：指场面宏大。 ㉟三寿：上寿九十，中寿八十，下寿七十。作朋：为友。 ㊱朱英：矛头饰的红缨。绿縢（téng 藤）：束弓套的绿绳。 ㊲重弓：二弓。 ㊳朱绶（qīn 亲）：红线。 ㊴烝：众。增增：密密层层。 ㊵台背：鲐背，像鲐背，指老人。 ㊶艾：青黑。㊷岩岩：山石高峻。 ㊸龟：龟山，在山东泗水县东北。蒙：蒙山，在山东蒙阴县。 ㊹同：会同，朝贡。 ㊺凫：凫山，在山东邹县西南。绎（yì 亦）：峄山，在山东邹县东南。 ㊻徐宅：徐人居地。 ㊼貊（mò 末）：指少数民族。 ㊽许：许邑，在鲁西。 ㊾儿齿：老人齿落复生。 ㊿徂徕：山名，在山东泰安市东南。 (51)新甫：山名，在山东新甫县西北。 (52)松桷：松木椽子。舄（xì 细）：大。 (53)路寝：庙堂正殿。孔硕：很高大。 (54)奕奕：神采飞扬。 (55)奚斯：鲁僖公大夫。(56)曼：广。 (57)若：顺。

【译文】

神秘庙宇是清静，广大而雕饰细密。威赫的姜嫄，她的德行纯正不邪僻。她是依靠上帝，无灾又无害，满足十月生产不迟。生下了后稷，天降赐他百种福。黍稷先后种后先熟，豆麦前后栽。拥有天下的各国，使人民都种庄稼。有黍有稷，有稻有秬。拥有天下的土地，继承夏禹的业绩。

后稷的后代，就是这太王，住在岐山的南面，谋划开始灭殷商。到了文王和武王，继承太王的事业，执行上天的讨伐，在那牧地的原野。没有贰心没有疑虑，上帝亲自看着你！消灭商朝的兵力，能够共同建功业。成王说：叔父，建立您长子的事业，使他在鲁做君侯，大力开发您的侯国，做周朝辅助的事业！

于是王命令鲁公，侯国建立在周东。赐给他山川，赐他土田做附庸。周公的后代，庄公的儿子，龙旂承接祭祀礼，六根辔头柔和下垂。不懈怠春秋祭祀，不差错献祭享祀。伟大的天帝！伟大的祖先后稷！祭献用红牛做牺牲，是享用是适宜的祭祀，天降的福既多。伟大祖先周公，也赐福给您！

秋天开始行尝祭，夏天修理牛棚，白公牛和赤公牛。牛角杯相撞声锵锵，带毛烧熟和切块烧羹。笾豆和大杯，规模宏大《万舞》洋洋。孝的子孙有吉祥，使您兴旺而盛昌，使您长寿而康强！保护那个东方国，鲁国江山要久常。不会亏损不会崩，不会震荡不翻腾。三个寿人作友朋，像山陵像山冈。

鲁公兵车有千辆，矛有红缨有绿绳，佩有二矛带二弓。鲁公兵有三万人，头盔饰贝缀红线，大军密密又层层。戎狄前来遭击抗，楚舒前来是戒惩，没有谁敢来相敌。使您昌大而盛炽，使您长寿而富庶！黄头发和鲐鱼背，老来相与进言事。使您昌盛而强大，使您老而又年轻！活到万又千岁年，虽寿而又无灾害事。

泰山石头高峻，鲁国人所仰望。拥有了龟山蒙山，于是扩充到极东。至于海上的邦国，淮夷纷纷来会同。没有不相率来服从，都是鲁侯立得功。

保有凫山和绎山，扩充到徐人居处。至于海上各个邦，淮夷和南蛮北貊，以及南夷各个邦，没有不相率来服从。没有敢不来归从，鲁侯命令全顺从。

天赐鲁公以大福，长寿保全鲁士子。居住常邑和许邑，恢复周公的土址。鲁侯设宴喜庆贺，有寿母和好妻子，也宴饮大夫众士。国泰民安的鲁国，既多受天赐福祉，使他生出黄发儿齿。

徂徕山上的松，新甫山上的柏，是砍下是剖开，是几寻是几尺。松树做椽粗又大，庙堂正殿高又大。新庙神采飞扬，是奚斯所盖；广阔而宏大，万民都说是顺洽。

商　颂

朱熹《诗集传》云："契为舜司徒,而封于商,传于四世,而汤有天下。其后三宗迭兴(《史记·殷本纪》称'太宗''中宗''高宗'使殷国复兴),及纣无道,为武王所灭。封其庶兄微子启于宋,修其礼乐以奉商后。其地在《禹贡》徐州泗滨,西及豫州盟诸之野。其后政衰,商之礼乐日以放失。七世至戴公时,大夫正考甫得《商颂》十二篇于周太师,归以祀其先王。至孔子编《诗》而又亡其七篇(按《诗》非孔子所编……"方玉润《诗经原始》："……然《颂》之编,不始于孔子。'颂'之名,自商始有之……愚谓颂之体始于商,而盛于周。鲁,其末焉者耳。然必合三诗而其体始备,亦犹后世之论唐诗有盛、中、晚三唐之分,此三颂之体所由辨也。而乃先周而后商者,何哉?盖先周者,尊本朝;后商者,溯诗源,编《诗》体例应如是耳。"

那

猗与那与①,置我鞉鼓②。奏鼓简简③,衎我烈祖④。汤孙奏假⑤,绥我思成⑥。鞉鼓渊渊⑦,嘒嘒管声⑧。既和且平,依我磬声。於赫汤孙⑨,穆穆厥声⑩!庸鼓有斁⑪,万舞有奕⑫。我有嘉客,亦不夷怿⑬?自古在昔,先民有作,温恭朝夕⑭,执事有恪⑮。顾予烝尝⑯,汤孙之将⑰。

【注释】

①猗(yī 伊):盛大。与:叹词。那:繁多,指武功。用"那"做诗题,是赞汤的武功多。 ②置:设立。鞉(táo 桃)鼓:有两耳的摇鼓,摇时两耳击鼓发声。 ③简简:和谐洪大声。 ④衎(kàn 看):使欢乐。烈祖:有功业的祖先,指汤。 ⑤孙:后代。奏假:奏告。假,通"嘏",告。 ⑥绥:安。成:平,太平,指汤取得太平。 ⑦渊渊:指鼓声。 ⑧嘒嘒(huì 惠):清亮声。管声:管乐声。 ⑨於(wū 乌):叹词。赫:显赫。 ⑩穆穆:和美貌。 ⑪庸:通"镛",大钟。斁(yì 亦):洪大调和。 ⑫奕奕:娴熟。 ⑬夷怿(yì 亦):喜悦。 ⑭温恭:温文恭敬。 ⑮格(kè 克):谨慎恭敬。 ⑯顾:《笺》:"犹念也。"烝:冬祭。尝:秋祭。 ⑰将:奉。

【译文】

盛大啊繁多啊,设置我的手摇鼓。敲鼓的声音洪大,快乐我有功业的先祖。汤的后代奏报,赐我太平好报。手摇鼓音深深,清亮的是管乐声。既谐和且平正,依伴着我的击磬声。啊,显赫的汤后代,和美的奏乐声!谐和的钟鼓声,《万舞》显得娴熟又有神。我有助祭好客人,不也喜欢平和声?从远古在从前,先民就是这样作,从早到晚温良恭敬,办起事来谨慎恭敬。顾念我的冬祭秋祭,扶助汤后代祭祀相延。

烈 祖

嗟嗟烈祖①!有秩斯祜②,申锡无疆③,及尔斯所④。既载清酤⑤,赉我思成⑥。亦有和羹⑦,既戒既平⑧。鬷假无言⑨,时靡有争,绥我眉寿,黄耇无疆⑩。约軧错衡⑪,八鸾鸧鸧⑫。以假以享⑬，我受命溥将⑭。自天降康，丰年穰穰⑮。来假来飨⑯，降福无疆。顾予烝尝⑰，汤孙子将⑱。

【注释】

①烈祖：有功业的祖先，指成汤。 ②秩：很大貌。 ③申锡：反复赏赐。无疆：无穷无尽。 ④斯所：此地，指宋国。 ⑤载：设。酤（gū 沽）：酒。 ⑥赉（lài 赖）：赏赐。成：平，指太平。 ⑦和羹：调和的浓汤。 ⑧既戒：既已完备调和。戒，备。平：和平。和羹的调味是和平的。 ⑨鬷（zōng 宗）假：祷告。无言：指默默祷告。 ⑩黄耇（gǒu 苟）：黄发老人。 ⑪约轵（qí 其）：用皮束车毂。错衡：雕刻车前横木。 ⑫八鸾：八个鸾铃。鸧鸧（qiāng qiāng 腔腔）：铃声。 ⑬以假（gé 隔）：迎神。以享：神受享。 ⑭溥（pǔ 谱）将：广大而长远。 ⑮穰穰（ráng ráng 瓤瓤）：丰盛貌。 ⑯来假：神来。来飨（xiǎng 享）：神受享。 ⑰烝：冬祭。尝：秋祭。 ⑱将：扶助。

【译文】

唉唉，有功业的祖先，天赐大福与功大相连，重重赏赐无边，直到你所在处所。既陈设清酒来前，赏赐我太平好极。也有和羹极妍，既已调和味和平。向神祷告默无声，当时肃敬没争喧，赐我与长寿相连，我的黄发有寿无边。革束车毂雕饰横木，八个鸾铃声连绵。迎神前来受祭享，我受天命大久延。从天降下安康，谷物众多又丰年。神的到来受享，降下的福无边。顾念我的秋祭冬祭，扶助汤后代祭祀相延。

玄 鸟

天命玄鸟①,降而生商②,宅殷土芒芒③。古帝命武汤④,正域彼四方⑤。方命厥后⑥,奄有九有⑦。商之先后⑧,受命不殆,在武丁孙子⑨。武丁孙子,武王靡不胜⑩。龙旂十乘⑪,大糦是承⑫。邦畿千里⑬,维民所止。肇域彼四海⑭,四海来假⑮,来假祈祈⑯,景员维河⑰。殷受命咸宜,百禄是何⑱。

【注释】

①玄鸟:燕子。 ②生商:传说有娀(sōng 松)氏女简狄,吞燕子卵有孕,生下商族祖先契(xiè 谢)。 ③宅:居住。殷土:殷国土地。芒芒:广大。 ④古帝:上帝。武汤:威武的成汤王。 ⑤正域:正其疆域。四方:四方四面,指天下。 ⑥方:遍。后:君,指各酋长。 ⑦奄:全部。九有:九州。 ⑧先后:先王。 ⑨武丁孙子:武丁好后代。武丁是汤九代孙,所以孙子指后代。 ⑩武王:指汤。 ⑪乘:辆。 ⑫大糦(chì 斥):大祭。 ⑬邦畿(jī 激):国都附近。 ⑭肇域:开始拥有。四海:四海之内,指中国。 ⑮来假:来到。假通"格(gé 格)",到。 ⑯祈祈:众多。 ⑰景员:通"广运",东西为广,南北为运。指大的国界。河:黄河。 ⑱何:通"荷",承受。

【译文】

上天命令燕子,降下卵来生出商,住在殷土一片茫茫。上帝命令武王成汤,征服疆域有四方。命令各酋长,统有九州作他们的王。商的先王祖先,接受天命不懈怠,武丁是汤后代最贤。武丁是汤贤后代,武王事业没有不胜任。打起龙旗车十辆,承担大祭行在前。国都附近有千里,人民所居紧相连。开始拥有那四海，四海君主来朝见，来朝见的人众多，国界与黄河相连。殷受天命很相宜，天赐百禄担在肩。

长 发

濬哲维商①，长发其祥。洪水芒芒②，禹敷下土方③。外大国是疆④，幅陨既长⑤。有娀方将⑥，帝立子生商⑦。

玄王桓拨⑧，受小国是达，受大国是达。率履不越⑨，遂视既发⑩。相土烈烈⑪，海外有截⑫。

帝命不违，至于汤齐⑬。汤降不迟，圣敬日跻⑭。昭假迟迟⑮，上帝是祗⑯，帝命式于九围⑰。

受小球大球⑱，为下国缀旒⑲。何天之休⑳，不竞不绿㉑，不刚不柔。敷政优优㉒，百禄是遒㉓。

受小共大共㉔，为下国骏厖㉕。何天之龙㉖，敷奏其勇㉗，不震不动，不戁不竦㉘，百禄是总。

武王载旆㉙，有虔秉钺㉚，如火烈烈，则莫我敢曷㉛。苞有三蘖㉜，莫遂莫达。九有九截㉝，韦顾既伐㉞，昆吾夏桀㉟。

昔在中叶㊱，有震且业㊲。允也天子，降予卿士。实维阿衡㊳，实左右商王。

【注释】

①濬（jùn 俊）哲：明哲。 ②芒芒：通"茫茫"，指广大。 ③敷下土方：治理天下土地。 ④外大国是疆：夏以外的大国划定疆。 ⑤幅陨：面积。长（zhǎng 掌）：增长。 ⑥有娀（sōng 松）：国名。方将：正兴盛。 ⑦立子：立女子，指姜嫄。 ⑧玄王：契的谥号。桓拨：武勇奋发。 ⑨率履：遵行。不越：不超出礼法。 ⑩发：行，施行。 ⑪相

土：契的孙子。烈烈：威武。　⑫海外：指遥远处。有截：整治不乱。⑬汤齐：和汤一样。　⑭日跻（jī 基）：每日上升。　⑮昭假：祷告。迟迟：久久不息。　⑯祗（zhī 知）：尊敬。　⑰式于九围：领导九州。　⑱球：玉。　⑲缀旒（liú 刘）：旗上的飘带，指表识。缀，表。旒，章。　⑳何：通"荷"，承受。休：美。　㉑竞：争。絿（qiú 求）：急。　㉒敷政：发布政令。优优：宽容。　㉓遒（qiú 求）：聚集。　㉔共：通"珙"，指美玉。　㉕骏厖（méng 蒙）：庇护。　㉖龙：宠。　㉗敷奏：施展。　㉘戁（nǎn 赧）：恐惧。　㉙武王：指商汤。旆（pèi 配）：大旗。　㉚有虔：坚强。钺（yuè 悦）：大斧。　㉛曷：通"遏"，阻挡。　㉜苞：树桩。指夏桀。三蘖：新生的枝，比韦、顾、昆吾。　㉝九有：九州。截：整治不乱。　㉞韦：国名，故址在今河南省滑县东南。顾：国名，故址在今山东省鄄城县东北。　㉟昆吾：国名，故址在今河南省许昌市东。夏桀：夏朝的末代君主。　㊱中叶：商朝中期。㊲业：大。　㊳阿衡：商代官名，指大臣伊尹。

【译文】

　　明哲的只是殷商，久已发现它吉祥。大水一片白茫茫，禹治水理天下四方。京城外划定大国边疆，面积既经增长。有娀国正在盛强，上帝立女生殷商。

　　玄王武勇奋发，受封到小国令通达，受封到大国令通达。遵照礼法不超越，遂即视察教令发。孙子相土真威武，在海外整理乱国。

　　上帝命令不可违，与汤齐名是一回。汤的降生正适时，圣敬之德上升时。向神祷告诚迟迟，上帝是神受敬奉，上帝命令导九州。

　　接受了小玉和大玉，作为各国的表章一流。担负上天的美意，不争不急求，不刚也不柔。发布政令平和又宽容，百种福禄都聚拢。

接受小宝玉和大宝玉，作为各国的庇护公。担负上天的光宠，施展他的英勇，不震惊不摇动，不胆怯不惊恐，百种福禄都来从。

商汤车子树大旗，坚强地执着大斧，猛烈得像团烈火，没有谁敢阻挡我。树根生了三枝杈，不能上长不能大。九州治理归一统，韦国顾国既讨伐，昆吾夏桀又治理。

从前商朝在中叶，确有威震立大势，诚然是天以为子，天降给他好卿士。这就是阿衡伊尹，确能辅佐商王事。

殷 武

挞彼殷武①，奋伐荆楚②。罙入其阻③，裒荆之旅④，有截其所⑤，汤孙之绪⑥。

维女荆楚，居国南乡。昔有成汤，自彼氐羌⑦，莫敢不来享，莫敢不来王⑧，曰商是常⑨。

天命多辟⑩，设都于禹之绩。岁事来辟⑪，勿予祸适⑫，稼穑匪懈。

天命降监，下民有严。不僭不滥，不敢怠遑。命于下国，封建厥福。

商邑翼翼⑬，四方之极。赫赫厥声，濯濯厥灵⑭，寿考且宁，以保我后生。

陟彼景山⑮，松柏丸丸⑯。是断是迁，方斫是虔⑰，松桷有梴⑱，旅楹有闲⑲，寝成孔安⑳。

【注释】

①挞：行动迅速貌。挞通"达"。殷武：殷王武丁。　②荆楚：荆州的楚国。　③罙："深"的本字。阻：阻碍处。　④裒（póu抔）：俘虏。　⑤截：整治。　⑥汤孙：汤的后代，指武丁。绪：业绩。　⑦氐羌：古代西北的两种少数民族。　⑧来王：来朝见。　⑨常：通"尚"，尊崇。一说常，指常君。《笺》："氐羌远夷之国，来献来见，曰商王是吾常君也。"　⑩多辟：多君，指诸侯。　⑪来辟（bì必）：犹来朝。　⑫祸适：指谴责。　⑬翼翼：整饬，整齐，有条理。　⑭濯濯：指光明。　⑮景山：在商故都西亳（bó博），今河南偃师县。　⑯丸丸：光直。　⑰斫（zhuó酌）：砍。虔：削。　⑱松桷：松树作椽子。梴（chān 搀）：长貌。　⑲旅楹：众柱。有闲：即闲闲，粗大。　⑳寝：正殿。

【译文】

神速是那殷商武丁，奋起讨伐荆楚。深入到它的险阻，掳获楚军作俘虏，整治了他们处所，汤的后代业绩树。

你们荆楚，住在我国的南乡。从前有成汤，从那远方的氐羌，没有敢不来进贡，没有敢不来朝见王，说对商这是尊崇。

上天命令众诸侯，设立都城禹治地。年年到时来朝见，不过问不谴责，不废庄稼不可懈怠田役。

上天命令向下监察，天下人民谨慎又惊惶。不敢越礼，不敢过度，不敢暇息。施令于诸侯各国，分封立国福禄有光。

商朝都邑整饬，是四方侯国的表率。威赫的声望，光明的威灵，神赐长寿且安宁，来保佑我的后生。

登上那景山，松柏挺拔正直。于是砍断于是运出，于是用刀削于是用刀琢。松树椽子太长大，众柱太大实难成，正殿落成很平安。

诗经

Theory on Literary Translation of the Chinese School

The theory on literary translation of the Chinese school owes its origin to traditional Chinese culture, including the Confucian and the Taoist school of thought respectively represented by *Thus Spoke the Master* and *Laws Divine and Human*.

It is said in the first chapter of *Laws Divine and Human* that truth can be known, but it may not be the truth you know, and that things may be named, but names are not the things. When applied to literary translation, this may mean that the theory on literary translation can be known, but it may not the unproven theory on the one hand, nor the scientific theory on the other, for neither literary translation nor its theory is science. As the names are not equal to the things, the translation cannot be equal to the original. As there is more difference than equivalence between the Chinese and the English language, the principle of equivalence can not be applied to the translation between them as between two occidental languages.

It is said in the last chapter of *Laws Divine and Human* that truthful words may not be beautiful and beautiful words may not be truthful. That is to say, there is contradiction between truth and beauty or between equivalence and excellence. A translation where equivalents are used may be called a faithful or truthful translation. When no equivalent can be found between two languages, the translator should make use of the best expressions or excellent expressions of the target language. That may be called theory of excellence.

In *Thus Spoke the Master*, Confucius said, "At seventy, I can do what I will without going beyond what is right." Professor Zhu Guangqian said that this has shown the mature state of an artist. I think it may also show the mature state of a literary translator. The literal translator has used the equivalents without going beyond the original in sound; the liberal translator has described the image without going beyond the original in sense; the literary translator has described the scene without going beyond reality. Not to go beyond the original is to be truthful or faithful, and the translator has reached the ordinary level of translation. To do what one will without going beyond the original is not only to be faithful but also to make his translation beautiful, in that case the translator has attained a higher level. To excel the original without going beyond the reality it describes is to attain the highest level.

What is literary translation? It is an art of solving the contradiction between faithfulness (or truth) and beauty. How to solve it? There are three methods, namely, equalization, generalization and particularization. When there is little or no contradition between truth and beauty, equalization or equivalents may be used. When there is contradction between them, generalization may be used to make the meaning clear, and particularization to make a deeper impression.

Confucius said in *Thus Spoke the Master* that it would be good to be understandable, better to be enjoyable and best to be delectable or delightful. When applied to literary translation, this principle means that an understandable translation is good, an enjoyable one is better and a delightful one is best. The ontology or theory of contradition between truth and beauty, the methodology or theory of equalization, generalization and particularization, and the teleology or theory of the understandable, the enjoyable and the delectable, all owe their origin to the Confucian and Taoist schools of thoughts.

But Confucius said less about what delight is and more about how to be delightful. In the beginning of *Thus Spoke the Master* he said it is delightful to acquire knowledge and put it into practice; In Chapter Six he told us how Yan Hui could find delight in reading though living in a humble lane with only a handful of rice to eat and a gourdful of water to drink; In Chapter Eleven, Zeng Xi told us his delight in an spring excursion. From these examples we can see Confucius' theory on delight or teleology, and his theory on practice or methodology. His theory is not scientific but artistic. Since literary translation is an art but not a branch of science, his theory can not only be applied to the practice but also to the theory of literary translation. As his theory has stood the test of time, it is as durable as scientific theories. A theorist on science who studies truth and the truthful should not go beyond what is truthful. A theorist on art or an artist who studies beauty and the beautiful may go beyond what is truthful and faithful.

The contradiction between truth and beauty in Chinese theory on literary translation has developed into a contradiction between equivalence and excellence. As Keats said, "Beauty is truth, truth beauty," we may even say beauty is a virtue, a kind of excellence. When we cannot find the equivalent, we may resort to generalization or particularization.

In short, literary translation is an art to create the beautiful.

This is the epistemology of the Chinese school. The contradition between truth and beauty or between equivalence and excellence is its ontology; the theory on equalization, generalization and particularization is its triple methodology; and the theory of the understandable, the enjoyable and the delectable or delightful is its triple teleology.

Xu Yuanchong
Oct. 2011

诗经

代后记:中国学派的文学翻译理论

中国学派的文学翻译理论源自中国的传统文化,主要包括儒家思想和道家思想,儒家思想的代表著作是《论语》,道家思想的代表著作是《老子道德经》。

《老子道德经》第一章开始就说:"道可道,非常道;名可名,非常名。"联系到翻译理论上来,就是说:翻译理论是可以知道的,是可以说得出来的,但不是只说得出来而经不起实践检验的空头理论,这就是中国学派翻译理论中的实践论。其次,文学翻译理论不能算科学理论(自然科学),与其说是社会科学理论,不如说是人文学科或艺术理论,这就是文学翻译的艺术论,也可以说是相对论。后六个字"名可名,非常名"应用到文学翻译理论上来,可以有两层意思:第一层是原文的文字是描写现实的,但并不等于现实,文字和现实之间还有距离,还有矛盾;第二层意思是译文和原文之间也有距离,也有矛盾,译文和原文所描写的现实之间,自然还有距离,还有矛盾。译文应该发挥译语优势,运用最好的译语表达方式,来和原文展开竞赛,使译文和现实的距离或矛盾小于原文和现实之间的矛盾,那就是超越原文了。这就是文学翻译理论中的优势论或优化论,超越论或竞赛论。文学翻译理论应该解决的不只是译文和原文在文字方面的矛盾,还要解决译文和原文所反映的现实之间的矛盾,这是文学翻译的本体论。

一般翻译只要解决"真"或"信"或"似"的问题,文学翻译却要解决"真"或"信"和"美"之间的矛盾。原文反映的现实不只是言内之意，还有言外之意。中国的文学语言往往有言外之意，甚至还有言外之情。文学翻译理论也要解决译文和原文的言外之意、言外之情的矛盾。

《论语》说："知之者不如好之者，好之者不如乐之者。"知之，好之，乐之，这"三之论"是对艺术论的进一步说明。艺术论第一条原则要求译文忠实于原文所反映的现实，求的是真，可以使人知之；第二条原则要求用"三化"法来优化译文，求的是美，可以使人好之；第三条原则要求用"三美"来优化译文，尤其是译诗词，求的是意美、音美和形美，可以使人乐之。如果"不逾矩"的等化译文能使人知之（理解），那就达到了文学翻译的低标准，如从心所欲而不逾矩的浅化或深化的译文既能使人知之，又能使人好之（喜欢），那就达到了中标准；如果从心所欲的译文不但能使人知之，好之，还能使人乐之（愉快），那才达到了文学翻译的高标准。这也是中国译者对世界译论作出的贡献。

翻译艺术的规律是从心所欲而不逾矩。"矩"就是规矩，规律。但艺术规律却可以依人的主观意志而转移，是因为得到承认才算正确的。所以贝多芬说：为了更美，没有什么清规戒律不可打破。他所说的戒律不是科学规律，而是艺术规律。不能用科学规律来评论文学翻译。

孔子不大谈"什么是"（What?）而多谈"怎么做"（How?）。这是中国传统的方法论，比西方流传更久，影响更广，作用更大，并且经过了两三千年实践的考验。《论语》第一章中说："学而时习之，不亦说（悦，乐）乎！""学"是取得知识，"习"是实践。孔子只说学习实践可以得到乐趣，却不说什么是

"乐"。这就是孔子的方法论，是中国文学翻译理论的依据。

总而言之，中国学派的文学翻译理论是研究老子提出的"信"（似）"美"（优）矛盾的艺术（本体论），但"信"不限原文，还指原文所反映的现实，这是认识论，"信"由严复提出的"信达雅"发展到鲁迅提出"信顺"的直译，再发展到陈源的"三似"（形似，意似，神似），直到傅雷的"重神似不重形似"，这已经接近"美"了。"美"发展到鲁迅的"三美"（意美，音美，形美），再发展到林语堂提出的"忠实，通顺，美"，转化为朱生豪"传达原作意趣"的意译，直到茅盾提出的"美的享受"。孔子提出的"从心所欲"发展到郭沫若提出的创译论（好的翻译等于创作），以及钱钟书说的译文可以胜过原作的"化境"说，再发展到优化论，超越论，"三化"（等化，浅化，深化）方法论。孔子提出的"不逾矩"和老子说的"信言不美，美言不信"有同有异。老子"信美"并重，孔子"从心所欲"重于"不逾矩"，发展为朱光潜的"艺术论"，包括郭沫若说的"在信达之外，愈雅愈好。所谓'雅'不是高深或讲修饰，而是文学价值或艺术价值比较高。"直到茅盾说的："必须把文学翻译工作提高到艺术创造的水平。"孔子的"乐之"发展为胡适之的"愉快"说（翻译要使读者读得愉快），再发展到"三之"（知之，好之，乐之）目的论。这就是中国学派的文学翻译理论发展为"美化之艺术"（"三美"，"三化"，"三之"的艺术）的概况。

许渊冲
2011年10月

图书在版编目（CIP）数据

诗经: 汉英对照 / 许渊冲译. — 2版. — 北京: 五洲传播出版社，2020.1
（许译中国经典诗文集）
ISBN 978-7-5085-4360-4

Ⅰ. ①诗… Ⅱ. ①许… Ⅲ. ①古体诗 – 诗集 – 中国 – 春秋时代 – 汉、英
Ⅳ. ①I222.2

中国版本图书馆CIP数据核字(2020)第013157号

诗经

译　　者：许渊冲
策划编辑：荆孝敏　郑　磊
责任编辑：王　峰
中文译注：周振甫
中文编辑：石　玉
英文编辑：鲁大东　郁　辉
装帧设计：北京正视文化艺术有限责任公司
出版发行：五洲传播出版社
地　　址：北京市海淀区北三环中路31号生产力大楼B座6层
邮　　编：100088
电　　话：010-82005927，010-82007837
网　　址：http://www.cicc.org.cn　http://www.thatsbooks.com
印　　刷：中煤（北京）印务有限公司
版　　次：2012年1月第1版　2020年4月第2版第1次印刷
开　　本：140mm×210mm　1/32
印　　张：24.75
字　　数：680千字
书　　号：ISBN 978-7-5085-4360-4
定　　价：148.00元